HOTTIE ON HER SHELF

HOTTIE ON HER SHELF

USA TODAY BESTSELLING AUTHOR
CHRISTI BARTH

This book is a work of fiction. Names, characters, places, and incidents are the product of the author's imagination or are used fictitiously. Any resemblance to actual events, locales, or persons, living or dead, is coincidental.

Copyright © 2022 by Christi Barth. All rights reserved, including the right to reproduce, distribute, or transmit in any form or by any means. For information regarding subsidiary rights, please contact the Publisher.

Entangled Publishing
644 Shrewsbury Commons Ave
STE 181
Shrewsbury, PA 17361
rights@entangledpublishing.com

Amara is an imprint of Entangled Publishing.

Edited by Alethea Spiridon and Heather Howland
Cover illustration and design by Elizabeth Turner Stokes

Manufactured in the United States of America

First Edition July 2022

At Entangled, we want our readers to be well-informed. If you would like to know if this book contains any elements that might be of concern for you, please check the book's webpage for details.

https://entangledpublishing.com/books/hottie-on-her-shelf

To the hottie on my keeper shelf.

Chapter One

Nothing drove home being another year older like waking up with a killer headache, dry mouth, and regret oozing from every pore.

Hallie Scott knew it was socially acceptable to be hungover the day after her thirtieth birthday. She also knew she was officially old enough to know better. To know that imbibing an entire pitcher of margaritas—even when shared with her bestie, Megan—would constrict her blood vessels. That the sugar in them—because Megan had insisted on passionfruit-flavored—would do a number on her liver. And that having to scream to be heard in the noisy bar would leave her throat scratchy.

Hallie knew all that because, as head librarian for Swan Cove, she prided herself on *knowing* things. But she also knew the evil drink-pusher who'd insisted on "kicking off her next decade in style" was a force not to be ignored or argued with. Aka, her hangover was actually a lot less painful than resisting Megan's insistence on a big celebration.

The hangover would be tolerable...if she was home.

Tucked up in bed under her fluffy duvet surrounded by books with a super strong mug of tea.

The other thing about being thirty, though? It made Hallie old enough to know a hangover was no excuse to shirk her daily opportunity to spread the wonders of reading. After all, she wasn't *sick*. She was simply suffering the consequences of her actions.

Which meant she was at work. In the quiet, serene confines of the Swan Cove Public Library, breathing in the heady scent of ink. Situated behind the checkout desk staring at the obnoxiously bright laptop screen while looking at the day's schedule of events.

It was the kickoff of their summer reading challenge. There were six boxes of T-shirts for it waiting to be unboxed and stacked on a table by the also obnoxiously bright poster at the entrance.

Hallie didn't want to do any of that. She just wanted to, well, moan. Maybe whimper.

Instead, she tightened her everyday ponytail *despite* how it exacerbated her headache.

The front doors of the brick building whooshed open. "Happy being thirty and a day!" Megan yelled.

Yes, *yelled*.

Inside a library.

No, it didn't technically open for another half hour, but the sound still made Hallie cringe.

"Library voice, please," she admonished.

"Yeah, yeah." Megan waved away the request as she bustled in. Megan lived her life in dramatic absolutes. She was always either bustling and rushing, or sauntering and strolling. Middle ground was unacceptable to her, whether in rate of walking or painting her walls. Hallie still closed her eyes every time she used Megan's bathroom, painted in plate-sized fuchsia and lime polka dots. "That was my test to see how hungover you are."

"Just like every test that's ever come my way, I pass with flying colors. I'm here at work. Vertical." Hallie smoothed a hand down her white blouse, tucked neatly into navy pants—although she was wearing sneakers instead of her usual pumps. Her sense of balance had been, well, *compromised* this morning. The thought of walking to work in heels promised to end with her falling off them and twisting one, if not both, ankles. Megan didn't need to know that part, though. "Dressed professionally and ready to welcome lovers of books into my sanctuary of reading."

"Methinks the librarian doth protest too much." Megan plunked down a pink and white striped canvas tote. "Your hair's in a messy pony. Your eyes are bloodshot. And I feel responsible."

Good. "You *are* responsible."

"Did you have fun last night?"

"That's not the point." Under the microscopic clarity of hindsight, the fun had not been great enough to struggle through the misery of today.

"You didn't think I'd let you be miserable this morning, did you? I've brought more presents. The perfect hangover food—donuts. And a concoction that won't taste as good but *will* make you feel normal, super fast."

Megan pulled out a white cardboard box…and a travel mug of something bright green. And thick. If Hallie had to describe it, she'd say it looked like something a sewer monster sneezed out.

"How about just the donuts?" She reached for the thickly glazed apple fritter.

Megan intercepted, shoving the drink into her hand instead. "Drink your medicine first. Trust me. Out of the two of us, who's had more hangovers?"

The joy of talking to your oldest, bestest friend was that

you didn't have to be polite. Hallie could be factual. Which was, after all, her *thing*. "You. By far. Probably at least by quintuple the amount."

"Ouch. But true. This will reboot your electrolytes and deliver a bunch of other healthy zings to your system. So drink up."

"Fine." Trying to be a good sport—because it *was* sweet of Megan to show up with remedies—Hallie chugged a huge swig...

...more than half of which ended up on her shirt as she choked out a spit take.

"What is in this? It burns *and* tastes horrible *and* is slimy."

Megan winced in sympathy. "Mmm. The burning is the ginger. The slime is probably the raw egg. The taste? Probably the bitter combo of kale, celery, and turmeric. Now keep drinking."

Hallie looked down at her previously white shirt, now wet, splotched with green, and sticking to her. "I need to change." Good thing she had all those boxes of reading challenge tees—although they were sized for kids.

"Not yet." Megan's bright pink-slicked lips zipped in and out of a grin. "I've got one last present for you."

Hallie gestured at her shirt. "I think you've done enough. Save it for my next birthday."

"Nope. This one's time sensitive. Sort of. I put your name on the ballot to be the next mayor of Swan Cove!"

Her brain *was* clicking along slower this morning. But that in no way explained the ridiculousness that Megan had just spouted. "Very funny. Now stay here at the desk while I go change."

Megan shoved the mug back at Hallie. To assuage her, she braced, pinched her nose shut, and took one more big swallow.

"I'm serious, Hallie," Megan said. "Today's the last day

to make changes to the ballot. Actually, it becomes officially locked in an hour. There's you and Mayor Montgomery. That's it."

Crap.

This time her mouth just opened in surprise. "Why on earth would you do that?"

"It's what you wanted." Megan spoke slowly, over-enunciating, as if trying to explain something as obvious as how blow-drying hair upside down creates more volume.

"No." Hallie lifted her hand to tick off points on each finger. "Not in any universe. Not in any reality. Not here. Not in Narnia, or Regency England, or Mars. Nowhere would I want to be mayor."

Now Megan's mouth fell agape. "But you *said* so. Last night."

Not a chance. As far as Hallie was concerned, being mayor ranked right up there with living in a world without air-conditioning and antibiotics. And joining a submarine crew despite her extreme claustrophobia. "I promise you I did not."

"You most certainly did. You were ranting on the walk home about what a bad job the mayor's been doing for Swan Cove. We were at the edge of the swan pond, and you pointed at the swans and said *they* could do a better job than Fitz Montgomery."

Hallie started to fold in half to bang her head on the desk. Then she remembered the pounding headache and, *slowly*, straightened back up. "That's *not* the same as saying I want to be mayor."

"I interpolated. Extrapolated? What am I trying to say?"

"That you lost your mind? That you overstepped?"

Megan tossed her head, which didn't have the usual effect, since she'd chopped off her long blond locks last week and gone with an angled bob instead. She worked in Swan

Cove's toniest salon, and considered her own hair to be a walking billboard for her services. She changed up her look every six months. "You're welcome, by the way. And happy birthday."

Hallie half stood to lean across the desk and grab Megan's arm. "Go fix it. Get my name off. Right now."

"I can't."

"Of course you can."

Megan twisted out of her grip with a crinkle of her nose. "First of all, there's only an hour left before the ballot's official, and I have to go open the salon. Can't be late. My little old ladies are sticklers for punctuality. And, secondly, only *you* can take it off. The clerk was very clear explaining that. Protects the validity of the electoral process. Otherwise, any contender could just stroll up and demand someone's name be stricken."

Hallie blinked, grabbed the fritter, and took a huge bite. She'd need the sugar for fuel, not just to zoom out of here, but to sustain her through the awkward conversation with the city clerk. Hopefully, they could share a good laugh about Megan's mistake/overreach. More hopefully, Hallie would be able to secure a promise from the clerk that nobody would ever learn that her name had even been on the ballot for a hot second.

She swiveled around, taking paper from the printer tray and a marker from her desk. It was electric orange, but she didn't have time to search for another.

She was about to do the unthinkable—open the library late.

But *more* unthinkable was running for mayor.

With swift strokes, she penned an apology note to tape to the front door. Turned out her hangover was good for something—it'd forced her to wear sneakers. It'd make the six-block run to city hall borderline doable.

Hallie slammed her hand onto the cardboard box. "Leave all the donuts. You can take the smoothie, because I'm definitely not drinking or wearing any more of it. And although I can't believe this has to be said out loud, do not ever again submit my name for anything official—not a marathon, not a blood drive, and certainly not an election—without checking with me first!"

Megan didn't so much as blink at her stern tone. "Nope. You were ranting, Hallie. You always do. You think too much and get riled up and rant, but then you don't take action. Whereas I'm great at action—lots less at thinking. You need me to help you get things done." She lifted her chin. "I still say this is the best birthday present ever."

Hallie grabbed her keys, pushing Megan out the door in front of her. "If you truly believe that, we might have to kibosh presents for the rest of our lives."

Yoga was great because it made Hallie feel virtuous about knocking out non-sweaty exercise that kept her flexible and halfway counted as meditation.

Yoga, however, did *nothing* as far as cardio was concerned. That was clear by the end of her six-block sprint. Apparently, the more appropriate and necessary present Megan should've given her was a gym membership.

Hallie collapsed against the cool wall of city hall's lobby and panted. A lot.

She wanted to blame the hangover, but that probably only accounted for, at most, half of her diminished capacity. She definitely blamed being thirty. It was now the worst birthday ever.

Sliding around the corner, she sank onto the stairs and glanced at the watch her parents had given her for high school graduation. Good. There was still time. Hallie didn't need a watch that allowed her to check her email and buy shoes. Her watch was a visual reminder of her parents' love and pride in her accomplishments. Their belief in her was worth ten times more than any tech gadget.

She'd climb the two flights up to the clerk's office after catching her breath. Or at least after the stitch in her side subsided—

"Did you check your email yet, Mr. Mayor?" a man asked in a brusque tone.

"It's not even nine a.m. and you just intercepted me two flights away from my office. *And* I've told you for years to call me Fitz."

Hallie froze.

Mayor Fitz Montgomery. The youngest mayor in the history of Swan Cove.

He of Montgomery Industries, MI Shipping, MI Lumber, Swan Cove Pies, Montgomery Harbor Inn, MI Exchange, Montgomery Center for Fine Arts... What wasn't named after his family in town was still owned by them, albeit with a cutesy name to appeal to tourists, like the Pie Time pie shop.

"Not going to happen," the other man said. "My job is to constantly remind you that you *are* mayor. Makes the rigors of the campaign easier to swallow when you're already holding the prize in your hand."

"I don't need your pop psychology, Derek," the mayor grumbled. "Just your campaign strategies. And I barely need that, since my name's the only one on the ballot."

Was that a cocky smirk in his smooth, baritone voice?

"Not anymore."

After a beat, the dry denial came. "Very funny."

Hallie slapped her hand over her mouth to muffle the giggle. Because it *was* funny that the mayor had echoed the exact thing she'd said to Megan.

"I know it sounds like a joke, Mr. Mayor, but it's real. There's another candidate in the race. A woman."

The derision that dripped off his words put a worse taste in Hallie's mouth than the neon smoothie.

After an overly long pause—was he grimacing? Unable to process the fact someone might have the temerity to run against him?—the mayor asked, "Who?"

"Hallie Scott. I don't know who she is."

The mayor seemed to, though, because he instantly filled in the info. "She's the librarian."

That was interesting.

Why did the mayor know her name right off the top of his head? Sure, their coastal Maine town was small—except for the summer months when it swelled with vacationers—but Hallie intentionally kept a very low profile. She didn't run in the same social circles as Fitz Montgomery.

"It doesn't matter who she is." Derek's dismissal swatted away Hallie's existence like it mattered less than a stable fly at the beach.

"Seeing as you're my campaign manager, a challenger such as Miss Scott should matter to you quite a bit." The mayor's voice was still smooth, but anyone with a modicum of self-preservation could hear that smoothness sheathed sharp steel.

The other man scoffed. "Her last name isn't Montgomery. That's the only pertinent piece of information you need when declaring how much more qualified you are than her."

That...that was *beyond*.

Hallie didn't want to run for mayor, but she also didn't want to be denied her basic right as a citizen to do so. She didn't believe it was required to be a member of the Montgomery family in order to do good for the town. She didn't believe her chances were impossible. Not great, sure, but not *impossible* simply because of her last name.

Most of all, she didn't believe some man named Derek had the right to dismiss her.

Hallie used both hands to push herself up from the stairs. Righteous indignation put pep back in her step as she rounded the staircase to confront the two men. Easy to tell who was who. Derek looked like almost every other man in Swan Cove—khakis, button-down shirt, brown hair with a swoop in the front. Aka, he wasn't the Adonis that was Fitz Montgomery.

The golden child.

Literally, with his picture-perfect, thick blond hair he gelled back, a jawline that could cut glass, and piercing blue eyes the color of the woad that Celtic warriors used to paint their faces before a battle.

Not that she'd noticed.

Just that you couldn't live in Swan Cove without seeing the mayor, well, *everywhere.*

"There are actually three requirements to run for mayor in Swan Cove, gentlemen. You must be at least eighteen, a registered voter, and have lived in the city for a minimum of one year immediately preceding the date of filing. Nowhere in the city charter is there a stipulation as to the last name of a candidate."

They both looked at her with mouths agape and squints of surprise. And that's when Hallie remembered her, ah, disheveled appearance.

The green stains covering the front of her shirt, the stains which were still wet enough to cling to the pattern of the lace on her bra. All the loose hairs that had slipped out of her pony as she ran. The sweat along her neck.

Yeah, she probably hadn't stunned them with her knowledge of electoral qualifications. More probable that they were, quite rightly, judging her for being so slovenly. Nobody should be out in public in such disarray.

Especially not someone trying to defend the moral high ground.

But it was too late to back away, pretend they hadn't seen her under the flickering fluorescents, and try again after a wardrobe change and five minutes with a hair brush.

"Who the hell are you?" Derek barked.

The mayor smiled. "This is Swan Cove's head librarian, Hallie Scott." Fitz used her title with pride, like he was introducing her around at a yacht club cocktail party. And he said her name like it was his own private pet moniker for her.

She'd seen him in action before. Despite his failings as mayor—which were many—Fitz Montgomery was an artist at personal connections. The eye contact, the warmth in his tone, the half smile. The utter genuineness.

Hallie wasn't falling for any of it. "I'm not just the librarian. I'm also a contender for *your* position."

"Contender?" Derek gave a long, slow up-and-down. "Hardly."

She'd endured snubs like that her entire life. They'd built up a callus on her emotional skin. Hallie didn't even feel his prick...which was probably what Derek's girlfriends all said.

Wow. She'd slipped right into full battle mode without even realizing it. "I heard what you two said about me just now."

"Eavesdropping? Classy." A sniff, as if Derek could smell whatever noxiousness was in the green stains on her shirt.

The mayor, however, had the grace to look chagrined.

Which didn't prove that he felt it, necessarily. Merely that he'd had manners drilled into him after years at cotillion class and club events. He dipped his burnished head. "I'm sorry, Ms. Scott. It's not sportsmanlike to trash talk your opponent."

"Point of clarification." Briefly, Hallie wondered if he even recognized the parliamentary procedure she was following out of respect for their location in city hall. "It's not sportsmanlike to *believe* that your opponent is trash."

Derek crossed his arms. "Why are you here? Did you wake up to the epiphany that there's no chance in hell you'll win and you came to take your name off the ballot?"

Would telling the truth take away an advantage? Possibly. But Hallie didn't intend to start her campaign out on a lie. Because, oh yes, she most definitely planned to run. "My best friend put me on the ballot as a birthday present. As soon as I found out, I ran here to take my name off."

Derek belly laughed.

The mayor let an infinitesimal smirk slip across his face before covering by infinitesimally straightening his tie. "Well, we can point you to the clerk's office and help you take care of that. Maybe next year ask your friend for a weekend trip to Boston."

The supercilious, condescending, patronizing nerve of these two! She'd been willing to give the mayor the benefit of the doubt and accept his apology as genuine.

Not anymore.

"That *was* why I came here. It's not why I'm here now. I've changed my mind." Hallie lifted her chin and glared down her regrettably pert nose at them. "To be clear, gentlemen, the two of you have changed my mind. I'm staying on the ballot."

Derek crossed his arms. "That's ridiculous. You don't have a chance in hell."

"You mean because my last name isn't Montgomery? Or because I'm originally from Crow Harbor?" Her hometown, a mere ten minutes away, was *literally* the wrong side of the tracks from Swan Cove.

"Yeah," Derek said with a shrug.

The mayor stepped forward, his arms spread wide in a classic nonthreatening pose like he was trying to negotiate with an unhinged hostage-taker.

"What he means to say, Ms. Scott, is that the odds are never in your favor when you run against an incumbent. A campaign would suck up your time. Your money."

She *would* give him points for proffering an explanation rather than an insult. "Not my money. We passed that campaign finance cap two years ago, remember? The town funds each candidate equally. Period."

And then, *then*, the mayor's gaze shifted over to Derek as if to check if what she said was true. It was appalling.

"You really don't remember an important ballot measure that passed during your tenure? We'll list that as reason number fourteen why I don't just *want* to run for mayor now but *need* to."

He put his hands together in a prayer position and tapped them against his perfectly aquiline nose. "Ms. Scott, I'm not trying to tell you what to do. I'm just pointing out facts. Facts that will indeed make it difficult for you to get through to an electorate that has proven to be happy with me as the face of this town."

"People are happy with what they know. Sure, they like vanilla ice cream…until they try caramel fudge ribbon and realize there's something far *more* to their liking."

His charming facade didn't exactly crack, but it did shimmer. As if she'd disturbed something in its depths. "You're calling me vanilla?"

This time, Hallie gave a slow up-and-down once-over to the criminally handsome mayor and decided it was okay to make a point with one *tiny* lie. "At best."

The shimmer of uncertainty smoothed out. The cocky grin returned. "Rich and decadent?"

Hallie waited a few seconds so that Mayor Montgomery could realize the unfortunate double meaning of his word choice. Great descriptors for a creamy dessert, sure.

Horrible descriptors for a man who held his position merely through nepotism. One who was beyond rich and probably had a lifestyle of disgusting decadence.

She didn't pay much heed to gossip about anyone. Fictions in her books were so much better drawn than ridiculous stories that flew around town. But with a face so handsome? Money to throw around like beads at a Mardi Gras parade? The probability was high that there were at least a few decadent episodes in his past.

Yup. Hallie knew it hit him when two vertical lines grooved between his dark blond brows.

"For your information, the two top-selling flavors at Baskin-Robbins vacillate between Pralines 'n Cream and Mint Chocolate Chip. My take on that? People prefer a flavor that isn't one note."

"So you're a reverse snob? My family's bank account is your issue?"

"Not at all." Mostly not. She'd have to watch herself. Reverse snobbery *was* just as wrong as actual snobbery. "My issue is that your family doesn't do enough for this town with all that money."

Those blue eyes lowered into a baleful squint. "For the record, I have nothing to do with my family's money. I make my own way."

Interesting.

Hallie *had* written him off as a trust-fund freewheeler, which went to show she'd need to dig in and do serious research on Fitz Montgomery. It also showed that she'd lazily made an assumption on appearances—the same thing she detested when people did it judging her background as a Crow Harbor native.

Maybe there was more to the mayor than she'd figured.

Maybe she had stepped into a monumentally more complex task than she'd realized…

Hallie couldn't let that immediate panic show, though. Only swagger and confidence. "Be that as it may, as mayor, you should have done more to work with the city's largest employer and biggest taxpayer."

"You…you…you can't go around spouting crap like that," Derek spluttered. "Who the hell do you think you are, lady?"

"There are a plethora of ways to answer that. The most subjective response would be to get all threatening and say 'your biggest problem.' I could get aspirational and say 'the next mayor of Swan Cove.'" Hallie threw back her shoulders. Yes, it made her stains all the more prominent, but this was a moment that called for a strong physicality with these jerks. "But here's the simple fact of who I am down to my bones. I am a *librarian*, a repository and hoarder of knowledge. Therefore, I am not to be underestimated."

With a sharp squeak of her shoes, she turned on her heel and made her way back down the hall and out the wide double front doors.

Only then did she let her trembling knees give way and sink onto the split-log edge of the flowerbed. Bravado was all well and good in the moment.

Living with the spur-of-the-moment decision she'd just made? Hallie wasn't at all sure she had it in her.

Not even to ensure that smirk got permanently erased from Mayor Fitz Montgomery's lips.

Chapter Two

Fitz never made the same mistake twice. Not knowingly, anyway.

So instead of tearing Derek a new one the moment the doors slammed behind the librarian, he jerked his head at the stairs and took them two at a time, which in no way burned off his anger.

He ran marathons. Lots of 'em, for charity. Was toying with doing an Iron Man in Florida in December just to escape the brutality of a Maine winter for a weekend.

He happened to know, however, that Derek's only exercise was riding eighteen holes in his golf cart. So it was... petty? Sure. But also gratifying to hear him huffing by the time they entered Fitz's office on the third floor.

Fitz shrugged out of his sport coat and hung it on the back of the door, then rounded his desk to settle in the big leather chair. Steepled his fingers, elbows on the desk. And waited.

For all that Derek's common sense had checked out during their conversation with the librarian, he seemed to be recovering it now. His campaign manager had definitely picked up on Fitz's mood. First, he paced between the coffee table and the wooden guest chairs, salvaged off a shipwreck in the 1800s. Glanced at Fitz a couple of times, a quick over-the-shoulder thing like he didn't want to be caught doing it.

Derek blustered. A lot. But he didn't have the spine—or the balls—to back it up when push came to shove. So Fitz let him stew in his own juices for a bit.

The man deserved it. He'd just fucking ruined the next four weeks of Fitz's life.

Finally, Derek eased into a chair, gnawed on his lower lip. "Look, you don't need to worry—"

"I damn well do!" Nobody would be able to hear them through the thick brick walls. "I've never run against *anyone*."

"Right. Because once a Montgomery's on the ballot, it's a done deal. That doesn't change, no matter how many names get added." A smug smile licked across his thin lips.

Oh, he'd regret that. Fitz would make sure of it. Because if Fitz had to be miserable, he'd make damned sure the man who *caused* it was doubly so.

"Let's break down how many things are wrong with what you just said." He circled one finger in the air. "Heck, let's toss everything in the mix. Talk about all the wrongness that's come out of your mouth in, oh, say, the last fifteen minutes."

Derek's neck audibly cracked as he twitched through a double take. "There's no need to be a jerk."

"You led off that particular parade, Derek. You're the drum major out there with that stupid tall hat with the fuzzy ball on top of it." Fitz whipped a pen out of the UCLA Bruins mug. Normally, looking at the reminder of his undergrad days lifted his mood. Not this time. He shook the pen at Derek. "One? An important lesson you'd damn well better take away from this morning. You don't trash talk *anyone* in a public space. Ever."

"It doesn't matter. She's nobody."

Jesus. How low of a worm did you have to be in order to actually believe that?

Fitz hadn't liked Derek from the first day his father foisted the man on him to head up the campaign. But arguing with dear old Dad almost never ended well. Better to save up for the truly big battles.

It'd been obvious from the start that Derek was a bootlicker. Not his, of course, but to everyone in power at Montgomery Industries. The campaign manager stayed behind the scenes, though, so Fitz hadn't worried too much.

It was his face on the poster, the billboards, the newspaper ads. He was the one who talked to constituents. And, more importantly, listened to them.

Derek did logistics. Undoubtedly reported back like a good little spy to his father. Ignoring Derek's pretentious snobbery had become routine.

Until today. The man had crossed a line.

Fitz had a reputation for being easygoing. A smooth-talking problem solver. He didn't bluster and yell.

Maybe it was time to turn over a new leaf...

"Hallie Scott matters because she's employed by the town. She matters because she's a resident of the town, a voter. Because she's a woman voter. Because she's a *person*." Bracing fists on the desk, he half stood. "Last but not least, she matters because she is my opponent. That ought to matter to you."

"You're blowing this all out of proportion."

Fitz sank back down, pulled out another pen to shake at Derek before laying it next to the first. "Second? Don't be rude to my constituents. Any of them. Even, and especially, the ones running against me. It's a bad look. It's disrespectful. I won't stand for it."

"A campaign is a war, for God's sake. Of *course* I'm going to throw down against the competition."

It was like talking to a wall. A pasty, stubborn wall dressed up in a pinstripe blue oxford. "Third. *Your* big mouth was the one throwing around the mocking remarks. Now *I'm* the one who'll have to pay for it, even though your job is to look out for me. You know I hate campaigning."

Was he whining? Yeah. Again, nobody could overhear. But of all the things Fitz didn't like about being mayor, campaigning topped the list. Spending a month reassuring people that he was the best, the only man qualified to lead Swan Cove. The biggest reason voters punched his name on the ballot, though? His last name.

Fitz didn't believe that was nearly good enough a reason. It left one hell of a bad taste in his mouth, but it was a legacy thrust upon him since birth. It'd disrespect the previous generations of Montgomery mayors, all the time and effort they'd lavished on steering the course of the town, if he just thumbed his nose and selfishly followed his own dreams.

"It'll be even easier this time." Derek flicked his wrist to swat away Fitz's concerns. "With someone sharing the stage, you'll get to talk half as much."

That was a problem in and of itself. Half the time to listen. To interact. To make an impression. Why would Derek think that went in the plus column?

Fitz's chair creaked as he sagged back. It didn't make him feel better to yell at Derek due to the whole not-getting-through-to-him thing. The dressing-down wasn't worth it. His time would be better spent grabbing coffee. Cleaning out his spam folder. Scheduling that emissions test for his car…

Derek jumped up, then double slapped the desk, beaming with confidence.

As if that would fix anything. "You're still going to win, Fitz. A Montgomery *always* wins in Swan Cove. I'll make sure history repeats itself." By the end of that weak-ass motivational speech, he was at the door, hand already cranking the knob.

Guess Fitz had instilled a little fear in him after all. The morning wasn't a complete loss.

The day had started...not *badly*. More precisely, it started in the shitter with the librarian's throwdown.

It didn't get any better from there.

Fitz remembered the relief he'd felt when gulping down his first mug of coffee. The always delicious turkey club from Monty's Sandwich Shoppe was a good lift halfway through the day. The rest of it stank like the badger carcass their family dog dug up and dragged inside when he was a kid. Until a spring break trip to the Yellowstone hot springs, that had remained the worst thing Fitz had ever smelled.

First, there'd been the meeting with the water department. Then a grip-and-grin with a delegation from their sister city, Kleve, in Germany. And by delegation, he meant three giddy high school kids and six chaperones. They didn't care about meeting the mayor. They just wanted to get out on a boat and spot some whales. Because, according to Gunther, "Everything is bigger in America—even the fish!"

Fitz figured he'd earned a metaphorical gold star in mayor-ing by not bursting their bubble and pointing out that whales were mammals. All in a day's work of presenting the best possible face to Swan Cove and the world.

Basically, the day had been meeting after meeting after meeting. He was *done*.

Fitz cocked an ear. Didn't hear a sound from the hallway—not at 5:01 in the afternoon. City hall emptied out faster than a dive bar when the lights turned up. He put his keys back in his pocket and hopped onto the flat metal banister of the stairs.

Then he *rode* all the way down. Even the loops at the landings.

Not exactly a specified perk of being the mayor. Not exactly something a thirty-two-year-old man should be doing in public. But he figured he'd make sure the day ended better than it started.

It worked. He plucked his keys back out, whistling as he pushed the wide exit bar to the back parking lot. Then his whistle petered out as did his mood. Because his parents were waiting for him at his car.

That couldn't be good.

A quick mental run-through told Fitz that he hadn't missed birthdays or anniversaries. If somebody was dead—Aunt Felicia, his sister Blake—he hoped to God they would've *called* with the news rather than waiting for his work day to officially end to conversate in the parking lot.

Fitz didn't have a clue as to why they were there. Why they'd felt a parking lot freaking ambush was necessary.

It was never wise to go into a discussion with his parents without any game plan or foreknowledge. It guaranteed a loss—whether of time, pride, or both.

He casually tossed his keys in the air. Never let 'em see you frantically trying to strategize.

"Good afternoon. Little weird that you're just standing out here. Did security ban you from the building? Catch you spray-painting 'our son's the mayor' with a smiley face under the exclamation mark?" Fitz said.

Preston Montgomery winced, his small head jerk making it seem as though Fitz's words had actually splintered a few cells of his brain. "Why must you be ridiculous?"

Better than the alternative. Dour. Grumpy. Permanently impaled by a stick up one's ass. "It's been a long day."

At that, his mother hinged forward slightly, presenting her cheek to be air-kissed. Dutifully, Fitz kissed the cheek he knew got regular applications of bee venom, which had always confused him, since his mom had screened in their entire patio to avoid being "terrorized" (her word) by a single bee.

He shook his father's hand next, since it was expected. Today, Dad wore his crimson Harvard crest tie. Must mean he'd been making the rounds up at the lab. Preston enjoyed intimidating all the MIT lab rats with it. Fitz, however, knew the MIT alums actually didn't give a rat's ass about his dad's Harvard degree. Same as him.

"I imagine so," his mom murmured. That was her MO. Caroline Montgomery especially liked to murmur in noisy restaurants to force the servers to apologize and lean in closer.

Fitz refused to play those games. So, he slapped on an innocent smile and asked, "You imagine what?"

"That your day was long. That it felt long, rather. What with starting with such a crushing disappointment."

How did they...?

Damn it. Why was Fitz even surprised?

Of *course* Derek had called them. Derek was first and foremost Preston's toady. His spy. Legit on his dad's payroll. Secondly, he looked out for himself. Doing his best for Fitz barely netted a bronze medal.

He had two choices: tap dance with them until they admitted that Derek had ratted out the confidential conversation of an elected official and a constituent—which would change their end game not at all—or...

...get on with the inevitable.

Fitz pocketed his key. "I'm frustrated at the last-minute timing of the addition. Less time for me to prepare to run against her. But I'm not disappointed. Democracy in action is a beautiful thing."

"Bullshit."

Tapping his toe on the asphalt, Fitz said, "You're literally standing on city property, Dad. Maybe keep your monarchial leanings under wraps while you're here."

"Democracy is fine. I call bullshit on you not being upset about the events of the day."

No doubt. Preston Montgomery wasn't big on tuning into the nuances of feelings. Something bad went down for his son, ergo Fitz must be pissed/crushed/etc. In his own way, Preston was sure of it because he cared.

How messed up was that?

"I was caught off guard, I'll grant you that. The more I think about it, though? It'll be fun. A race isn't much to get excited about when you're the only one running. I need that competitive spirit to kick in to get me to do my best."

Oftentimes, Fitz would make pronouncements like that simply to stir the pot with his parents. To try and prove to them that their side of an issue was not the be-all and end-all. Because, man, they used a crane to get up on their high horse about almost everything.

He *meant* this one, though.

Did he like the idea of doing more campaign homework? Nah. Not one bit. Fitz had slogged through a master of public policy at Stanford. He didn't shy away from hard work, but he hated memorizing budget stats and tourist stats and economic stats because, well, *stats*. He wanted Swan Cove to prosper. He just didn't give a rat's ass about all the numbers that told the story.

On the other hand...

Did he like the idea of the mental chess match he'd be thrown into against his beautiful—*no* denying that the librarian was beautiful—opponent?

Yeah. He did.

Fitz liked her...sass, too. The way Hallie Scott hadn't let being a mess hold her back from standing up for what she believed in was *impressive*.

A throat-clearing from his dad brought Fitz back from his reminiscing. Right. Parents were here to rip him a new one. Better get on with it.

For a split second, those sandy brows drew together as if Preston were about to unleash one of his classic rants. Or, what his dad referred to as 'not letting a teachable moment slip by.'

Then his forehead smoothed. He clapped Fitz on the back. "That's entirely the wrong attitude, son. We taught you better than that. You're in a competition every day. With yourself. To be better than you were the day before."

Ah, to be fifteen again and to willfully eye roll and damn the consequences! That was such a load of—

Didn't matter.

Fitz knew what they expected to hear. Spouting it was the fastest way to get them out of his parking lot. Because his dad's posturing came from a good place. Preston didn't pick on him to be a hard-ass. He genuinely wanted his son to be the best version—well, not of himself, but of the man Preston *believed* that he should be.

He clasped his hands behind his back. "I'll keep that in mind."

After clicking her tongue, his mother said, "I can't think how you allowed this to happen."

"What?"

She slid her ever-present pearls through her fingers (one strand for day, double strand for night. Fitz didn't love that he knew that. He also hoped that whoever his future wife was, wherever she was out there, she didn't wear pearls at *all*). "How could you let an interloper onto the historically one-person mayoral ballot?"

True to form, Preston piled on. "A Montgomery runs for mayor in this town. A Montgomery *is* mayor in this town. It's that simple, son."

"Well, it would be." Fitz crossed one arm over his chest, propped an elbow on his wrist and stroked his five-oh-seven o'clock shadow. "Except for one tiny caveat. A little thing you might've overlooked, not being intimately familiar with every line of the town charter the way I have to be."

"Which is?"

"As I said before, *democracy* exists. In America, and even right here in Swan Cove." Fitz threw out both arms wide.

"Oh, for goodness sake." Caroline's blue eyes, much more navy than his own, narrowed in contempt at his attempt to lighten the mood.

He shrugged. "Not my fault. I'm a pawn of the system."

"Fitzwilliam, that is enough. We're endeavoring to have a serious conversation with you."

He couldn't agree more. Because conspiring *against* democracy was deadly serious in his book. But he didn't want to go round in circles all night about it.

Most of the time, a solid 65 percent of the time, his parents were great. A little distant, a lot overly focused on upholding the family legacy and making sure their son was the brightest light in their corner of the universe, but good people.

He didn't like fighting with them. Didn't like disappointing them. Even though, by their account, he had a habit of doing both far too often...

So, Fitz went with a classic distraction tactic. "Seriously, Mom, this is your fault. Didn't your ancestors come over on the *Mayflower* seeking independence?"

"They were on the *Little James*. Right after the *Mayflower*." Her powdered cheeks immediately pinked up as she waggled a finger at him. "You always get that wrong on purpose."

"Because I love to watch you blush with pride when you harken back to your colonizing roots."

"Your roots, too."

"I know. And I know you want me to win. Trust me, I don't want to lose." Was that technically different from *wanting* to win? Maybe.

Definitely.

But phrased his way, it was the truth.

Preston smoothed his tie, looked out over the swan pond and the gazebo behind it. "It isn't that we *want* you to win, son. We *expect* you to do so. The town needs the steady leadership of a Montgomery. We're proven to know what's best for Swan Cove. No one else cares more about its success than the Montgomery family."

Yeah, see, that was the rhetoric Fitz didn't need. Or necessarily believe. That, in fact, pissed him off all over again.

Because he wasn't a medieval king, granted authority by God. He was just a man with an overhyped last name.

"Don't for a minute think this woman can beat you." Caroline took his hands and squeezed. "We won't let that happen. She's a nobody. You're a Montgomery."

"Well, I guess you've just written my entire stump speech."

The dry-as-Death-Valley sarcasm went right over their heads, because both parents freaking *beamed* at him.

"That's the spirit, son." Preston clapped him on the back. "Glad we're all on the same page. There's no one better suited to run this town than a Montgomery."

Another round of handshakes and air kisses and they left.

They left Fitz stewing.

Because his dad hadn't said that *Fitz* was the best one to be mayor, only that anyone with their last name was best. Not exactly a ringing endorsement. His biggest asset was… nothing *he'd* actually done. Accomplished. Chosen. Decided.

His own parents couldn't come up with a better reason than his name that he should be mayor? That wasn't enough of a reason. Not for him. Not for any of the voters.

Their lack of faith in him really shone through in this unwanted visit.

He'd been planning on going home to spend the night working on the stump speech Derek had drafted. But now? He needed to get far away from platitudes. Far away from anything campaign related. Far away from anything that lauded his brilliance at having his genes attached to the name Montgomery.

He whipped off a text to his best friend. Everett Reynolds had liked him before he had any clue about the heft and portent of Fitz's last name. Didn't give two shits about Fitz's family money and took every last opportunity to cut him down to size, because Everett didn't think Fitz got enough of that.

Blowing off steam at the pub would clear out the mood his parents had left behind like a bad fart. Tomorrow was plenty soon enough to pick up worrying about the campaign.

And the pretty librarian with the massive chip on her shoulder against him…*and* his last name.

Chapter Three

Hallie looked at the solid inch of latte-colored foam topping off the dark beer. She nudged it back to the edge of the table and gave the waitress with the neon-blue pixie cut a baleful glare. "Why did you bring me *alcohol*?"

Erin set it back on the coaster. "Because you're in an Irish pub. You're over twenty-one. It's the right thing to do."

"That's an unhealthy attitude. You shouldn't push drinks on unsuspecting customers."

Erin patted the front pocket of her black bar apron. "How do you think I pay my rent?" She gave a wink that involved half of her face.

"Stop hassling Erin. It was my idea, okay? I ordered it from her at the bar. On the q.t. Or it was supposed to be, until you made a federal case of it." Megan mouthed *I'm sorry* at the waitress.

"Are you kidding me? It was just last night that you got me drunk. Let's think back…how did that end up?" Hallie twisted her hair and shoved it over her shoulder so she could lean forward. "Oh yes, with you upending my life and launching me down the road to abject humiliation by sticking me on a ballot."

Placid despite Hallie's sharp tone, Megan sipped her own beer. "Which means that no matter how much you drink tonight, nothing worse could possibly happen."

"Categorically untrue. Hallie could agree to donate her kidney to a stranger in need. Or part of her liver. Living donations have been game-changers in the field of transplants," Randall said, with an inordinate amount of authority.

Randall worked at the pet groomer's. The constant barking was headache-inducing, so he wore noise-canceling headphones and listened to podcasts all day long. Hallie had tried to dissuade him otherwise, but he firmly believed himself to be an expert after a single podcast on whatever topic it covered.

Most of the time his tidbits were interesting. Sometimes hilarious, and often overly generalized. It helped to know the context. Easy, because he changed themes for each day of the week.

"Science podcast day?" Hallie guessed.

"Nope. True crime. Evidently, kidnapping people to harvest their organs is a lot less profitable for gangs nowadays."

"That's…reassuring?" Megan giggled and shrugged.

It'd be reassuring if they lived in San Francisco. Or Miami. Hallie didn't find it likely that a gang would trek up to the wilds of coastal Maine for their ill-gotten partial liver booty.

"I'm not donating a kidney. Not tonight. Although, for the record, if any of you ever need it, I'm O negative and would be honored to help save your life."

"What do you give someone as a thank-you present for that? Feels like a nice Bath and Body Works gift basket just wouldn't be enough."

Oh no. Megan was off on a tangent.

From experience, Hallie knew that Megan could literally hijack the conversation for the rest of the night, trying to get them to work out an appropriate organ donation thank-you. Ordinarily, it'd be fun. Oodles of laughs over their shared apps.

Not tonight, though.

Hallie tapped her knife against the glass. "Focus, people. Tonight is about this whole ballot…thing."

Megan reached over the plate of Reuben eggrolls to tap her nails against the frosty glass. "Which is why you need the beer. You stood up to the establishment. Thumbed your nose at it. We're celebrating."

"Are we?" Randall cocked his head and stroked his very hipster sandy-brown goatee. "I thought we were here to help Hallie wallow in the stupidity of her rash decision."

Ana, who'd been quietly cutting up the loaded potato skins for ease of sharing, set down her utensils with a definitive *clink*. She was the oldest of them all, at the ripe age of thirty-three. She often sat back quietly while they spun through a discussion, then joined in with a pithy statement that got them all back on track.

"No. We're here for an emergency summit on how we're going to make sure Hallie wins. Or at least determine if the odds are at all in her favor and what we have to work with."

The thing was, her friends were *all* right. Hearing it laid out like that, Hallie didn't know which aspect took priority. The only thing she knew for certain was that Megan had, after all, been *completely* on target with getting her a beer.

Hallie was still certain it had been the right decision to run, but the adrenaline of battle that had fueled her certainty when talking to the mayor had flattened. Soda-left-open-for-three-days flat.

"I'm not sure you can quantify *not* taking my name off

the ballot as standing up to the establishment."

"Are you kidding? You told off the hot mayor." Megan grabbed Hallie's hand and raised it overhead triumphantly. "You told off a *Montgomery*."

"In the heat of the moment." And why'd she have to quantify him by his hotness? It was a factor that Hallie had been trying quite hard to ignore. "I vented. I expressed a few opinions. I didn't organize a march or host a sit-in on the steps of city hall. I certainly didn't demand he take his *own* name off the ballot." Which would have been an epic conversational riposte.

Hallie had thought of it on her way back to the library (done at half the speed of her sprint to city hall. Actually, done at more of a sloth-like pace as the enormity of what had just occurred swamped her with fear. And regret. And the resurging waves of humiliation as she remembered her stained shirt).

"Why did you order all this"—Randall waved his hand holding a stub of pretzel covered in beer cheese dip—"if you weren't wallowing?"

"Or celebrating?" Megan added.

"Food is calming. It helps every situation." Hallie decided to be brutally honest. Her friends wouldn't judge her for being a fence-sitter. *She'd* judge herself, but they wouldn't. "And the thing is, guys? I don't honestly know what I'm feeling, which frustrates me above and beyond anything else. I'm a strong, fast decision-maker. I don't waffle."

Ana clasped her hands, then pointed her index fingers, each wearing a hammered silver ring, at Hallie. "Do you want to run for mayor?"

"No." It would take time, so much time. Gah. She'd probably have to use some of her precious PTO hours for campaign events.

"Do you want to be mayor?"

"No." Her only career aspiration *ever* was to be a librarian. To live and breathe books. To help others discover the magic of fiction. To spread the wonder and knowledge encapsulated in non-fiction.

Where was the wonder in going over the line item details of the town's water bills?

Ana leaned back against the green leather booth and fluffed her thick, dark waves forward to coil across her bright red tee. "Well, that seems clear-cut. You're screwed."

Randall laughed, coughed, and snorted simultaneously. "That's not helpful! Save that for when the three of us discuss how stupid this was in the parking lot *after* Hallie leaves."

Yeah, yeah.

It'd been impulsive, that was for sure, and not anywhere in her life plan, which was simply a five-bullet point list in her senior yearbook:

1) Graduate with honors from undergrad

2) Get *another* scholarship to pay for grad school

3) Graduate with honors again

4) Become a librarian

5) Fall in love with a man who would kill bugs for her and not complain about the teetering stack of books on her nightstand.

Honestly, Hallie was more than good with having crossed off the first four. She didn't think it needed a number six: lead the town with zero experience and simply a passion for responsibility and fairness.

Hallie didn't *do* impulsive. Except that it was too late to undo anything. So it was imperative she circle back and embrace the reason that had launched her off this particular cliff.

"I *do* want there to be a different, better mayor. No one else stepped up." She scooped more than her fair share of the potato skins onto her plate. Nobody else was stress eating.

They were just sympathy eating. That meant she deserved the ones topped with the most bacon. "You can't complain about a situation without bringing at least one solution to the table."

Megan's green eyes dripped with...pity? Yikes. "Oh, honey, you absolutely can. That's how complaining works."

"You chose to do something for the good of the community rather than take the easy way out and do nothing." Ana raised her glass in a toast. Her deep red lips, which contrasted so beautifully with her tawny skin that always looked tan even in the darkness of a Maine winter, spread into a wide smile. "That's admirable. It proves you'll be a good leader."

"While that strikes me as a vast overstatement, I'll take it." The first vote in her favor! Hallie beamed at her friend. "Thanks, Ana."

"However, we may be the only three people in all of Swan Cove who know you've got what it takes to assume the mantle of mayorship." Ana never pulled any punches. Megan and Randall were the *rah-rah* cheerleaders of their group. Ana stuck to the facts. Which Hallie *usually* appreciated.

"You need a mantle." Randall shook out his napkin and draped it around his glass. "A cape. If you win." His eyes flitted quickly among the three of them. His tongue darted out to lick his lips. "I mean, *when* you win. You'll totally win. I believe in you, Hallie. It was just a slip of the tongue. I'm still coming to terms with this big bomb you dropped on us."

Laughing, Hallie covered his mouth with her palm. "Randall. Stop. No need to backtrack. I know you've got my back. Just as much as I know that there's an exceedingly strong chance that I might not win."

Chance. Ha! It was all but guaranteed she wouldn't win.

Hallie, like Ana, also preferred to subsume herself in facts rather than hope. She'd taken a stand on principle, but in all likelihood, it would be no more than that. A grand gesture with no discernible outcome.

Aside from her abject humiliation.

Ana rapped her knuckles against the wood paneling that turned the booth into a semi-private compartment. "Like I said, tonight's an emergency summit. There's no point debating if it was a dumb idea to stay on the ballot. Or, rather, to have your name *put* on the ballot in the first place." She glared at Megan who responded simply with a "what did I do" quirk of her pierced eyebrow. "Let's talk through the viability of you as a candidate. See what we've got to work with."

Randall cautiously raised a hand and waited until Ana nodded. "Is that a polite way of saying 'see if she has a snowball's chance in hell of pulling this off?'"

"Hey!" Okay. Maybe she preferred his usual cheerleader role to this blunt honesty. But before she could splutter her indignation at the phrasing, a male voice floated over the top of their booth. It was overly loud, catching their attention.

"Short answer? No." A second behind his words, a head appeared. Followed by the tops of incredibly broad shoulders. His blue eyes crinkled at the corners in obvious amusement as he glanced at her, then her friends. Cheerful creases bracketed his mouth.

It was the mayor.

Hallie had thought she couldn't be more embarrassed than this morning when she'd accidentally overheard them dismissing her. Turned out she'd been wrong. Having the competition overhear her closest friends questioning her ability to win? That was indeed the lowest possible point.

She froze. What to do now?

She should go on the offensive. The mayor was, as of ten hours ago, officially her enemy.

No, she'd done that this morning. She should take the high road. Greet him magnanimously. Because he was a citizen of Swan Cove and thus just another potential constituent. An upstanding one with no current library fines (of *course* she'd checked immediately upon returning to work).

"Bar trivia's on Mondays, buckaroo," Ana said. "This is Thursday. Until then, you can keep your unsolicited answers to yourself."

Hallie had never loved her friend more. They'd always been kindred spirits and had bonded over the love of the written word. Ana ran the town's—or rather Montgomery Industries'—rare book shop.

Megan studiously did *not* look at the mayor. "Isn't eavesdropping rude? If someone belongs to the yacht club and the country club and is the primary representative of our entire city, wouldn't you expect them to have, I dunno, better manners?"

Not a hint of shame crossed his patrician features. "I wasn't eavesdropping. I'm sitting at the bar right behind your booth. And, well, you're all pretty loud."

That was probably accurate. They were worked up. But…oh, God…if the mayor heard them…who *else* had unintentionally overheard? Hallie wanted to pull a Wicked Witch of the West and melt into the floorboards.

Another man appeared next to the mayor. Hallie recognized his face, even if she couldn't dredge up a name. She *could* pinpoint that he came in every two weeks to pick up the newest thrillers.

"Hey. I'm Everett. I'll second that you were being loud. We're generally decent guys. We weren't trying to listen. But you've been talking smack about my friend here, so it's hard to tune you out."

Crap. Now she'd have to apologize.

Because Everett was cute, with horn-rimmed glasses, and a Henley taut across his pecs, Megan went straight into flirt-mode (which was her MO a good 98.4 percent of the time). "I'm Megan. And I don't think I mind at all being noticed by you."

OMG. A bar hookup was not the way to de-escalate the situation. Hallie had full faith in Megan's powers of flirtation—but that didn't make it *appropriate*. She wiped her hands and scooched out of the booth. "Mr. Mayor? May I talk to you? In private?"

The mayor looked over both shoulders. Then at her. "Will I need my security detail?"

Hallie's stomach twisted into a knot. Yes, she'd been, well, aggressive this morning in her approach. But did he really think she was calling him out for a fight? To settle the election here and now, in an Irish pub with fiddles blaring from the speakers?

"No. Of course not," she said swiftly as she rounded to meet him. "I would never disrespect the office of mayor or you personally with any physical attack. You can tell your security to stand down."

He threw back his head and howled with laughter. "I'm mayor of Swan Cove. There's no security. And I've got zero concern about you throwing down."

That was a tad demeaning. Her inner feminist flared to life. "Because I'm a woman?"

"Hardly. Women can kick ass. Because you're a librarian."

Hallie noticed that her friends—and his—were following the exchange with avid attention. She pointed to the open door right off the bar. The private party room looked empty, and once she closed the door, nobody would even know they were in there.

As soon as the door shut behind them, the mayor held up his hands. "Don't get in a lather that I'm insulting all librarians. I get the impression that you're Type A. Rule-following. More apt to use words than action."

"You'd be correct."

"So, we've established you didn't drag me back here to

beat some sense into me." He crossed his arms and half sat on the edge of a long, draped table. "What do you want from me, Ms. Scott?"

Now that it was just the two of them, it felt...*arch* to stand on ceremony with last names. Like she was trying too hard to prove a point. This wasn't 1922. "Call me Hallie."

"Okay, Hallie. You can call me Mr. Mayor." He waited precisely two beats—long enough for her outrage to flare to life—before laughing again. "I'm pulling your leg. Call me Fitz."

So that was how it was going to be?

Well. She could be equally laidback. Hallie pulled out a wooden chair and sat, crossing her legs, and was inordinately relieved she'd gone home and changed into clean clothes before arriving. "You enjoy laughing at my expense?"

"You walked right into that one. And, come to think of it, the previous one. If you give me a perfect setup, I'm going to spike the ball." He hinged forward from the waist. "I'm also going to assume you get that sports reference, despite all the librarian clichés."

How had he known?

She jerked in surprise. The wedge sandal she'd been attempting to casually dangle from her toes fell off completely. Because apparently the universe had decided that it was to be an all-you-can-eat buffet of humiliation in front of this man.

"You spent the day researching me, going through my yearbooks?"

Now Fitz jerked, jackknifing right up off the table. "What? That's creepy. No. I spent the day doing all the glamorous mayoral shit you want to take over. Why do you think I yearbook-stalked you?"

Whoops. She could *not* get a read on this man. Hallie toyed with her bracelet, heavy with bookish charms. "I...well...I was captain of my high school volleyball team."

Another laugh almost slipped from his lips. Fitz choked it back at her steely glare. "That's a handy coincidence."

Too much of one for her liking. And now that he was standing, he positively towered over her. Fitz had to be more than a few inches over six feet. Tipping her head back—which felt ludicrous, she asked, "Why'd you assume I'd get the volleyball reference if you didn't go scrabbling through my past?"

"I was making a point, attempting to, anyway, of not just seeing you as a librarian cliché."

Oh. That was thoughtful. Polite.

Damn it.

Plus, she still owed him an apology for spouting off with her friends where everyone and their dog could hear. It was necessary to give him something to make it right.

"I appreciate that. I do embody some of the ubiquitous traits of my career. A love of reading, a preference for tea over coffee, and...I occasionally take myself a bit too seriously."

His lips twisted downward. The veneer of charm cracked. "Whereas there are some who say I don't take myself seriously enough." There was a certain hollowness to his words. A shuttering coldness to his blue eyes.

Suddenly, unequivocally, Hallie *knew* that someone had hurt him. And it made Fitz Montgomery a tiny bit more approachable to her.

She tucked her hands beneath her thighs. "Sounds like Goldilocks would say that what Swan Cove needs is a third candidate."

"Do you have a daily goal to hit? Of book references to slip into conversation?"

"Of course. You only get one under-target day per week. Anything more than that, and you get dinged. Three of them, and my librarian's license gets pulled."

Fitz put his hands over his heart. Staggered back a few

steps until his shoulder blades hit the toucan on the vintage Guinness poster. "Stop the presses. You got my joke, and you built on it and volleyed it back."

"Another sports metaphor? Do you have a daily goal to hit of slipping *those* into conversation?"

Laughter roared out of him. And after only a second, Hallie joined in. Because that exchange hadn't been about maintaining their adversarial distance. It had just been fun.

He pushed off the wall, straightened the poster behind him, then extended his hand. "How about we start over?"

Hallie stared down at the long fingers. At how his cuff was caught on the big platinum and navy-faced watch. At the dusting of blond hair just below the edge of the cuff. There was something about the forearms...and wrists...on a man. Like a caffeine shot to her libido.

That extended hand had danger written all over it.

She sighed. "What would be the point? We're always going to be on opposite sides."

Fitz slid his hand into his pocket, smooth as a runway model. "*Always?* You're already planning to hold a lifelong grudge against me? At most, shouldn't it only last the month until the election? I'm polite. I donate blood, give to charities. Help little old ladies across the street."

She wriggled back into her sandal, then pointed her toe to draw a line across the green carpet. "As far as right now is concerned? That month is all that matters. You're over there. I'm here."

He stroked his chin. It had just enough dark blond six o'clock shadow to be as sexy as his wrists. "Do you want to bring back witch trials?"

What on earth? "Don't be ridiculous."

"Me, neither." Extending a finger, he tapped it against his lips. Which...were as sexy as the aforementioned stubble and wrists. She wanted to touch it all. "How about the speed limit along Main Street and Beach Road? Good with it?"

"The slower speed is to protect the heavy pedestrian traffic in those areas. It's both reasonable and appropriate."

"Agreed. Plus, we rake in a ton on speeding tickets. Not just tourists, either. The ticket fines cover the cost of resurfacing and filling in potholes."

Huh. So the mayor was more than a pretty face. An impeccably proportioned, handsome-as-hell face. While still an adversary, he'd at least be an interesting one.

Fitz looked down at the imaginary carpet line, took two steps closer to it. "Do you want to repeal the law prohibiting biting a landlord under any circumstance?"

It took biting the inside of her lip to keep from laughing out loud. "That's a real law on the books of Swan Cove?"

"Yep."

Randall had filled her in about plenty of old, weird American laws after a history podcast week. Cursing (technically) was a misdemeanor in Michigan. Delaware prohibited R-rated movies at drive-ins (doubtful it was enforced). Hallie had no idea that her own city had its own weirdly noteworthy law.

"No, I'm, ah, not prepared to wade into that particular issue."

Fitz tapped his chest with an index finger, then swung it back and forth between the two of them. "That's what I said when I first read it. It feels inconsequential but was clearly a hot-button enough topic to get passed. Better to let sleeping dogs lie."

They both chuckled together for a moment, just long enough to feel like they were in sync.

This pleasant banter was too nice, too easy. Too distracting. Too close to flirting. Hallie cleared her throat and tossed her ponytail. "What is the point you're trying to make?"

"Like I said, we start over. You can be all hopped up with micro-aggression and righteous indignation toward Mayor Montgomery, your opponent. But when we're not stumping? We're just Fitz and Hallie. Two people who agree on a lot."

That was true. They were getting along famously right now. They were having too much of a good time. It was an effortless push-pull.

It was dangerous.

He'd stepped closer again, so close she leaned back *and* tilted her head to look up at him. "Why?"

"Why not?" His hands gripped just above her elbows and pulled her to her feet. Warm breath with the faintest aroma of Guinness puffed across her cheeks. At least an inch of air still circulated between their bodies, but this close, Fitz's *presence* filled that empty space and pressed in on her. It felt like they were on the brink of something.

If she didn't know better, she'd swear he was on the brink of kissing her. Swan Cove's biggest playboy and most eligible bachelor. It was easy to see why so many women fell for his act.

Worse yet? She was on the brink of letting him. Hallie pulled out of his grasp. Stepping backward, however, banged her into the chair. She staggered sideways in a half spin and almost fell.

Until, of course, Fitz steadied her. Of course, because he was Mr. Smooth and she was apparently Princess Awkward in this cautionary tale.

As soon as her feet were planted again, Hallie brushed off his hands. "Now I know what you were doing all day."

Mild amusement flickered across his face. "This should be good."

"Once I announced my candidacy, you did a deep dive into *The Art of War*, didn't you?"

The amusement blinked away, replaced by a confused

squint around those blue eyes. "The book?"

"Yes, the book. Everything good and useful is in a book. And this one, by Sun Tzu, is studied by strategists and politicians and masterminds the world over."

"Well, I don't have a copy. What is it you think I got out of it today?"

"The most classic quote from it: keep your friends close and your enemies closer. This"—Hallie waved a hand over the carpet-scuffed line that was back between them—"*encounter* that just took place? Your attempt to keep your enemy close? It won't work."

She rushed out of the room before Fitz could see just how well it had almost worked. How her pulse still pounded. How her mouth was still parted, wishing for more.

Chapter Four

Pancakes or French toast? Fitz preferred not having to decide. It was why he loved breakfast events at the Guillemot Golf Club. It was a buffet, which meant he could load his plate with both. Plus, the chef put out warm maple, blueberry, and butter pecan syrup.

It *almost* made this campaign kickoff bearable.

Reasons why he'd still hate today?

One, his dad's cronies still treating him like a kid. One octogenarian had actually tried to tousle his hair while Fitz held the door open for him.

Two, the fact that a campaign event was hosted at a club where attendance was members only. C'mon—that was pure bullshit. Every adult citizen of Swan Cove deserved an equal chance to hear the candidates speak. But it was tradition that Guillemot kicked off the campaign, and tradition ran neck and neck with money when it came to what ruled this town.

Three, the way they'd sit through his stump speech but wouldn't ask him any substantive questions. Shouldn't they want answers from their mayor?

Derek had told him not to look a gift horse in the mouth. Still felt wrong, though.

And last but not least, four, sharing a table with Hallie Scott. His nemesis. Not by *his* reckoning. He'd tried, hadn't he? To smooth things over. To start on an even playing field. To be a decent fellow candidate and not a club-swinging neanderthal jerk of an opponent.

It hadn't worked.

"Fitzwilliam, you don't need all that syrup. You'll be drowning in sugar with that girl sitting next to you this morning." It was his old golf coach, Lawrence Fenton. The man wore old-fashioned plus fours *everywhere*. As if someone might knock over the chafing dish full of French toast and demand he show them how to put some English on a putt in the next five minutes.

"What girl?" All the kids were still in school. Was some over-eager teacher dragging their class here as a civics field trip?

"The one running against you. The librarian."

Holy hell. Lawrence *was* on the wrong side of sixty, but that was no excuse. "You can't call Ms. Scott a girl."

He waved the tongs, pinching two fat sausages. "Nobody's around to hear. You don't have to pretend to stick up for her."

"For God's sake, I'm not pretending. And I'm not sticking up for her. I'm sticking up for all women. *Women*," he repeated slowly, drawing the word out. "Anyone of the opposite sex old enough to vote."

"Ah. I see what you did there. Brought it back to being about the election. Well done." Lawrence dropped a sausage on Fitz's plate like a reward, winked, then ambled off.

That…had to be an anomaly. Hallie had the deck stacked against her—unfairly—because she wasn't a Montgomery. Her gender couldn't also be an issue. Not in the twenty-first century. Not in Swan Cove.

Could it? No. *Not* in Swan Cove. Fitz wouldn't stand for it.

"Ah, Mayor Montgomery." Olivier—God help anyone who accidentally pronounced it without that second "i" since he was named after the famous actor—leaned out to catch him as Fitz approached. "I see you broke out the seersucker on this warm morning. Perfect sartorial choice."

After spending thirty years as a costumer for the soap operas that filmed in Manhattan, Olivier had come back home to care for his mom after her stroke. He'd immediately started writing a fashion column for the *Swan Cove Bulletin*. And apparently felt it his duty to comment on every outfit worn by every person he saw in a day.

It cracked Fitz up when Olivier heaped praise on the oyster shuckers along the cruise ship dock for their "practical yet peppy" aprons. Because the man was never mean. He'd compliment a burglar on wearing slimming black while the guy robbed him blind.

"Thanks, Ollie. I wanted to make a good impression on you. It's your first election back home, and I'm hoping I can count on your vote." Fitz angled closer. Lowered his voice. "If you were compelled to tell your mom about my seersucker suaveness so she voted for me, too? Even better."

"You certainly look the part, my dear boy. Nobody else would even try to pull off that shade of green in seersucker. I approve."

"Thanks." He'd gotten the suit to attend the Kentucky Derby for a bachelor party. The invite had come with shopping links for "appropriate wear." The suit had lasted longer than the marriage.

"But I can't promise you my vote, Fitz. You're a good friend, but that doesn't make you a good mayor."

Grimacing, Fitz said, "Ouch."

"I didn't say it made you a *bad* mayor. I'm simply saying

I haven't made up my mind yet now that there's another candidate in the mix."

He was actually fine with that. "Fair enough."

"What's her style?"

Fitz...didn't know. He knew who Hallie was because he made it a point to be aware of all city employees, but he never *went* to the library. Never seemed to cross paths on Main Street with Ms. Scott until yesterday's disastrous meeting at the pub.

He vividly remembered the way the wet green stains on her shirt made it cling to her body yesterday morning. And last night...Well, he honestly didn't remember what she'd been wearing. Just the way her warm brown eyes had fluttered shut for a split second once he'd lifted her to her feet. The way her hair had flowed over his hands, the same brown as the cinnamon tea his Aunt Felicia favored. The tiny, dark freckle right below the outer corner of her left eye that he wanted to lick...

"Um, you know, like a librarian. That's your specialty, Ollie, not mine. She'll be up on the dais with me. You can figure out her style then."

"Looking forward to it."

Fitz made it a record-breaking seven steps away from the buffet before getting stopped again. He made sure to slap on a smile before looking up.

"Fitzwilliam." With a swift glance at the loaded plate, his father said, "You're going to finish that before the event begins, yes?"

"No." Talk about a fun realization. No shoveling it all down in the next five minutes. "That's the joy of having another candidate up there with me. I'll be able to enjoy my breakfast during her answers."

"You need to stay sharp, pay attention to what she says, in case you need to rebut. No slipping into a sugar coma."

"Dad, I'm thirty-two. I don't slip into sugar comas anymore. If you see that happen, call an ambulance, because it means I've developed adult-onset diabetes."

That earned him a frown that made the silver brows almost touch. "You shouldn't joke about it. You know Jerry McDonald has it. He's having a hell of a time getting his numbers under control."

Probably due to the fact that good ol' Jerry still posted up at the bakery for donuts every morning and finished every golf round with two scotches and a bacon cheeseburger. "You started it, Dad."

"Hmm." It was all the acknowledgment he'd get. "Try to throw her words back at her. Twist them. Cut her off whenever possible."

"Again, *no*. You taught me better than that. Nobody's going to vote for me if I'm rude to Ms. Scott."

"Nonsense." He made a minute adjustment to his black and gold tie tack. "Everybody's going to vote for you, regardless."

"Then there's no reason to be rude, is there?" Fitz grinned. Always nice to get one over on his old man. "See how I twisted your own words back at you? Clearly, I'm on fire this morning. No need to worry."

After a strong shoulder grip that would've made Mr. Spock envious, his dad looked him in the eyes and said, "Don't be cocky."

Man, there was no winning to be had this morning. Fitz kept his head down as he made his way to the dais. The six-foot-long table was skirted with red, white, and blue bunting. Guess he'd have lots of elbow room between him and Hallie.

He took his seat, pushed the microphone aside, and dug in. Tried his best not to make eye contact with anyone because that was just weird while chewing and being so far away from the rest of the tables in the ballroom.

But his gaze did a target-lock on Hallie as she walked up the steps. Navy blouse. Navy pants. Navy shoes. Either she was color-blind and dressing for safety, or...she really did have the clichéd style of a prim, boring librarian.

Except...there'd been nothing prim or boring about the way she'd looked at him when they'd been in a near-clinch, which made Fitz all the more curious about who Hallie Scott *really* was.

"Mayor. Good morning."

"Right back at ya."

She carefully set down her plate, with several chunks of pineapple sliding precariously close to the edge. "How are we supposed to eat and answer questions at the same time?"

He pointed at the first row of tables. "That's why everyone's seated so far back from us. Gives a spray zone."

Hallie's jaw was only halfway through dropping before Fitz laughed. "Oh, you're putting me on. Having a little fun at my expense. Again."

Way to put his foot in it. *Again.*

"Hell. No, I'm sorry. Just kidding around because I've had the same thought. This year's a big improvement. We'll each have time to chew and swallow while the other's talking."

"In that case, feel free to ramble. I was too nervous to eat, but this smells delicious." She dove right into her French toast.

"Not to freak you out, but I don't think I'll be talking much. You're the new variable in the equation. Nobody needs to listen to me rehash the same old, same old."

His eyes glued to her lips as she licked off a drop of syrup. "Throw a girl a bone, won't you?"

Fitz almost choked. The eternal twenty-one-year-old in him wanted to indeed give her a bone. If she'd phrased it like that deliberately, he was in trouble.

But before he could say anything—not that he'd thought

of a response that wouldn't result in an immediate glass of juice in his face—the president of the club stepped up to the mic.

Then he tapped it, resulting in the inevitable *thwomp* and immediate screech of feedback. Gerald would never learn. "Welcome to the campaign kickoff for Swan Cove's next mayor!"

Polite applause rolled through the room. Fitz would estimate at least thirty people didn't bother to put down their forks and participate. He glanced at Hallie.

She wasn't clapping. She wasn't eating.

Every bit of color had leached from her face. Either she was about to pass out, or she was terrified.

Yes, she'd brought this on herself. Or, at least, her friend had. But Fitz still felt bad for her. You didn't dip your toe into campaigning. It was more like being flung out of a helicopter in the middle of...whatever ocean had the most sharks.

With a casual nudge, he sent his knife off the table onto the floor in between them. Leaning down, he whispered, "It'll be okay. Just be yourself."

Maybe she heard him. Maybe not, since Gerald was still yammering away.

"Mr. Mayor, we'll lead off with a question for you." Gerald pointed at an elderly man practically vibrating with excitement. The club had a lottery every year for the honor of asking the first question of the campaign.

It usually terrified Fitz to think of how many tickets his dad probably bought.

"Mayor Montgomery, I'm Reggie Shaw."

"Reggie, no need for introductions. You think I'd forget the man who taught me how to drive?" Reggie had already been ancient when Fitz took driver's ed from him. It focused you, wondering if your teacher was about to slump over at any second.

He mimed putting his hands on the wheel. "Ten and two will get you through!"

Okay, Fitz *had* forgotten that old chestnut. He forced a smile and tried to share it with Hallie, but she only had eyes for her fruit. "What's on your mind, Reggie?"

"What are your thoughts on the expansion of the downtown area?"

Fitz swallowed hard. Hell.

The old guy was leading off with a hot-button issue. The plans weren't even official public knowledge—they'd only shared the proposal at a Chamber of Commerce meeting to gauge the response among businesses that would be the most affected.

There was a good chance Hallie didn't know about it. Or anything more than a rumbling, a hint. Plenty of people wanted to keep the downtown area intact. No buildings over three stories. No official expansion away from the already delineated six-block area by the harbor.

Plenty of *other* people thought growth was necessary, not just to expand tourism and bolster the economy, but because the population of locals had grown. Cygnet Labs was one of the top genomic research facilities in the country. Once they'd based their headquarters in Swan Cove, the population spiked by an additional 1,500—plus their kids and spouses.

Sure, the sixty-eight-building lab campus had its own cafeteria *and* gym *and* cleaners. But the bottom line was that Swan Cove was now bursting at the seams, both with people and with the demand for more services. And all those new people got visitors, which was why the centerpiece of the expansion idea was a hotel and marina.

Fitz didn't need to glance over the room to know that the split was probably fifty-fifty. Whatever he answered would piss off a good half of the attendees.

Number one rule of campaigning—according to Derek,

anyway? If you have to tell people something they don't want to hear, just *don't* tell them. Pivot. Make a joke. Change the subject.

As his gaze skimmed over the silver strands atop his dad's head, the answer came to him. Make a joke. "The obvious first thought is that my dad's going to want his name splashed across whatever might get built."

You couldn't blink without seeing *Montgomery* in some form on at least one of the nearest three buildings. Plus, it was self-deprecating, since everyone thought Fitz sponged off his family's trust fund.

Yep. The whole room chuckled. Crisis averted. The guy closest to his dad threw an elbow, and his dad tossed back a crumpled linen napkin. It was all jovial—until Gerald pointed his gavel at Hallie. "Miss Scott. If you would please give your answer to the same question."

"Oh." She blotted her mouth. Poked her glasses higher on the bridge of her pert nose. "Well, it can't be just a single question. You can't answer if it *should* be done unless you first assess *how* it should be done. Historical preservation is, of course, the delicate seesaw on which the whole thing balances. Do we preserve our history—and all the challenges that poses—to the exclusion of future growth? Do we find a middle ground, vis-à-vis rehabbing what is most pressing and pertinent to the historical sense of Swan Cove as a whole? Or do we embrace the fact that we have flourished as a community? Celebrate our successes by expanding accordingly for the betterment of all?"

Holy hell.

That was...a *lot* of words. All of which circled the generality of preservation vs. expansion, rather than diving into the specifics. It signaled to Fitz that this was the first she'd heard of the proposal.

He wouldn't just have time to finish his breakfast while

Hallie spoke. At this rate, he'd get a jump on lunch, too.

"Was that a yes or a no in favor of expansion of downtown, Miss Scott?" Gerald pressed.

"It was neither. If you'd been paying attention, that would have been clear. The question was too broad. I laid out the parameters of what needed to be delineated in order for a proper discussion to proceed."

She was still talking too much *and* hiding that she wasn't up to speed on the expansion plans while simultaneously knocking Gerald down a notch. Forget breakfast and lunch. Fitz wanted popcorn for this show.

Gerald shook his gavel at her. "You're talking in circles, Miss Scott. Please answer the question. That is, after all, why we've taken precious time out of our busy days, to learn where you, a complete newcomer to local politics, stand on the issues."

Yeah. Gerald had noted the smack down, and he wasn't happy about it either. Fitz pulled his phone from his pocket and started texting Everett under the table. *Campaign breakfast has turned into a WWE match.*

Hallie shook her fork right back at him. Syrup did indeed fly into the spray zone Fitz had jokingly pointed out. "You didn't make Mayor Montgomery answer the question. He got away with a single smart-aleck sentence before you moved on to me. I, at least, provided context for not only a more comprehensive debate but points which need to be solidified by the town council before we move forward at all."

Reggie stood again and poked his arm up and down until Gerald acknowledged him. "My apologies. My morning java hasn't kicked in yet, I'm afraid. You raised some good points. I didn't follow them all, but you sounded sure of yourself. I respect that. It's the key to good driving, you know. Surety in your decisions. You don't hang about, taking your time straddling a lane. When you want to move, you move. Safer for everyone that way."

After teaching driver's ed for...well, *forever*, Reggie found a way to turn almost every conversation back to something car related. Fitz knew that Hallie hadn't grown up in Swan Cove. She was probably confused as to why the man had veered off on that tangent.

"Here's what I'm sure of, Mr. Shaw." Hand over her heart, she beamed sincerity his way. "No matter what, we need more time added to the parking meters. Two hours doesn't give you enough time to get a haircut, have lunch with friends, and then do a little shopping. The maximum limit needs to be raised on the existing meters and, concurrently, if any are added to a potentially expanded downtown area."

Son of a bitch. She *did* know Reggie. Because as much as that man babbled on about driving with every other breath, he liked even more to complain about the tickets he amassed for staying over his meter time.

Hallie was...well, she was pandering to him, giving him exactly what he wanted. It was a beautiful move. Campaign-wise. Except...

Fitz knew that she'd unintentionally poured gasoline on a pile of tinder. Because there were many others in the room who knew how much revenue they brought in from meter ticketing. Plugging a meter with two dollars for four hours didn't compare to a fifty-dollar ticket for an expired meter.

All that cash rolling in was what prevented them from raising taxes.

And every person in this room knew that—except for Hallie, apparently.

Sure enough, just as Hallie leaned back in her chair with a hint of relief smoothing out the tense pull around her eyes, *chaos* erupted.

Everyone started talking at once. Fitz was too far away to isolate most of it. But from the closest tables he caught "you'll bankrupt us" to "you don't have the right to mess with our taxes" to, worst of all, "shows how little you know." Not to mention a few grumblings about how a nobody from Crow Harbor couldn't comprehend the reality of a balanced fiscal plan.

Man, that was going too damn far. Classist bigots.

It wasn't courteous.

It wasn't organized.

It wasn't mature.

It was like a bad comedy movie cliché of a campaign event imploding. Voices raised. Chairs pushed back. Gerald began banging his gavel. The kitchen staff even rushed out, taking protective positions behind the chafing dishes.

It'd be laughable in the retelling…someday.

Right now? Fitz was embarrassed his voting citizens were behaving like seventh graders. Mad at them for turning breakfast into a shitshow. If this was a taste of what the rest of the campaign events would be like, it'd be a painfully endless two months.

Worse still? Fitz couldn't do a damned thing about it. He had to wait it out and let Gerald try and get everyone back under control.

Not because he thought it'd in any way affect his chances at reelection, but because from his two brief interactions with Hallie, it was obvious she was fiercely independent. And that if he gave in to his chivalric instincts and smoothed things over and redirected the flow of crap aimed her way by the town's most upstanding citizens?

She'd probably throw the syrup-drenched plate at him.

Even though her face was currently beet red with embarrassment at so obviously having said the wrong thing and caused this mess.

Even though he could see her white-knuckling the edge of her seat.

Even though, even over the din, he could hear her panting as if she'd just run up the stairs of the Empire State Building.

So, Fitz said nothing, did nothing, aside from polishing off his breakfast. It didn't feel good, but that was pretty much par for the course of his entire tenure as mayor.

Chapter Five

Some people drowned the memory of a crushing defeat in ice cream. Or any junk food. Alcohol. Unwise flings. Unnecessary hair color changes.

All of that was just trying to erase the previous bad decision with a new one.

Hallie knew better. There were two important steps to recovering from a...misstep. An egregious mistake. Or...a series of misinformed choices.

One, acknowledge what went wrong. No excuses. Own the blunder and accept that no matter the good intentions behind it, it was not a success.

Two, figure out how to keep from repeating it. Research. Study. All the information was out there waiting to be corralled. Categorized. Comprehended.

Hallie was very much aware that she'd screwed up at the campaign breakfast. That her performance earned zero points. No gold stars. Frankly, they should've charged her for the breakfast after bombing so spectacularly.

Embarrassingly.

And given that Swan Cove was a typical small town with a stereotypical group penchant for repeating minutiae? The story of her self-destruction would no doubt be told and retold. Not just for the duration of the campaign but for her entire life. Probably even retold as legend for every campaign that ever kicked off until a black hole, eons down the road, swallowed the earth whole.

Yes, Hallie was feeling sorry for herself. A tiny bit. But she had a plan to fix it all.

She'd eschewed offers from her friends to help her wallow, bring her donuts, bring her tacos, and especially declined the offer to go "run off her shame" for a few miles. Hallie felt bad, but she didn't feel *exercise* bad.

Instead, she'd posted up at her home away from home—the library. Amassing the right knowledge, having it all at her mental fingertips, would change everything.

Hallie was surrounded by copies of the *Gazette* from the past two months. It'd been the logical go-to for info about the expansion plans, but all she'd found so far was a single line about it as a topic for a Chamber of Commerce meeting.

It slightly mollified her that she hadn't been oblivious to a huge issue—it simply wasn't public knowledge yet. But being mollified didn't fix the problem. It didn't give Hallie the information needed to weigh in.

So, she was also surrounded by books. Books on famous battles, both the insignificant and the major wins/losses and their strategies. The same for campaigns. This wasn't a one or the other approach—this campaign would be a series of skirmishes. Battles. Fights for supremacy.

And all of that was just to prevent being laughed off the dais again.

Yes. Being buried in facts was the way to go. Even if one stack of particularly thick military histories had toppled and crushed her pinkie.

"Hallie, dear, I heard what happened." Felicia Montgomery (yes, *that* Montgomery family, aka, aunt of the current mayor) strode briskly across the library, not bothering to temper her voice at all in respect to the holy temple of knowledge. Her peacock-bright kimono swished against her pants.

"You heard that I decided against ordering the Pulitzer winners this year? Nobody reads them. The cache of having them on the shelves isn't worth the budgetary hit."

"Don't be obtuse. You're too smart to get away with it." Felicia pulled her cheaters off the top of her gray head simply to give a pointed stare over the edges of them. "I heard you were eviscerated. No, that's not quite right. You, yourself, are to blame for much of it. More along the lines of self-immolation, am I right?"

Continuing to play coy wouldn't accomplish anything. Felicia had sources. And to *so* blatantly not beat around the bush like this, every single source must've raced to update her.

Hallie methodically lined up her pen parallel to the edge of her notebook before answering because acknowledging step one to *herself* was not the same as doing it to someone else. "I will admit that the campaign breakfast did not rise above my very low expectations. Aside from the food. That was surprisingly delicious."

"Of course it was. I stole the chef from a burgeoning four-restaurant empire in Chicago."

That was Felicia Montgomery, the unofficial fairy godmother of Swan Cove. Or, to be more gritty about it, their fixer. She had no official title or salary, but if something needed doing, Felicia would get it done.

"Well, if I don't need to tell you that the pancakes were as fluffy as cotton candy, then I guess we're all caught up." Hallie moved her palm restlessly over the burgundy leather binding of a Napoleon biography. She yearned to be inside its pages, sopping up all the info that would keep her from screwing up so royally next time.

Felicia squeezed her shoulder in a grip that would do a masseuse proud. That single squeeze gave a measure of solace—while also being awkward. Felicia wasn't a touchy-feely-hugging type. "I'm sorry, Hallie."

"Thank you." Good. That was done. They could move on.

The most comforting thing about Felicia right now was that she wasn't a wallower. She was brisk, efficient, and always focused on the next thing—whatever that might be. Even her hair, in its thick Princess Diana shaggy cut, was wash and go. Felicia *never* wasted time.

"Naturally, I'm curious why you chose to enter the ring against an incumbent. You're educated enough to know that drastically lowered your chance of even marginal success." After a sharp *tsk* with her tongue, the older woman sat across from Hallie. "But now you're in the thick of it. All that matters is figuring out how to move forward."

Hallie delighted in proper vocabulary at all times. There were so many evocative, interesting words that never got used anymore. With that caveat, though, she had to clamp her lips shut to not simply respond *Duh!* Which was absolutely the right word at the right time.

Felicia deserved a tad more respect. So, instead, Hallie waved her arms at the semi-circle of stacked books. "What do you think I'm doing? This isn't me sloughing off reshelving. This is all research."

"On what?"

"Anything and everything that could give me a leg up when it comes to strategy."

The wince was so big it was easily visible behind her iridescent purple frames. "I suppose we do need to backtrack.

My dear, you didn't enter into this race actually planning to beat my nephew, did you?"

Not so much *planning* as righteously indignant and thus momentarily certain of being rewarded thusly with a win. Aka, impulse rather than intellect, which very well might end up in ignominious defeat.

Hallie couldn't exactly come clean with that as her rationale, seeing as how it made zero sense. Luckily, she'd crafted a much better, albeit fake, thought process to share with people in her sleepless night between committing to running and the debacle of a kickoff breakfast.

Interlacing her fingers in a pose that might play better behind a podium, she said, "Taking a stand without being prepared to follow through is pointless. So, yes, I'm going to try to crush the opposition." Except, Fitz wasn't any run-of-the-mill opposition, not where Felicia was concerned. Her foot was so far in her mouth it was practically back down by her other foot at this point. Hallie bit her bottom lip. "Sorry that it's your nephew, but that's politics."

Felicia's hand covered her mouth. "Goodness. I don't want to laugh and insult you, but…honestly, I *am* inclined to laugh."

"That's fine. Truly." It wasn't even worth explaining how Megan had initially gotten her into this mess. It'd been Hallie's decision to stand up to Fitz and his toady Derek and not back out. She'd shoulder all the fully deserved mocking for it.

"I came here to offer you help in saving face. By getting a few key people to smile favorably on you—not enough to give you any shot at winning, I'm afraid that simply isn't in the realm of possibility—but so you wouldn't be…what was the word? *Crushed*."

"You're very kind."

Felicia had looked out for her from day one, at Hallie's

interview. Felicia had castigated the former head librarian for making a snide comment about how Hallie's summa cum laude wasn't very impressive from *Crow Harbor* High.

An unlikely friendship...mentorship?...had sprung up between them. She reveled in her wealth, but didn't look down at all on those who had less. Blunt and unconventional, she was probably the bane of her brother's existence. Hallie knew the older woman was truly sympathetic to her plight—and certain of her inevitable loss.

Felicia nudged away one book stack with a hand adorned with a diamond and sapphire encrusted watch. "You won't need these. Just leave it to me. I'll introduce you to a few people who aren't judgmental jackasses. They might not vote for you in the end, but they will help shut down the potshots people are taking at you for your background."

Her background. Right. Not the full scholarships, not the graduation with high honors. Her "background" meant coming from Crow Harbor. That was it. People sneered at her for her childhood zip code. How inane!

Accepting Felicia's offer was tempting, all right. As tempting as mozzarella sticks at midnight, drenched in marinara.

It was also just as bad for her.

Hallie only felt the tug of temptation for taking the easy way out for the length of a slow double-blink. That righteous indignation that had cemented her name on the ballot still burned just as hot in her belly.

Now, on top of proving to the rest of the town that she could be mayor, she needed even more strongly to prove it to herself.

Without any greasing of the skids by a Montgomery.

Without even the slightest help from, well, anyone.

Her gratitude for the offer, however, was boundless. "I can't thank you enough. I realize that your helping me might make things uncomfortable between you and Fitz. I couldn't be the cause of any family disharmony."

This time, there was no discreet palm to the mouth. Felicia dropped her head back and *guffawed*. "Our family wouldn't know harmony if the Mormon Tabernacle Choir sang to us. We're a disharmonious mess. Most of us. I adore Fitz. I believe the feeling is reciprocated."

That was incredibly sweet. Hallie tried to picture the slickly charming man getting all gooey over his stoic aunt. It was a pairing that couldn't be conjured into a mental image.

Mostly because every time she thought of Fitz, she thought of The Near-Kiss.

Felicia very much did not need to know the extent to which Hallie wished that she had *reciprocated* with Fitz.

"That's all the more reason for me not to put so much as a twig between you two. Besides, you helped me get the job here as librarian. That was a big enough favor to last a lifetime."

"I nudged a few ancient and stubborn fuddy-duddies who wouldn't recognize the future if it was laid out on their bed in La Perla."

"Felicia!" Hallie whipped her head around, checking to see if anyone was close enough to have overheard.

"Is there a rule against talking about lingerie in a library?"

Geez. "Not, um, *officially*." But there ought to be a rule about even mentioning lingerie if there was an age gap of more than, oh, ten years between you and your conversational partner. Felicia had to be sixty.

Hands splayed on the thickly lacquered desk, Felicia leaned forward. There was a fierce glint in her eyes that exactly matched her nephew's. "You were the best candidate for this job. Where you come from doesn't make a whit of difference. Don't you ever think otherwise."

Hallie knew it, deep in her bones. It was why she'd fought so hard for it. It was why she'd accepted Felicia's help back then.

This run for mayor, however, was a different situation. "I feel very supported by you, but that's all there can be. I need to do this all by myself." She hugged the nearest stack of musty books. "Knowledge is power, and knowledge is my stock in trade. I've got this."

The older woman steepled her hands and then tapped them against her lips. "My dear, I don't believe that for a minute. I can't wait for the day you prove me wrong, though."

...

Guilt was something that couldn't be cleared up with antacids. Fitz knew the churn in his belly wasn't from the French toast, and that it wouldn't go away until he made things right with Hallie.

He'd been stuck at the golf club for a solid hour after Hallie escaped the dais. Everyone wanted to shake his hand, congratulate him on the slam dunk of a campaign kickoff.

Every slap on the back increased his discomfort.

What had happened wasn't fair. More importantly, it wasn't *right*. Fitz didn't want people to vote for him solely on the merits of his last name. He also didn't want people voting *against* Hallie out of spite or bias or bigotry. That wasn't winning.

Fitz had stewed on it in his office for the whopping total of five hours until guilt had driven him out of city hall...and straight to the library.

After not finding her behind the checkout desk, Fitz started searching the stacks for the librarian. Maybe he should drop a book to see if the noise would get her to come running? But then he saw her, head bowed and propped on raised fists. Towering stacks of books hemmed her in, with piles of newspapers on the floor.

It was one of those moments where Fitz *knew* he'd take heat for interrupting. Clearly, something was wrong. It was just as clear that Hallie and he weren't exactly on "sharing" terms when it came to emotions. Especially not when he was probably the cause—if indirect—of her bad mood.

But he had to make this right. Now. Or at least before attempting to eat dinner.

So, he took two beats to catalog how pretty her thick hair was, curtained around her face. To notice the always-sexy nape of neck just barely revealed. Then *another* beat to ask himself what the hell he was doing, running down her sexy traits. It'd been a mistake to come so close to kissing her. And he sure as hell wouldn't let it happen again.

Fitz mouthed it silently, to drive it home.

When he couldn't think of any more ways to stall, he took a breath. "Got anything good to read in here?"

Lame. Lamest of lame. He'd had better game than that before he'd even sprouted whiskers.

But, hell, Fitz didn't know what to say or do around Hallie. She seemed dead set on them being enemies. He didn't know enough about her to *dislike* her, let alone brand her an enemy.

What little he did know—aside from when she was calling him out for not doing enough as mayor—he *liked*. To Fitz, opinionated was good. Interesting. Way easier to talk to than someone who simply agreed with everything.

Hallie also came off as driven. Responsible. Passionate. Close with a group of friends. All pluses. And he was supposed to hate her just because she was running against him?

First of all, that was just bad fucking sportsmanship.

Second…well…the harsh reality was that it was unlikely that she'd even make a dent in his numbers.

Third? Fitz didn't so much care who won the election—not that he could admit it. That would be a slap in the metaphorical face to the legacy of a long line of Montgomerys.

Even though *he'd* never wanted to be mayor…

Meanwhile, her head had jerked up at his words. "Are you trying to be funny? Or is this really your inaugural trip inside a library?"

Ah. She was one of the many who assumed he'd used his trust fund and legacy status to buy a degree. Probably didn't even know about his master's, not that Fitz trotted it out frequently in conversation. Having knowledge was enough. No need to convince everyone else that you had it.

But clearly the librarian needed to see his credentials. "Not by a long shot. I'll have you know I used to work in a library. At my alma mater."

"Really?" Cynicism spiked off both syllables. And her eyes, the color of his favorite Blanton's bourbon, narrowed.

Who would lie about *that*? "Yeah. Gotta pay for all those late-night pizza runs somehow."

Plus, the library had A/C.

Los Angeles' heat was a nice change, but also no joke for this Mainer. If he wasn't at the beach or a Dodgers game, Fitz made sure to keep all other activities indoors for his four years there.

"Prove it." Smiling smugly, Hallie crossed her arms.

Fitz tried to ignore how it drew her shirt taut against her breasts. Being annoyed by her idiotic request made it *almost* doable. "You think I saved my pay stubs? From twelve years ago?"

"No. If you really worked in a library, you should be intimately acquainted with the Dewey Decimal System." She stood. Went on tiptoe to bracket his eyes with her hands like blinders on race horses. "No peeking. What category is 796?"

"Sports." This, he could do. Like the lyrics to summer

camp songs he hadn't sung in decades, he'd never forget all the numbers he'd spent so many hours shelving under. Fitz raised an eyebrow. "Trying to throw me a softball? Figure that's the only classification a man would know?"

"Then what about 320?"

Shit. It was either economics, or—Fitz snapped and finger-gunned at her. "Political science."

Hallie dropped her hands. And her attitude. "I apologize."

"Forget it." Fitz never minded proving himself to people. He preferred it, actually, after so many instances of being accepted and handed things *without* proving himself, just because he was a Montgomery.

Plus, her pop quiz had been fun. How was it that every time they started arguing, it ended up being fun?

She moved her gaze in a slow circle, encompassing the tidy shelves, the windows just below the ceiling that flooded the room with light, and the comfortable blue and green chairs all over. "Then why haven't I ever seen you in here?"

It was hilarious how adorably sad Hallie sounded. Like he'd hurt her feelings by ignoring her cute pet. But the place wasn't a dog in a checked bandanna—it was a building, one which Fitz simply didn't need.

"Technology," he said succinctly. "I use the library only for ebooks, though. That way I can read on my phone between meetings and not live with the constant fear of breaking the spine. Way more convenient."

"Glad to hear you utilize at least some of our services." Hallie sounded 50 percent mollified, at best. Yeah, this place was definitely her pride and joy.

He could see why. It looked miles different from the brown and beige boredom jail of his youth. The children's area was colorful and just messy enough to be inviting. Random books were left on the end tables next to every reading chair to lure in readers. And he was pleasantly surprised by the coffee bar on the far wall.

"Hey, if you want to see me more often, I could come on in and check out a physical book every once in a while. Give you a chance to ogle all this..." Fitz waved a hand up and down his body just to see what sort of reaction it'd provoke out of her. Hopefully, it was shocking enough to distract her out of being so guarded against him.

"You're...you..." she spluttered. Her eyes rounded and her hands fisted.

She was so much fun to poke at. "Yes, I'm kidding."

The spluttering cut off abruptly. After a long sigh, Hallie rubbed at her temples. "Looks like I owe you another apology."

It was his entry point to getting her to drop the whole mortal enemies shtick. "I'd say it looks like you need to stop hating me for no reason whatsoever."

"Oh, I've got my reasons."

"Seriously?" The woman was freaking stubborn. Fitz yanked out a chair, flipped it around, and straddled it backward. "I don't drown kittens for fun, for Christ's sake. There's no rule that says you have to hate me to buckle down and try your damnedest to beat me."

Now that he was on her level? She flipped *over* the legal pad full of handwritten notes that he couldn't read upside down anyway.

Uh, he wasn't a trained spy. And he wasn't a sleazy jerk. But he was getting more annoyed by the minute.

Hands primly intertwined, Hallie said, "Hate is too strong a word. That would be saved for the monsters who dog-ear pages."

"I'm in the clear with my ebooks, but for the sake of the rest of the citizens of Swan Cove, I hope you're pulling my leg."

"Mostly." A hint of a smile ghosted across her lips. "But

animosity *is* motivating."

"Wow. You're saying that if you let yourself like me, you wouldn't stand a chance of winning?" That was an avenue he'd never considered as a campaign strategy.

"No, not exactly. Being at odds with you just gives me a leg up against someone who already has a *considerable* leg up."

Now he was torn between anger and amusement. If Everett was here, he'd be laughing his ass off, for sure. "You hating me is your *entire* campaign strategy?"

She lifted her chin. "No. Obviously not. It's a way to stimulate my adrenals to get my brain working at peak performance."

Oh, thank God. He could lasso that sentence and yank them back to a normal conversation, because he wasn't prepared for Hallie to go into detail about her animosity or her adrenals.

"Thanks for that segue. Your performance in the campaign is why I'm here."

Her lips pursed. "I'm on the brink of asking if you've come to rub in how hugely I crashed and burned this morning. But, since I'm trying to not make any assumptions about you—well, as of two minutes ago—I'll ask you to elucidate."

Her librarian-speak cracked Fitz up. "That makes me feel like a younger, skinnier Hercule Poirot. Compliment taken, thank you very much."

"Compliment unintended, but you do you."

Man, the woman wouldn't give him an inch! Although there had been a suspicious twinkle of humor—or sass?—in her eyes with that last comment. "I came with an olive branch. An offer to help. You've never done a campaign before, am I right?"

"Correct." Hallie tilted her head to indicate the shelves surrounding them. "As you can imagine, I was always more of an in-the-corner bookworm than a class president type."

"Your lack of experience shows." Hurriedly, he held up a hand to stop her before she lit into him again. "I'm saying that empirically, not judging."

Without a hint of emotion, Hallie gave a slow nod. "Noted."

Huh. Did she accept his criticism because he'd rolled out the fancy vocab with "empirically"? That'd been his hope. Hadn't expected it to work, though.

"I've done lots of campaigns. The early ones relied heavily on poster-making skills, but that won't come into play for this election."

This time, Fitz was certain her lips quirked into a smile. It even lasted a whole two seconds. "Maybe you just unwittingly gifted me the secret to beating you. An avenue you've yet to explore with the electorate."

"Glitter pens and puffy paint? Be my guest." And if she *did* make a handmade poster, just to prove her point? Well, it'd be game *on*.

"You shouldn't win simply because you've more experience. Fresh ideas can be equally good for the town." And, oh boy, that smile was gone and Hallie's feistiness tank was topped off.

"Agreed. I want to make it a fair fight. Otherwise, a win won't matter." He extended an arm, gesturing between them over the sacred, secret legal pad. "Let me show you the ropes of campaigning. Lend a hand to get you and me on the same footing. It's a job you haven't trained for. This isn't something you can pick up on the fly. Every misstep costs you."

"You're unbelievable."

Yeah. Fitz had figured the offer to be damned magnanimous of him. How many candidates would offer to *help* their opponents?

But then...he registered the tone of Hallie's words.

She was *not* catching the magnanimous vibe he was dishing out.

As verification, she shot out of her seat with all the wrath of a pissed-off sea demon coming out of the waves—minus any sexy, watery sleek sheen to her skin.

"You think I need a hand?" The librarian had evidently forgotten about keeping her voice down in the building o' books. That was definitely asked in her outdoor voice.

"Look, it isn't an insult. Nobody's good at something the first time they try it. It's no different than saying...you can't throw a seventy-yard spiral pass for the Pats in the Superbowl. Because you haven't had the training. It's a genuine offer, Hallie. Evening the playing field."

"I don't need your *handout*." Hallie spat the word at him. Her cheeks reddened. "Knowledge is power. And knowledge happens to be my stock in trade."

"Sure," Fitz nudged the stack of books closer to her, "but you'd have to wade through a lot of books to get what I could distill for you in a couple of nights."

Her gaze sharpened to a suspicious squint. "Nights? That's the real reason you're here?"

Fitz was lost. "Well, we both have day jobs, so—"

"You think you can distract me with more flirting?" Hallie pursed her lips like an actress posing on a red carpet. "Over candlelight?"

Now *he* was pissed. That she'd accuse him of such low-down tactics. "You have got the wrong idea there. We've never flirted."

"Your eyes flirt just looking at a woman."

Whoa.

That was flung at him like an accusation—but it was more of an interesting reveal on her part. One he'd think about the next time he needed an ego boost. For now, though? It just made things trickier.

Fitz spread his hands wide, palms up, in the classic nonconfrontational position. "This isn't a trade-off; sex for campaign tips. It is—*was*—a straight up, no-strings-attached offer of sharing expertise. For *your* benefit. I'd get nothing out of it," he emphasized. "I'd expect nothing in return. Definitely not flirting," Fitz couldn't resist adding.

"It's insulting that you think I need the help. It is reprehensibly insulting if you think you can turn my head with your smoldering eyes. You—your body—you can't turn my attention away from the campaign with it. Keep your lips and your offers to yourself, Mr. Mayor. It won't work!"

Fitz blinked. Smoldering?

What had crawled up her ass?

Yeah, they'd shared that one moment in the pub where something, maybe, *could* have happened. Nothing did, though. Thanks to his restraint. Was Hallie insulted or hurt that he *hadn't* crossed that line? Was that behind all this blowback?

Either way, he wouldn't stay here, letting Hallie shove his good deed back in his face like it was a coconut cream pie.

"Fine. Be the laughingstock of the town. Be content with votes in the single digits come election day. But when that all happens, remember that I tried to throw you a lifeline and keep you afloat." Fitz pushed out of his chair, mad as hell. "That's a mistake I sure as hell won't make again."

He stormed out of the library, wishing the doors weren't the electric whooshing kind so that he could've slammed them.

No good deed goes unpunished. That was his takeaway. And that was her last chance. Fitz would now throw himself into campaigning. He'd do it harder and longer and better than ever before. That'd show her.

Of course, then he'd be stuck being mayor for another four years.

Chapter Six

The entire car shuddered as Hallie gunned it over the railroad tracks. "Sorry," she muttered as Megan grabbed for the panic bar.

"No worries. I figured it was on purpose, to jolt us into realizing that we're officially on the wrong side of the tracks again." She pointed at the large WELCOME TO CROW HARBOR sign at the edge of the road.

It was true. The neighboring town couldn't be more different from Swan Cove. Her current hometown had the fancy science institute, the college, the yachts, B&Bs, and mansions, whereas Crow Harbor was the home of the *working* waterfront—commercial fishermen, processing facilities, boat repair, and marine transport.

"Uh, you grew up here, too, Megs. Maybe don't trash talk the place that made us who we are."

Megan pulled out her red lipstick to do final touch-ups at the light. "Just stating facts."

Ooh. That reminded her of Fitz so sanctimoniously "stating the fact" that she'd crashed and burned at the campaign kickoff. Hallie gripped the steering wheel tighter. How dare he? How dare he assume that she couldn't regroup all by herself?

It was bad enough that Felicia had offered to help out of friendship and, well, pity, but Fitz doing it was low. Pretentious. Arrogant. With a possible teeter toward misogynistic.

Was she overcompensating with her anger at him out of her embarrassment at sucking? Possibly. A tiny bit.

Fitz made a convenient target, though. Besides, didn't she get a warm-up? One event to test the waters? To feel out what it'd be like?

It was in *no* way a "fact" that Hallie couldn't reassess and come back stronger than ever at the next one. The nerve of the man!

And for him to be outraged that she saw through his sexploits. Sexploitation? He'd come sniffing around to try and turn her head with flirting and more almost-kisses. The very lowest of the low stunts. One of the oldest tricks in the book.

Did Fitz Montgomery actually think his shoulders were so broad, and his smile so charming, and that twinkle in his eyes so bright, and his chest so hard, and his hair so tousleable, that she'd go weak in the knees and forget they were enemies? It took more than a sexy body and a beautifully resonant voice to distract this woman!

"Uh, Hallie? Light's green. Light's been green for a while."

Oops.

Her foot jerked onto the gas pedal. "Thanks for coming with me tonight. You know my parents adore you. I didn't want them to spend all of dinner gushing about how *me* running for mayor is the first step to becoming president." Once the shy, quiet bookworm in the corner, *always* the woman who preferred to not be the center of attention.

"Hang on. You pitched a fit about running for mayor. You really want to be president?"

"Of course not. Never. Never ever." Talk about something she'd never hear the end of from her bestie. Megan would no doubt proprietarily insist on being the one to put Hallie's name on every ballot, as a tradition.

"The president does get a butler, and a valet. Or whatever the female version is. Tempted now?"

She turned at the house with four rotted-out boats on the lawn that had been up on blocks her entire life. "To be responsible for sending troops into war? No. Count me out."

"Oh sure. Get me all excited at the possibility of a butler bringing me an iced tea on a fancy tray and then just yank it away. You're such a tease."

That surprised a laugh out of Hallie. Megan was the femme fatale. The flirt. The fun one. Hallie was the opposite.

Of all those things.

"I think every man along the Maine coast, if forced to choose between us, would label you the tease and me the… well, the librarian."

"Fine with me. And I'll go ahead and change the topic if your parents get stuck in the rut of praising you too hard. If your head gets any bigger, I'll have to change your hairstyle."

"Very funny." Hallie parked right behind the bright yellow school bus that took up most of the driveway. Her mom was the driver. She always said that parking it at their house was a badge of honor. Pam Scott appreciated that parents entrusted her with their children every day.

"You know you're lucky to have parents who think you walk on water," Megan said as she patted *today's* hair, which was in two French braids with turquoise ends. A bitter aftertaste hung on her words.

Megan's parents weren't anywhere close to supportive like the Scotts. They'd stayed locked in an ugly, violent marriage until the day she graduated high school, blaming her often for keeping them stuck in it. Now split, they'd both left town and *never* checked in on their only child.

Hallie knew she was better off without them polluting her life.

She also knew Megan would always carry a deep wound from their heartless actions. So, she made sure to ask her to come along to visit the Scotts at every opportunity. That way Megan still felt like she had a version of a family.

"I know I lucked out with Mom and Dad." Hallie hip-checked her as they opened the gate and walked up the crushed oyster path. "Just as lucky as I am to have you as my very best friend."

"Buttering me up? You must really think they're going to pile on with the congrats for your candidacy. Frankly, I hope you're right. Your mom makes a great cake. I'll bet this is a celebration worthy of a pineapple upside-down cake."

"Oh, there'll be cake. Maybe even the matching celebration app of onion dip and chips."

That was the sole perk of being an only child. Her parents smothered her with love and praise. It was uncomfortable at times. Mostly good. Hallie was quite certain that constant building up of her confidence by them was the reason she'd had the strength to stand up to Fitz and Derek and leave her name on the ballot.

She couldn't wait to thank them for it.

And if she was honest with herself, she'd come home tonight needing a full dose of parental pumping-up, no matter how much she said otherwise to Megan. After feeling like a failure at the campaign kickoff, Hallie needed to hear that she was still smart and would wipe the floor with Fitz Montgomery.

The front door swung open before they even got to the steps. Her mom wore an apron over her brown jumpsuit uniform, but...no scent of pineapple goodness wafted out from behind her. "Get in here, girls. You don't want the neighbors gawking."

Megan kissed her cheek. "I kind of do, Mrs. S, or I wouldn't have dyed my hair blue."

"They've got enough to talk about already." She lightly whipped her kitchen towel at Hallie to hurry them along.

Hallie stopped in the hallway next to the coatrack, which was full even though it was May. There weren't enough closets in the tiny house to begin with, let alone a spare to corral all the coats Maine's weather necessitated. "Uh, hi, Mom. Geez. Don't I get a hug?"

"Your father's waiting in the living room."

Ahhh. She got it. This was a surprise party thing. She and Megan dropped their purses along the wall and brushed past the pot-bellied stove in its brick alcove.

Gene Scott sat in his prized recliner. The one that even when he was at work, Hallie hadn't been allowed to use, for fear she'd wear it out too soon. His gray hair was slicked back from his usual post-work shower. Fishermen never smelled good after a long day's work—unless it'd been a bad day's work.

"Hi, Dad." Hallie started over to kiss him, but he just pointed at the couch.

Okay. Strange. She and Megan dropped into the spots they'd used their whole lives. Her mom sat in the wing chair. Now what?

Oh.

Maybe they hadn't heard about the mayor's race yet. Maybe they were worried about whatever drove her to surprise them with a mid-week visit. There'd been no intention to give them a scare. Hallie had assumed the word would've spread—as it always did—between the neighboring towns.

"Thanks for letting us come over for dinner. I needed to see you guys."

"That goes for me, too." The Scotts treated Megan as if she were Hallie's sister.

Gene wiped a hand across his mouth. "We know why you're here."

"Do you?" They weren't just playing it cool. They were playing it vampirically dead cool. "Well, just to make sure we're on the same page, I have news. I'm running for mayor of Swan Cove."

"We know."

If anything, their furrowed brows had gone a furrow deeper. Her parents radiated disapproval and disappointment. Hallie looked at Megan. All she got was a *WTF is going on* squint in return.

And she was suddenly quite certain there wasn't any cake on tonight's menu.

"What's the matter? My whole life, you've celebrated my achievements. Applauded each and every step toward success." They'd been so proud when she officially "got out" via scholarships. Even *prouder* when Hallie had landed a coveted job in Swan Cove. They'd never once expressed any concern that she was aiming too high, or getting ahead of herself. "This is a big step."

Her mom nodded repeatedly, faster than a bobblehead. "It sure is. The trouble is, you don't have the right shoes for that step."

Huh?

"Don't worry, Mrs. S. I'm going to work with Hallie to put together a wardrobe for her campaign events. Make sure she spiffs it up a bit." Megan covered the ends of her colorful braids to hide them. "Classy, of course. No flash."

This was the first Hallie was hearing of Megan's plan.

It didn't thrill her. Mostly due to her strong *No Help*

stance, somewhat because it was insulting. She was thirty years old. She could dress herself just fine. And lastly due to not having any expendable income to waste on new clothes. Everything Hallie saved was earmarked for a trip to Venice. It was sinking by two millimeters a year. Time was of the essence.

She wanted to sit on the edge of the Piazza San Marco sipping an espresso garnished with a sliver of lemon rind and dangling a kitten-heeled mule off one foot.

Was it ridiculously specific for a fantasy? Yes, but she'd spent years laboriously conceiving it. There was no room in its execution for *galoshes*.

Her mom clasped her hands and leaned forward. "You're entirely right. We've always been so proud of you. Sweetheart, you've exceeded all our dreams for you. We love you so much."

"Okay, now I'm worried you're either sick or divorcing."

"Nothing like that. But even though you're all grown up, we still want to protect you. That's our number one job as parents. Aside from, in your case, twice weekly trips to the library." Pam's attempt at lightening the mood in the room fell flat.

It was obvious they were working up to something big. Something Hallie wouldn't like.

"I appreciate the library trips. And the protection—especially since I was a bit of a klutz growing up. But I *am* an adult now, and I *can* take care of myself. Completely. Without any parental aid."

"For the most part, yes. We've still racked up lots more years of life experience, though. You see the world through the optimism of youth. We see it through the lens of reality, which is how we can help protect you."

Geez. She wasn't a cynic, but she also didn't think good intentions and an open smile were all it took to snag a job or get a better deal on a new car. "What does that even mean?"

"I'm sorry, Hallie. You can't run for mayor. You'll lose," her dad said flatly.

Well. She hadn't seen that one coming.

A quick glance at Pam revealed no hope of her rushing to refute his statement. What the heck?

"First of all, I don't fail. I never fail." Hallie was no Don Quixote, tilting at windmills and impossible dreams. She identified a goal, then she worked her butt off to achieve it. The formula was unassailable in its simplicity.

Or at least…it always had been.

Until just a few days ago when she'd thrown caution to the wind and gone along with the plan to run for mayor. Been uncharacteristically spontaneous. Committed to doing a thing that Hallie was in no way certain she could actually achieve.

Aside from that, Hallie had a solid track record of delivering. There was no reason for her parents to be the least bit negative. Or worried.

No reason they should seem to be convinced that she'd *lose*.

"Here I thought we'd be celebrating tonight, that you'd be excited for me." There was a bitter tinge to her words, like the black crust on the edges of overdone toast. Because it hurt that they weren't behind her 110 percent.

She'd *never* felt that lack of support from them.

Hallie's only chance at winning relied on her confidence supercharging the campaign. And if her parents didn't believe she could do it…well, her own tank of confidence would run dry in a matter of days.

Hands running nervously back and forth over the bottom seam of her apron, Pam said, "Hallie, listen to your father."

Like hell.

Instead, Hallie jumped up to pace across the braided rag

rugs made by her grandmother. "Listen to him announce that I can't do something I'm already legally obligated to continue?"

Her mom tried to grab her wrist but failed. "You're upset."

"Gee, do you think?"

"She was really looking forward to your cake," Megan butted in.

It wasn't a true statement. Nor was it useful to the conversation at all, but since Megan was the only person taking her side, Hallie was grateful for the *attempt* at an assist.

"Don't you see, Ladybug? We're trying to save you from yourself." Her dad using an ancient pet name didn't soften his message at all.

The message Hallie got, loud and clear, from Felicia was that she had no chance of winning—and no chance of losing with at least a non-embarrassing margin without her help.

The message from Fitz was that there was no chance of a humiliation-free campaign without *his* help.

She had to prove her worth by doing it all without accepting any help. And now here were her parents piling on. The *last* people she'd expected to take a hit from.

"Didn't I get all As? Didn't I graduate valedictorian? Didn't I get full ride offers from four colleges? Haven't you always been impressed that I work the Sunday crossword in pen?"

"Of course. You've done everything you set your mind to. More than your dad and I ever dreamed of when we had a child."

"Then why don't you believe in me? Why don't you think I can pull this off?" Hallie sank to the floor, cross-legged, as she had countless times before. Times when she'd plead her case for a later bedtime, or to see an R-rated movie, or that they needed to start recycling because it would take everyone pitching in to save the planet.

All those times had felt like the world would end if she didn't change their minds. This time was more so.

Gene hitched up his sleeves before planting his elbows on his knees. "We believe in you, Hallie-girl. We love you to pieces. That's why we're speaking up."

"I don't understand."

"We believe that you're strong and smart."

"Oh, and stubborn," Pam added with a wan half smile. Then she tucked a strand of her bob behind her ear. Megan kept it sable brown for her gratis, every eight weeks no matter how busy her salon schedule. "Which can be useful. You can do almost anything you put your mind to."

It sounded like they hadn't forgotten her capabilities, which calmed Hallie a bit—but did nothing to settle her confusion.

Gene circled his hands where they dangled between his knees. "But the Montgomery family? They're *powerful*. That's a whole different kettle of fish."

They...they were scared for her?

Hallie dismissed it immediately as 99 percent ridiculous. The one percent that terrified her, well, she'd worry about that whenever it woke her up in a cold sweat in the middle of the night.

This was fixable.

Manageable.

She could make her parents see the truth of it in minutes, then maybe take the four of them out for dinner to smooth everyone's ruffled feathers.

"The Montgomerys aren't kings. They're simply a family. And from what I can tell, a more than slightly dysfunctional one."

Felicia certainly danced to the tune of her own drum. She often spoke fondly of her family. She just as often called them dyed-in-the-wool snobs, stuffed shirts, and idiots. Despite that, she wasn't the black sheep of the family.

Nope, that *dis*honor went to Fitz's Uncle Jeremiah, who'd been the mayor before him. Then...something happened. Nobody would say what, but he'd moved all the way to Miami and never came back. That sure had all the trappings of leaving in disgrace to Hallie.

"They don't just run that town." Gene tightened both hands into fists in midair. "They own it. Lock, stock, and barrel. How many businesses do you know about fall under the Montgomery Industries umbrella?"

Nearly all.

Some outright, some with business loans, some with silent financial backing. Common knowledge said it was easier to open a new business if it was Montgomery-approved and at least partially owned by them rather than doing it solo.

And those businesses included Megan's salon, and Randall's grooming business.

Were her parents scared for her friends, too? That would explain some of their overreaction.

"Preston Montgomery can snap his fingers and make things change in Swan Cove. Even here in Crow Harbor, some. That threat is always there. And everybody knows that a Montgomery can and will follow through on it." Pam shook her head. Then her entire body shuddered. As if in fear of some unspeakable recrimination, for crying out loud.

Drama much? Hallie pushed her fingers through her hair from ear to temple. "That's not how democracy works, Mom."

"Do you really want to take that chance?"

Oh my goodness. Hallie looked to Megan with a *can I get a WTF* but instead saw a similar unease in the tense lines bracketing her friend's eyes and mouth. And her dad had both hands braced on the arm of his recliner as if ready to push out of it and fight off any Montgomery minions lurking about outside.

Hallie loved them for being so protective. She just needed them to be more Team Hallie and a lot less Team Anti-Montgomery.

Wow. She'd have to find someone much better at slogans to come up with one for herself. That was pitiful.

"Yes. I believe I could effect positive changes in Swan Cove. I also believe that democracy works, that the citizens will vote for whomever they believe will do the better job. And I have to believe that I can make this happen without any recriminations from the Montgomerys."

Not that Hallie particularly *wanted* to extend full faith to Fitz. He was still cocky. Still believed, just like her parents, that he would win, regardless. Nevertheless, it was...decent of him to offer to coach her, to make it a level playing field.

Her mom waved a hand back and forth, like she was trying to erase the last thing Hallie said. "That's the part where we're worried you're too optimistic. People like the Montgomerys, they don't play fair. They stomp all over the little guy. We don't want you to be crushed."

"They're too powerful," her dad insisted.

"Maybe part of that power is due to people building them up into oversize figures. *Maybe* this will turn out to be a real-life reenactment of *The Wizard of Oz*—there's nothing big and scary behind the curtain. Just a man."

Megan's hand flew into the air. She started ticking off points. "Everyone almost dies in that movie. The scarecrow's set on fire. The poppy field, the attack by the flying monkeys—how is that supposed to reassure us?"

Uh-oh. Her parents had officially infected Megan with their doubts. "Because Dorothy gets what she wants in the end."

Very quietly, Gene said, "Dorothy goes home. Why not

do that?"

"Pull out of the race," Pam begged. This...this felt like there was something else behind this request. Something more dire Hallie wasn't being told. "If you have to run for mayor, then do it here, in Crow Harbor."

"I can't. I don't live here anymore. Being a citizen is one of the very few prerequisites for the job."

"So move back here." Gene slapped his armrest as if that made it a done deal. "You can stay in your old room until you find a place."

Just what every thirty-year-old longs to hear. "I have a job, a good job. My dream job. *In* Swan Cove."

"That's what we're trying to save, Ladybug. What if this run costs you the job at the library?"

This verged on ridiculous. They could what-if it to death. *What if* running for mayor made her ineligible to simultaneously run for state senator? *What if* it meant she could no longer play the lottery as an elected official?

"If they manage to fire me because I beat their son, I'll still be mayor. I'll simply rehire myself."

After a warning finger shake, her dad said, "Don't sass me, no matter how old you are."

"I was not sassing. I was stating a fact. The Montgomerys have no reason to hurt me if I lose, and no *way* to hurt me if I win. You'll just have to trust me on that." Hallie got up—not as gracefully as the last time she'd planted on the rug. This required twice as much room for her arms and legs and a sort of tripod approach to pushing up.

"Pull out of the race, Ladybug. Please."

"No." Another pleading glance at Megan.

Megan, who was as stiff as a board on the couch, twisting the multicolored rings on every finger. She'd brought her friend along to distract her parents. Her uncharacteristic quietness was *not* helping.

It scared her more than her parents' obvious trepidation. Residents of Crow Harbor built up everything and everyone in Swan Cove to mythic heights, but Megan lived there with her. Knew what was real, knew of the players if not on a first name basis with them.

If Megan was worried? Megan, who'd gotten her *into* this situation? The three people who loved her unconditionally and had stood by Hallie her entire life were telling her to quit.

They didn't believe she could even make a run at it.

Hallie's stomach flipped into a giant knot. What if they were right?

What if she *did* humiliate herself? What if her bad showing at the kickoff breakfast was the tip of the iceberg of horribleness about to be enacted?

What if Fitz's dad decided to play dirty and threaten her friends' jobs?

What if she let panic and desperation color her decision-making?

Good thing her mom hadn't baked a cake. Hallie's appetite was now as slim as...as her chance at getting more than five people to vote for her.

Chapter Seven

Fitz scrolled through the gag gift site...for three whole seconds before stopping on the perfect present. A whoopee cushion, classic for a reason.

He bought end-of-season presents for all the kids on the lacrosse team he coached—"present" was more palatable to him than "participation trophy." Mason, the clown of the team, would appreciate the hell out of this. His parents, not so much, but that was not Fitz's problem.

That only left fifteen kids to go...

Yeah, he'd need caffeine to finish this. Matching the personality traits of ten-year-olds to gifts required fully revved brain cells. And it mattered to Fitz that he nailed each one. Kids needed, deserved, to have their individuality recognized. He'd head for the lunchroom, grab a soda, and come back to it.

One step out of his office, though, and he saw the librarian coming up the stairs. Engage the enemy? Or retreat and lock his door? Damn it, if they were going to go another round, Fitz *really* needed that caffeine.

"Mr. Mayor." Hallie raised an arm to flag him down. "Do you have a moment?"

It was after five. Nobody else would be coming out of an office to save him. Fitz really needed to stop hanging out late at city hall. Too easy to be ambushed.

"Depends on what you want to do with said moment. If you're going to accuse me again of flirting to somehow distract you from running a solid campaign, then no. I'm fresh out of time and fucks to give."

Hallie's cheeks turned a dull red. "I deserved that. I'm sorry."

Sounded genuine. He'd take it. Holding grudges was never worth it. Hands in pockets, Fitz nodded. "Thanks."

"For the sake of my mental state, will you answer a question?"

That was a weighted approach. No polite way to blow her off now. "Is this part of the moment you want?"

"No. We'll call it a sidebar."

"Then follow me." He led her into the room with its single table and plastic chairs. One vending machine was half chips and half candy. The other was all soda. A yoga instructor (mid-life fling for one of the council members) had lobbied hard to swap the soda for all waters. They'd even held a poll. Not a single person who worked in the building voted in favor of making the switch.

And then the wife had found out about the fling, so they didn't have to worry about their caffeine disappearing anymore. Fitz fed in a dollar. "Want anything? It's on me—unless you'd then accuse me of trying to bribe you into losing the race."

"I deserved that one, too, but no more. And no, thank you."

"Suit yourself." He popped the tab. Leaned against the counter and crossed his legs at the ankles. Hallie wore another take on her librarian uniform: longish brown skirt, long-sleeved ivory top, and...sneakers? Same as the day she'd accosted him under the stairs. "What's with the sneakers?"

"Oh. I walked here. I try to walk everywhere I can. Hard to do in heels, so I change into these. I know it looks silly."

A lot less silly than the women who tottered around town on fashionable stilts, canted forward and with one hand out for stability as soon as they got within inches of a wall or table or car.

"Makes sense. If I had to wear heels, I'd write a line item into the city budget to be carried around in a palanquin like an ancient Indian prince." The raise of her right eyebrow was slight, but Fitz didn't miss it. "You're surprised I know what a palanquin is?"

Her lips pursed. They were slicked in a deep brown that almost matched her skirt. Like she'd been drinking wine and chocolate. Together. "If I say yes, will you be insulted?"

"A little. You don't own the corner in this town on having knowledge." Although if Hallie walked into his office and saw the whoopee cushion currently on his monitor, he'd have to jump off his high horse.

"You're right."

"And you're being surprisingly agreeable. It makes me nervous." After a long sip during which Hallie said nothing, Fitz decided to throw her a bone. "My college roommate watched Bollywood movies. Hari would binge them right before going home on vacation so that he could pick them apart with his mom. I kept him company. Maybe—though I'll deny it if Hari's mom shows up—we made a drinking game out of them."

"Ah. Fun." She could not have sounded more disinterested. Hallie swiped her fingertips back and forth over the edge of the bright orange molded plastic chair. Her gaze stayed fixed down on...the cookie crumbs on the table?

"Back to my question. When we were at the pub, something... almost happened. I think the not knowing for sure is what made me freak out on you. *Did* you almost kiss me?"

No wonder she wouldn't look at him. It was one hell of a question. Fitz would label that more than a sidebar. It was a potential minefield. He didn't know Hallie well enough to predict what would set her off. He just knew that he had an innate ability to do so.

Because this was just the two of them, and not a public event or, God forbid, a campaign event, Fitz stuck with his go-to: the truth. "Yeah. I was tempted to kiss you. Not to throw you off balance as a candidate, but because you're interesting. Unexpected. And pretty. More than enough reasons, in my book, to take a shot."

Her eyelids flashed wide. Those whiskey-brown eyes locked onto his. "I...did not expect any of those."

Fitz enjoyed catching her off guard. And pushed the advantage. "Did you almost kiss me back?"

"The truth?"

He used his soda to make a go-on gesture. "Please."

The restless motion of her hands stopped. "I'm not sure. I would've been tempted. Because you're *almost* handsome enough to make me throw common sense out the window. And because I dismissed you, judged you before I even knew you—it turns out that *you're* interesting, too."

Whaddya know? That was progress. Détente.

"See? When you drop the whole 'we must be enemies' thing, we communicate effectively." Pushing off the counter, Fitz led her back to his office. Their steps were overly loud on the tiled floor, the only sound in the deserted building.

"Effective because I complimented you?"

"Only after I complimented you first." Détente, but still with verbal fencing. Which was actually fun. Fitz stopped at the top of the stairs, waiting for Hallie to make the next thrust.

Instead...she laughed. No, she *giggled*. The giggles rolled out of her like bubbles bursting out of a champagne bottle. It was infectious. Well, that and Fitz knew how ridiculous it was for them to one-up each other over compliments. He burst out laughing, too. Their laughter echoed off the open stairwell.

Hallie was even prettier when she laughed. Might as well be the difference between a black-and-white movie and a colorized version. Her eyes sparkled, her beautiful smile brightened up like a freaking sun ray, and...oh, *hell*.

She had a dimple.

Dimples were Fitz's kryptonite. There was something about a dimple in a woman's cheek that revved him from zero to sixty in about a second.

She was leaning toward him, too, as she laughed. Practically touching. Not that Fitz could feel it, but he saw her hair drifting against the arm of his dress shirt as she shook with laughter.

It was comfortable between them. Maybe for the first time. Fitz was acutely aware that he was entirely alone in the building with Dimple Girl. And that it'd be the most natural thing in the world to drink up those adorable giggles with his lips.

That'd be...unwise.

Dumb.

Bad.

So he broke off first, striding purposefully straight into his office. Fitz made sure to ignore the couch, too. Sat down in his chair and celebrated the generous width of the desk between them.

Distance was exactly what he needed from Hallie at this moment.

"You asked for a moment." He was so tired of being

asked to reallocate the budget. Which he couldn't actually do—it took the approval of the city council. Or to make a parking or speeding ticket go away. Which he *also* couldn't do. Unlike everyone else who asked for a meeting with the mayor, Fitz didn't have a clue what she wanted from him.

"Yes."

When she didn't expand on that, Fitz leaned forward. "Is this in your capacity as a citizen of Swan Cove? Or as my opponent in the mayoral race? If it's a complaint about the upcoming season at the Performing Arts Center, my last name's on the building, but I don't get any say in the touring productions. Which I've explained to more than a dozen people since the announcement came out last week about that comedian who sets things on fire."

"It's about…well, not being your opponent, per se. More about being a mayoral candidate in general."

"Are you taking your act on the road? Running for mayor in multiple towns? Because there's you and me on the ballot. Pretty sure you've gone out of your way to establish that it's a *mano a mano* opponent situation."

"I think you were right," she said slowly.

Fitz kicked back in his chair. Interlaced his fingers behind his neck and grinned. "I'm all ears."

"You pointed out that the campaign was its own beast, but separate from that, we're simply a man and a woman who may have things in common. Who may like each other as people, no matter how we feel about each other as candidates." Hallie swallowed hard. Lifted her chin. "Who may be inclined to help each other."

No question she'd surprised him. Talk about pulling a one-eighty.

No question he'd have a little fun with it, too. "Ah. The classic supplicant making their way to bend a knee before the mighty leader." Fitz grinned even wider. "Did you come to me to ask a favor? There's only one response to that. To badly mangle the words of Don Corleone, someday you can do a favor for me in return."

Definitely no vestige of her dimple left as she scowled at him. "Why do all men find it necessary to quote *The Godfather*?"

"Why do all women find it necessary to quote *The Princess Bride*?" Thrust and parry. Fitz could keep this up all night.

After a moment of silence, Hallie dipped her chin. "Fine. Yes. I need a favor. You offered to help me before. Very generously and selflessly, might I add. To learn the ropes of campaigning. I'd like to accept."

Wasn't that interesting?

He tapped two fingers on his cheek. Enjoyed the hell out of watching her attempt—poorly—to hide her frustration. "Hmm. I don't know."

That got him an eye roll. Definitely frustrated. "Would your answer be different if I'd countered with whatever the next stupid line is in *The Godfather*?"

"No, but it wouldn't kill you to watch. The thing's a cinematic classic."

"Fitz, if I promise to watch the movie, will you please show me the ropes of running for office?"

"Why?" The front legs of his chair thumped back down. "Don't say to beat me. Don't say to ensure our town continues with the perfect blend of progress and reverence for the past. You were dead set on being insulted at my well-meaning, sportsmanlike offer to help. Sloughed it right off. Tell me why the about-face."

"Does it matter? I've already swallowed my pride to come to you, hat in hand. Isn't that enough?"

"No." Fitz held up a finger to prevent any possible eruption of temper. "Not to be a dick about it. The opposite, in fact. I don't want to unintentionally insult you again. Hell, I don't want to be yelled at again. Can't move forward until I know why you changed your mind."

"I was wrong."

This whole conversation was like a present dropped in his lap. "Again, fun to hear, since that automatically makes me right, but I need more."

"After my, ah, poor showing at the campaign kickoff, I needed an emotional pick-me-up. An ego-stroking boost. I'm an only child."

"Aha. The golden child, right? They think you can do no wrong? That you're the smartest, funniest, nicest, most beautiful woman in all of Maine? If you were arrested with paint can in hand for spray-painting curse words on a church, they'd insist it was all just a misunderstanding?"

Sheepishly, she nodded. "Exactly."

"Lucky you. I've got a sister, Blake. Plenty of times both of us wished for the magical perfection of the life of an only child."

Hallie pursed her pretty lips. "You don't get along now that the volatility of puberty has subsided?"

They'd have to talk to each other with actual regularity to get along or not. Even in a town this small, Fitz only saw his sister a dozen times a year. Holidays. Birthdays. Obligatory stuff. They'd drifted apart young as their parents pitted them against each other "to stoke the competitive fires."

He wished it were different. They'd never had much of a connection, good or bad. Aside from avoiding fights with their parents. Now it felt too late to start. Fitz would have to add that to the list of dreams he didn't get to pursue.

"My parents were always comparing us. Even with an age gap. Doesn't matter. You always want what you don't have, right?"

"I don't know about that. My best friend, Megan—she's

the one who put my name on the ballot, so we'll see if we're still best friends by the time the election's over—she's like a sister to me. I never missed out on having one because I had her." That damned seductive dimple flashed again. "Plus, all the only child perks."

"Best of both worlds." Fitz pulled a pen out of his mug to give his laptop an officious tap. "Back to your story. I'm intrigued for you to get to the part where I'm right."

Temper flared her nostrils. Then Hallie took a long, slow breath, tucked her hands beneath her thighs. "I went home to be soothed, to be told it was just a stumble and I would end up wiping the floor with you. And that I'd be the best mayor who ever mayored."

"Obviously." Fitz appreciated that she was *talking* to him. Not spitting out the story in anger, not rushing through it just to answer him.

Hallie's answer was conversational—something they weren't practiced at. Hearing this made him feel like he was getting to know Hallie. Not the librarian. Not his opponent. Digging a layer deeper into the woman who intrigued him.

She scrunched up her nose. "But that's not what happened. Instead of pumping me up, my parents begged me to drop out."

"Why?"

"They don't think I can win. No," Hallie shook her head, sending her hair tumbling over her shoulders, "they don't even think I can make a smudge on the final tally. That I won't simply lose, but I'll be crushed."

It didn't take his two degrees for Fitz to connect the dots. "Because I'm a Montgomery and you're not. Because Swan Cove's mayor is always a Montgomery."

"Yes."

Good thing he was twiddling with a pen. He would've snapped a pencil in half as righteous indignation poured like lava through him. "That's bullshit."

"Yes." Hallie pressed the heels of her hands to her eyebrows. "It means...more than you can know to hear you say that."

Oh, man. His reaction should be the norm, not the exception. Fitz wanted to scramble over the desk and cuddle her for comfort.

He had *never* before had the slightest inclination to cuddle anyone in this office. The institutional gray file cabinets and acoustical tile ceiling didn't make for much of a romantic atmosphere.

What was going on with him? She might as well be a box full of old-fashioned dark chocolate glazed donuts. Tempting, but stupid to engage with.

Fitz surged out of his chair to restlessly circle the office. "I'm serious, Hallie. People should vote for who'll do the best job. Gender, legacy, ability to race sailboats, or ability to quote Thoreau—none of that should matter. I know that isn't the case, but it's how it *should* be."

"Thanks. But if my own parents don't think I can attract even underdog voters, I clearly need coaching. I can't afford to hire an actual campaign advisor. And, well, you've already made the magnanimous offer to help."

"The offer stands." Then it hit him that if he really wanted it to be fair for her *he* shouldn't be Hallie's only option. "Or, if you aren't comfortable with me, I could find someone in Augusta to talk to you. My treat. To level the playing field."

"Thanks, but...that'd be weird. I can take your free advice. I can't take your money to hire an advisor. I just don't want to embarrass myself again." She tapped her fist against her mouth. "Because, yes, I know the breakfast was a disaster."

"You sure?" He pulled the coatrack sideways in front of him as a shield. "I still want to be able to father children someday. I don't want you putting a knee to the groin if I point out the ways in which you screwed up."

Laughing, she got up and stood the coatrack back up. Which left them all too close with nothing between them but...possibilities.

Hallie pointed at him. "No sugarcoating from you." Then she cocked her thumbs back at herself. "Zero threat of physical injury from me. I'm big on learning from mistakes."

"Me, too. Makes the screw-up sting less if it's worthwhile in the end."

"I may not win—"

Making a time-out gesture with his hands, Fitz took a large step away from her. Then he mimed doffing a hat and putting on another. "As your opponent and not your coach, I need to interrupt here. You're not going to win, Hallie Scott."

"We'll see, Mayor Montgomery." To his delight, she jumped up and pretended to knock the hat off his head. "But, *Coach* Fitz, if I'm able to change a few people's minds on issues, or at least get them *thinking*, that'd be a win for me."

Wow.

Hallie's approach was so different from his parents' *win the race or generations of Montgomerys will roll in their graves* attitude. She genuinely wanted to make a difference and that was freaking fantastic. He admired the hell out of her, because, yeah, swallowing all the pride to come back to him for help probably choked the air right out of her. He added gutsy and fun to the list of reasons why—

Hell.

—why she'd be worth kissing.

Screw strategy. Screw logic. Fitz was going with his gut. And maybe a part of his anatomy a bit lower, too.

Winging an elbow across the top of the file cabinet, Fitz said, "Here's the thing. I get that it wasn't easy asking me to help. Let me make it more palatable. Let me make you dinner."

Hallie's eyebrows zinged up faster than the express elevator in the Empire State Building. "Why?"

"Why not?" That logic had worked on her last time. No reason to reinvent the wheel.

Darting to his desk, she grabbed his ceremonial gavel (carved from the canoe of an 1800s Canadian fur trader, if the legend was to be believed) and rapped it on the desk. "Point of order. I'm laying down a ground rule. You never, ever get to use that phrase with me ever again."

"You enjoy complicating things, don't you?" Fitz snatched away the gavel and set it back on its stand. No need for her to get comfortable holding it.

The sparkle that had lit her eyes while they...bantered?... snuffed right out. "We haven't had the smoothest start. I don't want to risk misinterpreting a comment, getting riled over a friendly joke."

Aww, *hell*.

"I'm sorry. Genuinely. I don't want to say something that makes you feel bad, even by accident. That's the real reason why I want to have you over to dinner. I owe you."

"I don't get it." Hallie stepped right up to him until the tips of her sneakers butted against the tips of his polished brown oxfords.

"I, ah, regret what you overheard that first day in the stairwell. It was ungentlemanly, and unjustified. It was cheap, unsporting. I've been feeling like crap about it. I'd like to make it up to you with an apology dinner. And if you get bored halfway through, it could transition into our first coaching session." They were close enough that Fitz caught the surprised double-flutter of her long lashes.

White teeth bit into that luscious lower lip. "One dinner?"

"Gotta start somewhere." Fitz held very still, not wanting to spook her. Not wanting to make her feel pressured or give her any excuse to say no. Or any excuse to think of the reasons it'd be a bad idea to consort with the enemy.

Her sneaker squeaked loudly on the wood as she backed up a few steps. Then Hallie crossed her arms and looked at him with skepticism from beneath half-lowered lids. "So is this a coaching session or a semi-date?"

"Yes?"

"That's a very politician-y answer."

"We'll call that a freebie." At least that got a laugh out of her. Sort of a gurgle of a laugh, but Fitz'd take it. "Dinner, Hallie, tomorrow night. We'll see where the conversation takes us. No matter what happens, I'll coach you."

A crinkle appeared between her brows. He'd seen it before. Wrote it off as combative. But now...Fitz thought it was adorable. What did *that* mean?

"I'm compelled to state the obvious. You're a politician." If she'd called him a pus-oozing eel, there couldn't have been more disgust in Hallie's voice. "Can you be trusted? Are you a man of your word?"

"Not a politician. Mayor's my job title. It isn't who *I* am at my core. And I won't be acting as mayor when I coach you." He double thumped his chest. "Me, Fitz—I always keep my word. You can trust me."

Another wiggle of her teeth on her lip. "I'm not sure this is a smart idea."

"C'mon," he coaxed. "We're both smart people. Ergo, with us being the participants, it *becomes* a smart idea."

"You think by saying ergo it turns into a wise-sounding choice?"

Fitz wasn't sure if she was dithering or drawing the decision out as a way of flirting. He kind of enjoyed not knowing. "I think it's one dinner in a lifetime of dinners. Average life expectancy for a woman in this country stands at about eighty years. Times three hundred and sixty-five, minus a few for whatever reason, that's around twenty-nine thousand dinners. I'm asking for *one*."

Lightning fast, her dimple winked in and out of existence. "Okay." With another sneaker squeak, Hallie bolted out the door.

Fitz wondered if it was his charm, his logic, or the ability to do mental multiplication that swayed her. Then he wondered what the hell to do about all the problems that dinner presented...

Chapter Eight

Hallie opened the front door and threw her arms around Megan. "You're like Santa Claus. And a fairy godmother. And Glinda the Good Witch, because you know I need a literary reference and she wears an amazing dress."

"Hi, Hallie. Are you drunk?" Megan pushed out of her embrace to drop a tote bag on the couch. "You're not usually a big babbler."

No kidding. Words were meaningful, so she preferred to be precise whenever possible. "That's because I don't usually freak out. I'm the one in control. Controlled."

"Controll-*ing*," Megan corrected. The accompanying wink showed off her glitter ombre taupe to orange eye shadow. Hallie must've sent her SOS while her friend was prepping for a date.

Or, possibly, it was just a regular old Thursday. Megan liked to mix things up with her look. She said it was important to be a walking billboard for her salon...except Hallie couldn't think of anyone else in town over the age of fifteen who'd wear glitter eye shadow.

She shoved the door shut—okay, she slammed it. "Well, you're the one who wants me to end up controlling this town as mayor, so you must like it!"

"Freaking out *and* bitchy. I repeat, are you drunk?"

Whoops. It wasn't fair to take her nerves out on her best friend. "Sorry. No. Not yet. No drinking allowed whilst serious decisions are being made."

Megan plopped down on the pine-green sofa. It mirrored the view out of every window. Hallie liked to call it her treehouse. The second-floor apartment had exposed beams that led the eye to all the Eastern white pines that surrounded it. It was all cozy eaves and angles and diagonals.

"What serious decisions? You told me to bring over my three tops for you to borrow. That's about as serious as saying you're switching out the penne for rigatoni in pasta salad."

Hallie could launch into an obviously necessary lecture on how important it was to match the sauce to its ideal pasta shape. And that rigatoni trapped an oily vinaigrette better, while penne would catch and hold a thicker sauce like pesto. But that would only delay getting Megan's input on the *actual* crisis.

"The serious decision is what I'll wear to dinner with Fitz tomorrow night."

"Your maybe date?"

"Yes." Hallie *hated* that she couldn't appropriately label it. She spent all day, every day, putting things in their correct categories. Travel, faith, history, mystery—you knew what to expect when things were categorized. She had no idea what to expect with Fitz, which no doubt contributed to her current over-the-top freak-out.

Megan snorted. "I don't think there's much of a maybe to it. You said you had a moment at the pub, then your eyelashes fluttered in triple time. That automatically plops this dinner into date territory."

No. No, it absolutely did not.

Hallie picked up a soft corduroy throw pillow and plumped it. Punched it, just to shape it pleasingly, not to vent her tizzy or anything. "Your facts are fuzzy. I did not agree to a date. I agreed to dinner. And to accept the graciously offered apology-with-food that he owes me for being a semi-jerk. With free campaign coaching and the possibility of a date vibe *during* it."

"You make things more complicated than they need to be."

Hallie—*again*—had things she could say in response, things like how Megan let everything roll off her. How nothing was serious, or complicated. And that not everyone reacted well to that loose an approach to life. That she, for one, required structure.

But that would be an overgeneralization, another semi-bitchy attack, especially since she was aware that there was more to Megan than the laissez-faire attitude she projected.

And, again, it would delay getting Megan's input on the actual crisis.

"Look, I can tell I'm holding you up from your evening plans."

"Oh, do you like?" Megan stood, twirled, holding out the ruffled skirt of the fiery orange sundress. "I'm having dinner on the cruise ship. One of the cast members of their big musical show. I gave him fresh blond tips today. He flirted very well, so we're meeting up before he has to perform."

It was a marvel how casually Megan stated she was headed off to break a rule. "You're not supposed to sneak onto the cruise ships. They, in fact, very much frown on it."

"Not the guys who let me on the gangplank. They wink at me. Not a frown in sight."

Hallie literally could not imagine knowingly breaking a rule and being so okay with it, so glib about it.

Nah, she couldn't imagine doing it at all. "You know, once I'm mayor, I'll need to help enforce rules like that, in the spirit of maintaining the wonderfully lucrative partnership between Swan Cove and the cruise industry. I'll have to put my foot down when it comes to your ship-hopping shenanigans."

"That's the classic definition of a *tomorrow* problem. How about we concentrate on what's got you in such a state *today*?"

"I have nothing to wear." Hallie rocketed through to her bedroom to stare at the numerous outfits she'd laid out. The numerous, boring, unsexy, practical outfits. "All my clothes look like they were purchased by a librarian."

Megan leaned against the doorjamb. Her eyes widened as she took in the disaster zone. "I don't care what you say. You obviously *are* drunk, because…duh, you *are* a librarian."

"Yes, but I don't want to look like one."

"Hallie, I love you, but I've harped on about your boring, staid librarian clothes for years. You insist that you don't want to draw attention to yourself."

"That's true. I hate it when people stare at me." Hated it *so* much.

Hallie preferred to blend in with her books. Be like the old-school leather covers. Nobody looked at them. If opened, amazing worlds were revealed, but to a casual observer, you'd barely notice them.

Megan came all the way in, took both hands, and squeezed tightly. "You're no longer the know-it-all teacher's pet that everyone teased. You own your smartness now. You're a walking billboard for badass smartness."

"I know." School had been rough. College had fixed all that. There, Hallie had found likeminded people who worked as hard as she did. Who got an equal kick out of etymology and literature and picking apart themes. She'd found her lane and floored it.

Drawing her down onto a pile of nearly identical dark pants, Megan continued. "You're also not the poor girl from the wrong side of the tracks. Lots of people here don't care that you're from Crow Harbor. They just know that you're a kickass librarian with two degrees who knows every bookish thing there is."

"What I don't know, I *do* know where to find the answer," she corrected.

It earned her an eye roll. "Exactly. I get that there's lingering insecurity. Our childhoods mess everyone up in all sorts of ways, but you're too strong to let it shape you anymore. Too strong to be held back by insecurity, or fear of being judged and mocked."

Oh, God. Had she really been doing that? Still trying to blend into the background so nobody would point and snark and laugh? Still, at the ripely mature age of thirty?

What a waste.

How had she not figured this out a decade ago? With all of her vast—some called it obsessive—reading, how had Hallie not seen that she'd turned into a caricature of a librarian? How had her allergic-to-introspection bestie figured it out first?

Well, she wouldn't look a gift horse in the mouth. Hallie threw her arms around Megan, rocking back and forth a bit. "You're really smart."

"Sometimes. On some things," she said smugly. "Pretty much an expert at seeing what's right in front of me. Aka, you, my favorite friend."

She scooted back against the plethora of green throw pillows in all shapes and sizes. "Have you been dating a therapist? Or hanging out in the self-help aisle at the library?"

Megan stuck out her tongue. "The only place I hang out there is at the front desk to talk to you."

"Well, however it came to you, thanks for the truth

smack. I needed it."

"A little tough love can work wonders." The smugness was layered on as thick as the frosting on top of the Boston crème cupcakes from her favorite bakery.

That smugness rankled. And then it hit her. "Megan Eileen Lennox, did you put me on the ballot to shake me up and get me out of my rut?" If so, the payback would be ruthless and never-ending. A private intervention was one thing. This ultra-public, one-month humiliation of a campaign was something else entirely.

"No. No, of course not." Megan sounded shocked enough that Hallie believed her, but then a slow, sly smile unfurled across her lips. "Although that would've been brilliant. Totally justified. I'm mad at myself for not having that as the reason."

Hallie wanted to shove everything on the bed to the floor. She was practical enough, however, to know that would just create an extra hour of ironing for her this weekend. "I need a new look."

"Truer words have never been spoken." She crinkled her nose, picked up a cream blouse, then a white blouse. Then a taupe blouse. All with only two fingers, as though the clothes would taint her with their dullness if they touched her entire hand.

It wasn't as if a fairy godmother would, well, first of all appear, and then flick her wand and turn these clothes into *haute couture*. "Like you said before, though, that's for future Hallie to work on. Present Hallie needs a smoking hot outfit for dinner with Fitz."

"Why? Why does it even matter to you?" Megan demanded.

Because he'd called her pretty. And interesting.

Because he didn't seem in the least intimidated by her vocabulary.

Because he could quote Thoreau.

Because he had a charming and easy confidence that made her think he'd kiss like he had a PhD in it.

Hallie decided to summarize in reasons sure to resonate with her friend. "Have you ever seen the mayor? Talk about smoking hot. The man is, well, yummy."

"Your vast vocabulary, and all you come up with is 'yummy'? Yowza."

Okay. This was apparently painful honesty night. Grudgingly, Hallie allowed, "He's also nice."

"He's also the enemy."

"Right."

Squinting suspiciously, Megan asked, "Do you *want* this to be a real date? Is that what's going on?"

Hallie knew she *shouldn't* want that. It would be easier to keep focus if she locked Fitz into a single mental corner—opponent. Genghis Khan, Napoleon—two of the greatest battle strategists of all time. They probably never got distracted by date nights.

Who was she kidding? Napoleon was a big-time skirt-chaser, but just because he pulled off brilliant strategy interspersed with hot and heavy interludes didn't mean Hallie was ready to try that. She was still strictly an amateur.

"No. Of course not. Mayor Montgomery *is* the enemy."

"Correct. So why do you want to borrow my sexy tops?"

"Reminding myself that Fitz is the enemy gives me the motivation to go out there guns a-blazing." She whipped her shirt over her head, caught sight of the plain white bra in the faux Baroque gilt mirror, and winced. "I'll use my assets to befuddle him, dazzle him with my decolletage. Get the intel I need without giving him an inch."

Megan frowned. "Don't joke about inches. You're not ready for that."

"I can flirt. I've flirted successfully. I enjoy it."

"You flirt with safe men. The guy who changes your oil. Everyone with a Y chromosome at your librarian conferences. Fitz is nothing like those men."

Thank goodness. The thought whisked through Hallie's brain. Staying focused, flirty, but uninterested and unaroused? Hallie wasn't sure she was up to the challenge.

. . .

Fitz was used to the unending boredom of budget meetings. Of how the two-minute wait for the microwave to heat leftovers felt like two hours.

None of that compared to the tedium of peeling the slimy, limp shrimp in his hand. "How many of these do I need to do?"

"All of 'em." Everett glanced over his shoulder from the stove. "Don't leave a speck of shell. They need to be clean as a whistle."

The bowl was *mounded* with the glistening, gray, comma-shaped shellfish corpses. No. No way. "C'mon, man," Fitz wheedled. "You said you'd help me cook dinner."

"I am. I'm doing ninety percent of it." Everett used a wooden spoon to point at the food spread out on the island. "I cut up all the veggies for the shrimp Cobb salad. Toasted the bread. Made the balsamic tomato topping for the bruschetta. Baked a blueberry crisp. The one, *single* thing you're doing is taking the shells off the damn shrimp."

Fitz pulled off the tail, and thought about how chicken came without feathers in a sterile plastic package. Perfectly clean and ready to cook. Why couldn't Ev have planned for chicken? "It's the most *boring* thing. It should count for more. More than all the stuff you did put together."

"How about the fact I lied to my boss to cut out early, shopped for all this, and came to save your ass by cooking it all? What does that count for?"

"Everything." Shit. He'd been whining, which was ungrateful and unacceptable. Fitz wouldn't treat his worst enemy that way, let alone his best friend. "Sorry. You're saving my ass. Thanks."

Ev shrugged it off. They didn't hold grudges. They'd been friends long enough they knew there were times one of them would say something idiotic…and it'd invariably be balanced out by the other one doing the same down the road. "When are you going to learn how to cook?"

"When did *you*?"

"Grad school. Didn't want to be that nerd cliché living on pizza and Chinese takeout."

"That's not a cliché for nerds. It's for everyone in their early twenties." Fitz held his breath and plowed through four more shrimp. If he just went by feel instead of looking at them, it was marginally less disgusting.

"Plus, my brain needed fuel. My study group figured if we were smart enough to be brilliant biochemists, we could learn to follow a damn recipe."

"You couldn't have had that realization in undergrad, with me?"

"In Los Angeles?" Everett shoved at the bridge of his glasses. "I don't regret a single one of our many, *many* trips to In-N-Out. You shouldn't either."

He didn't, but he did get a kick out of his science teacher/assistant principal friend approaching cooking like a science experiment. They'd shared enough meals since the high school hired him on here (which Fitz had, ah, expedited with a poke to the school board superintendent) that Ev had proved his expertise over and over. Which made him the only person Fitz had thought to call for tonight.

"Seriously, thanks for dropping everything to help me. Once I realized I couldn't take Hallie out to a restaurant, I panicked. Flipped out."

Everett walked over to peruse the wine rack. "I'll say. You don't ask for favors. Ever."

Damn straight. "You know why."

"Yeah. You don't want to trade on the family name. You get enough handed to you on a silver platter from being a Montgomery, blah blah blah." He shoved a bottle in the freezer. Set a timer. "None of that applies to me."

"Thank God."

"I'm serious, Fitz. Remember the kidney pact?"

"Of course." They'd been a little drunk, tossing around the idea of getting tattoos. Science major Everett had kiboshed them due to some random (aka, unlikely as hell) article he'd read about the possibility of complications from them during MRIs. What twenty-one-year-old worried about getting an MRI in forty years?

They'd had more beer (because *college*). And somehow ended up making a pact—as best friends—to donate, should the need arise, a kidney or partial liver to each other.

The weird part was still wanting to do it sobered up the next day, which resulted in sneaking into the science building on a Sunday for Everett to test Fitz. Turned out they had the same blood type. The pact was a go.

"How come you'll ask me for a kidney someday, but this is the first actual favor you've asked of me in fourteen years?"

"Hey, with an ask that big in the offing, I didn't want to risk using up your goodwill on little stuff," he joked. And thankfully finished the last shrimp. Fitz scrubbed his hands and wished he could scrub his mind of the memory. He rarely threw his money at problems, but he'd pay anyone *anything* to avoid doing that again.

"I'm serious."

Hell.

They rarely did serious. They were guys, after all. But a

call to *be* serious had to be respected.

He wiped his hands on the dishtowel. It was covered with drawings of different types of roosters and "Cocks" was emblazoned in bright yellow at the top. It was a housewarming present from his Aunt Felicia. She'd laughed for five solid minutes at his expression when he opened it.

Maybe he should hide it for tonight...

"Look, it's my own messed-up thing. I don't ask for help. I don't ask for favors. I don't ask anyone for anything."

Everett's mouth twisted downward. "This whole Montgomery family legacy did a number on you."

"There are worse vices. I don't smoke. No drugs. I don't do illegal drag racing."

"Asking for help isn't the same as taking advantage of someone."

"It is if they feel pressured into saying yes." Fitz pulled out wineglasses. "Whereas I know you would've had no problem telling me to go fuck myself if you really couldn't get away today."

"True."

"Which brings me back to thanking you for saving my ass. *Obviously*, I couldn't take Hallie out to a restaurant."

Everett snorted. "You're a Montgomery. Right or wrong, you can do whatever the hell you want in this town."

"Technically..." Man, Fitz *hated* that was true, which was why he bent over backward never to take advantage. "...but I'd get a river of grief about it from my parents."

"Really? They care who you date? Are they arranging a marriage for you with some daughter of a West Coast scion of industry? Something to increase the Montgomery lands and holdings like you're an eighteenth-century duke?"

Generally, Fitz appreciated that Everett gave him a hard time. He didn't let him skate on anything, but would it kill the guy to let a couple things go without giving him a canoe full of grief about it?

He leveled a gaze at Ev hard enough to crack a walnut. "First, it's not a date."

With a clatter, the wooden spoon dropped into the pan as Ev raised both hands. "Don't even."

"It's just an apology dinner, open to the possibility of going in any direction."

Anger tightened every line and angle on Ev's face. "I don't skip out on work for just dinner. I brought my A cooking game because I thought this was a date."

That was fair. "Simmer down. If *I'd* called it a date, Hallie would've said no. I *want* it to be a date. If all goes according to plan, your awesome food will soften her up enough into accepting that it's a date. For right now, though? Not a date."

"Copernicus." As a scientist—and avowed atheist— Everett refused to swear "like a Christian." Instead, he used his favorite scientists, which confused everyone who didn't really know him. "Why does this have to be so complicated?"

"Have you met women, Ev? They're *all* freaking complicated. That's what makes the payoff so sweet."

"I'm just saying this feels more like a Scooby Doo episode than a night in the life of Swan Cove's esteemed mayor."

Fitz yanked out a chair from the dining table and straddled it backward. "Secondly, my parents would care if I took her to a restaurant because they'd brand tonight as me 'consorting with the enemy.' They're already up my ass about Hallie's name even being under mine on the ballot."

"Why do they care so much, if they're certain you'll win no matter what?"

"Winning's not enough. Having no contenders—that's the way Montgomery mayors roll." Fitz thought about it a little more. "*Maybe* I could lose. Not likely, but it could happen."

Everett dumped the shrimp into the pan, gave a quick

stir, then turned to face him. "Why do *you* care?"

"You've met my parents. You know they're as single-minded about me being mayor as a kicker is about centering the ball between the goal posts for his thirty seconds of game play."

"Forget your parents. Why do *you* care?" he repeated. "You've never liked being mayor. You oughtta be thrilled someone's challenging you. It's your get-out-of-jail-free card."

God, wouldn't that be nice dumping it all in someone else's lap? The constant worry about budget and prioritization and placating and juggling the tourist industry representatives.

If only...

But that'd make him a horrible person. Like a dad who pushed a stroller into a mall and then walked away, abandoning his baby.

It was his inheritance, after all. His duty to both the town and the generations of Montgomerys before him that'd been drummed into him from day one. Seriously. There was a pic of him as a newborn in a onesie that said *Future Mayor*.

Fitz checked his watch—a Chopard Alpine Eagle his parents gave him when he "won" the first term as mayor, engraved with his new title. He had fifteen minutes to clear Ev out before Hallie arrived. Which gave him little time to shut this whole conversation down.

Shouldn't take too long, though, since none of it was open for discussion. "I don't hold the post because I want it. It's my family legacy. Our duty to Swan Cove. A massive, generations-long pain in the ass. All that adds up to me not getting a vote in the matter."

"I've always said I'm smarter than you—"

Fitz almost tipped over the chair as he leaned forward to cut off his friend. "Which I've never bought. Your science degree isn't any better or harder than mine in public administration. It's just different."

"—but clearly I *am* smarter, if I have to point out to the duly elected leader of this town that he lives in a democratic state. Every vote counts, Fitz. Even yours."

Again, if only…

Chapter Nine

Thanks to Megan's help, Hallie's strategy for the night had streamlined.

Lull Fitz into complacency. Pick his brain.

Hopefully, dazzle him with her decolletage—only possible due to Megan's red ruffled off-the-shoulder blouse with white polka dots. Summery, flirty, but paired with jeans to keep it casual…and platform red leather pumps to keep it—what was it he'd called her? *Interesting.* If that worked, he'd be distracted by it at every campaign event.

Bottom line, she was on an intelligence mission. Not a date.

The only hitch in the plan? This non-date was better than any actual date she'd been on in years.

She'd been worried his house would befit, well, a member of the family that owned the whole town. Formal and/or fussy and big enough to house four families. Instead, Fitz's house, tucked away on just enough of a rise to glimpse the Atlantic through the trees, was, well, comfortable.

Nothing ostentatious. Mission style furniture with thick

brown leather cushions that looked like the perfect place to read—or nap. Big black-and-white photographs on the walls of the Southwest that she wondered if he took himself. Sultry, smooth jazz warbled out of the speakers. It was just right. The accent lighting was soft yet warm. Even the food had all been delicious, but more on the casual side than a multiple forks and courses approach.

Hallie was let-her-hair-down comfortable here. And the thing was? It wasn't his comfy house or the wine.

It was Fitz himself.

Their declared truce had changed everything. Well, her truce. He'd never been reciprocally gunning for her. It turned out that he was right. When you took the mayor's race out of the equation? When they were "just" Hallie and Fitz?

They were two people with *scads* of things in common.

In the long run, Hallie was aware that should worry her. At some point, the truce would have to be dropped. The reality of their situation was that they were engaged in a battle. And it wasn't like having co-captains of the cheerleading squad.

There could only be one mayor of Swan Cove. The other candidate ended up the loser.

But for tonight? It was a treat to relax and laugh across from a heart-stoppingly handsome man who didn't make a face at her penchant for big words. And he didn't retreat behind bruised male ego when she teased him, either. *Also* a rare event.

"You're wrong, Fitz." She put her napkin on the table and shoved her chair back a few inches. "In fact, you're so wrong that I may have to get up from this table and go find your friend and tell him just how wrong you are."

"Before dessert?" Fitz's arm—sexily exposed by rolled-up sleeves that showcased a tan that had turned the hair on his arm to pure gold, and the ropy veins that made Hallie's mouth go dry—shot out. He sandwiched her hand to the table. "You can't go now."

His hand was broad, with long fingers that promised to be nimble as they traced a woman's body. Hallie desperately wanted to flip her hand over and interlace their fingers.

But she wouldn't. That'd be like unlocking a gate… to a dangerous playground. The equivalent of running out into the woods in only a white bra and panties after hearing wolves howl and seeing a hooded figure carrying a chainsaw.

So, Hallie simply arched a brow. "Just like *you* can't claim that either of us had it as tough as Everett getting a master's of science in education, and then *dealing* with teaching actual children as part of it. Pretty sure that's harder than both of our master's degrees put together."

He let out a long sigh. And, to her great disappointment, removed his warm hand. "Whose side are you on, woman?"

That was an easy one. "The side of logic and reason. Always."

"Nothing but logic, huh?" Leaning in, his eyebrows waggled. "Does that mean you don't believe in ghosts?"

"No, I do not." Fun to read about, in *fiction*, sure.

In reality? They were nothing more than your brain playing tricks. Fear conjured an idea of a shadow at the corner of your eye. Memory placed faces in your cortex as you pined for important people in your life. Adrenaline ascribed normal noises of a house settling to mystical goings-on.

"Fairies?"

"Maybe. Nobody's really worked to debunk the idea. Plus, the legend of fairy-like creatures is found in the literature of multiple cultures, which ascribes it a higher chance of being based in truth."

Steepling his hands in front of his mouth, Fitz frowned. "Now for the deal-breaker. Aliens?"

Whew. She'd pass his test. "Indisputable. The law of averages alone says that given the vast nature of the universe, there must be other life forms out there somewhere."

"Right? When you look at our structures, down to cells and atoms, those could be considered universes, comparatively speaking. Plus, who built the pyramids if not aliens?"

Hallie started to answer, then she saw the crinkle of laugh lines around his eyes kick in. "You don't really want me to give you the answer to that, do you?"

"No, thanks. I'm good." They laughed together.

Hallie laughed a *lot* with Fitz. More of that being utterly comfortable with him magic. It was all going too well. They liked the same music, shows. They both loved to argue, even when ultimately agreeing on a subject.

It was too good to be true.

Was it all an act on his part? Hallie didn't feel like she was being hoodwinked. On the other hand, the man *was* a professional politician. It wouldn't be hard for him to fake enthusiasm.

Going more personal was the only way to get at the truth. "What was your favorite class in undergrad?"

He shrugged a shoulder dismissively. "Nothing in my major."

"Okay...that's not an answer."

He shifted in his seat. "How badly do you need to know?"

"After that attempt at a dodge and weave? Very badly." Not to savor the potential salaciousness of it. Hallie wanted to dive deeper into the layers of the man. Not even for her strategic plan to suck him dry of all campaign knowledge.

Just...because.

Fitz got up and cleared the plates. With his back to her, his voice had no trouble carrying across the open floorplan. "Social psychology."

Not at all what she'd expected. Although Hallie knew just enough to recognize there was far more to Fitz than met the eye. "That sounds like more than a simple one-hundred-level class to knock off a science requirement."

"Yep. Don't worry, I did the pre-req. No skipping the line for me, ever."

She was beginning to learn that about him, too. Fitz definitely didn't behave like his mom and dad, who expected the entire town to bow at their feet. They weren't mean about it, but they did accept the attention as their due.

Fitz didn't cut corners. Or abuse his mayoral powers. Or, from what she could tell, ever use the power of his last name. If he somehow lost his pinkie finger in a freak accident at the Superbowl? He still wouldn't use the spouting arterial blood as a reason to jump the line to the bathroom.

"Why a psych class, though?"

"It's what explains how the whole world works. Who you are and why you do what you do. Fascinating and necessary." He slammed shut the dishwasher.

Necessary? "You...took this to be better at public administration? That's a reach."

He sat back down after refilling her water glass from a chunky, hand-blown glass pitcher. "I took it because a kid in my dorm overdosed. First semester beat him up, he was homesick. Unprepared for the level of work required, couldn't find friends. Everett and I ate with him a couple of times, tried to talk to him in the elevator, but he was too miserable to make any effort."

"God, that's awful." It wasn't a unique story, but it still twisted Hallie's stomach. "Did he live?"

"Yeah. Transferred out the minute he was discharged from the hospital, but we helped him pack his things. Nobody else even offered. Like his misery was a contagious disease." He spiked his fingers through his hair. "Garrett thanked us. Can you imagine? We did the bare minimum as humans, after not doing nearly enough for weeks on end—and he *thanked* us."

The naked pain, even after all these years, that darkened his eyes till they were almost all pupil, was hard to watch. Hallie couldn't let Fitz beat himself up when he'd actually stepped up.

She took his hand and sandwiched it between hers. Hopefully, he could feel her empathy being squeezed into him.

"Your 'not enough' was much more than anyone else's efforts. I'm sure it *did* make him feel better, even if only for five minutes. An act of kindness is a powerful thing."

"I know that now, but I was pretty hard on myself at the time. Wanted to make damn sure I never failed someone again."

Her heart broke for the eighteen-year-old version of him who'd suffered, as well as today's wiser, but still repentant, version. "Oh, Fitz. You didn't fail him."

"Not just him. *Me.*" Fitz pulled back his hand to thump his breastbone with his knuckles. "I failed myself. I wasn't aware enough. Didn't pull my head out of my own ass-full of problems to make more of an effort. That's not the kind of man I wanted to be."

Talk about high-level self-awareness. Hallie's respect for him skyrocketed. "You were just a kid, still learning all these life lessons."

"Don't cut me any slack. I did screw up, but I used the whole thing as a springboard to do better. Joined PAWS."

Hallie did a quick mental review of the basic data she'd skimmed on him this week to come up with his undergrad school as UCLA. "'Cause you're the Bruins? That's adorable."

His side-eye was laser sharp. "It's cutesy as fuck. Ergo, a really horrible acronym, but it stands for Peer Assistance and Wellness Support. We got training in, well, how to listen to people. Not our job to fix things. Just listen. It's amazing how much of a difference that makes."

That was also impressive. Hallie clasped her hands and tapped them on her lips as she stared at him. *Really* seeing more and more of Fitz. Liking what she saw—and not just the thick hair and long eyelashes and dreamy lips.

Although those things did have to be mentioned as notable assets.

"I can see you'd be good at that. After all, you've been patiently listening to me all night."

"It doesn't require any training to listen to a beautiful woman be insightful and witty."

Good thing she was sitting down. Her knees had just turned to jelly.

"Wow. That sentence was sweet enough to be dessert, especially if it's true." Because Fitz Montgomery could wink and get any woman in town to come running. Heck, any woman on the entire Maine coast, and he probably *had*. Which made Hallie wonder how many times he'd said that exact sentence to *other* women.

A furrow appeared between his brows, as if he were able to see her churning thoughts displayed in a cartoon thought bubble, and he said, "Not a line, Hallie. I swear."

"You'll forgive me for being skeptical."

"No, actually. I won't. Why would I invite you to my home unless I genuinely wanted to be with *you*? Unless I wanted to make an effort?" He scrunched up his entire face, as if a skunk had just sprayed the room, finished off in a grimace that would win him a costume contest as The Joker. "I'll let you in on a secret. I didn't cook this dinner."

Aha! "I had a feeling…"

Talk about too good to be true. Charming, handsome, thoughtful, *and* a good cook? Not a chance in hell. It was disappointing, on the one hand, but Hallie did appreciate that he was leveling with her.

"I did peel the shrimp. Have you ever done it? I'd call it harder than almost the whole rest of the meal put together."

"Mmm. Like Everett's degree," she teased.

"Funny you should mention him. He's the one who made all of it. I now owe my best friend a massive favor. He skipped out on work to do this for me. I don't like owing people, but I do now—for you."

She didn't know what to say to that. Asking his friend for help did seem above and beyond. It did make her feel... special. It also made her wish more and more that this was, indeed, a real date.

"Well, thank you. And thank Everett too. I feel a tad guilty that he did all this work and didn't get to enjoy any of it."

"Don't feel too bad for him. One, I still owe him the aforementioned favor which I guarantee he'll collect. And two, this wasn't hard for him. It was a time suck that he hadn't planned on, but he's good at cooking. I doubt he slummed it on drive-thru for dinner."

"Thank him anyway."

Fitz dropped a nod. "I will, as long as you get that accusing me of not being truthful with my compliment wasn't an insult to me. It was an insult to yourself."

Darn it. He was right.

Hallie was the ultimate bookworm, good-girl, teacher's pet cliché, all grown up. She knew she was smart and successful. A good friend. A gold-star date? Not so much.

And...just maybe...she was letting reverse snobbery get in the way.

Fitz Montgomery was the golden child, the shining supernova in town. The man other men wanted to be and women wanted to...well, whatever they could get away with. It wasn't fair to punish him for her own insecurities.

Hallie dipped her head too. "I feel like you're using your

Psych 301 knowledge on me. And I bow to your wisdom. Your skills aren't rusty at all."

"No chance to get rusty. I still do volunteer shifts." Fitz drained his water.

It was impossible not to notice his Adam's apple bobbing up and down as he swallowed. So...masculine. So...large. "At UCLA? Aren't you a tad long in the tooth for peer counseling? How do you keep up with the modern lingo?"

"First of all, that's what the urban dictionary is for. And TikTok."

Her jaw cracked, it dropped so fast. "You're on TikTok?"

Fitz roared with laughter. "Of course not. I'm an elected official. I may not wear a tie to work every single day, but I've still got a sense of propriety."

"You were pulling my leg." More careful wording this time. Not an accusation of laughing at her like before. Hallie was deliberately being less accusatory. More...congenial.

Maybe it was the wine. Maybe it was the memory of how good his ass looked when he'd had his back to her, dishing up dinner...

"Just to see how easy it still was. And secondly, my volunteer shifts are on a suicide hotline. Mostly listening, letting someone know they matter."

Wow. *Wow.* Not only did it take up time, but it had to be an enormous drain on energy and emotions. Talk about something that could guarantee him reelection. Proof of just how much Fitz Montgomery cared about people—even total strangers.

Why wasn't his campaign manager shouting this from a bullhorn up and down the street? "Why haven't I read about this in the *Gazette*?"

Fitz winced, rubbed at the back of his neck. "Ah. It's a secret. You can't say anything. Nobody knows, except Everett. And my sister, who I finagled into writing me a character reference. Figured her PhD would make her come off as believable and honest."

"You just entrusted a secret that big...to your opponent?" She was flabbergasted.

"No. I entrusted a secret to Hallie, my dinner companion. But, if you're ready, I've got my first piece of campaigning advice ready to dole out."

Huh. He'd revealed this huge, selfless thing to her. A hugely *personal* thing. And now Fitz clearly wanted to skate right past any further discussion of it. Was he too modest to want her to compliment him? Well, if he was in the mood to share, Hallie had a question that had been burning in her throat all night.

She circled a fingertip around the rim of her glass, not looking at him. "As long as you're talking about things not covered in the local paper, I've been having trouble finding much information on the proposed expansion."

"It's not ready for public consumption."

That pat, full-politician response snapped her head up. If a Secret Service guy appeared behind him and a flag pin popped onto his lapel, he couldn't be any more of a politician. "Really? Because a member of the public—not your campaign team—brought it up at the kickoff breakfast. So, you're basically trying to drag on a condom right after I waved a positive pregnancy test at you."

All the color blanched out of his cheeks. "That's...that's some powerful imagery."

True. Hallie was even a little terrified at the thought. "Whatever it takes to drag a real answer out of you."

"Sorry. That was an autopilot excuse. One I regretted the minute the words left my mouth."

"Why?" The why mattered. It needed to be for the right reason. Hallie really, really wanted him to have a good one.

"Because we're past that surface-level bullshit. I owe you

more honesty than that, now that we're friends."

That was the *perfect* reason. "Great. Hit me with the facts."

"It was floated at a chamber meeting to gauge reaction. There's been no official movement." Fitz held up his hand to keep her from jumping down his throat again. "*Unofficially*, though? I'm aware plans have already been drawn up for a hotel and marina complex at the south end of town. Doesn't mean they'll be approved. Just means that the people pushing it are either optimistic or stubborn—or both."

Hallie drew a line with her finger along the border of a gray and blue stripe on the placemat. Not fidgeting. Mapping out the boundaries to the town. "The south end? That's where the marina access is for the fishermen from Crow Harbor. Would it impact them?"

"Yes."

She made the logical leap to the thing that took all the shine off the expansion idea. "Would it mean wiping out the fishermen's marina entirely?"

"Yes. They'd have to find a spot and build a new one."

Wow. Fitz really was bringing the honesty. "Would Swan Cove finance that, after shoving them out of the way?"

"Doubtful to hell no."

What a non-surprise. The town with all the money was going to spend it to make more, while negatively impacting the blue-collar workers in the neighboring town with no money.

"People will lose their livelihoods, at least for the short-term. Some forever. My father would likely be one of those affected."

"I'm sorry, Hallie." His tone was deep and sincere. "There are a lot of angles to this proposal. There's no clear-cut solution that'd make everyone happy. Or one that's obviously right, but I don't represent everyone. As mayor, my duty is to my electorate."

Truly, she wasn't trying to be antagonistic. Merely calmly interpreting his statements. "Funny how that sounds a lot like you're willing to screw over Crow Harbor."

"Then you're not listening hard enough." Temper hardened the lines of his handsome face. "My duty is to protect and advance Swan Cove. That doesn't reflect my personal feelings on the matter. Being mayor means shelving your own opinions sometimes. It's not all parades and meetings. It's hard. Which is why we should get back to the campaign advice I was about to hand out."

Hallie was impressed yet again. He'd made an extremely valid point. One that would probably keep her up nights worrying about the responsibilities of this job she was chasing.

It wasn't fair to keep hammering at Fitz on the topic. He was her fount of information, not the person pushing through the proposal. And since they weren't *really* on a date, she'd respect the Grand Canyon–sized leap he'd made to a new topic, take a deep breath, and move along. "Should I take notes?"

"You'll be able to remember this." A flash of even, white teeth and an eyebrow wiggle gave Fitz an evil, piratical look. "You won't like it, so it'll stick in your craw like a popcorn kernel."

That explained the wicked grin. "Lovely imagery."

Fitz clapped his hands, brought them to his lips, then flattened them on the table, as if smoothing out the nonexistent tablecloth. "You've got to be less of a…factual statistics machine. They won't help you make your case."

That was the big learned wisdom from an experienced campaigner? Geez. Good thing she'd at least gotten dinner out of the night. "I don't understand—facts are irrefutable."

"No, facts are boring."

"Sometimes. They're also necessary." Talk about a

personal assault. The only profession that might take more umbrage to his claim than a librarian was a statistician.

He clasped his hands behind his head. The movement drew his shirt taut along his chest and triceps. That outline of his muscles had Hallie licking her lips. *Yum.*

"Boring's no good. Death knell of a campaign. People can't feel good about you if they're snoozing off, or wishing they could be anywhere else to avoid more of the boring facts."

Irritated enough at that implied insult that she could ignore his distracting muscles, Hallie scooted to the edge of her chair. Anchoring her elbow on the table, she wagged a finger. "They need the factual information imparted so they can make a reasoned decision at the polls."

"Nope. Campaigns never come down to facts, or even the issues. It's all about how you make 'em *feel.* Like you're listening, and they're important. *Everyone's* important. That's your second piece of advice."

Hallie didn't buy it.

This was Swan Cove, after all. Status mattered. She'd heard that tables were assigned at the country club by what year the family had joined. His family was at the top of every list. "Don't you mean everyone with the right *pedigree's* important?"

Those blue eyes bored into hers like he was trying to push his response straight into her brain. "Damn it, that's not what I mean at all. I was being sincere. Every single voter—whether they agree with you or not, whether you like them or not—is important and deserves to be treated as such." Fitz snapped off each word fast, clearly pissed.

"Sorry. I shouldn't have made such a generalization." She'd fallen back on an instinctual pushback against snobbery. That's what happened when the *haves* chipped away at you for being a *have-not* your entire life.

Hallie had to admit, though, she wasn't sure how much of it was real and how much was perceived. There were plenty of residents, like Fitz's Aunt Felicia, who didn't care about Hallie's background or how much money she had. It was so much easier to let a few negative experiences paint everyone with a broad brush.

"I get why you did." Fitz stood up so quickly his chair teetered. He pulled Hallie up, too, with a tug on her forearm, then he slid his grip down to her wrist and placed her hand in the middle of his starched white button-down. "But here's the biggest takeaway of the night. *I'm* not my family. I don't think that way."

"That's becoming more and more clear." And that clarity was positively fascinating...

His tone lightened considerably. Lightly, Fitz stroked his thumb across the fingers still pinned to his pecs. "After all, they'd never condone consorting with the enemy."

They'd officially crossed the border of "just dinner" to "full-on flirting." Like many borders, it had been invisible and gone wholly unnoticed until Hallie suddenly blinked and realized everything was different.

She only had one move—to flirt back.

Hallie wiggled her fingers beneath his. Not to get away. Merely to flex against all that deliciously taut muscle. "Is that just fancy talk for pretending to like me?"

"There's no pretending." Cocking his head, Fitz pursed his lips to the side in a classic *I'm thinking* expression. He held it for a few long seconds. "I can't say for sure how much I like you, but I'm definitely intrigued."

"Me too."

"See?" Fitz gave her a cocky wink. "I told you we agree on lots of things."

Hallie had barely started smiling when he covered her mouth with his own. She'd never been smile-kissed before.

Because Fitz was smiling too. They didn't fit together *as* optimally…but it felt wonderful nonetheless.

Hallie opened her eyes. She wanted the up-very-close-and-personal view of Fitz's magazine-cover face.

Except…his eyes were open, too. His lips were an inch away from landing back on her mouth, but his blue eyes were locked on her face. And what she saw in them…

Pleasure, sure, even though they were barely one second past a peck, but she saw something else, too. Interest. Connection. A softness that could only be labeled as romantic.

Omigod.

Fitz really *did* like her.

And…she liked him right back. Fitz Montgomery. The mayor. The *competition*. The one she couldn't afford to let down her guard around. The one Hallie couldn't possibly feel…tender toward. Or lustful. Or anything in between.

Yet they clearly *did* like each other. A lot.

What was she supposed to do with that? Completely freaked out, she yanked out of his embrace.

"Thanks for dinner. And the advice."

And then, with desire still pinging like star fire through her veins, Hallie grabbed her purse and ran out the door.

Chapter Ten

Fitz's phone pinged. Pinged again.

And then so many times in a row that it sounded like a damned pinball machine.

He pulled over under the shade of the bookstore's green and white striped awning, then had a quick flashback to what a clusterfuck it'd been to get the awnings. Nothing changed in the historic downtown without a lot of discussion—aka, arguing—and going in circles in more laps than the Indy 500.

What drove him up a wall was that everyone wanted the awnings. All the fighting had been about the color, and then solid or stripes. That was a month of his life he'd never get back.

Before he walked out the door of city hall, he'd informed Derek that he'd be out for a bit. He'd walked a total of five blocks, and now Derek had texted him twelve times and sent two emails.

As far as Fitz knew, a cruise ship hadn't missed hitting the brakes and plowed into their marina. No smoke hung in the air. Nothing was literally *on* fire. And if aliens were invading

D.C., well, it could all wait until he finished his errand.

The text buried among Derek's dozen was, however, worth a response. Because when someone saved your ass on a daily basis, you didn't *ever* ignore them.

He sat on the green wrought-iron bench in front of the planters bursting with flowers. Mainers weren't patient about waiting to get their spring color going. If a late frost hit, they'd just buy more. The boxes in front of every store had more than one tourist framing a photo of them.

The phone only rang once. "Hey, David. Got your 911. Did you catch someone embezzling?"

The town accountant let out a choked-off gasp. "No! Do you think city funds are being embezzled?"

Fitz kept drilling down, trying to uncover a sense of humor in the guy. So far, the only thing he'd discovered that reliably made David laugh were GIFs of pets talking. "It was a joke. If they were, I sure wouldn't notice."

David did all his work—and carried a hefty chunk of the mayor's fiscal load, too. Fitz gave him an enormous bonus every year, from his personal bank account, for...well, doing his homework for him.

Fitz wasn't lazy. He also wasn't great with numbers. Swan Cove deserved better than his ham-handed attempts to wade through it all. He still put in the due diligence, scowled over every spreadsheet, but then had David sit with him and make sure everything was really on the up and up.

"Last I checked, which was fourteen minutes ago, our accounts were secure and unchanged."

"Great. So what do you need from me?" There was a slight pause. Fitz could picture the ultra-precise David checking the task list on his Outlook before answering.

"It's payroll day."

"Yep."

"I need you to sign the checks."

Archaic nonsense. He had to approve the checks being printed in the first place. Forcing him to hand-sign them was a waste of time. The secretary of the treasurer sure didn't sign the checks for every federal employee from GS1 to GS15.

Fitz had suggested a stamp of his signature. You'd think he'd suggested the Devil sign the checks by sticking his forked tongue in blood.

That wasn't how things were done in Swan Cove.

If one person had said it to him, a hundred people had said it. Including people who weren't even on the town's payroll.

"Yeah. I do this every two weeks, David. By noon, so they can hit the mail." The lack of direct deposit was another fight for another day.

"Derek said you were gone when I dropped the checks off on your desk. I was concerned."

For fuck's sake. Anger spiked through him like a heated pitchfork to his brain stem. Not at David. The guy was just acting on the information he'd received.

But *Derek*. Trying to micromanage him every second of the day. Obviously pissed that Fitz had taken unexplained time for himself and put the whole building on alert in a passive-aggressive play to get him back.

Campaign manager. *Not* a minder, not a jailer. The man thought he owned every inch of Fitz during campaign season. Probably because that's what his dad had told him, and because he was an officious little prick.

One problem at a time, though.

"David, have I ever missed signing payroll?"

"No."

"I appreciate your due diligence, but you never need to make a call about this again. Those checks will always be signed and on your desk by noon as long as I'm mayor, without any poking necessary."

"Okay. Thanks."

Fitz counted it a win that he simply disconnected the call. He wanted to chuck the phone across the street, right through the window of the chocolate shop.

Dealing with Derek wasn't a one-step process, though. Anything he said to him would lead to certain and immediate blowback from his father. Culminating in the often-repeated lecture about how it was the duty of the Montgomery family to look out for the town and do everything with its best interests at the forefront.

He *knew* that.

Most days, it was easier not to fight than have the same fight for the thousandth time, because no matter what he said or did, his dad ended up shoving that duty line down his throat. Like a goose being force-fed for its eventual transition to foie gras.

Fitz absolutely wanted to do right by the town. Swan Cove had its quirks and issues, but it was his home. All he wanted to do was help its citizens live a good, happy life.

A lot of days, though? It didn't feel like he was accomplishing that via his daily sojourns to the mayor's office. But yeah—one problem at a time. He was on a mission. And it wasn't speed-walking through downtown.

Pedestrians had already stopped him four times to chat. Mary Alice, the vet who kept watch over the eponymous swans in the pond, made him detour to point out how glossy their feathers were since adding musk grass to their diet.

Seth was on the sidewalk, checking in a big shipment of hops for the brewery. He told Fitz about the new bellini-esque ale experiment rolling out over the weekend and secured a promise to drop by for the keg tap.

That was the best part of his job. The one-on-one interactions. Fitz didn't begrudge a single extra minute of his walk.

Maybe...also...because he had no idea what sort of a reception he'd get at the library.

His pissyness with Derek must've reflected on his face. Nobody stopped him on the final block as he turned off of Main Street. Fitz didn't let himself pause under the library overhang with the purple and pink filled flower baskets. No need to officially gird his loins, right?

When he made a mistake, he owned it. Then he fixed it.

A quick scan of the bright room didn't reveal Hallie behind the desk or among the shelves. He peered into the glass-walled magazine reading room. Then into the conference room, full of babies and moms. Ah. Signage announced it as the La Leche League meeting. A different group of moms, and some dads, were in the kids' area doing story time on a rug that fit together as primary-colored puzzle pieces.

Still no Hallie.

This was good. He wanted privacy. And the perk of being mayor was that nobody blinked an eye at him going *anywhere* in town. So, Fitz nonchalantly walked right behind the checkout desk and through to the hallway where he hoped to find her office.

Whoops.

Not an office.

Fitz had entered the big room where all the books were processed. It was crowded with carts, long tables, and innumerable short stacks of books. A water cooler and coffee station made him assume it doubled as the break room, too.

Hallie had her back to him, filling a mug. Because he was alive and awake, Fitz took a moment to enjoy the view. Her long brown hair centered down her back in a braid that made his fingers itch to undo it. A silky pink blouse was tucked into brown pants that outlined the shape of her ass—which also made his fingers flex with the urge to squeeze it.

Ignorance really was bliss.

Now that he *knew* how soft her skin was, the scent of her, the taste of her...well, it made sneaking this look at her a study in frustration.

Not just because he couldn't grab her and kiss her *now*. Because he didn't know if he'd ever get to again. That thought had kept him tossing and turning all night. Last night with her had been hands-down great.

Until it wasn't.

Until he'd ruined it by kissing her.

Hallie turned around, startled when she spotted him, which sloshed water out of the mug in her hand.

"Shit. Did you burn yourself?" Fitz rushed across the room, dropping his bag on the table and quickly taking the mug.

"No. It just got my shoe. No updating the OSHA stats for the city over my jasmine tea incident."

"Damn it, Hallie, I don't care about that. I care about you getting hurt." He took her hand, pushing up her sleeve, looking for any redness or wetness.

"Really, I'm fine." Much softer, she added, "Thank you."

Fitz forced himself to let go of her hand, yanked off a wad of paper towels and knelt to blot at the carpet and her shoe. "For what? I'm the one who made you spill."

"You're not exactly an axe-murderer in a Halloween mask. The library is open for business, and anyone could've wandered in. I overreacted."

"I get the feeling your reaction was because it was me in the doorway. That you might've not even blinked at an axe-wielding maniac."

"Well, this *is* a lumber town. It could happen..." Hallie offered him a wry smile.

He'd take it. Because it really didn't sit well that she'd been so put off by his appearance. Proved that coming here to make amends was the right move. "Do you have a couple of minutes?"

"Sure. I am the boss, after all. I can give myself a break. Looks like you've done the same to come browsing at ten in the morning."

"Nope. My Kindle's fully stocked. I'm not here for books. I'm here for you."

Hallie slowly walked around the carts to shut the door. She kept her hand on the knob as she turned back to him. Couldn't have put off more of a *keep away* vibe if she'd wrapped herself in barbed wire.

Shit. He jammed his hands into his pockets to appear as nonthreatening as possible.

"Fitz, there was no need to step away from your duties as mayor to see me."

"How and when I handle my duties is entirely up to me," he snarled, and immediately realized how much of an asshole he sounded. "Sorry. Didn't mean to snap at you. That was entirely aimed at my campaign manager."

Her right eyebrow arched up. "Having a tiff, are you?"

"Ha. No." A tiff sounded civilized and reasonable, easily resolved over club sandwiches. This was so much bigger, and not fixable. "Derek thinks he owns me, body and soul, during campaign season. Causes some, ah, friction. Like this morning. I told him I was stepping away. He's been bombarding me with texts ever since."

To his immense relief, Hallie finally stepped away from the door. Came all the way back over to him and retrieved her mug. "Aren't you his boss? Can't you tell him to dial it back?"

"No, and no. It's complicated."

She sat on a brown padded folding chair. "Too complicated for a librarian, a mere first-time candidate to comprehend?"

How had he put his foot in it again? Especially since he was here to apologize. "Not at all. It's a family dynamics thing that will make me sound like I'm whining."

"Everybody needs to vent, Fitz. Remember our rule? When it's just the two of us, we aren't opposing candidates. Simply Hallie and Fitz." She toed out another chair from beneath the table. "So go ahead—let it out."

It wasn't why he'd come, but it was an invitation he couldn't refuse. Everett was the only person in town he could open up to about this—and Ev was probably sick to death of hearing about it after all these years.

Fitz sat heavily, whooshing out a breath. "Derek's employed by my dad. When my uncle quit as mayor, Dad told me it was my time to step up. That had always been the plan—hence the degree in public administration—it just happened way sooner than anticipated. I'd been away at school for so long. Dad knew more people, had the connections, got all the balls rolling. Derek was one of those balls."

"Easier to go along than start from scratch yourself. It just happened to be one of those smart choices that didn't turn out as well as expected. I understand."

"Yeah, especially since I hate campaigning."

This time, he was treated to a full, genuine, spotlight-bright smile. It turned out to be the pace car for rolling laughter that had her shoulders shaking. "After only one event? I'm right there with you."

"See? Another thing we have in common." This was going...better? A rocky start, for sure, but the prevailing winds had definitely shifted to favorable.

Fitz relaxed a little. When they weren't fighting, talking with Hallie was...a combination of easy and invigorating. Like a shot of tequila with a lime and Corona chaser.

Hallie lined up the spines on the book stack closest to her. "I've lived here long enough to notice the power structure in town. Your father touches almost everything."

"Yes." Could've said a lot more, but that'd be opening a

Pandora's box. Fitz was immensely proud of how his family had shaped Swan Cove. How they'd thoughtfully expanded it over the decades. How they'd pivoted to bring in the more modern laboratory to not be dependent on the old standbys of lumber and tourism.

But he also hated that the Montgomery fingers were in every pot. Hated the automatic kowtowing. Hated the assumption that whatever a Montgomery said was true, the best way, the right thing, the only way.

On the bad days? Fitz likened it to being a mob boss, without all the shooting and decapitation and bribes, of course.

"So Derek's his toadie?" Twisting around, she pulled an enormous red leather-bound *Complete Works of Charles Dickens* from a cart. "Like Uriah Heep in *David Copperfield*, or Iago in *Othello*."

"Yes. Or, to be more topical, like Kissinger was to Nixon."

Dropping the book with a thud that shook the entire table, Hallie clapped. "Ooh, excellent reference. I think you win that round."

Damn it. There she went again. "Hallie, there doesn't always have to be a winner and a loser with us. We can be equals."

"I don't think that would ever be possible. Even if you and I believe it, the whole town has you and your whole family on a pedestal high enough to touch the moon."

Fitz had wanted to be an astronaut until he was twelve. That was the year they toured NASA and he learned about the possibility of astronauts wearing diapers in space. His career path pivoted immediately. "That's fanciful of you."

"Not entirely." With a tug in the middle of yet another stack, she brandished a copy of *The Right Stuff*. "Couldn't help it. Shelving puts so many ideas into my head. The course of my entire day can be changed depending on the books I handle."

"You do live in the tiny house equivalent of a city. You should probably handle *Our Town* every day."

"Mr. Mayor, you are quite well read."

"I like books." Then he did a neck swivel so slow that he heard each vertebrae crack as he looked around the big room, near to bursting with paperbacks and hardcovers. "Probably not as much as you, though."

"It is about quality, not quantity."

Fitz put a finger to his lips, shushed her dramatically, stretching to look at the door and the row of windows up at the ceiling. In a stage whisper, he asked, "Are you allowed to make a sexual innuendo in the library?"

Her pretty eyes with flecks of gold widened and held that way for a second. Then Hallie burst out laughing. Loudly.

"Pretty sure you can't make noise in a library, either," he drawled.

"Good thing I'm in charge and can do what I want." From beneath half-lowered lids, she smoldered intensity at him. "Sound familiar, Your Mayorship?"

"Cut it out."

"Couldn't resist," she shot back.

"Fair enough." The knowledge that she was teasing, that Hallie didn't actually *believe* that, made all the difference.

"We could easily sit here bantering all day."

Yeah, he really could. Fitz had the feeling that'd be one of the best days of the year if it happened. Couldn't say that, though, not after pushing himself on her last night. He dialed back his intensity.

"I can think of worse ways to pass a day."

"I'll bet the taxpayers who provide both of our salaries wouldn't be thrilled, however. So why don't you tell me why you popped by?"

Guess it was time. Time for the fun to end—potentially.

Fitz scraped his chair back out. Retrieved the paper bag he'd carted across town. "To bring you this." He pulled out a round baking dish with a lid carved to look like an apple. "You left last night without getting your dessert."

"Oh. Oh, Fitz. That truly wasn't necessary."

"In the overall breadth of your sweet tooth, no. But the blueberry crisp was an excuse to get me in here to do the necessary clearing of the air."

She'd been in the middle of lifting the lid, already bent over to sniff at it. Hallie froze. "What?"

Why the surprise? Did she really think he was that much of an egotistical jerk to not apologize? He shoved his hands into his pockets. "You know—make amends. Grovel. Humble myself in my wrongness and beg forgiveness."

After a quick sniff that made her lashes flutter, she replaced the lid. "I don't understand. You haven't done anything wrong. You cooked me dinner."

It wouldn't be right to start off the apology by accepting false credit. "I peeled shrimp and *arranged* dinner to be cooked for you," Fitz stipulated.

"Fine. But you were the perfect host. It was a warm, wonderful evening, one of the best I've had in a long time." As she spoke, her hands molded the air as if holding an actual conversational ball. "You don't need to apologize for anything."

Confused as hell, Fitz was still determined to make this right. Two long steps brought him around the table to her. "I do. For God's sake, Hallie, I made you feel so bad that you literally *ran* out of my house. I assume I crossed a line by kissing you, for which I'm truly sorry, but if it was something else—or something in addition—just tell me."

She just looked at him. Said nothing.

"I don't want you feeling so uneasy around me that you have to run away. It made me sick last night to realize I'd made you so uncomfortable. I—"

"Stop, Fitz. Just stop." Hallie jumped up to put her soft palm across his mouth. "Will you be quiet? For a minute?" When he nodded, she dropped her hand. "This is embarrassing, but I'd rather be embarrassed than let you wallow in guilt."

That'd be Fitz's vote too. He didn't risk saying it out loud, though, since he still didn't know entirely what her reaction was about.

"Thank you, for bringing the dessert, for apologizing." Her hand briefly touched his cheek. Then she clasped her hands behind her. "The thing is, though...I didn't leave because you made me feel bad. I left because you made me feel too *good*. Too much. That's what scared me."

Well, well, well. Fitz shifted his weight back onto his heels, considering. *That* little revelation was unexpected. Both that it'd happened and that she'd admitted to it.

He mimed a semblance of the Boy Scout salute. Maybe. Close enough that Hallie shouldn't know the difference. "You swear you're not mad—or hurt?"

"Absolutely not."

"I made you feel good, huh?" Yeah, that came out smug as all hell. In a world where everyone from car-share drivers to restaurants to movies pushed their good reviews out constantly? Fitz figured he was entitled to enjoy getting one himself.

Especially one that had zilch to do with his family, his name, his title, or his money.

That prim twitch to her lips that they must teach in Librarian 101 came back. "That's a basic biological reaction. Don't get too smug about it."

Hallie tightened the end of her braid. Fitz was learning that she did it the same way Everett pushed his glasses up his nose, as a thinking moment. A three-second excuse to not respond, to not meet your eyes. It often made him wish he had a beard to stroke for the same ploy.

Aside from not liking the itch, or the way they caught food and kept him from feeling the softness of a woman's lips on his chin.

"I'll accept the dessert because it smells divine. But you see why I won't accept your apology. Instead, I'll offer one to you for running out so ungraciously."

Fitz batted away her words with a lazy swipe of his arm. "Yesterday's over. I'd rather focus on tomorrow."

"What's tomorrow?" Her skeptical squint was becoming familiar, too.

"We should go on a date. Not an apology dinner. Not coaching. A real, not masquerading as anything else, date."

"Why?"

Fitz flipped through possible responses. Everything from the childish *why not* to a six-point explanation. But if a picture was worth a thousand words? A kiss was worth at least a *million* of 'em.

So, he simultaneously flopped into a chair and snagged her waist to draw Hallie onto his lap on the way down. Before his ass hit the seat, they were kissing. Kissing like they'd never stopped the night before. It was hot and wet and more than a little frantic, as if they both realized how close they'd come to never doing this again—and what a fucking mistake that would've been.

His hand moved up to curve around her cheek to gently adjust the angle until Fitz could've sworn there was a click.

Optimal position achieved.

Hallie's hands were all over his head. That was fine. He let her drive the position. Fitz was busy running his hands over her thigh, down her calf, and up her ribs to knead at her perfectly plump breast.

Little huffs of need escaped from her mouth into his. Fitz

provided growls of desire, while Hallie added near purrs of pleasure. The way her weight rocked back and forth on this cock was maddening.

And fantastic.

And Fitz never wanted her to stop—unless it was to get naked, which they couldn't do right now. Talk about a slap of cold water to his libido.

He grasped her face in both hands and broke off the kisses. "*That's* why. If you liked it so much last night, I'll bet you'll like it even more when we do it again."

It was gratifying to see that it took a couple of seconds for her eyes to refocus. "We can't."

"For God's sake, woman. I want you. Let me know if I'm wrong, but it feels like you want me, too."

"Well, yes. I do." She licked her kiss-swollen lips. "Quite a bit, if truth be told."

"There you go. Unless—are you secretly married?" Fitz pinched her ring finger. "If not, there's nothing standing in our way. Aside from the whole being at your work right now. Let's say there's nothing standing in our way in about six hours."

Hallie marched over to the bulletin board over the sink, snatched down the flyer with the list of campaign events and brandished it. Nearly gave his nose a paper cut. "We're running against each other. The ballot box is standing in our way."

He crumpled it up and—thank God—sank it in a beautiful airball in the *furthest* trash can. "I'm not planning on taking photos and turning them into campaign posters. We had this fight already. Candidates Montgomery and Scott can't date. Hallie and Fitz can do whatever they want."

It earned him another down-the-nose, prissy glare. Man, those turned him on. "That's semantics."

"Yep." It was kind of fun going ten rounds with a word

nerd. "Would you feel better if we kept it on the down-low?"

"Would *you*?"

Sneaking around? Yeah, that sounded sexy as hell. Plus, it'd halve the potential for daily lectures from his dad. "It'd make my life less complicated, I won't lie, but I don't want you to think I'm reluctant to be seen with you."

"You are, though. And I share that reluctance."

Deliberately, Fitz palmed her butt. "Do you share my longing to get my hands on you without any clothes in the way?"

"Perhaps." After another tighten of her elastic, she added, "It's something to be explored."

She was so damn full of attitude, and it *delighted* him. "Okay. Secret fling, here we come."

Grimacing, she said, "Nope. No labels, either."

What man in his right mind would argue with *that*? "No problem. No strings. No witnesses. Just what feels good. Tomorrow night?"

"Not tomorrow. I need to prep for the next campaign event."

It stung, a little, that Hallie *could* wait, when Fitz was raring to go right this minute. Shoving his hands in his pockets, he asked, "Got your competitive edge on, huh?"

He'd expected her to come off cocky. Instead, Hallie massaged her temples with a rueful squint. "Well, if I follow your advice and abandon my rational plan of sharing statistics and examples based on facts, I'm going to need time to come up with a new plan."

Hell. Fitz wanted to help, but he didn't want to be *responsible* for her choices. "Hallie. Don't dive into a new strategy just on my say-so. You might regret it. Think about what I said. More importantly, think how it relates to you and how you could tweak your current plan to simply be less... ah..."

"Tedious?"

"Sure. We'll go with that." He'd been thinking boring AF. Good thing he hadn't said it out loud, but the simple fact was that today's society took in information in short bursts. Anything long and they tuned out. She deserved to at least have the attention of the voters.

"I can pivot, as you'll see, Mr. Mayor."

There was the expected cockiness. If Hallie thought she'd shut him up? Ha! With an unrepentant smirk, Fitz said, "I can't wait to see you pivot. Preferably in lingerie. Or less."

"If you're lucky, perhaps you'll see both." Then she shimmied as she walked across the room and out into the library.

Fitz couldn't deny how very much he liked her blend of seriousness and sass. *And* sexiness.

Maybe she was right. Okay, very probably Hallie was right. The odds were stacked against them.

But who didn't enjoy trying to beat the odds?

Chapter Eleven

"If I'd known all campaign events focused on food, *I'd* have run for mayor years ago." Randall broke a whoopie pie in half and offered one to Hallie.

She waved him off. Her embryonic campaign was on thin enough ice. Talking to constituents with chocolate cookie stuck in her teeth would ring the death knell on it. "Please. You're twenty-seven. You weren't old enough years ago."

"In California, you can be governor if you're eighteen."

Trust Randall to argue with a ridiculously random fact. Hallie zipped up her navy windbreaker. The gusts coming off the ocean today were fierce. She tapped on the oilcloth front of his yellow slicker. "In California, it isn't fifty degrees in May at lunchtime. You'd rather be here, legit experiencing all four seasons. You love the excuse to break out all your different weights of coats."

Ana stepped away from the busy takeout window of the lobster restaurant that was the stanchion of the wharf. "Plus, you come to the wharf at least twice a week. It's the same food you eat then. It isn't special just because Hallie's sitting behind a giant bunting rosette."

Even if she won the election by some miracle, she'd certainly never get a big head with *these* friends. Always known for her bluntness, that was a particularly pointed barb. "Thanks, Ana. For the reminder I'm not special."

"I didn't say—sorry. Low blood sugar. Gimme that." Ana snatched the other half of the whoopie pie and gobbled it down. She was dabbling in training for a half marathon and it made her hungry all the time.

Dabbling because she hated to run but wanted a legit excuse to head to the warmth of Fort Lauderdale in February. Hallie had sat on the bleachers and read her book while Ana did laps at the high school track. That counted as support, right?

Randall shoved his sunglasses atop his head, brown hair disheveled from wearing his big headphones all morning at the groomers, and looked at the growing crowd and the line at the white and blue framed takeout window. "If you eat this well as a potential mayor, I wonder how much better the food is if you run for governor. Or president."

Oh, Hallie had to shut that down *immediately*. Her heart was in her throat, her stomach was in knots, and she'd woken up with a headache from clenching through her nightguard from stress. Tension. Anxiety. Fear. You name it.

There would be no wondering about a bigger variation. If she escaped *this* race without an ulcer and her first white hair, that'd be enough.

"First of all, I have zero political aspirations beyond this race. And, secondly, the events coincide with food because it's an easy way to bolster attendance. Everyone has to eat, even on a Thursday. It helps drum up extra business for the establishments on the wharf, which is a good thing for both candidates to claim. Trust me, I'm not in this for the free lobster roll Poseidon's Kitchen will hand me at the end of it."

"I'll be with you in spirit, but I may not last till the end," he warned. "We've got a poodle coming in that's bad tempered. If Cora can't handle her alone, she'll text me."

"Aren't all poodles bad tempered?" Megan asked as she scooted into their little circle with a basket of fried clams. The black half apron for her styling scissors and combs was still tied around her waist.

"No snark allowed," Randall said with a warning finger shake. He was a passionate supporter of every pup that crossed his threshold. "All dog breeds have their good and bad highlights."

"C'mon. I call 'em like I see 'em. Poodles are as temperamental as Mrs. Eliopoulos if the water is one degree the wrong way in the shampoo sinks."

Randall rolled his arms in an enormous circle, then clapped. "Oh! We should do campaign sound bites on TikTok for you, Hallie!"

That was a horrifying suggestion. Social media was *not* Hallie's thing due to the whole introvert/preferring to always be in the background entirety of her personality.

"That's not the place for our girl." Megan sniffed, as if the very idea smelled worse than the seagull guano at the end of the dock. The cruise ship crew scraped it every week before letting any passengers deboard. "Hallie making videos? Even twelve-second ones? No way. She forgot her one line in the Christmas pageant and fell over instead of doing a somersault."

Great. There was a memory Hallie kept in a mental vault behind bulletproof glass, titanium doors, and a concrete box to avoid ever revisiting. But the one thing you could count on best friends for, besides hugs and unconditional support? *Embarrassment.*

"When was this? How did I miss that hilarity?" Ana's indignation sped her words out in a near screech.

"Well, she was only nine," Megan conceded. "Having avoided performing since then, I doubt she's improved to where videos would be a good idea. But you do have a point, Randall."

"I always do. You just don't always deign to acknowledge my brilliance."

Megan turned to Hallie, eyes wide. "You need a social media presence. ASAP. We didn't think of that."

Oh, Hallie had thought of it and dismissed it as painful and avoidable...until her friends ganged up on her, at least. "There's no doubt a lot we haven't thought of yet." That's what happened when you cannonballed into a new adventure without any planning. It made Hallie all the more relieved that she'd accepted Fitz's generous offer of coaching help.

If he'd still follow through with it after today.

"I'm only here for twenty minutes, too. Same for her." Megan pointed at Elaine Alsip, who was sitting on a wrought-iron bench clasping her late husband's walking stick with its swan's head handle. Their family had been here almost as long as the Montgomerys. And every time she came into the library, she paused in front of the romance shelf, sniffed, and muttered "low class trash" with a withering stare at Hallie. "She's got a blowout with me. Prep for her daughter and grandkids arriving tonight."

Oh. A little, no, a *lot* of Hallie's bravery melted away. Even with a crowd of easily sixty people, she'd been counting on the presence of her three besties, if only to flick her eyes at them for a moment in the next hour and get a warm smile in return.

The trick was to not let them see how close she was to falling apart without them. Hallie squeezed Megan's arm. "I appreciate you guys coming out, more so for all your help the past few days. Coming up with a new campaign strategy would've been impossible without you."

"You're Woodrow Wilson." Ana slurped up corn chowder from a mini bread bowl balanced in one hand.

Hallie raced through everything she knew about the president—admittedly, not a lot—and couldn't come up with anything that related to her. He'd been a war president, for crying out loud. "Is that meant as a compliment or an insult?"

"He said *I not only use all the brains that I have, but all I can borrow*."

That was actually completely on the nose. Hallie filed it away in her permanent mental quote collection. And, truth be told, she couldn't wait to share it with Fitz. He'd get a kick out of it.

"Ha!" Megan waved a clam strip. "Fun quote. Smart guy."

Randall's side-eye hit her so hard that Hallie practically heard it crunch against Megan's face. "Seeing that he won the Nobel Peace Prize and gave women the vote, you could say so."

"He didn't *give* women the vote, we took it." Ana stuck out her tongue at him. "You ought to be ashamed of yourself. You parade around, out and proud in your rainbow scarf, but deep down, you're just another bastion of the patriarchy."

"You take that back. It is utterly hurtful."

Ordinarily, Hallie enjoyed her friends' banter. Today, it was just static over the rapid beating of her heart because her new campaign strategy was a risk.

Not to mention it was the *only* one they'd come up with. So she backed away toward the dais with a wave. "Gotta go do the thing. Thanks again." When Hallie turned to look for the steps, she bounced right off Fitz.

He steadied her with a hand above her elbow. "Is running over the competition your new strategy, Ms. Scott?"

"No. Sorry."

But he might feel like he'd been run over by the end of

the event, Hallie thought. Guilt grabbed on to the nerves circling her belly in an epic round of crack the whip.

Fitz looked like an action figurine of Sporty Mayor. A cream half-zip pullover revealed a blue oxford with a light brown tie with a clam shell pattern. Well-weathered boat shoes, of course, that Hallie assumed had logged plenty of nautical miles on one of the Montgomerys' three boats. The wind tousled his golden hair artfully, which wasn't fair since Hallie *knew* it was teasing random, messy strands from her French braid.

Men had it so easy. No wonder Ana had snapped at Randall, even though more than a hundred years had passed since the passage of the Nineteenth Amendment. Unlike Fitz, Hallie would be judged on her messy hair. So, she unzipped her windbreaker and removed it. It'd be cold, but at least she wouldn't be a bulked-up frump next to him.

"It's nice to see you." He leaned in closer to murmur in her ear. "It'll be even nicer to see even more of you."

"Fitz!" Hallie yelped. Then she frantically scanned the crowd to see if anyone had noticed. "You can't flirt with me at a campaign event."

"Which is why I said it softly. Nobody overheard."

It appeared to be true. People were still digging into their lunches and getting settled on the folding chairs spread in rows down the wharf. She blinked at him slowly. "Oh. I'm not used to being stealthy."

"The trick to being stealthy? At least, according to my many rewatches of the Clooney/Pitt Ocean's franchise, including the awesome all-female versions?" He winked. "Be normal, be yourself."

Did he really think that made it easier? Or even doable? Even though she did appreciate his taste in movies... "Those are two opposing tactics. I can pretend to be normal. If I'm being myself, then I'd be paranoid, screeching like a seagull every time you moved your hand within touching distance of me." Hallie considered this. "I'd probably have shifty eyes, too."

"Good God, woman. We're not about to steal a royal baby. We're just not announcing to the world that we've discovered an interest in each other."

Hallie licked her dry lips. "I'm no good at lying."

Fitz roared with laughter. "Then you're *definitely* not suited to be a politician." Offering his arm, he led her up the stairs. They settled themselves on the dais.

Hallie was grateful the ocean was at their back. She wouldn't be squinting at the glare from it. And everyone else would be, which meant less focus on her wind-whipped hair. Also? Their table was draped in a tablecloth with the enormous red, white, and blue bunting rose at the front. That gave her license to fidget and cross her legs with nobody the wiser.

It felt odd not to have notes, though. Ana had insisted she leave her tablet at home to give the appearance of utter confidence in her seemingly off-the-cuff responses, which she'd practiced, nonstop, for three days.

The jingle of anchor chains and the creaking of the dock's planks should've been a soothing, familiar lullaby to Hallie. She often came out here for lunch, dinner, or just to relax in front of the ocean's constant swells.

Not today.

Today, the soothing noises jangled on her already frazzled nerves. Either she was about to turn herself into a target of loathing…or…she was about to do the same to Fitz. It felt vaguely sleazy, which Megan had pointed out probably meant it was the correct political maneuver.

The logic was solid. Still, it wasn't the way Hallie liked to do things. Which *Randall* had then pointed out probably meant it'd have a higher shot at success than her previous campaign outing.

It flat out felt wrong. Hallie covered the microphone in front of her. "Fitz."

"Yes? You ready to attempt to kick my ass?"

Hmm. That had come out more than a tad condescending. Her sense of wrongness scaled back by 5 percent. "Right now, we're only the candidates up here."

"Yup." He hooked a thumb over his shoulder to the sign swaying next to them. "We're the only two names on there."

"No, I mean, we're not Hallie and Fitz who really like laughing and kissing together."

"Correct. We've got our game faces on. Candidate Scott and Mayor Montgomery. Gloves are off." Fitz covered his microphone, leaned closer, while keeping a fixed smile on his face and his eyes on the crowd. "But in two hours, we'll take off our politician masks and go back to being ourselves."

After licking her swiftly chapping lips, she asked cautiously, "And you won't be mad at me, no matter what I do?"

"Is that a threat or a promise?" He threw her a devastating wink. "Of course not. I'm rooting for you, remember? I want this to be a strong campaign that shows the electorate the strengths and weaknesses of both candidates. Do your best. I can take it."

Then at least her conscience was clear.

Twenty minutes later, Hallie was as much of a mess as her hair. And she no longer gave a rat's ass about her conscience.

The crowd was chatty. Closer to boisterous, really. The outdoor setting and the food turned several of them into hecklers. Rather, they heckled *Hallie*. For the most part, Fitz was left in peace. The only people who had yelled anything at him had been praising his sailing skills and long-ago lacrosse skills. Neither of which, Hallie was *damned* certain, in any way translated to the administration of a city.

It was different from the reserved, stodgy club atmosphere of the first event. Hallie felt like she was in the front seat of a roller coaster without any safety bar. She hadn't practiced being shouted at, interrupted.

It was tempting to consider not going ahead with her plan under these less orthodox conditions. Except...scrapping this plan, postponing it, left Hallie with exactly *no* plan to survive the event.

"You're not even from here." The man with a solid line of salt-and-pepper eyebrows had a razor-sharp edge to his tone. "What do *you* know about Swan Cove?"

And there it was. The "outsider" accusation. Expected, since the *Gazette* had run full bios on both candidates this week. On the front page. Fitz's bio had led off with the descriptor of "favorite son of the town and next scion of the Montgomery dynasty."

Hallie's? "Raised in Crow Harbor."

Fitz leaned forward, mouth right up against the mic. "That's an unfair question. A low blow. There's no requirement to live here your whole lifetime to be the mayor."

Wow.

He'd leaped to her defense, *while* running against her. It might not be a great move as a candidate, but it sure made Fitz a truly excellent person. Hallie's toes tingled with the warmth of that gesture, but she still needed to handle the heckler herself.

Channeling the patience of Gandhi, she said, in a remarkably calm tone, "I've lived in Swan Cove for six years. What specific depth of knowledge do you feel Mayor Montgomery has over me? And in what way does it enhance his job performance?"

"He knows us!"

Now, there was an opening. *Finally.*

Peripheral vision showed Fitz to still be wearing his flat,

professional politician smile. Interesting. She twisted to really look at him. Zero warmth or recognition crinkled around his eyes. That smile appeared to be frozen in place.

So she took a shot. Leaning into his mic for effect, Hallie asked as pleasantly as if offering ketchup with fries, "Mayor, what's that man's name?"

Oh, that unfroze him all right! Heat burned into her like a laser from his glare. The muscle in his thigh twitched.

And she waited.

When he didn't answer, she lifted the mic from its table stand to right in front of his lips. Those talented, firm lips that, huh, still weren't moving at all.

"Sir, would you like to introduce yourself? To, well, both candidates, apparently?"

"I'm Fergus Nutley." His eyebrows were still a single pelt. Evidently, he didn't care for Hallie showing the weakness in his candidate. Then he'd better buckle in, because she was just getting started.

"It's a pleasure, Fergus."

"Yes." Fitz talked right on top of her. "Why don't you hang around once we're done and I'm grabbing my lunch? We can get to know each other." With an outstretched hand— but eyes that still burned—he included her. "Ms. Scott, you're welcome to join us."

"I'd be delighted to, for a short while. It'll be helpful. I like to get all of my talking urges out before going back to work at the library. Like draining a septic tank."

Yes, it was both a weak and rehearsed joke, but it turned out that neither Hallie nor any of her friends had any latent stand-up talent. The fact that three people chuckled at it was an enormous win in her book.

"Thanks, Fergus, for reminding everyone I'm a proud lifelong resident of Swan Cove. Not that the zip code on my birth certificate should sway anyone's vote." Hand over his heart, he gave a mini bow.

Of course, that earned Fitz as big a cheer as if he'd just hand-carried the game-winning touchdown across the entire length of the field.

It was also the best segue Hallie could hope for. The time for attack was nigh. "That could be both a pro and a con, Mayor. You see, longevity in a place, in a role, can lead to lackluster performance."

"Now who's tossing out low blows, Ms. Scott? Never accuse a man of lackluster performance. Certainly not without firsthand knowledge." And then Fitz tossed that devastatingly sexy wink at the crowd.

They ate it up with a roar. She couldn't blame them. He *did* have a reputation as a ladies' man, which was not at all what she'd been trying to attack him for. Talk about a backfire.

Surprisingly, Fitz was known for his love 'em, leave 'em, but still like 'em policy. No string of bitter, broken hearts in his wake. It was as if the women considered themselves privileged just to have had the shot. Like Academy Award nominees.

Hallie had to win this tug of war with him to control the crowd. "I want to be clear. I am in no way accusing Mayor Montgomery of neglecting or slacking in his duties."

"Where's the fun in that?" It was Elaine Alsip. She was aged enough to get away with being salty. And on her bench, disturbingly close to the dais and thus easy to overhear.

"I came here to see a throwdown. Isn't that the point of finally having two candidates?"

Oh, dear. That shout-out had been from a lobsterman in a heavy oilcloth slicker and boots. This was the time of day they started dropping off their catch at Poseidon's Kitchen, but...a good 99 percent of the lobstermen lived in Crow Harbor. This guy was stirring up trouble just to be a jerk, *not* as an actual concerned citizen.

Fitz took a sip of water, leaned back, and lifted an eyebrow. It was a clear indication he was leaving Hallie to sink or swim on her own, which she deserved after lobbing the first real attack. So, this was it. Her big plan. "Here's how the current administration"—she gave a graceful game-show hostess presentational wave to Fitz—"has fallen short of their promises."

Shelby Kirk, a columnist for the *Gazette*, waved a hand. "The mayor promised to date me back in high school. Can you make him follow through on that?"

"I can't make him do anything." This time, Hallie did a super slow neck roll, channeling a snowy owl, and pursed her lips to give Fitz the most dramatic *I see right through you* stare ever. "Evidently, no woman can."

Aha! This time the crowd roared in laughter *with* her. *At* Fitz. It was a glorious sound. It spiked Hallie's confidence by 1,000 percent. It gave her, frankly, the guts to continue.

"Campaigns are when a candidate makes promises to you. Bribes, really." She made finger quotes. "'If you vote for me, I'll do all these wonderful things.' Like a sophomore class president promising to allow video game play in study hall, but...have you ever heard of a teacher allowing that?"

A soft rumble of nos filled the air. She had them.

Eye contact was a bridge too far. Hallie stared at the tops of heads. And very much made sure not to so much as flicker an eyelash in Fitz's direction. "Empty promises are useless. They leave you feeling twice as let down as if the candidate had never dangled that carrot covered in tasty blue-cheese dip in front of you. I firmly believe the mayor had good intentions, but if he doesn't fulfill those promises," she lifted her empty palms, "he's no better than a used car salesman that fudges the truth on how long a car with a hundred and fifty thousand miles on it will last."

Just as Ana had predicted, that simile brought Fitz into defense mode. He rustled next to her, no doubt abandoning his relaxed posture. "I've accomplished plenty in *both* my tenures as mayor."

"I'm sure that's true. However, I'm shining a light on what you didn't accomplish." And she went in for the kill. "Because you promised to add funds to the arts program in all of the schools. In *both* of your campaigns."

The bland, expressionless mask was gone, but so was the practiced politician look. Fitz now wore the focused, interested, small squint that popped a vertical line between his brows he had when the two of them were alone at his house. Like they were debating for the fun of it, rather than with an audience of more than fifty.

"Introducing an initiative doesn't magically make the funds appear. I tried. I put the measure up for discussion. It was the school board that didn't approve the shift of funds from other programs."

"Perhaps you should've sussed that out prior to making an empty promise," Hallie retorted. Her adrenaline had layers of adrenaline now as she rolled on. "You also promised to borrow close to a million dollars to pay for the installation of a fiber optic communications network at all of the town's buildings. I can confirm that no such network has been put in at the library, or even broached."

Murmurs rippled through the crowd. Hopefully, from other downtown businesses who suddenly remembered that they didn't have it, either.

Fitz shook his head, regret showering off of him with that simple movement. "It was deemed to be an overly optimistic reach once we got into the nitty gritty of a bond statement."

Still, an unfulfilled campaign promise. And she had more. Hallie pointed over the heads of the crowd. "You paved over the gravel and oyster shell parking lot for this wharf, but you'd promised to do the same in front of the community center, the historical society, and the VFW."

"I prioritized small business support." He drilled his finger into the table. "This is where the tourists spend their money when they get off the cruise ships. Money that keeps our town solvent."

"Money that keeps the Montgomerys solvent, you mean. As your family owns or has a controlling interest in seventy-eight percent of the businesses on the wharf and downtown. But I imagine, to no one's surprise, your family doesn't own so much as a smidgen of the community center, the historical society, or the VFW."

Shelby jumped to her feet. "These are harsh accusations, Ms. Scott. Do you have any proof?"

"Oh, I do. I have stats and facts to back up every statement, which I'd be happy to email you afterward. But for now? Well, I hate to be a cliché. Bad enough that I'm a Taurus who's very stubborn. Anyone who lives with a Taurus knows we dig in our heels over the littlest things." Hallie grimaced, got a couple of knowing snorts. Geez, she really stank at a planned-out joke.

"Worse still that I'm a librarian who has shushed a person or twenty this month alone." A little more laughter. "But librarians have a bad reputation for burying people in piles of dull facts. I definitely don't want to *bore* anyone."

Next to her, Fitz sucked in a sharp breath. Guess he'd realized that she'd steamrolled him by taking his own advice.

This time, the roar of laughter was accompanied with hearty applause. Just like that, Hallie felt the tide began to turn her way.

She hoped it wouldn't make Fitz turn away from her.

And the last feeling she took the time to register before continuing to argue with him was how…incendiary it had been to spar with him. In front of everyone.

Aka, Hallie very much wanted to jump the mayor at that moment.

Impossible, of course. They had the rest of the event to get through. Then lunch on the pier with whoever chose to stay, and then straight back to work for both of them.

But their excellent debate had been stellar foreplay for whenever they were able to be alone again. Hallie very much hoped that'd be soon.

Turned out that she wanted the current mayor—naked—almost as much as she wanted her next breath.

Chapter Twelve

Fitz loved sailing, being out in the open water, pitting himself against the elements.

He loved cross-country skiing in pristine snow and having a moose cross his path.

And he *loved* listening to people. Not blowhards droning on and on. Not idiots self-aggrandizing. But people opening up about what mattered to them.

When he could mix giving them the safe space to talk *and* the opportunity to help them, it was a good day. Pretty much the best days he had as mayor.

The trick of it was getting both sides to listen to each other before they started swearing and hurling insults. Fitz had a window about as wide as a spider's filament to make that happen. Right now? He was tightrope walking on that single thread and hoping for the best.

Ravi Patel pounded the side of his fist on the conference table. "You have to cut down those trees that fell in the ice storm. What landed in the water is acting as a makeshift dam. It's disturbing the delicate balance of the watershed."

It was a fair point, and expected from him. Ravi headed up the Coastal Bays and Estuaries program. Well, he was technically the head of one of the genetics sequencing departments at Cygnet Labs. Apparently, when your brain was world-class brilliant, heading up town environmental committees was a fun activity. A hobby—just a far more respectable one than the way Fitz and his friends spent their downtime watching Red Sox games.

"Nature versus nurture." Raquel Milligan, from the Park and Leisure Services advisory board, held up both hands like a set of scales. "Also see *nature is red in tooth and claw*. In other words, let nature do what it will and stop trying to control it."

Ravi's right eye twitched. "That's not what either of those phrases means."

Fitz used his pen to push the box from Frosted 'n Frozen, the ice cream and donut shop, closer to the man. Sugar usually helped soothe people—or at least stuff their mouths—long enough to let the other side get their argument out. Aside from his last name, that store was probably most responsible for his success as mayor.

Wendy DeLuca tapped her crazy long, tapered orange nails against each other. "Besides, do you know how expensive it'll be to cut them down? That's an unforeseen chunk of budget yanked away."

"Unforeseen?" Bruce Barnett's snort was loud enough that Fitz half expected to watch a loogie sail across the table. "You're on the Tree and Landscape committee for a town in *Maine*. You didn't foresee that harsh weather would at any point, every damn year, impact your trees and landscapes?"

Bruce was a...character?

Sure, that was the kindest descriptor. Those who *weren't* kind called him loud. Harsh. With assholish tendencies more often than not. But he owned a fleet of ships based over in

Crow Harbor, was proud he'd built it, one by one, and then clawed his way across the tracks to live in Swan Cove.

Hell.

Which meant his fleet would be seriously impacted by the plans for the new marina/resort.

The man could be a jerk, but he also put in more volunteer time than five other people combined. Bruce downright loved this town, the way anyone loved the realization of a dream. Fitz appreciated the hell out of the guy...when he wasn't busy trying to calm the storms Bruce always left in his wake.

Yes, Wendy's comment had been idiotic and indefensible, but it didn't mean Bruce should be allowed to make her *feel* idiotic.

At least Ravi had picked up a strawberry glazed. That should buy Fitz time to calm things down. He loosened the knot of his tie and undid the top button. It'd make everyone feel like he was digging in and in the trenches with them.

"Look, I know everyone seated in this room wants what's best for Swan Cove. We don't have to necessarily agree on what that might be. We just have to find a way to interweave all these solid requests while still respecting where everyone is coming from." Fitz finished by leveling a warning glare at Bruce.

"We don't have the money to do the full removal of those trees and plant new ones. Ms. Scott reminded us yesterday about that."

Hallie's pointed accounting of where he'd fallen short on campaign promises had been, well, a brilliant strategy for which he applauded her...

...as well as a gigantic pain in the ass. He'd been dodging questions from all quarters ever since. Derek was doing a crap job of shielding him from the brunt of them. Fitz had *thought* this meeting would give him an hour of peace from being hounded.

Stifling a sigh, Fitz asked, "About what?"

"How you promised to plant ten more trees a year in the historic downtown."

Really?

Should've read whatever stump speech that had featured in a hell of a lot more closely. Swan Cove was exactly two things: the harbor front and the forest, with maybe an inch of neutral ground in between. Fitz wanted to do right by the environment, but Mother Nature could take out twenty trees a year around here and nobody would notice.

Aside from Wendy and her tree census committee members.

"Even if we had the money to do both, finding the labor is a problem. Everyone in the landscaping business is booked. This is their high season." Raquel gave a smug head toss—which didn't really come off, since her hair was too short to flip. "We've already scheduled all our plantings on behalf of the committee for a year from now."

Raquel loved being smarter than everyone. Or she loved believing it. Bruce didn't suffer fools. Ravi just wanted his ecosystem restored no matter what. And Wendy—it was better to tell her what to do and get her enthusiastic about it as if it were her own idea.

None of them were partial to compromise.

Fitz glanced at the clock on the opposite wall. He needed to wrap this up, get changed, and get over to the high school. Coaching sessions were back-to-back-to-back with the tryouts for the travel club lacrosse team in a week.

An idea slammed into his brain with the pinpoint accuracy of an ice-cream headache. The high school…it was the answer. To everything.

This could end up being one of those days where Fitz felt proud to be mayor, rather than just trapped by family legacy and responsibility. He sat up straighter. "What you've all brought to me as a problem is, in fact, an opportunity. Summer school will start soon. Those kids hate being cooped up all day."

Wendy giggled. "Mainers *all* hate being inside once the sun's shining."

"Not all." Ravi dusted the crumbs from his fingers. "At Cygnet, we have phototherapy boxes at every desk to combat seasonal affective disorder. With those, you never need to go outside."

Scientists sometimes went too far to find a technological solution for everything. It was May now. Just freaking walk outside! Fitz couldn't wait to tell Hallie. She'd get a laugh out of Ravi's avoidance of nature.

Unless it meant telling her the entire story, which included the reference to her and where he'd fallen down on the job. That wouldn't leave either of them in a laughing mood.

Hell.

Bruce's scowl broadcast that he didn't like where Fitz was going—even though he'd barely begun. "Why do we care about delinquents who couldn't be bothered to do their work during the school year?"

"Nope. None of that." Fitz didn't raise his voice, but it was as cold and sharp as an icicle. "Summer school's to give extra help. It isn't a punishment."

"My niece Charla missed a whole month from a serious case of mono." Raquel spoke with a ferocity that had Bruce edging away from her. "She's not a bad student. She's simply trying to catch up."

"Sorry." Bruce bobbed his head, thick white hair waving over his forehead. "Guess things were different in my day."

"That must be it," Fitz said with a forced calm. Raquel could be a force when riled up and he didn't have the energy to referee. "Look, teachers try alternative methods of reaching students in summer session. More interactive, more out of the box. We'll take advantage of that." He pointed both index fingers down the table. "Ravi, could you find someone at Cygnet who'd be willing to do a lesson on why dams are both good and bad? What the trees are doing in their unfamiliar environment?"

Rubbing his hands together like, well, a mad scientist, Ravi said, "That won't be a problem."

Fitz didn't want him to randomly recruit. He'd sat—well, zoned out—through too many of his sister's lengthy opuses on science factoids. "Someone who'll make it fun, and not just a recitation of facts," he specified.

"Scientists are fun, Mr. Mayor." Another gleeful hand wringing. "You have no idea the hijinks we get up to in the lab."

"I'm sure I don't." Ravi was a nice guy, and wildly passionate about his work, but what did he consider hijinks? Shadow puppets in front of the light boxes? Yeah, Fitz wanted to pass that nugget on to Hallie, too.

Wendy broke a donut into quarters, then took about three crumbs off of one piece. "How does a science lesson get my trees planted?"

Fitz planted his palms on the table and slid them forward until his chin barely cleared the wood. "The students will do it, with a botany lesson attached, and a little P.E. credit for the sweat equity. Heck, we could even cover mythology, too, with Persephone and Demeter." He jerked upright, counting off his points on his fingers. "It slashes the labor costs, educates the students, and maybe even gets a couple of them excited about some part of the whole process."

Raquel beamed. Wendy clapped. And Bruce crossed his arms, as if giving his blessing to the whole thing. "That's a more than acceptable solution, Mr. Mayor."

"Your committees will need to do the work." Fitz shoved back his chair and stood, slipping on his suit coat. "Come up with people to do the lessons, get the equipment, chaperone. You should all meet again to hammer out the details as soon as possible. Or, you're welcome to stay here and continue. If you'll excuse me, though, I'm out of time."

There was a round of handshakes, an increased buzz of enthusiasm, and smiles as he closed the door behind him and wiped a hand across his forehead in relief.

What a great day. Man, he loved it when he could mediate to an equitable compromise. He couldn't wait to share the story with Hallie. This was politics the way it was supposed to work—without the bullshit, without the angles. Simply helping the town to be a better place to live, which made him think about the proposed marina deal again. It really would be good for Swan Cove.

As good for his town as it'd be *bad* for Crow Harbor. Technically, that wasn't his problem. Technically, he should be laser focused only on the benefits to Swan Cove. That was his job as mayor.

As a member of society, though, the idea now sat in his belly as heavily as a caliente burger and chili cheese fries from Tommy's back in his undergrad days. One town shouldn't flourish by pushing down another.

All his good feelings from the meeting resolution fizzled away. He and Hallie were on opposite sides of this thing. How would they get past it? And all the emphasis on legacy—Fitz didn't want to go down as the Montgomery mayor who wiped out dozens of Crow Harbor jobs as a side effect to this epic expansion.

He slapped out a frustrated rhythm on the polished wood of the balustrade. It echoed all through the open stairwell.

"Fitzwilliam. What do you think you are doing?"

Amazing how after more than three decades, his mom's voice could still freeze him in place with that spear of disapproval.

He turned to see his parents coming off the elevator. "Mom. Dad. What are you doing here? Remember the rule about not barging in during the workday without an appointment?"

"It does not appear that you *are* working. Or rather, if this is how you spend your days, loitering in the hallway, perhaps Ms. Scott was right to lambaste you publicly."

Ah. That's why they were here. To rip him a new one. So much for his buzz of accomplishment.

"If I told you I'd been in back-to-back meetings since ten, would that make a difference?"

"No. A public figure doesn't make excuses, Fitz. A public figure doesn't make the mistake that needs to be excused in the first place."

Yeah. This wasn't the day to mess with him. Because he'd had people throwing his so-called mistakes in his face all day long. Some accusations were true. Some were wildly overblown, seeing as how he wasn't a monarch ruling singlehandedly. Either way, he didn't need the people who were supposed to support him making digs on top of everyone else.

Especially not after just accomplishing an actual mayoral task so damn smoothly.

"You know what?" Fitz drummed another riff. "This isn't a mistake. And it doesn't require an explanation."

Caroline shifted her underarm clutch to a stranglehold in front of her with both hands. "We won't air the family's dirty laundry in the hallway. Let's go in your office."

"I don't think so." They'd set up camp and berate him for letting down the vaunted and lengthy legacy of the Montgomerys.

One, he knew that tune and *hated* it. Two, this was *his* life. If Hallie was strong enough to stand up to him and the entire town, he could damn well stand up to his parents. If he'd screwed up, he'd own it. He'd try to make it right, but he wouldn't be lectured at like he'd forgotten to turn in his homework.

This time, his mom put a hand on his arm. An "all is well" pleasant mask lifted her cheeks and eyebrows, in case anyone walked by. God forbid a person know that the Montgomerys bitched and argued like everyone else.

"The conversation we want to have with you isn't appropriate to conduct where passers-by could overhear."

Two could play that game. He donned his own mask of professional courtesy. "In that case, I'm certain it's not a conversation I have the time for today. Feel free to check with my assistant and schedule something for a week or so from now."

"Fitzwilliam." Preston's rumble of his full name was low and stern. "This cannot wait."

"Unless there is a surprise invasion by Canada—or, I guess, a water attack from Greenland—it *can* wait."

His father gripped his other arm. "You've got bad press, son. Front page. It must be managed."

"Nope. Freedom of the press says otherwise. The *Gazette* can write whatever they damn well please. I don't have to like it. You don't have to like it. If it isn't libelous, it gets printed."

"There's a very small window in which the reports of yesterday's debacle can be handled." Preston leaned forward until his chin was over his polished-daily black oxfords. "That woman can't be allowed to make you look bad."

That woman? Fitz cringed. And got righteously mad on her behalf, too.

"Ms. Scott didn't make me look bad. She held up a mirror. What was reflected had more than some truth in it. I mean, she didn't bother to list all the occasions when I did come through on campaign promises, but that's not her job." Fitz wrenched away from his parents and stalked down the hallway to stop outside the door with the flag of Swan Cove hanging on the wall next to it. "That's all I've got to say on the matter."

"Fitz—"

"No more. I'm doing my level best to uphold the family legacy. I'm genuinely sorry if I'm not doing it up to your expectations. If you want to register a complaint as a citizen, again, talk to my assistant. If you want to set up a convivial family dinner where we talk about the chances of our team winning the July yacht race, let me know when. Otherwise, we're finished."

Fitz slipped into his office and locked the door for good measure, even though it felt ridiculous. Then he leaned back against it, fingers at his temples, and let out a long breath. That wasn't anywhere close to fun.

"Fitz. About time you got in here." Derek hinged up from where he'd been lying on the couch. "We need to talk damage control."

Son of a bitch.

Well, it wasn't as if he could step back outside to avoid the guy. The parental units were probably still there, fuming and huffing.

Fine. He'd do this now, waste his high from the tree meeting, get all the shit out of the way at once, and then go refind his good mood on the lacrosse field, helping kids reach their potential.

Yeah.

Fitz stripped off his jacket, tossed it on the couch, making Derek flinch. "We don't need to talk damage control. You've been supposedly *doing* it since yesterday. Be a man of action, not words."

"The thing is, people don't want to talk to me. They want to hear from you."

"Tough. You're my campaign manager. This was a

campaign, ah, incident. So—manage it." He didn't want to hear excuses. After all, this was precisely the reason his dad had saddled Fitz with his toadie. Spinning the facts was supposed to be Derek's wheelhouse.

Fitz yanked open the bottom file cabinet drawer where he'd stowed his gym bag. Derek could stay and watch him change, or he could spit it out and get the hell out.

Derek stood. Came right up to the edge of the desk, shot his cuffs with all the self-importance of Al Capone. "People want an accounting of every campaign promise you made, from both runs, and which ones are still unacted upon."

As they should. Frankly, Fitz was disappointed he hadn't done it himself prior to kicking off the campaign. He pulled out his cleats, let them clatter noisily to the floor. "Give it to them."

While he didn't scuttle away, the immediate hunch to his shoulders and several-step retreat made it clear that Derek was horrified by the demand. "I...I can't do that."

"Why not?" Talk about the wrong thing to say. Fitz was *over* Derek only being willing to pursue his own agenda... or Preston Montgomery's. "A solid, oh, ninety-four percent of those promises were things you dreamed up, things you slid into speeches after I'd okayed the draft. Ah, didn't think I noticed, did you? Things you swore would get people fired up about voting for me." Fitz yanked his tie from its knot and hurled it across the room. The breeze probably ruffled Derek's hair. "Things you never researched or strategized to see if they were actually viable."

"That's...that's not my job," he blustered. "I do what it takes to get you elected. You're responsible for the four years that go by afterward."

Fitz sat hard and started unlacing his shoes, but he only did one before he let his arms dangle between his knees. It was pointless. Derek wouldn't change. He certainly wouldn't change his allegiance to Fitz rather than his father. People like Derek always followed the money. Probably not a chance in hell he'd admit his errors, which wouldn't solve the current crisis, regardless.

Hallie was in the race for mayor because she believed, deep down, that she could do a better job than the current mayor.

Fitz needed to believe that *he* could do the best job as mayor. That *despite* his last name, he'd do right by the town.

That started here and now.

"You know what? You're right. This is at least partly my fault. I was a kid, a newbie the first time around. Doesn't excuse me letting you pull the same crap the second time. I took the easy way, fell in line."

"And it got you elected." Derek picked up the nameplate that spelled out his title. The one that had been sitting on the desk, without interruption, for a good hundred-plus years. He waggled it in the air between them.

"No one ran against me!" Fitz thundered. "I could've run on the basis that we should start a herd of alpacas and use them as therapy animals, and I would've gotten voted in. Making promises that can't be fulfilled, or that I have no freaking idea of how to implement, is wrong. I won't do it anymore."

"You have to." Earnestness poured off the man like sweat off a marathoner at mile twenty-five. "Ms. Scott isn't real competition, but she might pull over enough voters who think they're pranking you to make the results look bad. You don't need to start your next term under that cloud."

It was obvious that Fitz's point had space-shuttled right over the man's head. "Or she could win."

A half laugh choked off into a gasp. "I won't let that happen."

Not *you're the best mayor, so obviously the people will*

elect you.

Not a pep talk version: *you can dig deep and make sure that your passion for this town shines through and the voters will do their thing accordingly.*

No. To Derek, it was simply that a Montgomery had to win, whatever the cost. No matter if Hallie turned out to be a combo of Churchill and Roosevelt who mayored for a few terms then ended up being the first female president in a landslide.

Fitz was done with his attitude. Done with the way he supported the legacy and not the man trying to live it. "You won't have a choice, Derek. You're fired."

Silence filled the office. Fine with Fitz. He'd said all he'd intended. So, he took off his shoes and swapped into white socks. And then, prominently, put his shorts on the desk, topped off by his jock. That ought to send Derek running.

The nameplate slid from his hand. Its metal edge probably put a nick in the old desk. "You can't fire me. I don't work for you."

"And right there's the problem. I need a campaign manager who listens to me, whose sole agenda is getting me reelected. *Not* propping up the vaunted legendary status of the Montgomery family. *Not* leaping to attention every time my father snaps his fingers."

"We'll just see about that."

"I'm putting out a press release tomorrow saying that you've stepped down from the campaign. Anything you do on your own time is up to you, if anyone will listen. The key thing is that *I'm* not listening to you anymore." Then he stood and began unbuttoning his shirt.

Derek all but leaped to the door. "You'll regret this."

"I doubt it. But if I do? That won't be your concern. Your vote, however, would still be welcome." And Fitz flashed his signature campaign smile.

"You're nothing like your uncle."

The door slammed behind Derek. Well, it tried. The latch didn't catch, so it rebounded into the wall. The man was all about denting up his office, leaving his mark on the way out.

As long as he was gone, for good, Fitz didn't care if he'd need to be in here tomorrow with a can of spackle.

Weird parting words, though. Yes, his uncle had been the previous occupant of the office. What was that supposed to mean? Was Fitz a better mayor? Worse? Had Uncle Jeremiah been under his dad's thumb? Had he forged his own path?

As soon as he got in his car, Fitz turned on Bluetooth and called Everett.

"Life sucks."

"Heavy the head that wears the crown." Mocking laughter rumbled through the speakers. "Let's see—you're still rich, you're still mayor, and you've still got a solid thirty years ahead of you to work on getting as smart as me. What could suck?"

"My parents showed up at work to, well, the only word is *scold* me. For embarrassing the family by letting Hallie turn the tables at that event yesterday."

"You're still sore about that?"

Fitz swallowed his impatience as Mrs. Fernmueller pulled the red wagon with her obese beagle in it across the street at a solid clip of one step per minute. "No. I'm actually pretty damn proud of her for coming up with it. She found my Achilles and slashed at it. It was a great job."

"Proud of getting ripped to tiny pieces by a girl." Everett inhaled a reverse whistle. "Yeah, you're a goner for her, that's for sure."

"I just want a solid, fair race. Not like that last Superbowl that was a fifty-five to ten blowout."

"Right. Would you feel the same way if your opponent didn't look great in a dress? And flutter her long lashes at you when you hold her hand?"

Would it be out of the question to get out, drop Mrs. Fernmueller into the wagon too, and drag it across the street? "Cut it out. This has nothing to do with Hallie being a woman."

"It's funny how you think you believe that."

Maybe he burned rubber once the street was finally clear. "Anyway, I'd just kicked ass in a meeting. Felt like a superhero. Then my parents pulled a pop-in to drip their disappointment all over me. I escaped them, but Derek was lying in wait in my office."

"Derek the dickhead."

"Derek the done. I fired him."

A sharp hoot bounced all around the car. "That's the best news I've heard all month. I'm only sorry it took you this long. Good for you. We should celebrate."

"That's why I'm calling. Not to celebrate. More along the lines of *life sucks so come split a pizza with me once practice is over.*"

"You know I'm your guy for any and all pizza needs, but I say you're wasting energy being miserable."

"Did you not just listen to the recap of my shitty afternoon? I earned the right to say today sucks."

"That's one way to look at it. Or..."

"Or what?"

"Or you could remember how you never wanted to be mayor in the first place. How it got forced on you. You're working too damn hard on something you don't even care about. What if you put this much effort into something you do care about?"

And immediately, Fitz thought of Hallie...

He knew Everett was calling back to the nights they'd stayed up late talking in undergrad. When Fitz had confessed that he didn't want to be mayor, but couldn't come up with an escape plan. How he'd truly wanted to *help* people—and didn't see politics as the way to do it. How much he liked helping kids work up to their potential on the sports field. How he most enjoyed the coaching role he fell into as mayor sometimes, too. That one-on-one connection that really made a difference.

Pipe dreams, though.

His sister's big brain couldn't be wasted on politics. Blake had her out from the family business as soon as she skipped a grade and fixated on science. Her work could save lives—or fix 'em—globally.

So, Fitz was the only one to take on the family mayoral mantle, to stand up for the town the way generations of Montgomerys had before him.

He didn't get the chance to follow his career dreams. But he just might be able to put that untapped energy into getting Hallie…for at least a little while…and then he'd think on what his future held and what he really wanted out of life.

Chapter Thirteen

Hallie tucked her feet underneath her to curl her toes into the soft leather because the seats were heated—a luxury she didn't have in her ancient Honda. Yes, it was a beautiful, warm spring day out, but she'd never been in a Jaguar before and wanted to appreciate every tiny bit of luxury in its sleek, beetle-green body.

"Isn't this car horribly inappropriate for our winters?"

"Oh, it's useless," Fitz said with a surprising amount of cheer. "Barely clears the ground. A dusting of snow takes it out of commission."

"So you've got a seasonal car, the way I switch out my closets?"

"Yep. It was a reward from my grandfather when I finished grad school."

Aww. Sweet, if still surprising that the gift would be quite so significant, but maybe when you had Montgomery level money, a pricey sportscar *wasn't* significant. "I guess if it's a present, it isn't outrageously extravagant. It's pure sentiment."

"Half sentiment, because I really was crazy about the old

guy, and half feeling like I'm in a James Bond movie when I drive it." He looked her way, then back at the solid corridor of pines that lined the road. "You can tell me if you think it's stupid. If you think that I should sell it and donate the proceeds to a worthwhile charity."

Interesting. Hallie doubted his father would've batted an eye at the thought of multiple cars. Mostly, because she'd seen Preston Montgomery driving no less than three different cars around town. Everyone recognized them, because he'd sit at stoplights once they turned green and keep talking to whoever had waved at him on the sidewalk.

"Ah. Is that because of the backlash against that billionaire space race last year? Feeling guilty about enjoying your wealth, rather than spreading it around?"

Fitz poked her knee. "Huh-uh. I asked *you* the question. I want to know if all this"—he gestured at the gleaming dashboard with its wood inlays—"seems selfish and wasteful. To you."

"Honestly? No. Not if it makes you genuinely happy. If it were me, I probably wouldn't have two cars, but I *would* splurge on a bathroom with heated floors and a shower with twelve jets."

"That's specific."

Indeed. "I saw it on a travel show about the world's greatest resorts." She'd practically crawled across the rug to plaster her face to the screen and absorb its full glory. "Haven't been able to get it out of my mind since then. Bucket list, you know?"

"Worthy goal. I was in an eight-jet one in Switzerland, and, if you were wondering, it's as mind-blowing as you'd imagine."

"Mmm. Thanks for the verification." Hallie looked at his expensive watch, the haircut that probably cost more than her last five put together. He'd opened the door to discussing his wealth. She'd shove through it a bit more. "I answered. Now it's your turn. Do *you* feel guilty about your wealth?"

"Are you asking because you resent it? Or do you really want to know?"

Hallie wasn't sure of the answer, but she felt like she was suddenly the one under the spotlight rather than Fitz. Having the tables turned on her wasn't what she'd expected. "Yikes. We're going there?"

"It's the elephant in the room between us. Would rather clear the air and move past it."

Hallie appreciated his willingness to communicate, to engage, to not sidestep uncomfortable things. And yes, the, ah, disparity in their fortunes probably did need to be addressed. No doubt Fitz had dealt with fortune hunters more than once.

But they had a bigger issue to discuss first. Or this surprise overnight getaway might fizzle out before they even parked the car. "See, I don't think your family owning the town is the elephant wedged behind your gear shift. I think it's what happened at the campaign event four days ago."

"What happened to our sharp division between being candidates and being Hallie and Fitz?" He reached over to rub the ruffled hem of her pink dress between his fingers. It rode high up her thigh, so the rough scrape of his touch shot chills up and down her leg. "I don't think Ms. Scott, the candidate, would wear this."

She was delighted he'd noticed. "Correct. This is a dress intended to flirt and inveigle, not articulate long-range planning and steadfastness." Since Fitz had picked her up with only twenty minutes' notice and asked if he could whisk her away. The word *whisk* had extreme romantic connotations to Hallie. She'd only packed frivolous, flirty things.

Including underwear.

"Flirting—and what comes after—that's the whole plan.

We're off the campaign trail tonight, Hallie."

"I know."

She'd debated with herself about whether to bring it up at all. If this was just a frantic one-night stand at, say, a convention, no way. But whatever this evolution between them was? It was predicated on the fact that she and Fitz had somehow become friends. Friends who wanted to lock lips, but friends first.

And friends deserved honesty. "But...what I *don't* know is if you're mad at me. I don't want to keep treading on eggshells."

"What?" Spraying gravel, Fitz swerved onto the shoulder and stopped. "First off, I don't play those games—pretending everything's fine for the sake of appearances. If I was mad at you, you'd know, because we'd be back in your driveway, finishing the argument."

That dissolved the weight that had been tightening her chest for several days now. "Good. Not good that we'd be arguing, but I'm glad that's your approach."

"Second, why do you think I'm mad at you?"

How to answer truthfully and still spare his male ego?

Then again, why was she worrying about that after what he'd just said? They'd only been driving the winding roads of the coast for an hour. If this all blew up, they'd just turn around, call it an experiment. Not a failed experiment, because there were no such things. Good or bad results, an experiment *yielded* results.

She rubbed her lips together, sticky with gloss that matched her dress. "Because I more or less eviscerated you at the campaign event."

Fitz chuckled. "I'd expect a librarian to be more precise with her words, and less prone to exaggeration."

"You're right. Eviscerate was over the top."

"And you're jumping the gun on the toast I'd planned for

tonight. So, there's no champagne or flowers for punctuation. All you get are the plain words." But he did gather her hands in his and squeeze. "Hallie, you were magnificent. You wiped the floor with me. You didn't drag me through the dirt. You used facts and strategy and you sure as *hell* were not boring. Way to go."

Little bubbles of satisfaction fizzed through her brain. "Really?"

The crinkles at the corners of his eyes infused an extra hit of warmth in his gaze. "Really."

"Thanks."

"I mean, you might've laid it on a *little* thick. Drove your point home with a hammer, then a sledgehammer, and then a pile driver."

Hallie gurgled with laughter. God, she was just so relieved they were indeed able to wall off what happened on the dais. "I believe in being thorough." Then she remembered to truly *be* his friend and not just his opponent. Because it turned out that Fitz deserved a compliment, too. "When my friends and I finally got into serious opposition research mode, a lot of positive things you've done in your tenure as mayor were revealed."

Fitz rolled his eyes with those gorgeous thick lashes she coveted. "Now you're just throwing me a bone, out of pity."

"You champion underdogs, like me."

"If you're not the underdog, you don't need a champion. I like to put my talents where they're needed."

Fitz might be downplaying it, throwing up a smokescreen of modesty, but Hallie wouldn't let him get away with it.

She'd uncovered a lot that she hadn't even known about his career. She wasn't a political creature; she kept her head down and focused on the library almost all the time. It was only a few big issues that had stuck in her craw and gotten her to rant that fateful night to Megan.

"You aim for balance between departments, without pitting one against the other or playing favorites. You're stellar in a crisis. That hurricane two years ago? It was the first one to hit Swan Cove in over a century. Nobody was prepared. You were, quite literally, the calm in the storm. I remember being legit impressed at the time, long before your seductive smile worked its wiles on me."

"Thanks for noticing."

Now she was on a roll. "And employee satisfaction has spiked every single year since you were first elected. That's got to be a direct trickle down from the top. You make people feel cared for, important."

He shrugged. "I try."

"I can tell."

"Then we're good?" He waved a hand in the air between them.

"I think we're *very* good."

Fitz pressed a kiss to the back of her hand, then pulled back onto the road. "And to answer your earlier question, I don't feel guilty about the family money. It's not *my* money. Not yet. I've got a trust, but I do plenty of spreading around to important causes."

"I saw that from the tax returns you released." The list of charities he contributed to was both long and thoughtful. And they weren't all notoriety magnets, either. It'd given Hallie another window into a deeper part of Fitz, one that she admired.

"The eventual bucket of money's no different from the heirloom silver and the mansion passed down through the generations and, well, the responsibility of caring for the town."

"Swan Cove isn't a puppy. Or an herb garden. It isn't your responsibility."

"You clearly didn't sit through the fifty million parental

lectures that I did on the topic."

"How about you bullet point it?"

"The Montgomery family must protect the town. No one else can safeguard it as well as we can, with, yes, our wealth and care and decades of knowledge passed down." He used a stentorian tone that sounded far more like his father than Fitz. Overlaid with a tinge of…bitterness? "It's a legacy, a duty. Not something I had a choice in at all."

Hallie mulled over that. Given her hand-to-mouth upbringing, she'd never once considered wealth to be a burden, or a millstone of responsibility. She'd, yes, made assumptions that the Montgomery money made everything easy.

It was a good reminder that *nobody* truly had it easy. That her viewpoint was just as skewed coming from Crow Harbor as Fitz's might be from growing up in Swan Cove. And if she really was going to try to lead this town, she needed to open her eyes and drop her preconceived notions about its citizens.

Geez. Had she been a reverse snob this whole time? Holding a grudge against Fitz and his family *because* of their wealth?

That stopped right now. "I'm sorry. I never thought about how it could constrain you or limit your choices. How your family determined more than your last name. It sounds… difficult."

"It's a privilege, for sure. But yeah, not my dream. First world problem, though. I have a job in a place I love. Grass is always greener though, you know?"

"I'm beginning to."

"I wanted to do a stint in the Peace Corps." Fitz rubbed his palm over his forehead, as if burnishing the cherished dream. "Roll up my sleeves, really dig in, and give the kind of help where you see immediate results at the end of every day. Dig an irrigation ditch that transforms a village. Help administer vaccines. Rebuild homes after an earthquake."

That was...uncanny. "I did too. It was my dream all through high school. I read books about explorers and missionaries and memoirs of humanitarian aid trips."

"Why didn't you join?"

Just like that, Hallie felt a kinship with Fitz. "My parents. My mom's a school bus driver. Dad's a fisherman. They had a blue collar, hardscrabble life. Their whole aim was to make sure I didn't have the same. Every decision in my life, and theirs, was about whether it would lead to my getting a stable, good job with benefits and the guarantee that I'd never struggle financially. Two years with essentially no income—even to make the world a better place—would've been a, well, *selfish* choice for me, after everything they gave up to help me get my Master of Library Science."

"I get it." Fitz turned off the main road at a street that was barely more than a mile marker.

"Why didn't *you* join?"

"My parents." He grinned at her as he echoed her reply. "They told me it'd be selfish of me to go off and give my time and energy to strangers when the inhabitants of Swan Cove needed me."

The coincidence was almost laughable. They had so much more in common than she'd ever imagined. "Maybe we should abandon the campaign right now. Run off together and join the Peace Corps. That'd show everybody." Hallie was joking, but the thought of running off with Fitz wasn't that hard to build out in her mind. Not anymore.

"You'd really run off with the enemy? With your competition?"

"Not with just any enemy, or any random competition. Definitely not with Sandra Gurlick. She's been angling to win Best Small-Town Library and wants to rub my face in it."

"You haven't won yet. I'd remember if Swan Cove got

that award."

"No, not yet. But it's on my radar—as is Sandra." Hallie marshaled her courage. "I did run off with you today, though, without knowing where we were going. It isn't Namibia for two years, but consider it symbolic."

"I do. I was nervous as hell you'd turn me down, but the Peace Corps is a big commitment, and you and I already have jobs." He stopped the car behind a row of peony bushes bursting with pink and white blooms. They clumped along the back of a tiny cottage. "So, can we put a pin in that idea? Because I had a different plan for tonight, one that took a not inconsiderate amount of effort."

Hallie waited while Fitz came around to open her door and, thankfully, pull her up from the low-slung seat. "This trip—I thought it'd just be us having dinner at your family's cabin I've heard about."

"I don't want my family anywhere near you—not even in picture frames. Besides, I wanted to give you an experience that's more special than my usual weekend getaway."

Anticipation tingled from the soles of her feet all the way up her legs. This was getting more exciting. "You mean you didn't drive an hour away just to avoid the possibility that we might be seen together?"

"This location isn't about hiding. It's about giving you a special night. A custom-made-for-Hallie night."

Oh.

Fitz hadn't just made an effort. He'd made an effort personalized *for* her. That was...pure romance. The kind that filled four shelves in the back of her library. Hallie was gobsmacked that he'd gone to whatever trouble this all was. For her.

What on earth had been the catalyst for all this? All she'd done was...debate him. Engage in a delicious back-and-forth exchange of facts and wits that had left her panting and her pulse pounding.

Had Fitz experienced the same effects?

The strong salt tang to the air told her she'd see the Atlantic as soon as they rounded the side of the wood-shingled cottage. "I'm a librarian. What could be so special for me?"

"You'll just have to wait and see." Fitz grabbed their bags and led her up the oyster shell path to what was clearly the back door. "Pick up that lobster in the flower bed. There should be a hide-a-key in its belly."

"You'd think twenty-first century technology would've left hide-a-keys in the dust. Shouldn't there be voice print recognition, or a retinal scan?"

"I'm sure there is back at Cygnet Labs. I wouldn't be surprised if my sister does a full biometric scan just to grab a stapler refill. But this B&B is a little more old school."

"A B&B? I figured this was a solo rental cottage." Hallie twisted around. "I don't see any other buildings."

"They're spread out for privacy, but there's a main building, with a kitchen, so I promise you'll be fed."

"That was my goal for the weekend, being fed," she teased. Both hoping that he'd get her subtle double entendre and worried that she wouldn't have a strong enough follow-up if he *did*.

So much heat flared in his eyes that Hallie took a step back. An answering warmth pooled between her legs in response. "Don't joke, Hallie. I wanted us to get away from all that campaign crap. Just be ourselves. If all we do is sit on the porch and watch the water, that'll be good." He angled forward to whisper in her ear, "But I'm hoping like crazy that we don't."

It was *precisely* what she hoped. Hallie just hadn't known when to expect it. There weren't any rules she was aware of for taking it one day at a time. Plus, there was the whole complication of them being opponents.

And the *added* complication of Fitz being the end goal of every woman within a hundred-mile radius. Handsome, charming, powerful, and topped off by being genuinely nice. And Hallie being just a librarian.

The benefit to being a librarian, though, was that she read a *lot*. She might not have racked up as many, ah, intimate encounters as the rumor mill attributed to Fitz. There were, however, hundreds of literary sexual experiences filling her head that she couldn't wait to enact with him.

She gathered up more moxie than it had taken to first sit on that dais as a candidate and said in an attempt at a throaty purr, "It...doesn't even have to be the bed."

Fitz threw back his head and laughed, his Adam's apple working up and down. "Whatever, wherever, sweetheart. You name it, we'll do it."

That was more than a bit terrifying, like those restaurants with eighteen-page menus. Too many choices. Hallie handed over the key. "Let's lower those expectations. No paraphernalia or anything that requires stretching before or after."

"Good to know your limits." After juggling the bags under one arm, he opened the door and bowed. "Welcome to your getaway, Ms. Librarian."

Awash in curiosity, she stepped into the cottage. Immediately, her eyes went to the wide glass double doors that looked out across the bay. The view was stunning, but as she walked closer, other items drew her attention, like a top hat, balanced askew on its brim. A decanter of deep red liquid with a calligraphy tag around the neck that read *Drink Me*.

An oversize pocket watch balanced against a gilt-edged mirror with fanciful etchings of caterpillars and rabbits chasing each other around the frame. A set of leather-bound

Lewis Carroll books were propped on the fireplace mantel by a jaunty bronze of a standing rabbit in a vest.

"Oh my goodness. This cottage is all about Alice in Wonderland?"

"Yes. Each cottage has a literary theme. I couldn't think of anything more appropriate for my librarian."

Hallie was so very touched by his planning. No man had ever planned a date specifically tailored to her preferences. Heck, she wouldn't have even known what to ask for, really. Fitz's thoughtfulness blew her away. It was the most romantic thing anyone had ever done for her. And they weren't even officially dating.

Hallie was suddenly glad they didn't have a label for what they were doing, because it wasn't like any other relationship she'd been in. They'd started off as enemies, softened a bit to rivals, and then become friends. Only a good friend—rather than someone who just wanted to get her horizontal—could plan a trip like this.

She spun in a circle, taking in more special details like the quote stenciled on the wall over the hot tub, and the hearts embroidered on the bed's copious throw pillows. "This is absolutely marvelous."

"I'm relieved you like it. I know some people have their... what are they called...fandoms?" Fitz rubbed at his forehead, looking adorably muddled and out of his element. "My sister has very strong views on the different film versions of *Pride and Prejudice*. Couldn't tell you what they are, but I have heard her go on about them multiple times. So, I couldn't risk booking us the Jane Austen cottage."

"I've always loved Alice. She's an ordinary girl who falls into a fantasy world. What could be better?" Hallie threw her arms around his neck. "Thank you." Just as quickly, she squealed and pivoted away from him. "Is that a mushroom?"

She pointed to the three-tiered tray laden with tiny

sandwiches and pastries. The top layer had macaroons and exquisitely detailed marzipan mushrooms.

"A full afternoon tea comes with the room. It's in the book, right?"

"Yes. Yes, it is." It was like the Disney film come to life... except with a king-sized bed smack in the middle of it.

"We get dinner, too. Later. Whenever you're ready."

"I adore everything about this."

Fitz pulled out the tufted red-velvet chair at the table centered in front of the windows. "Do you want to start with tea?"

How chivalrous. He'd brought her out here but was letting Hallie call the shots, set the pace. Part of her wanted to ooh and ah over each story-centric item. Take a million pictures for her rarely used Instagram account and then dig into the tower of sweets.

Priorities, though. First and foremost, Hallie needed to *show* Fitz how very grateful she was that he'd made such an effort. "I think it'd be more strategic to work up an appetite." She tossed off the cream scarf she'd tied around her shoulders for the drive. It floated to the chaise lounge in three long swoops. Then she hooked a finger in the neck of his bright green polo shirt. "What do you think?"

"I think we've found yet another issue on which we're in full agreement." Fitz wrapped one corded forearm around her waist, lifted her off her feet, and spun her in a circle. "How about we see where else we can meet in the middle?"

Hallie chortled as she tipped her head back. "That's a horrible pun."

"Then I should stop talking." He took advantage of her exposed neck to nibble a line of kisses from her earlobe to her collarbone. Combined with the spinning and her closed eyes, Hallie felt like she was floating, anchored only by his lips.

When Fitz put her down, she realized he'd unzipped the back of her dress. The ruffled straps dipped down to fall at her elbows and the front gaped open to reveal the pink and black polka-dotted bra she'd ordered from Victoria's Secret the night Fitz first suggested they...explore spending time together.

"Oh, Hallie. That is one sexy bra. I'm torn between wanting to stare at you *in* it, and wanting to get you *out* of it." He traced a finger along the lace-trimmed edge of it, raising goose bumps in his wake.

"I don't know if it will help inform your decision-making, but"—she shimmied so the dress fell to the floor in a swoosh—"there's matching panties."

His eyes bugged wide for a split second.

First, Fitz used one hand to tug his shirt over his head. The motion exposed a muscled chest. Hallie almost wanted to stop and picture him at work raising and lowering the sails on his boat to create all those firm pecs and abs.

Second, he turned on his heel to cross to the tea tray. When he came back to her, he'd kicked off his shoes. And a devilish grin lit up his face. Then he slid whatever was in his hand beneath the top seam of her panties.

Fitz stepped back to hurriedly undo his belt and strip off his khakis. Hallie took the opportunity to look down. A small strip of hand-lettered card stock stuck out of her panties. Matching the theme and the tag on the decanter, it simply read *Eat Me.*

Hallie backed up until the edge of the chaise hit her calves. She had to do it by feel because there was absolutely no chance of her looking away from Fitz as he removed the navy boxer briefs. A dark gold line of hair arrowed down from his belly button.

She wanted to scrape her nails down it.

She wanted to lick it.

She wanted to grind against it.

She…*wanted*.

Hallie abruptly let her knees give in and sank onto the chaise. Because he was naked. And he was magnificent. Belatedly, Hallie remembered her plan. As he kicked away the briefs, she scrambled to get into position. Arms overhead, hanging off the curlicued frame, one leg hanging off the side and the other propped against the cushioned back in an open invitation.

If Fitz followed the instructional tag he'd so carefully placed.

But she was rewarded when he straightened. With a low growl, Fitz jumped onto the end of the chaise. Hallie squeaked, but as it rocked back and forth, he stroked the top of his head against her bare stomach, and she forgot all about the possibility that the entire thing might tip over.

He removed the tag with his teeth, then gave a sharp shake of his head to send it across the room. "You'll find I'm excellent at following instructions."

"Less talking, more doing." Who even was she? Hallie never gave guidance during sex. Heck, Hallie never had sex with the late afternoon sun streaming through a wall of plate glass, either, but Fitz's appreciation made her bold, eager.

And even though they hadn't *had* sex yet, she was beyond certain that he wouldn't make her regret a single out-of-character action or word, and that he'd just roll with whatever happened.

He scraped his teeth down the center of her panties. That was it. A single scrape had her *writhing*. Heat bloomed in all her extremities. All of 'em. Every last square inch of flesh and bone.

Hooking a single finger under the edge of her underwear, he slid them off one leg and left them dangling off her other ankle, as though he couldn't take the time away from touching her to remove them fully.

She *adored* feeling so desired.

Flat and wide, his tongue swiped along her core. Once. Twice. The third time, Fitz added two fingers up and inside. At that point, Hallie was trembling with need, with being on the brink, with pleasure saturating every cell of her body.

Fitz rolled on the condom she hadn't even noticed him retrieve. "This time, I think we'll leave the bra on for my viewing pleasure, but be assured this is just the warm-up round. I'll need to taste *all* of you in about five minutes."

"What happens until then?" Hallie asked breathlessly.

"This." Fitz drove into her, long and thick and in a smooth motion that had Hallie bowing completely off the chaise. He planted his hands just above her shoulders. "And this." Then he kissed her, his tongue mirroring each stroke of his hips. In unison, their bodies moved together in a sensuous dance that came as naturally as breathing with him.

Hallie brought her hands down to knead her fingers into his ass. To urge him harder, faster, more.

Fitz obliged. He gave her everything she needed. The sweetness of his kiss contrasted with the rhythmic, insistent pounding of his lower body. And his deep groan let her know he was as close as she was.

Hallie opened her eyes, wanting to memorize the exact moment that he drove her over the edge. She discovered his eyes were already locked on hers. That unexpected connection shattered her into a hundred million separate shivers of pleasure.

As Fitz swallowed her cry, he picked up his pace. Moments later, he shuddered against her. His eyes squeezed shut.

Only then did Hallie close her eyes, the moment painted forever on her mind, and her limbs boneless.

Fitz let his entire weight drop onto her for a second. Then, with a Herculean groan, he shifted to lie along her side.

"I want to make a clever Wonderland reference right now, but you've drained all my brain cells out my dick."

"Don't ever tell anyone, but I can't think of a thing to say either. Except *wow*."

"That works for me." Fitz raised himself on one elbow to place a noisy, wet kiss on her cheek. "I'll double down on that wow."

"We didn't make it to the bed," she murmured, ridiculously pleased with the idea. "We're wild."

"We're only getting started, sweetheart."

"That's one campaign promise I fully intend to hold you to, Mr. Mayor."

Chapter Fourteen

Fitz sat on his haunches, dipping his hand into a plastic baggie and tossing feed to the swans.

It was less fun than ripping off bread pieces the way he had as a kid. But back then, their swans died of a horrible diet pretty much every year, until a zoologist on a shore excursion watched it happen. He marched straight into the then mayor's office and called out the entire town as swan murderers who needed to stop fattening their swans like foie gras gooses in a feeding chute.

Now the town's eponymous swans had their own dietician. *No Feeding* signs were posted at the base of the wrought-iron fence encircling the pond. Sometimes being an adult and *knowing* things sucked the fun out of life.

"Mr. Mayor." The *Gazette*'s editor touched his fingers to the brim of his straw hat.

"Thanks for coming out."

Bronson Shepherd hitched up the knees of his pants to hunker down next to Fitz. "I haven't done an off-the-record park meeting since I left the *Boston Globe*. This is a nice flashback. It'd be even nicer if you're about to give me a scoop that'll get me a Pulitzer."

"I'm all for shooting for the stars, Bronson, but a Pulitzer? Really? C'mon." Fitz hoped the man was kidding, but...Bronson wasn't known for his sense of humor. He *was* known for spending all day, every day, and many nights at the *Gazette* offices. And doing anything to chase down even the smallest story.

"Then why'd you drag me out here on the low down?"

Right. Because it was such a hardship to sit in the spring sun for a seven-minute chat. "Need to ask you a favor."

His bushy salt-and-pepper eyebrows inched up. "Officially?"

Fitz looked around at the gazebo, the trees ringing the square, and the quartet of swans fighting for the feed he'd thrown. "If it was official, would we be shin deep in swan shit?"

"Hopefully not."

"I read the *Gazette* today."

"I should hope so. Don't you read it every day?" Bronson's voice rose. The aroma of the anise mints he constantly had tucked in his cheek wafted through the air. "How the hell else do you keep a finger on the pulse of this town without reading the paper?"

"I *am* the mayor," Fitz said drily. "Knowledge *is* reported to me without always going through the filter of the fourth estate first."

"Don't be cheeky. That was your uncle's shtick."

Huh. Nobody ever talked about Uncle Jeremiah. It was like when he moved to Miami, he'd been erased from the collective town memory. "What do you mean?"

"Eh. Don't mind me."

The guy was a talker. Stepping back from a topic wasn't something Fitz had ever heard him do. "Bronson. What about my uncle?"

"He didn't take his job seriously. He mouthed off, got cute about town business. Smarting off doesn't actually prove that you're smart, especially when your actions prove otherwise."

That was curious, and pointed. "Did Uncle Jeremiah do something wrong as mayor?"

"Ha! More like did he do a single damn thing right."

Coming from the objective editor, that sounded like the tip of an iceberg. "Is there something I should know?"

"Doesn't matter now. He's gone. His mess was cleaned up."

Fitz stood and brushed off his hands. A cold anger moved through him at being kept in the dark. How was he supposed to do right by the town if important things were kept from him? He might not want to be mayor, might even resent it some days, but as long as he held the office, he would damn well do his very best for Swan Cove, every single day.

"I think it does matter. I think I deserve to know, both as mayor and as his nephew."

Bronson straightened, then tipped back his hat. "You should ask your father. Or that tame accountant of yours that does all the work. Since he did the cleanup."

Holy shit. There really was something big. Everyone said there wasn't a single secret in Swan Cove that Bronson wasn't aware of. "I'm asking you. Clearly, neither David nor my dad saw to bring me into the loop."

Shifting his weight from foot to foot, Bronson said, "That's not why you called me out here today."

"Damn it, Bronson, stop obfuscating!"

"Ha." He laid his index finger on the side of his nose. "A word like that means you really are sneaking around with that librarian and trying to up your game."

Hell. What had tipped the guy off? Fitz wiped a hand across his mouth. "I'm not sneaking around with Ms. Scott.

She's my opponent, for Christ's sake. And again, I have to insist that you tell me about Uncle Jeremiah."

The older man jerked a shoulder to indicate they should walk toward the water's edge. As if truly worried that someone else might overhear. Once they were shoulder to shoulder at the seawall, Bronson stuffed his hands in his pockets. "He embezzled town money."

Four simple words, but Fitz could not comprehend how they made *any* sense all strung together. "What?"

"We used to have a city manager who did all the admin and budget stuff. The mayor's role was mostly ceremonial. Not even a full-time job. Jeremiah fired him when he started getting wise to the mayor's fiscal shenanigans. Struck the position from the line items, then went another two years before anybody caught on and called him on it."

"What happened?" Because he'd never heard so much as a whisper about this. Sure as hell hadn't seen any proof of it in the city budgets or documentation. A crime of this magnitude had to leave a trail of evidence.

"All the money got put back into the accounts. By your dad, I'm guessing. Or maybe your Aunt Felicia. Jeremiah made up some story about an opportunity in Florida and got the hell out of Dodge."

What Fitz had been told, while he was still off in grad school, was that his uncle had a medical condition which was exacerbated by the harsh Maine weather. Not life-threatening, but painful. And that an old friend was building a new high-end condo in Miami and offered Jeremiah the penthouse.

What with the location and the scant details about the "old friend," Fitz had assumed his uncle had come out of the closet. He'd been happy for him, and a little disappointed he'd never gotten an invite to go down to see the new setup and meet the mysterious old friend.

He was reeling. "Why doesn't anyone know? Why didn't you report on it in the *Gazette*?"

Bronson's matter-of-fact delivery shifted. He took off his hat, fanned himself a few times. Then he put up a hand to shade his eyes and kept his gaze fixed on the pale blue line where the horizon intersected with the Atlantic. "It's a delicate situation, what with his last name being Montgomery..."

"No," Fitz ground out from between clenched teeth. It was impossible to comprehend that this man, with his storied career in big papers in Boston and Seattle, would have compromised his ethics and not blown this story wide open. "It's not. Not delicate. Not tricky. It's cut and dry. Accountability matters."

"Not if you're talking about a Montgomery. No harm was done in the end, since all the money got returned."

"I don't care if you're talking about Santa Claus! The man engaged in criminal conduct. Put the entire town in jeopardy. *Everyone* deserved to know. And what about whoever cooked the books to hide the evidence after the fact? Is that person still working in my city hall right now?" Disgusted, he paced away, but then paced right back, because it was the only way to get answers.

"I'm sorry, Mayor. I swear to God I thought you knew, back when it happened and then when you took office. I assumed your family told you."

"So you thought I was complicit? That's not any better." Then it hit him. "Did you accept a payoff? Is that why you stayed quiet?"

No response, just that thousand-yard stare at the water, and the slow fanning with the hat.

Fitz snatched it away. "Damn it, I demand to know who in this town has dirty hands."

"My wife left me."

"Yeah. Years ago."

The color drained from his ruddy cheeks. "She ran off with her high-school sweetheart, after meeting back up at a reunion. I didn't take it well. Went out, got plastered, tried to drive home. Rear-ended your father. Preston wasn't hurt, the car only had cosmetic damage, but I smelled like I'd bathed in bourbon, and he noticed. Promised to keep it quiet, as long as I came through when he asked for a favor."

"This situation with Uncle Jeremiah—not reporting on it was Dad calling in the favor?"

"Yeah."

One problem at a time. Fitz handed back the hat. "You ever driven drunk since? Endangered anyone else?"

"No. I swear. I went into therapy to deal with Laverne leaving. My head's screwed on straight."

"Have you covered anything else up for my family or anyone?"

"No. Mr. Mayor, that's the truth. But once you took office and things looked to be back to normal, there wasn't any point to—"

He broke off.

Fitz knew what wasn't being said. There wasn't any point to a lawsuit, to maybe losing a point on his driving record. To losing the goodwill of the man who owned so much of Swan Cove.

After sucking in a long breath, he puffed out his cheeks and blew it out slowly. Bronson was right on one count. Eight years later, it wouldn't do any good for him to ladle out recrimination and judgment. "Thanks for coming clean with me. I won't lie—I'm disappointed. I'll keep your secret, though. Sounds like it isn't mine to share."

"Thanks."

Now the reason for this meeting was twice as awkward. Fitz considered walking away. He didn't want to be perceived as trying to influence the man. He didn't want to be perceived as anything like the rest of his family after that story. But… this wasn't about him. This was about Hallie, and he had to do right by her.

"Look, I'm not asking for a favor. No wink and a nod. You can say no, and there'll be no harm, no foul. I wanted to talk to you about your column space on Ms. Scott."

"The librarian?"

Fitz led them back toward the swan pond. "The other mayoral candidate, yes. You should write whatever *facts* you want, but you've printed two op-eds with a derogatory slant on her being from Crow Harbor."

"I gotta run something."

Of all the things Fitz was responsible for as mayor, that for *sure* deserved to be filed under Not My Problem.

"There's plenty of other things going on in Swan Cove to opine about. Folks in Crow Harbor work hard, *do* a lot to support *this* town. It's insulting to them and to her to suggest Ms. Scott can't be mayor because of the zip code she was born in."

"You're right, of course. And on a personal level, I agree." Bronson leaned on the arrow-tipped top of the fence around the pond. "Fanning the flames sells papers, though."

"This is the first two-person campaign in over a century. There'll be plenty to cover."

"You should know, since we're laying all our cards on the table, that it wasn't my idea. Your campaign manager suggested it."

"Derek? I fired him." And hearing that made Fitz feel doubly solid about the decision. Little weasel.

"Yeah, well, his directive came down before that."

Fitz stabbed his fingers through his hair. Huffed out an exasperated breath. "He doesn't speak for me. My father doesn't speak for me. And the only directive *I'll* give you is to be fair and objective. Period."

"Even when it comes to the downtown expansion?"

Oh, for fuck's sake! He wasn't a feudal lord trying to scoop up the profits of everyone on adjacent land. "Especially then."

The newspaperman had the bit between his teeth and pressed on. "Because, you know, it'll benefit your family's bank account more than anyone else's, which some would see as at odds with your decision-making power as mayor."

"Bronson, you know better than that. The entire city council votes."

"You won't sway it for your personal benefit?"

Enough was enough. Fitz knew it was Bronson's job to ask the uncomfortable questions. It was a genuine kick in the gut, though, that anyone would even suspect Fitz of pulling strings. "Okay, we're *on* the record as of right the fuck now."

Shaggy gray eyebrows arched up. "Whatever you say."

"We are only at the preliminary, investigatory stage of the proposed downtown hotel and marina expansion. It has not yet been put forth to the council for a vote to conduct further discussion. We're nowhere near a vote on acceptance. That's something the next mayor would handle."

"Got it."

He white-knuckled the railing, blocking out the *hi how ya doing* squawks of the swans. It wasn't that hard when Fitz heard Hallie's voice in his head. "What everyone should consider is that this expansion would, yes, benefit Swan Cove, but it would also have a significant negative economic impact on Crow Harbor."

"How negative? Do you have solid numbers?"

Uh, not his job to be an informant. Bronson would have to do his own legwork. "As mayor of Swan Cove, this town is my sole priority. The *people* of this town, however, ought to have a healthy respect and consideration for our neighbors to the south as part of the decision-making process."

Bronson's mouth formed into a soundless O. "Are you sure that's the message you want to put out, Mayor?"

"I am."

After a long searching glance, Bronson nodded. "Glad to hear it from you."

"Not half as glad as I am to get it off my chest."

The older man resettled his cap, then looked over both shoulders like they were players in a Cold War espionage drama. "Off the record, again, between you and me. I've been keeping a lid on a dirty scoop on your librarian."

"She's not *my* librarian," Fitz automatically spit out.

"Whatever. I've got reliable intel on something she'd want kept under wraps. Something that could tank her campaign."

Fitz didn't believe it for a minute. Or if it was real, it was something as shockingly truthful as her hometown zip. Like...Hallie got a B in P.E. her sophomore year—stop the press!

"If it's an actual fact, and not just shady gossip, I won't tell you what to do with it. But, two things. One, consider the source, not to mention if the fallout would be deserved. And two, I don't want to hear it. Not a hint or a whisper. Period. I won't run a smear campaign."

"Your choice." Bronson narrowed his eyes, his years of flogging stories showing in the network of lines fanning around them. "And maybe your loss."

...

"You know it reeks in here, right?" Hallie desperately wanted to breathe through her mouth, but she didn't want to risk inhaling a flyaway piece of snipped hair. The salon ought to come with a warning label for those with respiratory sensitivities. "Of enough ammonia to clean up a murder scene?"

Megan froze with the paintbrush halfway between the color pot and the foil strip on Hallie's head. "Hey, I don't come to your place of business and say it smells."

"That's because books smell *wonderful*. They smell like possibilities." And if you closed your eyes and thought hard enough, they also smelled like places and people and food and drinks and love and laughter.

"They smell dusty."

She met her friend's laughing green eyes in the mirror. "Bite your tongue."

Megan grabbed a glass off a passing tray carried by the receptionist. "Here. Drink your wine, that's why we serve it. To both cut down on nerves and to distract you from the stench."

"Aha! You admit it smells." But she took the wine because that was apparently the kind of wild woman Hallie had become this month. A middle of the afternoon wine drinking and sex having Bohemian.

"Yes, chemicals do smell. It's the small price of beauty." Megan's face was thunderous, but her touch of the brush to Hallie's scalp remained gentle. "Whereas I'm fairly certain I've gotten a mildew allergy from the contents of your library."

"Why are you so mean today?"

"Because you've been grumpy since I picked you up for breakfast. You've grouched at me, snapped at me, and sullenly pouted. And now, in front of other customers—who we sort of hope will be *returning* customers—you've compared this lovely, upscale salon to an embalming room."

It was all true.

Hallie remained steadfast that everything *she* had said was true as well. Which didn't excuse most of it, especially not taking out her bad mood on her best friend…even though it *was* Megan's fault she was in the race for mayor and thus currently battling intermittent waves of panic and misery.

It was the nicest salon in town. Crystal chandeliers in the waiting area, with an elegant black and white aesthetic. Each station had a mirror in a unique, artsy silver frame. And each station was individually leased by the stylists—from the owner, Montgomery Industries. Aka, Fitz's dad, who was spearheading the expansion project.

If Hallie campaigned against it, would he retaliate? Cancel Megan's license, as his toadies would surely inform him she was Hallie's BFF?

Thoughts like those were why Hallie swung in wide arcs between elation at the wonderful nights she'd spent with Fitz and a soul-churning panic that increased as each day grew closer to the election. And an ever-growing third emotion—the determination to not be bullied into changing her beliefs or dropping out.

Hallie pulled her attention back into explaining her, yes, bitchy mood to her friend. "Megan, I love you, but I don't believe in what we're doing here today. I let you all talk me into it because I always bow to majority rules with our group, but it feels…cheap."

"It won't once you're standing at the register," Megan said with a smirk.

Great. Maybe she could chug a second glass of wine before that happened? "It's a cheap ploy," Hallie clarified.

"It's a makeover, which is something you've needed pretty much since the day I met you. Every time I've given you a trim at home, I've begged to do more. Just because you *are* a librarian doesn't mean you have to look like one."

Now Hallie had to stand up for her entire profession. "Librarians don't have a 'look.' We don't get handed a uniform when we pick up our graduation hood."

Megan didn't so much as pause in her application as she immediately spit out a laundry list. "Scraped-back hair into an unflattering, un-poufed ponytail. Hair with no verve or depth of color to it. Boring clothes in neutral colors that are so modest you could pass as a Mennonite some days. Mascara—dark brown only, because God forbid you wear black and make your eyes actually pop—and gloss."

"*Sparkly* gloss, some days." But Hallie let her eyes flutter shut. She knew it was splitting hairs.

"You're like a kid insisting we include their half birthday in their age."

"Specifics matter. Plus, you've never once objected to my mom making you a half-birthday cake."

"Here's a specific. You're a naturally pretty woman." The brush clattered onto the metal tray. Megan framed Hallie's cheeks with her hands and beamed at her. "Period. By anyone's standards, but you don't *embrace* it."

"It isn't part of my persona. I'm a nerd. A booklover. And time spent shopping, or trying out new looks, or deciding on eyeshadow palettes, well, that's all time that could be spent reading." After all, her days were packed.

There was the book to read on the elliptical at the gym. The breakfast book. The lunch book. The self-improvement after-dinner book. And then the book to read before falling asleep. Hallie had barely fit it all in *before* this campaign.

Now, with her research and speechwriting and strategizing, she was down to a scant two books a day. And when she'd been with Fitz over the weekend, for the first time in her life, she'd gone an entire *day* without opening a book.

Okay, she'd skimmed a few lines in the vintage *Alice's Adventures in Wonderland* with the embossed gold letters on the burgundy leather cover on the mantel, but that didn't count as reading. It was merely appreciating the ambiance.

"You're also a woman in the prime of her life." Megan pinched her cheeks before returning to the foiling.

Flashing a smug grin, Hallie said, "My life's pretty darned prime right now, thanks to you-know-who." Of *course* she'd told Megan all about her romantic getaway with Fitz. No need to swear her to secrecy; the stakes were obvious.

"This has nothing to do with your super hot fling," Megan whispered in her ear. "I approve, by the way."

"Thought you might." Megan spent an inordinate amount of time trying to talk Hallie into joining her in flirting with the cruise ship crew. Or into dancing with a good-looking tourist at the pub. Those things had never sounded as intriguing as heading home to finish her current read.

Fitz, however… She didn't want to read a book while she was with him. He was plenty fascinating and fun and enough for Hallie.

"I've been pushing a makeover all this time for your own self-esteem, so you know you look as good as you possibly can." Megan flourished her comb at the mirror. "So that every time you walk by a window or a mirror, you see a woman at the top of her game. What if you were a book?"

Hallie buried her nose in the glass of sauvignon blanc. "I'd smell better than I do right now."

After an appreciative snort, Megan rolled on. "You've ranted a zillion times about how the cover matters. The synopsis on the back—"

"The blurb," she interrupted. "Do you not listen to me at all?"

"Whatever. I'm about to prove that I do. The blurb can be great and the reviews can be outstanding, but you say that the cover needs to pop to really sell it."

Hallie did say that. Constantly. It was the only way to catch random browsers, whether in person or online.

Now she got it. There was an instantaneous flip from hating the makeover to realizing she both needed and wanted it. "For goodness sake, Megan. Why didn't you put it in book terms from the start?"

"We're sprucing you up for you. Not to win a man, but to

win an election." She brandished the color brush overhead in a Statue of Liberty pose. Impressively, without a single drip. "Because the cover matters to catch the eye of the random voter. You've got to put in the effort."

It sounded like the time in the salon chair wasn't all Megan had planned. Sure, she was pro-makeover now. However, it'd already been an hour. An entire hour without a book in her hand. Or her phone, rendering her unable to text Fitz. "Isn't it enough that *you're* putting in the effort today?"

"No. Think long-term, Hallie. You've got to do your hair *and* makeup *and* wear the outfits Ana and Randall are picking up for you."

That was new information. Hallie didn't like the sound of it one bit.

Ana's style was Goth biker chick—which always looked incongruous in her shop surrounded by leather-bound first editions. And Randall was...bright. Bright colors, bright patterns. How could they be trusted to choose appropriately conservative and professional looks for a political candidate?

"Nobody said they were dressing me up like a Barbie doll."

"Because we thought it was better to ask forgiveness than permission."

Knowing them, she wasn't surprised, but it was still presumptuous. And, in a backward way, highlighted even more that she might live in Swan Cove, but had the finances of a Crow Harbor native. "I appreciate the thought, but you'd better text them and call it off. My budget can't handle a complete wardrobe redo."

"We know." Megan squeezed her shoulder beneath the black cape. "We're each buying you an outfit as our contribution to your campaign."

"Now I can't be so much as peeved. That's incredibly generous. Thoughtful. Sweet. You're all wonderful." Hallie sniffed. Blinked in triple time to avoid being that woman who bawled in the salon.

"You know what?" The woman in the chair next to her leaned over, despite the stylist holding a comb and curling iron in her thin helmet of gray hair. "You go ahead and text your friends, Megan. Tell 'em to add another outfit to the pile. On me."

"Mrs. Vormelker, you're the best." Megan beamed at her. "Let me get you another glass of wine." She bustled off.

Hallie was blindsided, in the best possible way. "Thank you so much. You don't even know me."

"Sure I do. I came to your last event." She stuck out a hand. Bits of hair slid off the side of her cape. "Agnes Vormelker. I'm a department chair up at Cygnet Labs."

"Hallie Scott. If you don't mind my asking, why are you being so kind to me?"

"It's a tangible way to support your campaign. I'm voting for you." Pursing nude lips, she continued after a brief pause. "To be clear, I started out just being thrilled I had an option to vote for a woman."

Well, that was the thinnest of thin ice. "I agree that it's exciting to take such a huge stride for our gender, but I wouldn't want to win just because Mayor Montgomery gets a five o'clock shadow. That's a step *back*."

"That was only my initial knee-jerk reaction to learning you were on the ballot. Then I wanted to do it to stick it to those snobs who say you can't be mayor because of your hometown. Piffle. I'm from a backwater, one stoplight town in Alabama where they still fly the Confederate flag. Didn't stop me from scraping and getting my PhD and heading up a department at the most prestigious genomics lab in the country."

Ouch. Okay, it wasn't exactly a surprise, but it did sting to hear that even after presenting herself at several events, some voters still weren't interested because of her high-school zip code. "You've come far. That's impressive."

"But *then* I realized what I really wanted to do was vote *against* the mayor."

Oh, geez. Hallie hoped nobody was listening, although the inside of a salon had more eavesdropping going on than the six square blocks around the White House. "Mayor Montgomery isn't evil."

"Indeed not. Quite the treat for these aging eyes to linger on, too." Agnes stuck out her elbow as if trying to poke Hallie in the ribs...even though she didn't come close. "I've got no bone to pick with Fitz Montgomery, other than his last name. Preston Montgomery treats this town like his own personal fiefdom. He's out of control."

Hallie did not disagree. She'd just assumed her viewpoint was a solo endeavor. "I don't want you to punish the mayor for the sins of his father. If there *were* sins..."

"To truly take out an opponent, you have to hit 'em where it hurts. Nothing would hurt Preston like an attack on his vaunted family name. Fitz is simply collateral damage. The most direct hit I can make."

Mention of collateral damage filled her with fear again over what the Montgomery scion might do to strike out at Hallie. Would her friends, her family, be used to hurt her, to put her campaign in a tailspin?

Then she homed in on the fervor in Agnes's raspy voice. That sounded targeted, not at all a generalized dislike. "What, ah, injustice was visited upon you by the elder Montgomery?"

"I had petitioned to change the route of a smaller cruise ship, really more of an overloaded sailboat. A yacht, really. Easy to fit into our harbor. Of course, it'd boost the economy with further tourist dollars, and *he* denied them a license to berth here in Swan Cove because of the theme."

Hallie was scared to ask, but even Agnes's stylist had

paused her curling, raptly following the story. "Which was…?"

"It's a lesbian cruise. All-female crew, too."

Oh, boy.

Girl.

Whichever. "Can he do that? Mr. Montgomery's not the harbor master."

"No, but that one *is* in his pocket."

"Lou Fonseco?" Her stylist huffed out a breath. "He brags about it. Getting his monthly 'bonus'—which you or I would call a payoff—from Montgomery Industries. As if the offer of a free wine spritzer from him would be worth the boredom of listening to his self-important bullshit."

"See? It's common knowledge. Anywho, Preston didn't find the cruise 'wholesome' enough to live up to the high-class image of his carefully curated, jewel box of a town. I have proof he's the one who kiboshed it."

It all shocked Hallie. She was certain Fitz didn't know about any of this, and that he'd do his utmost to fix it once told the story. He did adore an underdog. "If you have proof, Agnes, shouldn't you complain?"

"To who?" Agnes accepted her wine and downed half of it in a determined gulp. "His son, the mayor?"

"Well, yes. I feel like Mayor Montgomery would give you a fair listen."

"He might, but he wouldn't be able to change his father's mind. From what I hear, he doesn't have anything to do with Montgomery Industries."

Hallie believed, completely, that Fitz would *try* to do the right thing, but, sadly, she agreed with Agnes that his father would *not*. "You could take your proof to the *Gazette*."

"Hmm. Possibly. I'll give it a good think, but your rational suggestions just made me all the more decided to vote for you." She lifted her glass. "Enjoy your outfit."

"See?" Megan tidied her station. "You have to put in the extra effort to win this election. For people like Mrs. Vormelker. After all, you wouldn't turn in the first draft of a paper without spiffing it up."

"You've got me there."

"Speaking of winning…" Megan leaned over, braced herself on the back and arm of the molded chair, and dropped her voice to a whisper. "I've been doing some digging—I think they call it opposition research—on Fitz with all my clients. I've learned a thing or two. *Not* the kind of things you've been busy learning under the covers with him."

"No. Nope. Please stop." She had to shut that down *now*. "Exposing a dirty secret wouldn't be right—if Fitz even has any at all. I'll win on the facts and the facts alone."

"That's very high-minded of you."

"Thanks."

Megan straightened up and snorted. "It wasn't a compliment. Playing fair and having ethics—sheesh, this isn't a T-ball game, Hallie. It's politics!"

"I'll be mayor on my terms or not at all." But Hallie did wonder…

…what exactly *had* Megan unearthed?

Chapter Fifteen

Tonight *sucked*.

Fitz had told Everett this would happen before he left. Everett had laughed so hard and so long that Fitz had been forced to hang up on him.

Tonight was the traditional mayoral candidate dinner, graciously hosted by Swan Cove scion Preston Montgomery. A tradition of sitting in the fishbowl of a restaurant so other diners could parade by, press the flesh, and, as Everett put it, bend the knee to the king. Of course, he was referring to Preston, not the actual mayor.

It was a tradition that had begun more than a century ago…even though nobody had run against the Montgomerys since that first time. It was a ridiculous, embarrassing, self-aggrandizing tradition that Fitz fucking *loathed*.

Tonight, though, it was so much more than that as it was Fitz's parents having his opponent/God-forbid-they-label-it bed partner to dinner.

There was bad.

There was the Red Sox losing the pennant in Game 7

bad. There was losing your internet before a Zoom meeting with the entire country's mayors where you were supposed to give a speech bad.

And then there was *tonight*. A whole new level of utter shit. Awkward and messy and stilted.

Oh, and not to be forgotten was the fun-fact dump Bronson Shepherd had gifted him about his dad and the secret cleanup of his uncle's mess. It was a fight Fitz hadn't had yet. He was still mulling over the strategy of broaching it at all. The events were in the past, and there was no revisiting. The wrong had been righted, with the money repaid to the town and the books cleaned up. Clean enough that Fitz had never caught so much as a whiff of the wrongdoing.

So, Fitz was stewing and second-guessing himself, both as a mayor and as a son.

The waterfront restaurant hosting the train wreck of a night was like a second home to Fitz and his family. Magically, even without reservations, the best table in the place was always available for the Montgomerys. *Not* a table by the wall of windows looking out at the Atlantic and the marina. No, the prime spot was right in front of the enormous stone fireplace, which roared year round. Everyone walked by it from the host stand, and again on their treks to the bathroom. It was a see and be seen kind of table.

And it's where he sat tonight, with his parents and, you bet he'd harp on it, his as yet unlabeled lover/opponent.

Hallie looked gorgeous. She'd confided that she'd borrowed the white lace top from her friend Ana and the flowy blue pants from Megan. Fitz had to consciously keep moving his eyes off of her because he just wanted to drink her in, which definitely would've tipped off his parents seeing as how he'd *never* brought a girl or woman to dinner with them before.

"How did this tradition start, Mr. Montgomery? Of your

family hosting the mayoral candidates?" Hallie scooped some of the lobster thermidor out of the shell.

Yet another tradition. Nobody got to order individually. The hosting Montgomerys decided the menu for the entire table. Fitz had forgotten until Hallie looked at him, confusion wrinkling her nose, when a waiter set down the iceberg wedge salad without taking her order.

Fitz decided it was less of a tradition and more of a total dick move. His dad asserting his power every chance he got. Of course, he *was* pissed at his dad now, so his objectivity wasn't at peak performance.

His mom set down her knife and fork, then patted the ubiquitous pearls resting at the neckline of her peach and cream block sweater. "We had an outsider marry into the family. There'd been a few lean years, and Robert Dufort brought a healthy influx of capital when he proposed. He'd been a blockade runner during the Civil War."

"For the North?" Hallie asked.

Aww, it was sweet how she assumed the best. Fitz wasn't holding his breath on that score, however.

"That was the thing with blockade runners." Preston gave an avuncular "let's not nitpick" chuckle. "They didn't so much choose sides. They simply followed the money. Which, in part, was why he was so agreeable to changing his last name to Montgomery as a condition of the betrothal."

Fitz had never heard this story. Or maybe he had years go, but his grandfather had tended to drone on and on and on with family history. Frankly, he was glad he'd been in ignorance about this particular ancestor. "So, if you cut through the crap, he was hiding. A traitor. Running from the authorities."

"Not running." Preston smirked. "Looking for a place to relocate. A place to settle down and start fresh."

His mom continued the moral whitewashing. "And

marriage to the right woman guaranteed him that. Robert was, by all accounts, a savvy negotiator. It was his idea to insist on being mayor. And it kept the office in the family once he changed his name. A win-win all around."

No way.

Clearly, the moral ambiguity in his family hadn't started with the situation with dear old embezzler Uncle Jeremiah. Fitz desperately wanted to shoot Hallie a *do you believe this bullshit?* look. Couldn't risk it, though. He sure couldn't wait to debrief with her tonight.

In bed.

Naked.

Son of a bitch. Those thoughts were off-limits while sharing a dinner table with his parents.

This wasn't his first rodeo of a public argument. Fitz kept his voice modulated, his eyebrows high, and a *isn't that interesting* uptick to his lips. "You call a man who didn't have the strength of principles to pick a side in a war that tore this country apart a winner?"

Preston's face slipped into an identically polite mask. "You've no place lambasting his strength, son. Do you realize the courage it took to weave his ship in and out, when literally every other ship on the sea was gunning for him? That's a man with a spine of steel. A man who won't back down."

"He refilled the family coffers, was a good husband to your great-great-great-grandmother, produced three children, and led this town." Caroline lifted her wineglass in a wordless toast to long-gone Robert.

"So, you're painting him more as Rhett Butler than as a war criminal?" Hallie smiled over the rim of her water glass. "The way I see it, for all his failings, Rhett was a far better person than Scarlett."

Fitz wiped his mouth to hide his grin. That was his librarian, always bringing the conversation back to books.

And, handily, trying to dispel the growing tension at the table with a subject change.

"Those are fictional characters, Ms. Scott. We're discussing a real leader of this town." The cutdown by his mom was swift, and it surprised Fitz. He knew Caroline belonged to a book club, that she always had a stack of books on her nightstand. She wasn't anti-reading or anything.

Was she anti-*Hallie*?

Hallie blinked twice, but she didn't back down. "You can have a spirited discussion using the filter of fiction. It can be much more productive. Makes things less personal."

"She's trying to help me, Mom." Fitz tapped the center of his pale gray tie. "Since I'm clearly not excited by this reveal of family lore."

"Good or bad, family is what counts. Robert did a lot of good in his day, and he kept the line of Montgomery mayors unbroken."

Fitz had been raised to believe that was a good thing, a necessary thing. That nobody else had the means or the institutional knowledge or the genuine good intentions to take care of Swan Cove as well as the Montgomery family could and did.

He was no longer swallowing that hook, line, and sinker. "Well, he cheated, especially post-Civil War. It wasn't what you'd call a liberated time. A man taking his wife's family name was unheard of."

"That's enough." Preston shook his fork. "You will continue that line, Fitz, so I won't have you badmouthing it."

"There's no guarantee."

"Of what? You respecting your ancestors? We raised you better than that."

Were they really that single-minded? Deliberately, Fitz lifted his glass and clinked it against Hallie's. "There's no guarantee I'll win. Ms. Scott here might just surprise you."

Preston burst into loud, rolling guffaws, loud enough that other tables looked over and smiled at the obvious good times going down. "It would surprise me, indeed. Oh, that's hilarious."

"I disagree." Fitz infused the two words with icy steel.

Hallie set down her fork and lined it up parallel to the knife clinging to the edge of the plate. And then she beamed at him. "No, thank you, Fitz. I can stand up for myself. You shouldn't be forced to defend my chances of beating you, but it is chivalrous that you'd try. And I'd take a Lancelot type over King Arthur any day."

His dad's chuckles barely died down. "Please. We all know this is a stunt, Ms. Scott. I genuinely don't understand why you're wasting your time with it, but that's your choice. Regardless, your attempt at a run against a Montgomery cannot be conceived as anything more serious than a publicity stunt."

"I'm not seeking notoriety. It's costing me money, energy, and time. It's certainly beating down my ego to a microscopic sediment." Hallie had followed Fitz's lead, keeping her voice low and calm. The rest of the room wouldn't have any idea that she was in the most epic showdown he'd ever had the privilege to watch. "So, I assure you this is a serious run, and not a stunt."

"Then you're a fool," Preston spat out, his brows coming together ominously.

"And you're ill-mannered to speak that way to a dinner guest."

Wow.

Wow. Fitz didn't know if he should applaud or run and grab the fire extinguisher to cool these two off. She'd been worked up and worried about this dinner, intimidated at the prospect of meeting the couple who owned the town.

Fitz had pointed out that she had a good relationship

with his Aunt Felicia, and an *extraordinarily* good one with him, so clearly the Montgomerys weren't as scary as she was making them out to be.

But to say she was holding her own was the understatement of the decade. And his father...wasn't. His face was the same red as the lobster shells on every plate. His mom's had blanched to the color of the lobster meat. A vein popped out along Preston's temple, pulsing and dark.

The thing was, though, Hallie was right. No matter what the circumstance, Preston had overstepped. So now what? If she didn't want him to run interference, what *was* Fitz supposed to do as the charged silence dragged on and on?

...

Hallie wasn't a newbie to being insulted, overtly or discreetly. She'd grown up a nerd, on the wrong side of the tracks of a town that every other town along the coast looked down on. She'd become a librarian. Well aware that she'd been a lifelong easy target, Hallie genuinely didn't get perturbed by much. Not anything aimed at her, at least. If somebody badmouthed her friends or family, she'd become ferocious, but she took very little personally.

Preston Montgomery didn't know that about her, though. He'd been an inconsiderate, snobbish jackass. And Hallie knew why. Not because she dared to run against his precious next-in-the-dynasty son. Okay, maybe a little that, but mostly because she was from Crow Harbor and daring to reach for the stars in his wealthy, privileged, better-than-everywhere-else hamlet.

That she couldn't let go unanswered.

Nobody was better. People were different, vastly, but nobody was better. Especially with the egregious display of pomposity Preston had just put out there. So, she'd fired back.

Preston Montgomery would always be aware that Hallie Scott had gotten the better of him. She'd had the simple joy of watching him and knowing her words had hit the mark, but Hallie wouldn't let him writhe there on her verbal harpoon.

Then he'd have cause to retell the story and slant it to where Hallie was the gauche attacker. Blame her snarky zing on her being a Crow Harbor ruffian with zero respect for people of quality.

Nope.

She picked up her fork and began digging at her lobster again. "But I know you *aren't* ill-mannered, Preston. I realize you were simply testing my mettle to see if I had what it takes to stand up to the slings and arrows of the campaign trail. I appreciate you, as the defender of the town, putting me through my paces. It was considerate of you."

Please, please, take the peace baton offered. Don't drag this out and make it even more uncomfortable.

"Quite, ah, quite right." His words were slow at first, disconnected. Then his blue eyes, identical to his son's, sharpened. "Good to see that you're so savvy, Ms. Scott."

"I know you only have the best interests of Swan Cove as your motivation, like we all do. Far and above any personal preferences." Somebody's foot—presumably Fitz's—pressed insistently on the top of hers.

Hallie got the message. She'd made her point. Time to pivot. Although her last attempt at seemingly innocuous small talk had led to the disastrous blockade runner reveal, so she didn't think any topic was safe.

To her immense relief, Fitz jumped in. "Why didn't Blake join us? She always comes to this thing."

"Your sister always comes because it has always been a simple family dinner. She's very busy at the lab and had no desire to sit through a long political discourse."

"That makes two of us," Fitz joked heavy-handedly.

It was enough, though. Hallie had collected herself, taken two more bites, and was ready to jump into the fray once again. She'd thank him later—with exquisite slowness and attention to all that naked detail—for his intervention.

"Mrs. Montgomery, is there any issue you're particularly interested in that's come to your attention as the de facto matriarch of Swan Cove?"

"I support the issues most important to the mayor. It is paramount to not have division in a family."

"Oh, I agree. My parents and I are quite close. If I don't show up for dinner at least bi-weekly, well, I'd better have at least a broken limb as an excuse."

"It takes two casts and a concussion to get out of a Montgomery family dinner." Fitz cocked his head to the side. "Unless you're Blake, I guess, since she slid out of tonight so easily."

"Your sister's work has the potential to be life-changing. Her work with the human genome could transform the future of autism, cancer treatment, auto-immune diseases."

That was...vague. Genuinely interested, Hallie asked, "I don't think one gene covers all of those conditions. What's her specialty?"

Caroline waved her wrist as lazily as Queen Elizabeth in her golden State coach. "Whatever piques her interest."

Fitz hooted. "You don't know! You tune out when Blake gets that PhD lecture tone in her voice, same as me."

"You *will* not tell—" Caroline broke off. "Hel-*lo* Lloyd. It's been ages. So good to see you."

The fireplug of a man didn't have to bend far to air kiss her cheeks. He wore a tan sport coat over a mint green polo. "You're a sight for sore eyes, Caroline. I've been at the bar all by my lonesome."

"What a shame. You'd think the manager of the town's bank wouldn't have to dine alone. You're far too important to go solo. I'll bet you kept your status a secret, you wily man. Escaping a rough day at the salt mines?"

"You got it. Plus, I'm officially a bachelor for a while. Roni's going to be disappointed she missed you."

Hallie followed the conversation, face lifted, neutrally pleasant expression in place. But Caroline didn't pause to introduce her to the man, nor did Preston, her official host for the evening. If she didn't know better, she'd say the elder Montgomerys were content to pretend she wasn't there.

"Where is she tonight?"

"Tending to her mother." He grimaced, showing teeth so perfect they had to be dentures. "Knee replacement. She and her sister are trading off weeks of playing nursemaid."

Caroline plucked at his sleeve until he leaned over. Behind an upraised hand, she said in a stage whisper, "You hired an *actual* nurse, I hope?"

"Of course. The old lady only wants attention from her daughters. She wants a trained and appropriately pricey professional for everything else." He shook Preston's hand, then circled the table to shake Fitz's. "Mr. Mayor."

"Good to see you, Lloyd." Fitz put an arm across the back of Hallie's chair, effectively including her in the conversation. "Have you had a chance to meet Hallie Scott? She's our fantastic librarian, and a formidable opponent for me in the campaign."

Ohhh, she appreciated him *so* much at that moment. It was like the cherry on top of her telling-off-Preston sundae.

Lloyd hustled right over, which, to Hallie, signaled he had to be in sales rather than simply a trust fund social flitter. "Lloyd Saxby, president of Harborside Bank."

"Nice to meet you. Your tellers are always personable and accommodating."

He thrust out his chest, palm on it like Napoleon. "You bank with us?"

Awkward. No. Quite simply the interest rates were better at big corporate banks.

"The library does. You've no idea how quickly all those late fees add up and need to be deposited."

"Ha!" He grabbed her hand that he'd just relinquished and patted the back of it. "You're like a meter maid, making money for the city off stupid transgressions."

She didn't care for the condescending pat, but it was obvious Lloyd was making an effort, and more so than two of her tablemates, so she'd cut him some slack. "I prefer to think of myself as a conduit to information and entertainment, but sure, that, too."

Then Lloyd slapped Fitz on the back. Big toucher, that one. "It's a hoot to see you breaking bread with the enemy, Fitz."

A meter maid and a hootable enemy. Wow. This guy was a real charmer.

Fitz looked at him with a blank expression as if Lloyd had just accused him of pogo-sticking into church. "Ms. Scott's not my enemy. We both want the same thing—what's best for Swan Cove."

"Not much of a delineating rallying cry, you wanting the same thing." He guffawed.

Fitz continued as if the other man hadn't spoken. "And we do this at every campaign event. You should come out to the one this weekend at the community center. We're talking about ways it could expand."

"*After* the marina expansion, of course. Bigger money there than at a community center. Funny you should mention that. My nephew mentioned just the other day it'd be great to have a mini-golf course. Indoors, of course. Big fun for the entire family."

"We'll both make a note of that," Hallie said hurriedly. It seemed prudent to remind Lloyd there were *two* candidates.

"Feel free to think on it more and send over any additional suggestions."

"Will do." With a wave, he left the table.

Too bad. It'd been nice to have one more person who didn't actively loathe her in the conversation.

"I noticed what you *didn't* say, Ms. Scott." Disapproval rolled off Caroline thicker than the layer of butter she'd slathered on her poppyseed roll. "You really ought to bank with Lloyd."

It'd be useless to ask how her personal finances were any of Caroline's business. Clearly, the woman felt *everything* in Swan Cove was her business. "Then he really ought to lure me with better rates. I've got to accrue every cent I can."

"Money is not all that matters. The optics matter."

Hallie couldn't wait to see Megan's eyeroll when she told her that quote. "See, the only people who think money doesn't matter are the people who have oodles of it. Now, if the mayor here threw the town budget out the window and doubled my salary, *then* I'd consider banking local."

"No can do, unless you want to pull a double salary and actually be the meter maid?" They both laughed at the ridiculousness of it.

Preston and Caroline did *not*.

Preston placed his fork, tines down, on the plate. Then he caught the eye of the nearest waiter and lifted his chin, indicating it was time to clear for the next course. Was he like Queen Elizabeth? Was everyone supposed to stop eating just because he was done?

"Well, I suppose the optics don't actually make a difference in your case since you won't actually become mayor."

He'd hammered that point home tonight. Again and again and again.

"Dad!" Fitz said harshly. His voice boomed above

the clatter of silverware against china, and the buzz of conversation, loud enough to have several couples near them neck-twisting like owls to ogle them. "Enough."

"I'm not being insulting, or mean. I'm simply stating the fact that not only is Ms. Scott not a Montgomery, she's from Crow Harbor. She won't win."

That was the moment.

The one where Hallie realized that even if she *did* win by some miracle, she'd never be truly accepted. Not by the old guard in the town. Not by the Montgomerys, who owned and ran everything and were friends with everyone. And they definitely would never accept her as Fitz's girlfriend.

Not that they'd talked about that. Hallie and Fitz had spent almost every night together for the past two weeks. Texted constantly. They were twining together like two vines…but they hadn't even driven by the border of discussing dating after the election. They were happy and that was enough.

For now. Well, until *right* now.

She'd been tilting at windmills this whole time—and look how badly that ended for Don Quixote. Concentrating on facts and figures, expecting they would be all the ammunition necessary.

How could they be when the bias against her was pure snobbery and wholly emotional? How could she possibly fight that? For the mayorship…or for the chance to keep her handsome, caring lover?

Chapter Sixteen

Fitz raised an eyebrow as he realized Hallie was trailing behind him. "I thought it was only women that went to the bathroom in pairs. You know you can't go in there with me, right?"

"Did you actually expect me to stay at the table with your parents by myself?" she said in a stage whisper. "That's just cruel, Fitz."

"I'm not abandoning you to bolt out the door. Nature calls. It's a standard and universally accepted excuse for leaving the table."

"Actually, speaking of doors, can you, well, hold it for another few minutes?"

"Sure."

Hallie peeked around the corner, then led him out the glass door to the patio and nipped them away from the patrons to the delivery entrance. A row of bushes hid it from view. She put a hand to his cheek. "Are you okay?"

Weird question. Fitz turned to kiss her palm. "I'm young, I've got enough to live on, and a beautiful, intelligent woman sharing my bed every night. I'm damn okay."

"I mean...you seemed pretty argumentative in there with your parents. Almost like you were already mad at them, didn't want to tell them, but took it out on them anyway."

Very perceptive. If only his parents could read him as well... "After how poorly they treated you tonight, you're actually trying to protect them?"

"Oh, no. Your parents have not endeared themselves to me one iota. I'm trying to protect *you* from lashing out and saying something you might regret."

There it was. He all but heard the squeak as the lock on his heart unlatched.

Nobody had ever stood up to the Montgomerys, let alone to defend their son. The way Hallie cared about, well, the people and things she *cared* about, the passion and loyalty—it was amazing. Her friends. Her parents. Her adopted town— running for a job she didn't even want because she thought the town deserved better.

And now him.

Fitz had tried to resist falling for Hallie. It'd complicate their easy little fling. It'd make it harder to walk away when it inevitably had to end. Turned out it was impossible *not* to fall for her.

"That's... Thank you. For looking out for me."

"Of course. We're not opponents right now. This is a Fitz and Hallie moment, out here. What's wrong?"

He couldn't tell her. Could he?

No. All he had was one person's story. No corroborating evidence. No admission from anyone actually involved. Fitz didn't want to spare his uncle or his father the blowback, the humiliation, if it was true, but he didn't want the town distracted this close to the election by something that happened years ago and had zero relevance to the current campaign.

"You're right. I am pissed at my dad. I heard a rumor that, if it's true, is pretty damning. Can't ask him about it, though, until I get my ducks in a row. If I accuse him without having the facts to back it up, he'll deny it. There'll be a huge fight. I won't get the chance to bring it up again. I lose the element of surprise."

"Talking to your father requires a whole strategy?"

"Yes."

"But you're sure he's in the wrong?"

That was a tricky one to answer. On the one hand, he'd repaid the stolen money to the town. Technically, doing what was the mission statement of the Montgomery family—protecting Swan Cove.

On the other hand, the fact Preston actively worked to hush up the incident sure made it look like his dad had been protecting his brother, Jeremiah, far more than Swan Cove.

Slowly, Fitz said, "I think he did the right thing, ultimately, but for the wrong reasons, and that's a big problem."

"That's admirable, Fitz. Plenty of people wouldn't worry about the why, they'd just move along."

He looked down at her, at the way the moon made a nimbus around her hair. The new cut and highlights she'd put in still looked like Hallie, but turned up a notch. A soft breeze carried the scent of some blooming tree, and a few petals fell on their shoulders.

"I'm not so admirable, because all I want to do right now is kiss you. Doesn't matter that there are thirty people on the other side of those bushes, and a hundred people inside. My parents waiting for us."

"Well, if none of that matters, then why aren't you kissing me already?" Her tone was pure sass and challenge.

"I like how you think." Fitz was still grinning as he lowered his mouth to hers.

Hallie rose up on tiptoe to meet him halfway, because

she threw herself into sex with the same focus and interest that she attacked a stack of books. It was adorable—and arousing as fuck.

He lifted her off the ground with one arm around her waist, twined his hand through her hair to angle her head just so, and then *devoured* her. It had to be fast. They could be discovered any second.

Fast and hard.

Their teeth clinked a couple of times. Finesse was out the window. It was all need and heat and lust. Their mouths fused together into one long, unbroken kiss. Fitz was so turned on he thought he might burst through the zipper on his pants.

Hallie twined her legs around his, both her hands cupping his skull as if to prevent him from moving so much as a millimeter away from her mouth.

Like that would happen. Not when Fitz was engulfed in its sweet warmth. Hallie tasted faintly of the chardonnay they'd been drinking. She smelled of flowers and citrus, and she felt like heaven melting in his arms, moaning, and rubbing against him with a fervor that ought to be striking literal sparks from their clothing. Fitz ran the tip of his tongue along the satiny inside of her lower lip, and then finished off with a nip of his teeth.

God. He wanted to sink his teeth everywhere. To give... yeah, to give the first hickey since he'd accidentally left his last one on Maria Silverman under the bleachers during freshman homecoming. Leave a mark so he wouldn't have to be so nonchalant to the world about Hallie.

So that everyone would know she was *his*.

Damn it, that was a stupid instinct. Stupid enough to throw cold water on the moment. Fitz eased back, set her on her feet. "When you go back to the table, tell them I had to take a call. That'll give me time for this whole situation," he gestured to the tenting at his crotch, "to disappear."

"Pick up where we left off later?"

"You'd better believe it."

...

Okay. Fitz's kisses had fueled her up. Hallie could take whatever nastiness the Montgomerys dumped on her. They were his parents, they loved him. That had to count for something, right?

Maybe she should ask them to tell funny stories about him as a kid, and abandon trying to have a decent conversation about the town and maybe being mayor and just play to their strengths. Because they clearly weren't budging on the whole *your last name must end in -gomery to know what is best for Swan Cove.*

"Good that Fitz didn't come back first," Caroline said as Hallie sat down. "We'd like to broach a subject with you."

Excellent. Hallie crossed her arms on the table and leaned in with a big, open smile. "That's why I'm here; to discuss any topic you care to put on the table."

"Information has come to us regarding your parents."

Hmmm. Come to them? A spy pigeon flapped through their window with a note taped to its foot?

Doubtful.

More likely they'd done opposition research. More likely that…oh! "Is there any chance a certain ex-campaign manager brought this to you?"

Preston drew himself up even more ramrod straight. The I-beams holding up this restaurant had nothing on the spine of a self-righteous man. "Fitz had no right to fire Derek. He's savvy and knows far more about campaigns than my son. Just because he sent him packing doesn't mean Derek's not still working on the campaign behind the scenes."

This was bad. Fitz would go ballistic. Should she tell him?

Should she wait for him to find out organically? Maybe wait until after tonight's promised sex, when he was loose and practically comatose and *then* tell him?

With a raised eyebrow, Hallie asked, "What does Derek think he knows about my parents?"

"That they've declared bankruptcy," Preston said in a flat tone.

Disbelief washed over Hallie, followed quickly by worry, bookended by anger. "First of all, you shouldn't pass on rumors like that unless you're certain they're true."

"Derek heard it from the lawyer who filed their papers."

That was very, very bad, for all sorts of reasons. "Then he should be disbarred. What about lawyer-client confidentiality?"

"The man's handling a bankruptcy. No doubt he feels confident your parents aren't in a position to sue him." Preston's whole attitude screamed *who cares about the little people*. It was infuriating. "Besides, no names were used. It was all couched in vague terms and hypotheticals."

"Then it sounds like nothing more than an ugly rumor to me."

Caroline tsked. "There's no point going around in circles. It doesn't matter if you believe it. We know it to be a fact. We're sharing that with you, in the spirit of generosity, so you aren't blindsided at a campaign event."

"Why would it even come up?"

She waved a hand in the air, weighed down with an enormous platinum wedding set. "Swan Cove is a small town. Somehow, word spreads. One never knows how it starts."

"Regardless, this gives you time to think about the ramifications. To you. To the campaign. What sort of spotlight your parents might be in at this difficult time in their lives."

Hallie didn't know what to say. All of her emotions had whirled together and then backed off. Shock, probably. At least the numbness kept her from yelling at Fitz's parents… and from getting in her car and racing to confront her own.

Why didn't *they* tell her? And if they didn't want her to know, shouldn't she respect that? Let them keep their pride?

Would continuing to run put them at risk, though?

She had lots of questions and no answers. No Fitz to rescue her yet, either. So, Hallie did the only thing she could, a remedy as old as politics itself. She drained what was left of the excellent wine.

Half an hour later, the buzz had dissipated, thanks to coffee and dessert, but that was okay. Hallie sought a different sort of buzz.

"Did you ever read *Peanuts*?" she asked Fitz as he let them into his apartment.

He hung their jackets. "The comic strip? I guess. Long time ago."

Hallie was at ease in his place now. She walked right on in without waiting, past the living room to the hallway leading to the bedroom. "There's one where Linus is super aware of his tongue. He tries not to think about it, but that only makes him think about it more. Lucy calls it dumb, and of course, when she walks away, suddenly all she can think about is her tongue."

"I like all the weird and wonderful places your mind wanders, but you lost me with that one."

She crooked her finger so he'd join her. "When you try *not* to think of something, you only concentrate on it more. Like an earworm."

Fitz pretended to spit. "Worst things ever. Worse than hiccups."

"You know what *does* work? Not thinking. Not talking.

Distraction."

"Oh?" Laughter rolled out as Hallie pushed off his sport coat. "What did you have in mind?"

She unzipped his pants. If there was the slightest chance he did still want to be mature and talk through his feelings about his parents some more, then her mouth on him ought to cut that right off at the pass.

"I find I do my best non-thinking naked."

"Is that so?" Fitz hitched in a sharp breath as she squeezed his already hard shaft. "Don't you want to move this to the bedroom?"

"Nope." As soon as his belt was undone, the pants slid to the floor with a quick jiggle of his feet. Hallie shoved both hands under the waistband of the black boxer briefs. She liked to cup his balls—both for her pleasure and his safety—when stripping him.

"How about you let me undress you, at least?"

Always considerate, that was Fitz to the core. He'd take his time, though, which might allow him to start *thinking* again. No, thank you.

Hallie whipped her shirt overhead, kicked her sandals in somewhat the direction of the door, and shimmied out of her skirt. While she accomplished all of that, Fitz removed her bra. That was enough for now.

Planting the tips of her fingernails just above his nipples, she slowly raked them down his chest. Slow enough to feel goose bumps pop up. Slow enough to feel his nipples harden.

Slow enough that his penis was tapping against her thigh in eagerness before she made it to his belly button.

Moonlight streamed through the wood slatted blinds, painting his already obvious abs in strips of shadow. Hallie brought her hands together at the narrow trail of hair; a signpost pointing to his most erogenous zone. At the last possible millimeter, she swept them apart to continue raking down the insides of his thighs as she knelt.

Fitz jerked, then let out a frustrated groan.

See? He was already speechless. Her plan was going great.

His hands caressed her bare shoulders. She loved when he cupped them, stroking down her arms. The broad palms and long fingers covered so much of her at once. So many nerve endings jumped to the surface simultaneously at his touch.

"Remember when you mentioned thinking about your tongue?"

"Yes?"

"I'm thinking about it a *lot* right now."

Ah. Hint received.

Gurgling with swallowed giggles, Hallie delicately swiped the very tip of her tongue across his tip. Down an inch to do the same thing at the oh-so-sensitive ridge encircling him. Then she sort of strummed back and forth over it. His hips jolted. Thumbs dug in hard enough it almost felt like he was trying to lift her.

"That's very good. That's some top-notch non-thinking going on right there."

Rather than respond, Hallie switched to licking. Long licks up and down, with a swirl around the tip. She pulled her arms in so the outsides of them rubbed against the crinkly soft hair on his thighs, because Hallie couldn't get enough of touching him.

Not just holding hands, or kissing, or actual intercourse. Hallie loved to touch Fitz *everywhere*. It was a sybaritic pleasure of which she constantly partook. Even at dinner, fully clothed, she'd rubbed her knee against his.

Because even that little bit of contact was better than *not* touching him, which kind of made her sound like an addict to this big, sexy, smart man.

Hallie was, surprisingly, fine with that. Sort of. She was

fine with it for now. When they inevitably would have to stop seeing each other after the election? She'd be *far* from fine.

And that was why she shouldn't be thinking, at all. Grabbing the base of his shaft, Hallie focused on sucking in as much of his length as possible. As much of the long, velvety, rock-hard man that she could fit.

Fitz's hands were moving faster, almost restlessly, over her skin. Up her neck. Tangling in her hair to pull her closer. He half bent, half crouched to reach her breasts.

"God, Hallie, I've got to have more of you." He crouched all the way down, anchored his shoulder just past her hips and lifted her in a fireman's carry.

That worked for her, too. The show of brute strength sent a surge of moisture pooling between her legs. Plus, now his hands were roaming all over her butt. Hallie couldn't breathe very well in this position, but that was a minor inconvenience next to having her breasts rubbing against the planes of his back.

He carried her into the bathroom, snatching a condom from the counter, and then through the door into the bedroom. There was a definite bounce from the drop as she landed on the big bed. It *delighted* Hallie, as did the way Fitz crawled up from the foot of the bed, a low growl escaping his throat, to position himself right on top of her.

He seemed as eager as she was; just as barely balanced on the edge between desire and out-of-control lust as she was.

But he stopped. Holding one heck of an impressive plank, he barely let the tip of his penis graze her outer lips. "Hallie," he said gruffly. "Look at me."

Oh. Ha. Her eyes had closed in anticipation of the zing of pleasure from that vigorous first thrust inside. Shadows obscured half of his face. The other half was all taut lines from the struggle for control. "I see you, Fitz."

"You do. You see me like no one else does. Be with me,

Hallie."

He...he meant *in* the moment, concentrating on the here and now, right?

"I'm with you," she said, not entirely sure of what she was promising. She dug her nails into his lower back, trying to press him forward.

Instead, he held her gaze for several moments. Locked onto each other, ankles intertwined, lips a breath apart, Hallie felt...penetrated, like they were fully sharing the moment in a tender way they hadn't previously. Pressure filled her heart, her chest, her head.

And then he slid in with slow caution.

Fitz maintained his rhythm at that maddeningly deliberate pace. It made her impending orgasm build in a different way, grow from a different place.

Hallie's thighs began to shake. Heat streaked through her limbs, down her chest. Coalesced between her legs. Her hips spasmed. Through it all, Fitz remained unhurried, although the heaving rasp of his breath showed that he was also at the brink.

They didn't speak. Didn't have the air to moan. And he barely blinked, still with his eyes on hers.

So she saw the flicker of...something move his features right as pleasure broke through her in a massive storm of satisfaction.

Her eyes shut in the aftermath as he let out a deep, feral cry and then collapsed half to the side of her. It was the most intense sex Hallie had ever had, which derailed her goal for the evening, because now a million thoughts raced through her brain.

They were all about Fitz.

About how she didn't know how she'd be able to walk away from this.

From him.

Chapter Seventeen

The secret to campaign events nobody had ever told Fitz was that they could be fun when you had a partner. Someone to riff off of, to joke with, to banter—

Reality check: it was just *Hallie* that made them fun.

She made everything more fun.

Her random spewing of book quotes and references to characters. Her earnest belief that a good night kiss had to be the very last thing done before they fell asleep. The way she made him feel twelve feet tall when he told her how he'd helped mediate or mitigate a problem. The way she laughed with and at him—when deserved.

They'd had sex in the forest—in a tent.

They'd had sex in the boathouse—in a canoe.

And right now, he'd locked them into the dressing room at the community center. No shows or rehearsals scheduled for a week. The crowd from the event were led to believe they'd slipped out the back door. So they were stealthily cuddling on an ancient couch, the stuffing worn so thin the individual springs made themselves known against his ass.

"You did great today," he said, nuzzling her neck. Soft strands tickled his nose and forehead. Hallie's lips were nibbling along the edge of his ear. They'd turned on the makeup lights around the mirrors, which gave a soft glow to the dark room.

"*You* did great." Hallie had a propensity to be exact that Fitz found crazy endearing. "I did acceptably, which is a nine hundred percent step in the right direction from our first campaign event."

"Then, my passionate wordsmith, you should agree that a nine hundred percent increase more than qualifies to be called great."

"You've got me there." They laughed. She wriggled on his lap, a study in sensuality and torture.

Fitz wouldn't ask her to stop for the world. "Did you have a good time? Doing the Town Hall?"

Her deft fingers worked their way down, undoing the buttons on his starched white shirt. "Never thought I'd say this, but I did."

"Me too. People are asking good questions about the proposed expansion. They've been on autopilot during campaign season for far too long. No matter who wins, this has been good. Shakes things up."

"So I'm...what? The metal cage that rolls around balls for bingo?" Hallie tickled her fingers in a circle, twining through his exposed chest hair. He'd never been so glad he'd abandoned the undershirts his dad had always insisted upon.

"More like the agitator in a washing machine, I think." Fitz grabbed her wrist, flipped it over, and dropped a slow, soft kiss into her palm. "I've never played bingo. Not up on the tools of the trade."

"Whaaaaaaat?" Hallie drew out the word until it practically had a thought balloon over it reading *ACCUSATION*. "You're the mayor of a small town. Isn't it in the bylaws that you have to participate in a bingo game at least once a year?"

"You're exposing your weakness to the opposition." Fitz flipped up the hem of her pink, scoop-necked sweater and tickled her stomach. Once she'd squealed and batted him away, he continued. "Haven't you read the bylaws yet?"

"Three times. Used a highlighter."

"Of course you did." Fitz should've known better, because he knew *her* better by now. The budget spreadsheets made her eyes glaze over, but she still studied them. Hallie didn't cut corners when it came to educating herself.

"I assumed it was like being president—some things don't get divulged until after you've taken the oath of office."

That was freaking hilarious. "Like you said, I'm the mayor of a small town. What kinds of secrets do you think we're hiding?"

And now *Hallie* was the one convulsed in giggles. "Really? You know how much I read, and you're seriously going to ask me what I *imagine* might be kept from public consumption?"

He'd enjoyed the Harry Potter series as much as anyone in their generation. However, Fitz didn't think for a second that wizards blended into the population in plain sight. He wasn't so sure Hallie shared his conviction… Better nip that in the bud.

"I'm telling you right now, on my honor"—he covered his heart with his hand—"that there's no portal to a magical world under the swan pond."

"What about a dead body, weighted down with rocks and perhaps mechanic tools?"

The woman constantly astounded him. "What the hell sort of books have you been reading?"

"Everything," she said with a blissful sigh.

A sigh eerily similar to the ones she made when he was

buried inside of her. Fitz tried not to take it personally.

He resumed slowly tracing the neckline of her sweater. And if his fingers dipped into her cleavage, well, Fitz blamed gravity. "Bingo's too plebeian for the elderly here. They prefer bridge, which I did learn how to play at my grandmother's knee."

"Are you any good?"

God, no. It'd have to be something major, like knee replacement surgery at eighty, to drive him to the edge of boredom and park himself in a bridge game. "No. I never play. I make the rounds and flirt with whoever's losing at each table so they have an excuse for their poor play."

"Aren't you a giver," she intoned drily.

"I support the citizenry however I can."

Hallie finished unbuttoning his shirt and tugged it from his pants. "In Crow Harbor, everyone plays five hundred. Megan told me she was at a wedding where a guest refused to dance with the bride because he had a winning hand and wouldn't stop."

Fitz threw back his head, cracking up. "I'll bet she holds that over his head for the rest of his life. Deservedly so, of course."

"Are you a good game player?" She'd scooted backward off his thighs so just her legs were draped over, which was good, but not *as* good as the previous position.

It meant Hallie wanted to talk. Her preference was for looking at him intently when they talked. They had to be the only couple in the world that turned a light on for a post-sex cuddle and chatting session.

But Fitz had discovered he liked it too. Liked watching the expressions flicker across her face at what he said, or as her mood changed. He could read her now like...well, like a book. And that added an extra layer of intimacy to it all.

Not that Fitz had been *looking* for intimacy. Apparently,

though, sometimes good things snuck up on you. He *felt* it. The rightness, the ease when they were together. He was sure Hallie felt it.

Fitz was equally sure the whole thing would implode if he brought it up before the election. They'd made an agreement that this was just for fun and it'd be over in a matter of days. Only a jerk would distract her, get her all in her head, throw her off her game by telling her how very much he wanted more. How the allure of sneaking around didn't seem to be as awesome as the idea of holding her hand as they walked down the street.

Nope. He wouldn't be that jerk.

Rubbing the backs of his knuckles down her cheek, Fitz asked, "Are you asking do I win? Or am I a good sport, regardless?"

Her pale pink lips pursed as she considered. That pursing made him want all the things from that pair of lips. "Both, I guess. I'm just curious. I'm curious about so many facets of you."

Well. Wasn't that interesting?

It wasn't being a jerk if Hallie opened the door a crack. Fitz could throw out a test balloon, toss out the seed and see if it sprouted. Dip a toe in the water.

Yeah, clearly he was nervous if he was thinking of all these stupid old-timey sayings instead of just pulling the trigger.

Hell.

Without changing the speed or firmness of his caress, Fitz casually said, "There's no rush. Before you know it, winter will be here. We'll be snowed in with nothing to do but play games."

Her fingers stilled for a few seconds where they were circling around his belly button.

Did it prove she'd registered his hint at a future together?

Or just that her wrist had grown tired of being torqued sideways? If Hallie was following his train of thought, was she on board with it? Or ready to jump off and find another ride?

Man, Fitz could barely stand himself with all the aphorisms. He sounded like all the residents at the retirement home. If Hallie could hear his thoughts, she'd probably run away at a full sprint.

Fitz wouldn't blame her one damn bit.

When her fingers restarted their motion, they trailed up to teasingly brush across his nipples. "You know"—and her voice got low and breathy—"I can think of something else to do where we both win…"

"If you're speaking of sex, Ms. Scott, I'm shocked. Shocked you'd be so brazen."

"You've got your hand down *my* pants."

Yup. "Couldn't resist." It seemed a more prudent course of action than pursuing talk of a hazy future that wasn't a realistic option for them, and one in which Hallie hadn't necessarily expressed any interest. A man had his pride, after all. Not to mention a libido. "Isn't that why we locked ourselves away in here?"

She jolted upright, her hands flying from him as though his skin had scalded her. "I thought you were kidding. You really want to have *sex* in *here*?"

How did she not get it? Fitz was insatiable for her.

He didn't think it was because they were sneaking around half the time. It was Hallie herself. Her quick brain that constantly challenged him. Her sharp wit. The way she gave everything 100 percent effort. How she moaned and melted into him with every stroke and touch…

"Hallie, I want to have sex with you. *Anywhere.* Everywhere. I genuinely can't think of a location that would make me turn down that opportunity."

"The dining room table at your parents' house."

After staring at her for a beat too long, he glanced down at his crotch. Slowly, accusingly, he dragged his harsh stare back to her beautiful brown eyes. "Why would you say a thing like that? Why ruin a righteous erection? You just verbally stamped it down like you were trying to stamp out a cigarette." Fitz winced as if in pain. "You're a brutal, cruel woman."

Hallie was giggling, of course.

That had been his intent, *always*, to make her smile or laugh or ecstatically sigh. Fitz would never forget this moment with Hallie laughing. With the makeup lights putting an angelic glow around her head. It was the moment he realized where all this sappiness was coming from. Why it was gathering in a corner of his heart like tumbleweeds against a fence.

Fitz had fallen for Hallie Scott.

The mayor had fallen for the town librarian.

To be specific, Fitz was certain that he was falling in love with her. *That* wasn't supposed to have happened. They were supposed to be having fun, making the best of an impossibly antagonistic situation. This was…so much more. More than he'd planned on, more than he'd imagined.

More than Fitz knew what to do with. Like…what the hell to do next? Tell her? Wait to tell her after the election? Not tell her and wait to see if *she* said something along the same lines?

No. That wasn't fair, putting the onus on Hallie. Fitz was the one complicating the situation with all these feelings that refused to be ignored. He'd own them, tell her. And then hold his breath for her response…

"I wasn't planning on having sex in a green room today."

"Then you need to think bigger, Ms. Scott. Outside the box."

She gently tweaked his nose. "Let me finish! I was,

however, *hoping* to have sex with you today, somewhere. So, there's a strip of three condoms in my purse, in case that information is at all useful to you."

"Teamwork. We just executed perfect teamwork, which is exactly how I'd describe the fantastic sex we have, by the way."

"It *is* fantastic, isn't it?" Hallie wriggled her eyebrows smugly, then she curled back along his chest. A soft palm flattened right over his heart.

Fitz swallowed hard. Reconsidered.

This wasn't the time for a romantic revelation, or the place. Not on a couch that probably hadn't been cleaned in a decade. Not in a room that held the pervasive smell of hair spray and Febreze.

Not when things were humming along so smoothly between them.

Fitz circled back to the simplicity, the safety, of sex. He caressed her leg from her ankle all the way up to where heat pooled at the seam of her pants. "Honestly? I was on the verge of agreeing with you, but then I remembered your strip of condoms. I think we'd better do a test."

"*Three* tests," she corrected.

"Of course. My scientist sister insists that being thorough in data collection is key."

"Ugh." Hallie's head lolled back into the cradle formed by his arm. "Now you've reminded me that we've got an event at Cygnet Labs in three days. I'm a book girl, the very opposite of everyone up there. I don't speak scientist."

Fitz was right there with her. Luckily, he had a solution. "Then don't."

"Not your usual top notch campaign coaching—I don't get it."

"You know Blake works there. She's all science, all the time. My mother was horrified when she visited her at grad school and discovered she used a beaker from the lab instead of a measuring cup. Blake had baked blueberry muffins for breakfast. Mom was scared there were some residual killer germs or mouse DNA lurking in them and she was on the brink of transforming into a mutant creature."

Hallie harumphed. "A scientist would never risk cross-contamination like that. And I'm almost as certain a daughter wouldn't risk her mom's life like that."

"Correct on both counts. Let's just say my mom has the same lack of interest in science as we do, layered on top of a deep distrust for what happens on the microscopic level."

"So, once your mom didn't turn into an aqrabuamelu—"

Fitz cut her off with a double tap on her clavicle. He didn't want to let her words just wash over him. He couldn't guarantee he'd memorize all her random references—especially the literary ones—but he did have an intense curiosity, both about the world and what took root in Hallie's brain. "A what?"

"Hybrid mythological creature in ancient Mesopotamia. Body of a scorpion plus the arms and face of a man. I didn't see any sign of Caroline morphing into one at dinner the other night."

"No. Plus, this visit was a good fifteen years ago." God, it was so nice to just hold Hallie and talk about nothing. More relaxing than a beer and baseball. "Point is, Blake's a science nerd."

"Redundancy alert."

Ha. "Does the book nerd really get to call out the science nerd? Or do you cancel each other out?"

"Fine. Go on." Hallie squirmed into a position that put her lips up by his neck again and proceeded to drop soft, light kisses in distinct rows, back and forth.

"Blake does, however, have other things that occupy her time. She's a black belt in tae kwon do. Adores musicals.

Can't draw a stick figure and won't admit it, so she won't talk art at all. Super into politics, too. Good thing you're running against me and not her."

She shot her index finger up. "You're telling me *not* to talk to the people at Cygnet Labs like scientists, but rather just talk to them like normal people."

"Yep."

"That's both obvious and brilliant. Thank you." Hallie arched her back to look down at him. "Do we have to declare a mayoral winner? Can't we keep politely arguing and discussing for, oh, a year straight, like Katherine Hepburn and Spencer Tracy?"

Fitz would like nothing more. "Their movies only lasted ninety minutes."

"Ah, but their real-life affair lasted twenty-six years."

"I don't think we'd get anyone to come out and listen to us for twenty-six years straight."

Laughter gurgled out of her. "I don't think we'd get anyone to come out and listen to us for twenty-six *hours* straight. I was just warming up to discussing expanding this very community center when they called time."

"You don't mean you listened to Lloyd's suggestion about a mini-golf course." He said it as a statement, not a question, because there was no freaking way she would have.

"No. But racquetball courts would be good, and upgrading the study rooms with electronic whiteboards." Hallie tapped her finger against her lips. "Why not do a real expansion?"

"You don't want mini-golf. We have a climbing wall. What are you thinking of?"

"It's a great facility already. Big. Never full to bursting."

Fitz preferred using it to the too-small, too-old, always-packed gym at the yacht club. Or the golf club. "That's because people up at Cygnet use their own facilities."

"So why not make it inclusive to Crow Harbor residents? They don't have anything like it. It'd be a great lift to getting through the long winters. You'd be helping their mental and physical health with increased socialization. It'd establish more of a community between the two towns."

He'd thought Hallie was going to suggest something fun but expensive, like a heated connecting skyway to the library. Fitz hadn't expected *that*. Letting her down sucked, but he wouldn't give false hope, either.

"I don't have that power."

"Come on. If not the mayor, then who?"

Talk about a naive viewpoint. "I'm mayor, not emperor. Not Thanos, either. I can't snap my fingers and do whatever I want."

Hallie swept her legs off his, then scooted to the opposite end of the couch, sitting upright as though presenting an argument at an event. "You don't know how much you can do until you try pushing the needle. This town welcomes thousands upon thousands of tourists every week, from cruise ships to day trippers. It *can* be welcoming."

"Sure. And the Queen allows tours of Buckingham Palace, but only a few rooms. Not her private sanctum." Fitz didn't understand why she was pushing so hard. Nobody had asked for this. Crow Harbor residents weren't petitioning to join. Yeah, in *theory* it was a good idea, but trying to make it happen would be downright ugly, especially with the downtown marina expansion muddying the waters at the same time. "Opening up a private perk of residents to outsiders would cause, well, a ruckus is downplaying it. There'd be an outcry loud enough to be heard all the way up in Canada."

She jumped up, pacing to the empty costume racks and back. Her arms flailed out and up. "Owning the town isn't enough. Raking in the extra profit from the expansion, from the extra jobs, that can't be your dad's only contribution. You and your family have got to *lead* it, not let snobbery get in the way."

"You're calling me a snob?"

Hallie paused, then pursed her lips. "Not *you*, per se."

"Gee, thanks. Glad we haven't devolved to name-calling."

Hallie seemed...mad. This casual mention of the community center had escalated to a full-blown fight and Fitz didn't know why. It was like there was a bonfire all laid out at her feet that he'd accidentally struck a spark to.

What was really going on here?

A sharp flick of her hand turned on the overhead lights. "I'm calling anyone who isn't open-minded enough to share their largesse with their less fortunate neighbors a snob."

Fitz stood up, too, and tried to figure out how to defuse the suddenly volatile situation. And figure out what he'd done to send Hallie into such a snit.

"You're painting with broad brush strokes. Swan Cove's tax dollars paid for the community center. If we open to Crow Harbor, other towns may demand equal access."

She threw out her arms again, signaling utter frustration at his comment. "What would be wrong with that?"

Hell. So many things. She sounded like a heckler in a campaign audience. She *didn't* sound like a woman who'd spent the last few weeks poring over budget reports from the last eight years.

She didn't sound like *Hallie*.

"You're thinking as a regular person instead of a fiscally responsible leader. Where does it stop?" Fitz pointed to a row of show posters tacked to the wall. "How do you tell a card-carrying Swan Cove resident their kid can't audition for the spring play because Crow Harbor kids filled up the audition slots? I'm not saying it's impossible. I'm not saying it isn't a worthy goal."

"I should hope not." A sharp tug pulled the hem of her sweater back into place. "Equity across class lines is more important than following borders on a map."

In theory. Something to shoot for as a society, for sure. In actual practice, though, Fitz had to account for every dollar spent by Swan Cove—dollars collected from the people that, yes, lived inside its borders.

"Equity is the people who paid for a service getting to use it. You want to raise taxes in Swan Cove when we have to pay for all new gym equipment in a year because the usage increased by three hundred percent?"

That rocked her back. Literally. Hallie shifted her weight onto her heels, then stared down at the floor as if waiting for an answer to appear on the cement floor. Fitz waited her out silently. Since he didn't know what button he'd pushed to kick off this fight, he didn't want to say anything more than the bare minimum.

Finally, Hallie muttered, "Non-residents would have to pay membership fees."

Keeping his voice calm and nonconfrontational—although he was sure getting worked up by her attack at this point—Fitz said, "Membership fees keep the lights on and staff at the desks. They don't cover big things, which you'd know if you dug into the numbers instead of going off on an emotional tear about snobs and ordering me to use my practically nonexistent power."

Hallie held herself stiff as a board. Arms crossed, back straight. "I might not know as much as you, but I've only been at this for a month. You have years of experience to rebut my suggestions. Or better yet, come up with fresh ideas of your own. Like how to expand Swan Cove *without* hurting Crow Harbor."

Indeed, but it wasn't anywhere close to that simple. "Look, I'm just saying it isn't something that can happen without a lot of strategy and time and careful presentation. Not something that can be rushed through to win votes."

"You don't have to worry about winning votes, about changing things to benefit anyone besides your father's cronies. You just make sure your last name is on the ballot."

Holy shit. Fitz couldn't believe she'd thrown that in his face. He crossed the room in three swift, long strides to stand right in front of her. "Hallie, that's not fair. And it's not true, either."

With all the lights on now, it was easy to see the dull flush of red that crept up her cheeks. "I'm sorry."

He wasn't just mad that she'd said it. Her cutting words *hurt*. "You've sat on every stage with me. Heard me discuss issues, take stances that aren't necessarily popular with the movers and shakers in the room. You've watched me work, side by side with you, for over a month. And you're going to accuse me of not *trying* to win votes?"

"No, you're right. I shouldn't have made that accusation. Not to you, anyway."

Aha, now they were getting down to it. Fitz realized her unexpected rant wasn't about him at all. So, he tried to shove past his own hurt to whatever had wounded *her*. "Is this about my parents? About dinner the other night?"

Hallie huddled even more tightly into herself. "Frankly, yes. They were civil. They paid for the dinner that they didn't allow me to choose for myself, didn't make a scene in a crowded restaurant when I disagreed with them, but they weren't always polite to me. Or even nice."

"I agree. I told them as much the next day." Not even over the phone. Fitz had shown up at the house with no notice—which was enough to freak out his mom on principle alone—and read them the riot act. Said he'd been ashamed of them as parents and as people. "I told them that how they'd acted toward you was inexcusable and they owed you an apology."

"It hasn't come."

It was the smallest, quietest voice he'd ever heard from her. Fitz *hated* that his parents had made her feel so small. Hated more that he couldn't fix it. "I can't force them, Hallie. I wish I could. I sure as hell tried to shame them into it, but they're adults who make their own choices."

"I know. That's, um, sort of my point."

Oh. She was worried about them skewing the election results.

Fitz wouldn't allow it. He'd lead off all of the remaining campaign events by reminding people that ballots were confidential and that they should vote their own mind—not be influenced by anyone.

With gentle tugs, Fitz got her arms uncrossed so he could grip her hands. "My parents can't force people to vote for me. You're winning voters over. I see it happen at every event. What you say is resonating with people. Maybe they're sick of only Montgomerys on the ballot. Maybe they're tired of me. Maybe you've got a stronger message, or all of the above. You can't let one bad dinner get you this worked up. It doesn't mean the election's lost."

Hallie…wasn't squeezing him back. "I'm not this upset about the election."

"Then what is it?"

"It's us, Fitz. You and me." She pulled free and walked down—aka, the length of the room *away* from him—to the shelves full of wig heads. "Our secret…whatever this is. It's no good."

No. No. Fitz wouldn't let her give up on them. Hallie just needed to clear away all the distractions and focus on how well they *did* work together. "Uh, I think what we've got going on is very good. Extraordinarily good."

"In this about-to-expire secret bubble of ours, sure, but we've clearly got no future together. Your parents don't accept me as just a member of their town. If they found out we were dating, they'd go nuclear with their disapproval."

No point in lying. "They'd be surprised. Bottom line, though? They want me to be happy. And God, Hallie, you make me happy in ways I didn't even know I needed. They'll come around."

"It isn't just your parents. Lots of people in Swan Cove look down on Crow Harbor. There've been hecklers at the events attacking with that."

"Yeah, they do, and that bias is wrong. We'll work on that, as a community. It's also generalized. Has anyone specifically been rude to you at the library since you were hired?"

"No."

Fitz pushed his point harder, because he knew there were good hearts inside perhaps a shallower veneer of most people he'd grown up with here. "Sneered at you? Said you weren't good enough because you were from Crow Harbor?"

"Well, no, only since I started running for mayor, but—"

"Sounds like you're holding on to this prejudice with a death grip. My parents were total jerks, but once they get to know you, it'll be different. Same with anyone else who you call a snob. I get that you've been the victim of it, but times—and people—are changing. You've got to allow for that to happen."

"You're very optimistic, whereas I'm realistic. We were kidding ourselves. There's no point continuing to pretend. You and I just won't work. The mayor and the librarian who lost the race to him? No."

Fitz couldn't lose her. He couldn't let her walk away from him, not over something that wasn't even about the two of them. "See, you're conflating the election with our actual lives. It's a blip, a two-month experience that's about to end." Desperate, Fitz threw out a compromise. "Why not hit pause until *after* the election? Let the dust settle, and in a few weeks we'll start fresh?"

After picking up her purse, Hallie shook her head. "That's simply postponing the inevitable. No matter who wins, things won't be any different for us after."

And then she walked out the door.

It was over.

They were over, before they'd even had a chance to really begin.

Which was proof enough that being a Montgomery didn't mean getting everything you wanted…

Chapter Eighteen

"Good event, Ms. Scott." Fitz shook Hallie's hand.

She didn't *want* him to shake her hand. Even though they were on a dais in front of the fire station bay doors, with a crowd of fifty staring at them, Hallie wanted him to take her in his arms and hug her until she felt whole again.

Since there was zero chance of that happening, she returned his brisk shake. "Same to you, Mayor." Hallie didn't know what else to say. Technically, the end of this event was the same as all the ones in the prior weeks, because they'd never been anything but cordial opponents to the watching world.

But underneath, Hallie had known she'd see Fitz in a few hours, in private, and be able to tease him about the oceanfront wind tousling his hair and the wolf whistle it elicited from the very recently divorced-and-on-the-prowl Kelley Goss. Or kiss him proudly for the way he'd so skillfully arbitrated the shouting match over whether the fire department should go before or after the police in the Memorial Day parade.

Now Fitz was closed off from her, completely, because

she'd slammed the door shut.

Better to have done it now than in a few weeks, when she'd be a few weeks more head over heels for him. It saved Hallie's heart from, oh, an extra four hundred layers of scabs. It'd been the sensible choice. Sensible like a librarian…or a mayor.

Except Hallie didn't feel like either of those personas right now. She felt like a woman whose heart had been removed and repeatedly driven over by a thresher. Or whichever specialized tractor cut things up the most.

"Hallie! Thank goodness I found you." Randall hooked his arm through hers. Today he had three adorable yappers—two terriers and a pug—on leashes twining around his ankles.

"How hard was it to find me? I'm smack dab in the heart of town, with a microphone, and this event is listed on posters and websites."

"I looked other places first. It was hard." He pointed down at the panting mutts. "And you are needed, ASAP. A huge crisis that only you can fix."

Libraries really only had two versions of a crisis: a fire or a flood. It was a beautiful May day without a cloud in the sky—and without any billowing smoke. And why would Randall know about a library crisis? He certainly wouldn't enlist her to help with a dog-grooming crisis.

But Hallie was a rule follower. The rule was that when the word *crisis* was used, you dropped everything and helped.

She did take time to slowly remove her sweater from the back of the chair and fold it into her purse. That gave her a few extra seconds to drink in Fitz. The perfect break at the cuff of his tailored pants. The way his shoulders lifted the suit coat into a wide wall of light gray fabric. The little crinkle between his brows as he looked at Randall quizzically.

Being this close to him was both wonderful and horrible, like that first bite of the tip of the pizza that was so fantastic—

and scalded both your tongue and the roof of your mouth.

Randall dragged her down the stairs long before Hallie was ready to leave Fitz's proximity. He hurried her through the milling crowd and around the brick side of the firehouse. There, he gave a sweeping, courtly bow—one that looked very much at odds with his hot pink Bermuda shorts paired with a cream Cuban shirt. "You're welcome."

"For what?"

"I just rescued you."

Ohhhhh. That certainly made more sense than an actual crisis, but Hallie planned to make Randall squirm a bit and *admit* he'd lied to her. "What about your crisis?"

"Oh, it was real. The crisis was you being stuck with Fitz without the cushion of a pre-scripted event. Megan told me I had to evacuate you before any painful small talk got eked out."

So much for his squirming. The man was unrepentant.

He was also supposed to be uninformed about her very-much-in-the-past…by four days…relationship with Fitz. Trying to channel the snootiness of a Julian Fellowes heroine (what she wouldn't give to be wearing a shirtwaist dress and a giant hat tied down with a chiffon scarf!), Hallie declared haughtily, "I'm an adult. I can make small talk with my opponent."

Randall fanned himself with his straw trilby. "Nobody should have to shoot the breeze about the weather with their ex. That's a crime against humanity."

Yikes! Hallie shot out her hand to grab his wrist. Probably too hard, since he yelped and dropped the hat. The dogs immediately clamped onto it for tug of war. "You *know*? How do you know?"

"Megan had a client bring in three grandkids for trims. She got stuck. She'd planned to extricate you but was forced to call in reinforcements. I was happy to help." Randall's dark eyebrows drew together into a single caterpillar-esque line as he snatched back his hat. "I'm peevish about you not divulging this delicious secret romance to me from the start, but we'll save that dressing-down for *after* you've pouted and cried for a week and gotten him out of your system."

Funny how when you thought you couldn't feel any lower, Fate took a jackhammer and drove you six feet closer to the earth's crust. "I'm sorry. We'd promised each other to keep it a secret, because it wasn't an official thing, which meant it wasn't just my secret to divulge. Only Megan and Fitz's friend Everett knew because they were in on it from the start."

Randall palmed her shoulder in a quick, reassuring caress. "Your reasons—whatever they might've been—were, of course, valid. As is my right to have a teensy snit when you're up to it."

Ohhh. She dropped to a crouch, petting the pug to have a moment to swallow past the tears clogging her throat. Her friends were amazing. She'd find a way to make it up to him, pre-snit. Ana, too.

It was such a relief to be able to talk about her secret ex-boyfriend. Wow. When her life sounded like a nineties sitcom episode, it meant things had spiraled out of control.

"Fair enough. To reiterate, I am sorry. And as far as the other thing…it's going to take me a lot more than a week to get Fitz out of my system. I'm not sure I'll ever do it." In fact, it was taking a shocking amount of concentration to prevent leaning around the corner, scraping her cheek tight against the crumbling mortar between the bricks, and scanning for another glimpse of Fitz.

"Please." Randall dismissed the notion with a flick of his wrist that set the hat flipping back onto his head. "Handsome, rich, charming, thoughtful, ab-tastic men are everywhere. We'll get you a rebound hottie. Might not tick *all* the same boxes, but two out of five will still deliver a good time."

"I don't want a rebound. I definitely don't want rich. I want *Fitz*."

Randall cocked his head to the side and then tapped a finger against the soul patch she tried every week to talk him into shaving off. "I'm confused. Megan told me *you* dumped *him*. Did she get it wrong?"

"No." Petting the dog helped her tamp down—pretend to ignore—her feelings. Maybe she'd get a dog. Definitely not a cat. The spinster librarian-with-cat cliché was too depressing. "But I just got a jump on the inevitable. Fitz would've realized soon enough that we couldn't make it work. Or his parents would've forced him to do it."

He cocked his head to the other side. "I'm more confused. You fell for a man who still does whatever his parents order him to do?"

"No. I wasn't being precise in the description. Fitz wants, above all else, to live up to the duty, the responsibility, to take care of the town that his forebears have passed down to him as a sacred legacy."

"That's a heck of a lot."

"Yes. Yes, it is. Too much for a person to carry, in my opinion." It genuinely made Hallie sad to watch Fitz be jailed by the constraints of his family legacy. He so very much didn't want to be mayor—but also didn't want to abandon his family's post and all the citizens. It was a damned-both-ways scenario. The fact that he continued to choose the selfless-but-miserable option—well, it couldn't last forever. Hopefully, he'd break free before the *next* election. "Anyway, his parents would eventually remind him of this crushing duty, and he'd dump me. Or would have. That's why I jumped the gun. Not because I didn't…well…enjoy his company."

Randall pivoted, craning his neck left and right as if checking to be certain they were still alone. "Hallie? Were you—*are* you—in love with the mayor?"

"I don't know." She scrunched up her face, thinking, wondering if it even mattered putting a label on it now that they were over. "There was always this concrete wall in my head, with a flashing sign that said *this can't work out*. But the wall was crumbling, and I'd fallen hard for him. Very hard. Check out the bruises on my heart hard."

"I take it all back. No rebound sexcapades for you." He waved his arms in a big X, like a lifeguard signaling a swimmer to come in with semaphores. "That's the wrong prescription."

"Is there a right one? I'll pay whatever it costs." She stood, lifting a Boston terrier up with her. It was even softer. Could it be available? Because crying into her pillow every night was only setting herself up for a mold issue down the line.

"Yes. You need to throw yourself into a project."

Hallie's projects consisted of reading…and researching what books she wanted to read next. Or reading about the fascinating hobbies dabbled in by the characters in her books. In real life, a project sounded daunting. "Like that macramé planter you and Ana worked on after her long-distance fling with Werner fell apart?"

"No. That wasn't therapy, either. We were testing YouTube tutorials to see if they're actually useful or just staged."

All she really remembered was the hideousness of it lying in a knotted lump in Ana's living room for months on end. "And?"

"And have you ever seen that planter hanging in either of our houses?"

"No, thank goodness. I figured someone from the future hopped in a time machine and sent it back to the seventies where it belonged."

Randall clapped his hands twice, snapping her out of the macramé musing. "Your project—an all-consuming one—

should be running for mayor."

What? *Randall* had been the one who used the fancy app to design her campaign poster. Did he think that was just another fun project with no real-life application? "Uh, that's what I've been doing. Have you not listened to any of my stump speeches?"

"Yes. Blah blah new blood blah blah blah new ideas. I mean that you have to *win*."

"Please refer to my previous comment."

"Hallie, you're trying. I'll give you that, but until a few days ago, you were also sleeping with the opposition. That's not exactly cutthroat politics."

Dammit, he was right.

She'd dropped her guard. Still argued the issues, of course. Vociferously. But it had been more of a drawing back the curtain to show an alternate view than trying to take Fitz down. It'd morphed into a clash of ideals rather than a cage match from which only a single victor could emerge.

"So what do you suggest?"

"You need help from someone who knows things. Me? I've got enthusiasm and the random knowledge that can fill in topical jokes in a dull speech about parking meters. Patent granted in 1938, BTW."

"Hilarious," she drawled.

"Megan and Ana don't know anything either—aside from how much we wish we could do a better job of helping you."

"I don't need help. I've got facts and—" It was beginning to sound like the same rant she'd made to Fitz when she'd so snottily turned down his offer of help, which she'd ended up regretting.

Hallie tried never to make the same mistake twice. That was a perk of lifelong learning. Being slapped in the face with the truth that history would repeat itself unless you actively made the choice to change something.

In this case? That "something" was her stubborn self. And she knew exactly where to go to find assistance. Or rather, to *whom*. "Randall, you were a champion. Thank you for the rescue. Thanks even more for the pointed but stellar advice. If you'll excuse me, I'm going to go execute it." She handed over the pooch.

"Execute? You can't joke about things like that, Hallie. Not in today's political climate."

"Not assassinate. Sheesh. I'm executing—putting into motion—the plan you just handed me on a silver platter." Hallie kissed him on the cheek, then darted back into the dispersing crowd. She'd noticed someone earlier out there and was counting on the fact that everyone and their dog would stop to greet Felicia Montgomery and she'd still be here.

Sure enough, she was on the bright turquoise wrought-iron bench where Hallie had spotted her during the event.

"Hi. Hello. Could I take you for coffee?"

Wordlessly, Felicia lifted her cardboard cup. And a single salt-and-pepper eyebrow.

"Oh, right. I might as well be upfront. This isn't a request for a social chat. I need to ask you for a favor. Coffee, or donuts, or whatever you like is on offer. You could come to the library, not that it's that comfy. We could go down to the beach—" Hallie broke off, noting two things. First, that Felicia's mandarin-collar silk dress didn't look appropriate for beach combing. And secondly, *yowza*, she was babbling. Rambling. Nervous as all get out.

"Aren't we friends, my dear?"

Not sucking down margaritas on a Friday night type of friends, but Felicia had helped her secure the librarian position. She'd been her champion. She'd been the first Swan Cove person to be friendly to Hallie. Her constant pop-ins were full of wry observations, a keen appreciation for books, and sage advice.

"Yes. We're friends, and I'm grateful for it."

A sharp elbow banged against Hallie's. "Then tell me what you want and stop acting as if you're asking me to give you a piece of my liver. Which, for the record, I'm quite open to. It regenerates, you know. If you're my blood type, you're in luck."

The older woman's matter-of-fact attitude went a long way to calming the raging case of nerves that had turned Hallie's stomach inside out and set her tongue to warp speed.

"Actually, I'm O negative, a universal donor. You should be asking *me* for a hunk of my liver."

"That'd be more my brother's speed. Preston doesn't consider a weekend well lived unless his liver's curled up in the fetal position, whimpering."

Evidently, she'd lost all control of the conversation. And thinking about Fitz's dad would only get her ire up and derail her more. "Regardless, I don't actually need an organ transplant, but I do appreciate the offer."

Felicia set her cup on the ground, then folded her hands in the lap of her deep red skirt. "Spit it out, then."

"Here? Out in the open?" Hallie didn't even want to *think* these thoughts in the open, let alone verbalize them. Sharing her, ah, vulnerability should happen in a dark room the size of a closet.

Elbow cradled in her palm and wrist tipped backward, Felicia patted her own cheek. "Now I'm intrigued. What sort of favor can't be asked on a park bench? Not sexual favors. I'm far too old for you. Do your parents want to explore the idea of a threesome? Are you sussing me out on their behalf?"

Organ transplants and threesomes. What on earth kind of favors did Felicia Montgomery get asked on a daily basis by the residents of Swan Cove? "Um, no. At least, I'm not here as their intermediary. I don't really have an, um, bead on their thoughts on the subject."

There she went again, letting the woman lead her astray. That wasn't the behavior of a mayor-in-the-making. Hallie had to either speak out now, or drop any pretense of having the ability to win this race...let alone run the town after that.

"All right." Felicia waved off her suggestion in a singsong tone. "I'll stick a pin in that. For now."

Hallie tucked her hands under her thighs to prevent fidgeting. Or worse, overly gesticulating with them. "It pains me to *ever* ask for help, but—"

A peremptory hand flap cut her off. "Why?"

"Why what?"

"Why don't you like to ask for help? There's no shame in it. You think Armstrong would've trod the moon without a full crew helping him get up there? And that string of presidential firsts—Catholic, then Black, then a woman—they didn't claw their way up to leading the most powerful country in the world as a solo act."

"No," Hallie said slowly. She had, quite literally, never looked at it that way before. It...felt almost like cheating. Too easy, too simple, and yet with the same reward in the end. "I suppose not."

"Do you think it makes you appear weak?"

Yes. Absolutely. Didn't it?

Stalling, Hallie forced out a dry laugh. "Are you going to charge my insurance a hefty fee for this therapy session?"

"I'm serious. Call divulging the truth my fee for this yet-to-be-named favor."

As if this wasn't already hard enough! "Well, then, yes. I've always been the smart one, the one with all the answers. It was what set me apart. Hard work, proving myself, was the only way."

"The only way to what?"

"To do better than my parents. To be more. It was their dream for me, and it became my own. To escape Crow Harbor, get a scholarship, get my dream job."

"It's certainly one way—you've proven that—but steadfastly refusing help is not the only way, I promise you. Perhaps that's a good lesson to instill in a child to keep them motivated. However, harder is not always better." Then she winked. "Although there are certain unmentionable circumstances when harder *is* better."

Hallie swallowed down a half laugh, half snort. Maybe Felicia *would* be fun to throw back margaritas with, despite being old enough to be her mom. "I came to ask you for help out of desperation, not from a position of strength."

"Well done." Felicia patted her leg. "Part of being smart is knowing what would be better served to call in for reinforcements."

"Be a team and not a dictator?"

"Precisely."

"In the spirit of being fully truthful, I'm still quite desperate, but I have received your excellent point. I'm absorbing it, and I promise to strive to apply it whenever appropriate."

"Splendid. Now, what do you need?"

Hallie pointed at the platform still draped in bunting and with the *Montgomery vs. Scott* sign overhead. "I need to know how to win this campaign. How to be a good mayor."

"Those are two separate items."

"Long-term, yes. Short-term, though, my weaknesses in campaigning serve to point out where I'd be a weak mayor, which is mainly in the numbers department. I do words. Words are my thing. Numbers are the thing I ignore whenever possible."

"You don't have to be good at numbers to be mayor."

"Dealing with the budget is a big part of the job."

"Not always." Felicia stood abruptly. "Walk with me. You were right. This should be discussed with a modicum of secrecy."

What could be secret about Excel spreadsheets? Although, at this point, Hallie was willing to acknowledge it might be necessary to make a smelly potion of eye of newt just to understand them.

"Before you think me the worst aunt in the world, I'll say I adore my nephew. What I'm about to tell you, I would've gladly shared with him—had he asked. One who seeks help often gets more than they expected."

This sounded...juicy. It definitely sounded like more than the phone number to a guy three towns over who would agree under cloak of secrecy to explain budgets to her. "I couldn't agree with you more. Fitz is a good man. He's just possibly not the *right* man to lead this town."

"Ha! Don't I know it. The boy's miserable. He's so busy trying to do the honorable thing that he isn't making time to do what he wants." Felicia slanted a glance at Hallie. "Or perhaps he has made a bit of time...lately. I've had my suspicions."

That look contained far too much certainty, not that Hallie would confess a thing—especially since there was no longer anything *to* confess. "You'd have to take that up with the mayor."

Although it wouldn't surprise her one bit if Felicia had sniffed out their secret romance. She didn't appear to run the town's government or businesses, unlike the men in her family, but she did seem to have eyes everywhere and an uncanny ability to know *everything*.

To her surprise, Felicia wasn't leading her to the privacy of the shore. Instead, they seemed to be headed toward the *Gazette* office.

"Before you moved here, there used to be a city manager,

in addition to the mayor. Someone to run the store while the mayor was the public face. Someone to deal with the budgets while the mayor greeted tourists and gave stirring eulogies."

Well, that was brilliant. "Like the Prime Minister and the Queen of England?"

"Far less glitzy, but yes. Fitz's idiotic and disreputable Uncle Jeremiah wiped out the position when he was mayor."

"Why? The division of labor seems so much smarter." It sounded like an utterly foolhardy decision.

"It was." Felicia tucked her arm through Hallie's and leaned closer. "It also enabled the city manager to discover that Jeremiah was embezzling. He fired him under blatantly trumped-up charges sweetened with an immense severance package and got rid of the position from the books so nobody else would catch him."

Her head was reeling. The previous mayor—Fitz's uncle—was a criminal? And he'd cooked the books too? How was this a secret?

She almost burst out with that question, until the oh-so-obvious answer popped into her head. There'd been a cover-up, of course, to keep the Montgomery name and legacy pristine.

While she didn't for a moment suspect Fitz of being involved, it did cement her belief that it was more than time for someone with a different last name to be the town's figurehead. "How long did that work?"

"That only bought Jeremiah another year in office before it all fell apart." Felicia paused at the old-fashioned Dutch door to the *Gazette*. "But the position of city manager could be brought back. It would take some convincing of the council. Not much, I'll bet."

"It would solve my worries about not having the budget experience to help Swan Cove."

"Precisely. You don't need to be an expert at everything.

You can hire someone with better qualifications and know-how. That's my two cents on how to help you both win and be a good mayor." She pushed inside, a bell ringing. "Oh, good. Sylvia, I'm pleased you're the one holding down the fort today. Will you please help Ms. Scott here go through old editions to gather information on Eli Koppelman?"

A woman with a deeply lined face that proclaimed her at least ten years past retirement squinted through purple-framed cheaters. "The old city manager? Are you stirring up trouble, Felicia? And if so, might I say it is about *damned* time."

So...not a complete secret to the town. Interesting. That might make it an easier sell to the council if any of them were aware of the illegal acts that precipitated the job being cut.

"I'm not *doing* anything." Felicia tugged her forward and then flourished her arm at Hallie. "Ms. Scott, as a thorough mayoral candidate, is merely educating herself on the history of Swan Cove's management."

"Right." She shoved her glasses to the top of her head. Gave an open-mouthed wink. "If that's your story, I'll stick to it."

Felicia put a finger to her lips. "I'd prefer you not mention this visit at all."

At this point, Hallie was wishing they were all dressed in trench coats. This had a distinct film noir feel to it. Aside from sneaking around with Fitz, it was, well, the sneakiest thing she'd ever done.

Sylvia shrugged. "We go way back, you and me. You say it never happened, then it didn't." Tapping stubby fingers on the blotter, she stared at Hallie. "You'll vouch for her?"

"I'll do better than that." Felicia patted Hallie's shoulder. "I'll *vote* for her."

Welling up wouldn't be very mayoral. It took some rapid eyelid fluttering to beat back the tears, though. Felicia *believed* in her. On top of that, asking for help *hadn't* been the humiliating train wreck Hallie had anticipated.

She couldn't have Fitz, but she might be able to be a success at this mayor thing, after all. It would have to be enough...

Chapter Nineteen

Strolling through a hospital wasn't on Fitz's list of top ten ways to spend a Friday afternoon, but with Hallie by his side, it should've been a *little* fun. Everything was, with her.

Well, she was by his side. But he was miserable.

They'd insisted together on adding today to the list of campaign events, but not to campaign. Healthcare workers had been stretched far beyond their capacity the last few years. For many, taking time off to grocery shop was nearly impossible, let alone nipping out to listen to mayoral candidates speak.

So, Hallie and Fitz had decided to do a walkthrough of the wards, handing out cookies and lemonade, and thanking as many as they could. The cookie-making was *supposed* to have been done together. Hallie had promised to wear an apron and nothing else.

Yeah, none of *that* happened. Once they broke up, Everett had conscripted his home economics classes to bake the cookies. Not to make Fitz's life easier, or so he claimed, but to teach the students that even small acts of charity can make a difference.

Fitz had been grateful.

Hallie had passed along her thanks to Everett directly. And now here they were, sharing the event they'd dreamed up, and not having any fun at all.

At least, he *assumed* that was true for Hallie. That she was as sad (aka, heartbroken) and awkward (aka, freaking uncomfortable) and at odds (aka, ready to tear her hair out while simultaneously screaming and kicking a wall) as he was.

She looked beautiful. Like a...what were those flowers around the swan pond? A tulip. A pink top with a scalloped neck that reminded him of the shape of petals was tucked into grass-green pants. The colors perked up the drab grays and greens of the hospital decor. The prettiest thing about Hallie, though, was her smile. The big, bright smile full of warmth that she bestowed on every nurse, doctor, and orderly.

The smile Hallie gave him when they shook hands at the hospital door? It'd been perfunctory, at best. Still probably more than he deserved, because he'd hurt her.

Not knowingly, of course. Fitz had counted on her to have faith in him. To believe that he'd find a way for them to be together, once they put all this election craziness behind them. It was his fault for not acting sooner, for not doing more to shore up that faith. He'd let her down.

Fitz would regret not stepping up sooner, not confessing that he was falling in love with her. He'd regret that for the rest of his life.

"This went well, I think." Hallie tilted her chin up, waiting for his response.

"Yeah. They seemed to appreciate our taking the time. You had a great idea."

"*We* had a great idea," she corrected. "Being on different tickets doesn't mean we can't overlap on the important things."

That sounded just like the Hallie of a week ago. Of course, there was still a cluster of staff around them, which explained her cordiality. "Thanks, all the same. No press, just connecting with people—this was the best event of the whole campaign."

"Agreed."

Then that awkward bubble of silence descended, the one that surrounded them every time they finished spitting out either arguments or shallow pleasantries.

It sucked.

"Look, Hallie, I—" Fitz reached for her arm, but just as his fingertips grazed her cool skin, a nurse stepped between them.

"Mr. Mayor? May I have a word?"

Hallie faded away from him, like a sun ray being blocked by a cloud. Damn it. "What is it?"

"In private?"

Strange. He followed her around the corner into an empty hallway. "If you're angling for the cookie recipe, I can't claim any knowledge. The Swan Cove High School home ec class made the magic happen."

"No, this is about your mother. I assumed, since you didn't say anything, that you didn't want people to know she was here. I can take you to visit her now."

"My mother?" That was out of left field. Not just sick, but sick enough to be admitted? "What's wrong?"

"Is that a test, Mr. Mayor?" She winked, like she'd already peeked at the answer grid to a pop quiz. "You know I can't divulge patient information."

The nurse wouldn't tell him, because Fitz, as the devoted son, was already supposed to *know* all about his poor sick mom.

"Right. Of course." He threw her a two-fingered salute.

"We get a lot of VIPs here. Good to see you're doing everything to protect their privacy."

"Absolutely. And I promise we're treating your mother like one of those VIPs. She's in the presidential suite, right around the corner."

Way to be low profile. Why did his mom *need* a hospital room that had a sitting room attached, a convertible sofa bed and an oriental rug when she evidently wanted her admission to be so under wraps that she hadn't even told *him*?

It was just a few steps through a secure doorway before she knocked on a half-shut door with a green light softly glowing overhead. "You can go on in. If she wanted privacy, the light would be red."

If she knew Fitz was out here, it'd probably be red with sirens going off after the way he'd dressed her down for being rude to Hallie at the dinner.

"Thank you. And thanks for looking out so well for my mother."

When he first entered, Fitz didn't even see the hospital bed, just the room set up like a hotel version of a sitting room. Green-shaded lamps keeping it warm yet dim, a brown leather sofa. A brass and glass coffee table that no doubt offended his mom's sense of classic style.

It took turning right in the large suite to find his mom. She was propped up in bed, wrapped in a quilted cream bed jacket. So...snazzy for a hospital patient, with tidy hair, but her ubiquitous pearls weren't around her neck. There was a smear of blood on the cuff of her jacket near what must've been an attempt-gone-wrong at an IV site. IV tubing came out of the opposite arm propped on a pillow and her skin was both pale and gray at the same time.

"Mom, what's going on?" Fitz rushed to her side, carefully kissed her forehead, and curled his fingers around her hand.

She frowned—probably at his uninvited pop-in. "It's

nothing."

Nice try. "I don't care how great your insurance is. You don't get a hospital room unless there's something very much going on."

"*You* might not." She lifted her bruised arm, winced, then slowly tapped her sternum with the hand skewered to the IV. "I'm on the frequent flyer plan. I check in every few months, get some meds, and go home a whole new woman."

"Mom, don't brush this off. Tell me what's wrong."

Her eyelids fluttered shut. "I didn't want to burden you."

The dramatic martyrdom wasn't anything new. It was, in fact, one of Caroline Montgomery's signature moves… and thus one Fitz was expert at countering. "Well, I didn't want to inherit Dad's overbite, but I did, and braces fixed it. You tell me what's going on with you, and I'll do everything I can to help fix it. Or better yet, find the right trained medical professional who can."

"There's no fixing this, I'm afraid. I must simply live with it." She must've heard Fitz's sharp indrawn breath of utter frustration because her eyes popped back open to lock on his. "I have multiple sclerosis."

A gut punch would've been easier to take.

Panic hit first, then sorrow for the struggle ahead for her to live with a chronic disease. Then Fitz remembered that his totality of knowledge about it came from a mystery series he'd read back in college. Better fact-check the biggest question in his head. "It isn't fatal, right?"

"No, my darling boy. You are stuck with me."

"God, I'm so sorry." He squeezed her shoulder and then wondered too late if her joints were sore. "Why didn't you tell me?"

"I didn't want to be a distraction. You've made no secret of your distaste for campaigning. Worrying about my condition wouldn't be prudent on your part."

"So you *just* found out?" Then why had she mentioned being a frequent admission at the hospital? Before Fitz crowned himself most unobservant son on the planet, he needed to lay out how *much* he'd overlooked.

"Well. No. I found out about eighteen months ago."

"Christ, Mom." He toed over a chair that looked like it belonged at a castle's dining room table and straddled it backward. "How can I spoil you with feel-better flowers if you don't tell me you're feeling lousy?"

"I'm not at my best when I'm having a flare up. Forgive me for taking the time to wrap my head around it before broadcasting my chronic illness to the world."

Wow. "Not the world, Mom. Just me."

Of course, he got her urge for privacy. At *first*. But what did it say about their relationship that she still hadn't confided in him after a year and a half?

It said that no matter how much he tried, he'd never be the son Caroline Montgomery wanted him to be. Which, to Fitz, was a giant neon *Stop Trying* sign.

Fitz wondered if his sister knew about all this. Probably. With Blake being a scientist, his parents had probably texted her for advice from the start. Which was fine. This wasn't a sibling rivalry thing. Strictly a parents versus Fitz thing.

Sometimes, Fitz wondered why he still tried. He loved his parents. He wasn't sure if the feelings were reciprocated. They seemed to love the mental image of their son carrying on the family legacy. Whether or not they loved the actual flesh and blood version of Fitz that followed his own mind? That was still up for discussion.

Well, God forbid they discuss their feelings. The Montgomerys had two settings—disappointment and pride. Nothing else ever seemed to register.

"Truthfully, it took me a long time to get to the acceptance stage." Caroline licked her lips. "It has been a struggle."

That admission must've cost her dearly. Fitz wouldn't push any harder, for today. He poured some water from the plastic pitcher (for this fancy room, it gave the illusion of frosted glass) and guided it to her mouth. "Would you please remember, going forward, that you can lean on me?"

"Thank you."

He pulled the tray closer so she could reach for more water herself. "I'm going to go home and google everything. New drug trials, alternative therapies."

Hallie would've enjoyed digging into this research with him.

Damn it. No matter how hard he tried *not* to think about her, he didn't succeed for more than ten minutes at a time. Because he freaking missed her so damn much.

"There's no need for you to trouble yourself. I have a good team. I received my official diagnosis at the Mayo Clinic."

Yup. That was his mom. Name-dropping, no matter the subject. Fitz propped his chin on arms crossed over the back of the chair. "Why are you in here now? What happened, specifically?"

"Oh, it's my eye. Optic neuritis. High-dose steroids are already turning it around. This isn't the first time. At least I know what to expect."

I don't, Fitz thought. He wondered if that was why the lighting was so dim. Did it hurt? Could she see? But it seemed as if his mom was parsing out precisely as little information as she wanted him to have.

"It still sounds scary. Did something happen to make it reoccur, that maybe you could work to prevent? A drug? A lifestyle change?"

"Since you ask"—Caroline folded the sheet more neatly across the muted blue blanket—"my condition *is* exacerbated by stress. Your poor campaign performance has been extremely stressful to witness. I tried not to let it get to me, but..." Her voice trailed off as she pointed at the blood pressure cuff rhythmically squeezing her upper arm.

Fitz scrubbed his palm over his mouth.

Trying to tamp down his bitterness, he looked at the drawn blinds, the fake candle sconces, the muted plasma screen TV showing a travel show about waterparks (proving his mom hadn't figured out how to work the remote). He looked anywhere but at her. Because she was sick. *Hospital* level sick. Clearly, not up to taking the full force of the anger that fired through his veins.

All the while knowing that she was using that sickness to try and manipulate him. Was this the famed Montgomery family legacy? What he'd bent over backward to live up to?

After swallowing hard—and then again—Fitz managed a measured tone. "You can't lay that on me. Especially after not bothering to let me know that you had an illness that *could* be affected by stress."

"Another day of IV meds and I'll trundle off home to rest. As long as you win next week, I'll be able to relax and fully recuperate."

"That's not fair. It's also not something I could begin to promise to make happen."

"That much is clear, but we've solved that for you."

"We?" Fitz didn't like the sound of that.

"Derek brought us some useful information."

Fitz bit back an oath. "I fired his ass."

"That's a fight for a different day. Luckily, he is loyal and has continued to work for the family. It turns that out the librarian's—"

"Ms. Scott," he corrected. She wasn't a job. She was a fully fledged person.

"Her father, over in Crow Harbor, is bankrupt."

"That's awful."

Oh, man, that sucked. Fitz knew how close Hallie was to

her parents. She'd take on their struggles as her own.

Hell. If Hallie even knew. It finally registered that it'd taken Derek's muckraking to dig up that morsel. Maybe she didn't know yet.

It was probably weird that he wanted to be there, to hold her hand when she found out. To support her while she was a pillar of strength for her parents. Weird because they were definitely over, except that her deciding they were over in no way turned Fitz's feelings off.

It'd sure make his life easier if there was a...love spigot her words turned off.

"No, Fitz, it is a very useful piece of information. You can immediately begin spreading that morsel around so that Swan Cove realizes a Scott isn't qualified to handle the town finances. That will guarantee you the win."

Oh hell. The bankruptcy must be the scoop that the *Gazette*'s editor tried to share...

Then it hit Fitz. One of his parents must be who gave the scoop to Bronson. He didn't know which was worse: digging it up in the first place or trying to spread it around like poison.

It was wrong on so many levels.

Fitz didn't believe in dirty politics. Didn't believe in turning over every single private piece of a person's life to try and find the few times they'd been human and made an error in judgment. You didn't win by making the other guy look bad. You won an election by making yourself look appealing to the voters.

He wanted to blame it on that little creep Derek, but this had his father's fingerprints all over it, too.

Not to mention that Hallie's dad in no way deserved to have his name blackened, his secret outed. Mr. Scott wasn't the one running for public office.

This was a shitshow, no matter how you looked at it.

And if his mom could bring it up from her hospital bed?

Well, he'd damn well end it right here, too.

Fitz stood, flipped the chair back around into its original spot, then shoved his hands in his pockets. "I don't want a guaranteed win. I only want to remain mayor if I earn it, which I won't do employing these tactics."

Caroline's head flopped back against the pillow. "Why must you make everything harder on yourself? This is just like when you made friends with that exchange student your junior year. You would've had a stellar final project if his limited command of English hadn't held you back. We offered to get you paired with someone else, but you insisted on helping the underdog."

"You don't slough off less than perfect people. Min was great. We learned a lot from each other. He didn't hold me back." Fitz cocked his head. "You know he lives here now? Works up at Cygnet Labs. I helped them lure him here after he got his doctorate at MIT."

"The point is, we can finish this farce of a campaign with a few simple sentences whispered in the right ears."

"It's only a farce if you *interfere* with it. Democracy, Mom, the thing I'm supposed to be protecting."

"You're protecting the family legacy."

Nope.

Not anymore, because a legacy stained with wrongdoings wasn't something he wanted to uphold or protect anymore. The thing with Uncle Jeremiah was bad. What if it wasn't the first such incident?

The impossible weight of family history lifted right off Fitz's shoulders.

Aaaaand he was done with his mom's guilt and guiding, too.

Done with her machinations. Done with the impossible task of pleasing her. Fitz would send her the obligatory flowers. He'd even go down the Google rabbit hole about MS, because Caroline was his mother.

But he was absolutely done with letting her run his life. Fitz wasn't entirely certain how to stop her. That was a problem for another day. The intent was what mattered now.

"You keep making this about the family name instead of what's best for Swan Cove. As the mayor—at least for now—I won't stand for your games. I've already shut down Bronson. I won't use the information on Gene Scott, and I'd better not hear a single person alluding that they know about it. I'm genuinely sorry about your stress, but I'm not stealing this election. I'm not letting you and Dad do it, either."

Fitz kissed her forehead in farewell and tuned out the sharp words his mother hurled at him as he headed back into the hallway.

He didn't want a single voter to check the ballot box because of his name. And he didn't want the conditional love from his parents to be only because he shared that name. It was tempting to put the same ultimatum in front of his father, except Fitz had no clue how to enforce it, how to put a hammer behind his words.

Hallie probably had some good Norse myth stories about Thor and his hammer she'd share if she were here.

What a mess, especially when he remembered Hallie broke up with him because of his name. Kind of made him want to rip off the monogrammed cufflinks at his wrists and chuck them into the Atlantic.

And there were still five days until the election. Five days to figure out how to make the expansion still palatable to his town while protecting another, even if nobody else cared. Fitz had to take a stand, which could make him persona non grata around here.

What the hell else could go wrong?

Chapter Twenty

When Hallie's mom opened their front door and saw Megan, her face dropped. "Oh. I...didn't know you were coming."

"As soon as she heard where I was going for dinner, she basically hopped in my car. You know Megan adores your cooking." Hallie hugged her mom and wondered why she was so taken aback. Her parents had always treated her best friend like another daughter. Not like a *guest*. Not like someone who needed a formal invite. This was weird.

She'd needed Megan to come along as a buffer. Hiding that she knew about their purported bankruptcy wouldn't be easy because Hallie didn't lie to her parents.

But if it was true? And they hadn't told her? That was their choice, and she'd respect it, no matter how it complicated her campaign.

At least, that was one way to look at it. The other way was to stop pretending, confront them, and warn them that certain crapbags who owned Swan Cove might spread news of their downfall in a public forum, which would humiliate her parents.

Hallie had no idea which option was best. Luckily, Megan would keep the conversation flowing because she didn't know any of this, which was lying by omission. Which Hallie hated.

If life was this stressful campaigning for mayor, what would it be like if she was actually elected?

"Hi, Mrs. S. I can't resist your tamale pie. Or getting a big helping of hugs from you and your hubby." Megan gave a hug but used it to make a face at Hallie that indicated she was confused, too.

"Well, that's always nice to hear." But Pam stayed in the doorway, blocking their entrance.

"Mom, aren't you going to let us in? Because the flies are sure using the open door to crash the party."

She gave a whole body shake, as if the flies were actually doing zoomies up her green apron. "Fine. Yes." And then she tucked her bob behind her ears *five* times before Hallie stopped counting. It was her mother's classic nervous tic. The question was—why was she nervous?

They beelined for the living room, but Gene called out, "In the kitchen," so they U-turned back into the hallway and into the kitchen.

Its look was *nobody could afford to remodel since the seventies*. Fake mahogany cupboards, cracked yellow linoleum, and an avocado refrigerator that Hallie had to avert her eyes from every time she had the flu because it doubled her nausea. Pam kept it spotless. They ate most meals at the kitchen table.

It wasn't even set yet. Her dad was in his usual seat (back to the door, ever since his binge of *The Sopranos* convinced him it was the safest seat). When he spotted Megan, his hand rose to his temple as if a puppet master had yanked on a string. "Oh. Megan. This is—"

"A surprise. Yes. We get that," Hallie said. "What is going on with you two?"

After a wordless exchange, Gene got up to hug first his daughter, then Megan. "I'm sorry, but you know what? This is fine."

"Huh. Mrs. S. gave me the 'fine' treatment, too." Megan scooched closer to the doorway. "If you want me to leave, just say so."

"No." He snagged the sleeve of her rainbow-striped cardigan. "Stay. We *want* you to know. We just weren't brave enough to tell you. We hoped that Hallie would take care of that for us." Gene pulled out two chairs. "Sit, girls."

If there'd been creepy organ music playing, the tone of the room couldn't be more sinister. "Is one of you sick?"

Once all four of them were settled, Gene reached for his wife's hand. "No, but we are bankrupt."

Talk about a good news/bad news situation.

Imminent death being ruled out gave Hallie about a half second of relief before she processed the rest of his statement. So, the cat was out of the bag, but they didn't need to know she'd gotten a heads-up on that status. "I'm so sorry. That's awful."

"It's just rotten," Megan said, reaching across the table to squeeze their hands.

At least them bringing it up meant she could get all her questions answered, because Hallie didn't understand.

They'd worked the same jobs their entire lives. They weren't blowing their money on Nigerian princes (well, not after that first time, thanks to Hallie's intervention). Maybe they'd…oh…balanced the checkbook wrong? Because, yes, they were that archaic they still had a checkbook in its little pleather case. "Are you sure?"

"We've already started the process with the lawyer. It isn't a threat. It's a done deal."

Looking back and forth between her parents didn't wring any more info out of them. Sheesh. So she prompted. "What happened?"

"Planning and hoping doesn't always work out," Pam said. There was a catch in her voice that tore at Hallie's heartstrings.

Gene cleared his throat. "We used all our savings to buy a share in a fishing boat."

Holy crapballs. That sounded, well, like it would've wiped out their savings. It sounded expensive.

Her mom's arms spread wide. "A whole fleet of 'em."

This story was only getting more dire.

Gene karate-chopped his hands down, parallel to each other. "Sharing the ownership allowed for us to make technological upgrades." He made another double-chopping motion. "Then we'd share the wealth. It was a solid plan. Until the boats were lost in the hurricane last fall."

"All of them?" Megan squeaked. Very high. Very loud.

"Enough."

That in no way should've led to bankruptcy. Hallie was more confused than ever. "But didn't the insurance safeguard against you losing your money?"

Gene scrubbed his palms over his eyes and then left them there, pressing against his browbone like he had the biggest headache in the world. Which he probably *did*. "We had to cut corners. Everyone who bought in was a lifelong fisherman or captain. We'd never had boats sink. Didn't need the insurance."

"Oh, Dad." It didn't lessen her sympathy. No, it increased it, because Hallie was certain her dad was beating himself up over the poor choice on top of being broke.

"It wasn't just your father." Pam patted his hand, stubbornly jutting her chin as she looked both women square in the face. "We agreed to take the risk. It was my decision, too. Don't blame him."

It'd been a brave move. Risky and ill-advised, yes, but

thoroughly brave and strong, which was how Hallie had *always* thought of her father. "I don't blame either of you, not for trying to get ahead a little."

Megan nodded. "You regret one hundred percent of the chances you don't take. Better to not live with regret."

Pam's eyes welled up. Gene rubbed the back of his hand across his lined forehead.

Hallie *hated* that they'd been so worried about talking to her. They were a family. All four of them. And they'd get through this together. "Can I help? Get you back on your feet?"

"No, thank you. We'll manage. We got ourselves into this, and we'll pull ourselves out. We're just…" Pam's voice drifted off. And then, to Hallie's horror, her mom started full-out crying. She alternated words and hitched-in breaths. "We're so sorry, sweetheart. We must be such a disappointment to you."

Never. Never ever. Hallie rushed over to hug her mom. It was from behind, and awkward, but still felt necessary. Once she sat back down, she laid it out. "Don't let me catch you thinking that, let alone saying it. My love and respect for you hasn't diminished one bit. It was a mistake. A very well-intentioned one, however."

"But we feel so awful—this could reflect badly on you."

Well, yes. Hallie refused to add to their guilt, however. Breezily, she waved it off. "That's highly doubtful."

Gene hooked his thumb at the window in the general direction of their downtown. "Greg over at the diner told us a man was nosing around, asking questions about us."

"Maybe he's heard about the crazy fun time that is your monthly pinochle game." Megan wriggled her eyebrows comically.

It didn't work as a distraction. Gene doubled down on his frowning until his eyebrows practically touched. "I'm serious.

For a stranger to come to Crow Harbor and know my name? There's something hinky going on there. That jerk running against you is the only one who'd care to spread the news that your family can't handle money."

That...had not occurred to Hallie.

She was certain her dad was half wrong. Fitz would never, ever pull an underhanded scheme like that. No way would he have been on board with the plan of making her parents' downfall public knowledge. Not because of their intimate relationship, but simply because he'd never run a dirty campaign.

His father, on the other hand? Preston would do it in a hot second. Had, in fact, all but promised as much over dinner. Her only hope had been that they'd gotten it wrong somehow. And it hadn't been much of a hope.

"Well, if that's the case, I should be apologizing to *you* for disrupting your life. For opening you up to public ridicule."

"Bah. We brought this on ourselves, like your mother said."

The more Hallie thought about it, the more she burned with righteous indignation. Megan kicking her under the table wasn't helping—mostly because she had no clue how to interpret said kicks.

This was a private matter. Her parents were good, hard-working, salt-of-the-earth people who didn't deserve to be dragged through the mud. This experiment of hers had gone too far.

"I should drop out of the race. That's the most surefire way to spare you a public humiliation."

"You're not listening." The chair squeaked badly as Gene rose to grab four beers from the fridge. He moved slowly, as if his entire body was sore from holding in his confession. "I know what I did was stupid. I'm man enough to take my licks."

"Of course you are. Still, it doesn't sit right that *my* life should make a spectacle of *yours*. Not just as your daughter who loves you, but as a person."

Pam spread her hands wide, palms up. "It is what it is."

For crying out loud. That had always been her mom's reaction to bad news. Not defeatist. Just accepting. It drove Hallie nuts.

"Maybe not. If I drop out of the race, whoever knows about this won't bother going public with their findings. Your secret will be safe. And six weeks ago, weren't you the ones trying to convince *me* to drop out before *I* got humiliated and lost?"

Gene slapped his hand down on the table. "We can't let you do that. We can't let you leave here tonight until you promise to stay in the race."

"Why?" It made no sense. Why would they fight her on this? And why *now*, of all times?

Another wordless exchange between her parents. Pam knuckled the wetness from underneath her eyes. "Because we were wrong, sweetheart. As long as you want to win, and want to try your hardest, then you've got to keep going."

"All we ever wanted was for you to do more, to have more than us." The beauty of her dad's oft-repeated simple statement filled her with gratitude.

It was also a karate chop of a truism to her head because it made Hallie realize that nobody had ever said that to *Fitz*. That he'd never been told *his* wants were a priority. Nobody had given him that gift of freedom.

It broke her heart all over again.

Her family looked to the outside world like it had so much less than the Montgomerys, but in Hallie's estimation, the Scotts had so very, very much more.

She'd continue on with her campaign, for the simple reason that she wanted to and still believed that she could do a good job.

It wasn't all Hallie wanted, though. Now she wanted to figure out a way to heal Fitz's heart. Whether he won or lost, it seemed clear that he didn't want to be mayor. Not just to her, either. The people closest to him saw it, too.

She wanted to help him figure out what he *did* want. Maybe, if she was lucky, that would include her.

Because to hell with the town and his parents. People that would use her parents' bankruptcy to vote against her weren't people she respected. Kindness mattered more than legacy or money. Compassion. Caring. That was what being mayor should be about. Not spreading nasty gossip or snickering over misfortunes.

Did she sound naively optimistic? Undoubtedly.

But her parents believed in her, as did her friends. And Fitz. So she'd work to nudge along everyone else by doing her best, which would include being with Fitz again. For real, this time. Hallie still didn't have a clue how they'd get there.

Aiming at a goal with all her heart, though…she was *great* at that.

• • •

Fitz glowered at the back—and the enormous cow-print backpack—of the retreating freshman. "Why do kids keep barging in here and interrupting us?"

Everett sighed as he shut the door. "There's a sign above the lintel. Says Open Door Policy. You've walked by it a hundred times. My *job* is to be available to the students at all times."

"Your job is to discipline the students. Isn't that the main skill set of an assistant principal?"

"Meh." Everett loosened his tie printed with baby Yodas. "You take the good with the bad. Nothing in my job description, however, stipulates being available to the *mayor* at all times."

Didn't that get encompassed by the description of best friend?

And it wasn't like he dropped by on a daily basis to hang out. Today's visit was an emergency. A necessity. Otherwise, Fitz would've embarrassed himself by...standing at the swan pond screaming at the sky and shaking his fists? Heading into the bar and ordering six shots of Jager at once?

Or, the worst case scenario, going to the library with a guitar and serenading Hallie to beg her to give him another chance.

Fitz couldn't sing. Couldn't play guitar, either. So dropping in on Everett at the high school was the only option that didn't get him ridiculed and worse, pitied, two things that pretty much guaranteed he wouldn't win the election.

Fitz looked at the poster of a line of penguins walking, with the last little guy coasting on his belly. It read *Mediocrity: just because we accept you as you are doesn't mean we've abandoned hope you'll improve.*

"Okay. You got me. I pulled rank and used my title so your guard dog of a secretary would let me in without an appointment."

A sharp laugh barked out. "No reason to bother next time. Susan thinks you're a hottie. She'd escort you straight over a bleeding, crying student if it got her a date with you."

Fuck. He was done with people saying they wanted something from him, which, admittedly, was a bad reaction from a guy trying to get an entire town to *want* him to work for them as mayor.

"It wouldn't." Fitz tried to ignore his irrational anger. Susan had a mini-crush. She was nothing like his mother who only wanted him for what he represented instead of for who he was inside. So he dug deep for a lighter tone. "First of all, I'd stop and administer first aid to the kid. Secondly? I'd never date Susan. She's a power walker. I mean, good on her for exercising, but those people look freaking ridiculous. Like they have to pee."

Two thumbs up signaled his friend's agreement. "You've probably got another five minutes before we get interrupted again. It's the end of the school year. Tensions are high. Mistakes are being made, desperate measures being taken. Want to finish your rant?"

Fitz had, technically, already finished. He'd told Everett the whole sordid story of what went down in his mom's hospital room. How she wanted to cavalierly ruin the Scotts just to make sure the Montgomery name remained on the door of the mayor's office.

How she'd kept her serious, major illness from him. How he wanted things to be different with his parents, but nothing ever changed.

The freshman had barged in right before Fitz rounded off with a soliloquy about how much he missed Hallie. How sitting next to her at events was torture. How he wanted to be with her no matter the consequences.

Everett didn't need to hear that. Not again, anyway. He'd already heard it plenty over the past week as he tried to keep Fitz distracted with a full viewing of the Fast & Furious series.

He shoved to his feet, rubbing the back of his neck. "Preston and Caroline have been manipulating me since the day I was born. Which, by the way? Even *that* wasn't my choice. Mom had a scheduled C-section because she wanted to get it over with in time to make her annual girls' weekend of Christmas shopping in Manhattan."

Everett one-fingered his glasses higher up his nose. "Dude, I agree with every nit you've ever picked against your parents except that one. Her body, her choice. You gotta drop that from your list of complaints."

Agreed. Fitz hated that it'd even slipped out to the front of his brain. It was proof he was way past the end of his rope. "Why do you think you've never heard me mention it before? I'm just so damned mad. So frustrated."

"It's about time."

"What's that supposed to mean?"

"Uh, that they've treated you this way forever. Your unflinching sense of duty's kept you from doing anything about it. The way you want to honor your family legacy is admirable, but it's gone on too long."

"The town's still here, the duty's ongoing."

"Nope. That's where you're wrong. The town's here—and so are other people willing to step up. This isn't a ragtag settlement back in the 1600s that you're holding together with grit by the skin of your teeth. We're a functional society. Sure, we need a figurehead. It doesn't have to be a Montgomery, though. It doesn't have to be *you*."

Fitz had come to that conclusion himself. It had hit him like a bolt of lightning the first time Hallie did great at a campaign event.

She cared. She wanted to do right by Swan Cove. She was smart enough, for sure.

She'd be a good mayor. That took the onus off him. Theoretically.

Except...he knew his parents would continue to do everything in their power to defeat her efforts. And at this point, Fitz felt it was weighted more toward them maintaining the status of the family name rather than choosing what was best for the town, let alone what was best for their son.

"They won't let up. They won't let me step aside. I'm trapped. I do my damnedest to do my best for this town while I'm trapped—"

"You do." Everett lifted a hand to start ticking off points on his fingers. "You're calm in a crisis. You *listen* better than anyone I know, including our trained school counselors. You always step up, lend a hand when needed. You're universally likeable. You follow through on every commitment, including the ones you hate."

"—but that doesn't stop me from feeling the metaphorical metal teeth sinking into my ankle, holding me down, keeping me stuck where I don't want to be."

"Fuck. All right." Everett rolled his neck, cracking it. "It was bad enough watching you give up Hallie. I can't watch you give up on yourself, too."

Acting like there was an obvious other path out there... it couldn't be a cruel joke on his friend's part. The sneaky bastard had an idea. "What's the alternative?" Fitz asked cautiously.

"You're loyal to a fault. So I've kept my mouth shut. I knew you'd have to be pushed to your limit to listen to this suggestion. Sadly, I think you're ready to hear it."

Now Fitz counted off on his own hand. "Uh, I don't like my job. I'm unfulfilled by it. I don't *like* my parents. Or respect them much anymore, even though I'll always love them. Pretty sure I met the woman of my dreams and was on the brink of deciding I was in love with her. And I lost her because of the aforementioned job and parents. Yeah, you could say I've hit my limit."

"You need to turn the tables."

The revelatory suggestion might as well have been in Finnish. Fitz didn't understand it at all. He leaned an elbow on the institutionally beige file cabinet. "Is there more? I'm willing to turn in my man-card if I can get an instruction manual to skim..."

After rolling his eyes up to the acoustical tiles with at least two dozen pencils impaling them, Everett gave a sigh that indicated further explanation would be as painful as carving it line by line into a totem pole.

"Fine. I'll spell it out. You need to expose *their* dirty secrets."

"Whose?"

"The Montgomerys. Preston and Caroline. Not your aunt, obviously. She's awesome. And not your sister, either."

Yeah. Those two had never pushed him to run for mayor. Never acted like their family was single-handedly responsible for keeping every citizen of Swan Cove upright and breathing, either. "Because Blake's in her own science-land bubble ninety-nine percent of the time."

"Right. Your *parents* are the problem-causing Montgomerys. We need to get you out from under their thumb and prove that their mightier-than-thou shtick is just an act."

"They're not perfect," Fitz murmured.

He thought about his mom caring more about appearances than sharing her genuine, frightening illness with her son. Thought about his dad's quarterly trips to D.C. to "visit an old friend," which he'd admitted to Fitz was code for visiting his mistress.

Everett snorted. "That's an understatement."

"But they do bend over backward to pretend that they're—no, that *we're* all perfect. That our last name magically confers some extra helping of brains and patience and fortitude and saintliness."

"It's not pertinent to this current emergency discussion, but as your friend and former roommate, I have to point out that you are definitely *no* saint."

"Thanks for that." Fitz cupped his ear. "Hear that? It's my grandparents rolling over in their graves."

"You don't curl up the tube of toothpaste as you go."

Yeah, they'd fought about that at least once a week. Even after Fitz bought Everett a case of his own to shut him up. "Why bother?"

"You always have to order last at a restaurant in case

someone else's order sways you. Do you know how annoying that is?"

"Why do you think I do it? Bugging you is one of the high points of my day." They grinned at each other, relishing their shared years of history. It was just the break Fitz needed to get his feet back under him.

"I'm just saying that *everyone* has things they regret. *Every* family has black sheep."

Hell.

Fitz lunged forward, arm raised in the unspoken signal for a high five. Everett did not leave him hanging. The sharp slap of sound reverberated through the office. "You're brilliant."

"Can I get you to record that? Maybe do a TikTok I can show the students?"

"Are you even allowed to be on TikTok with your job?"

"Sure, but it's a time suck. I'm not on it. The school has a secret account. We use it to check on students we're worried about, see if they're displaying warning signs of bullying, self-harm, suicide."

"Man, I thought my job was bad." Fitz sat back down, crossed his forearms on the desk, and leaned forward. "You've come up with a win-win scenario. I don't have to publicly shame my family. I just have to *threaten* them with exposure."

"You mean your uncle's backpedal down to Miami?"

Fitz had filled Everett in on the secret and ignominious *real* reason behind his uncle's relinquishing his title as mayor and moving to Florida. "Yeah. That's a scandal they've already bent over backward to hide."

"I think you're right. They'd do just about anything to not have that revealed."

"On the one hand, the citizens of this town deserve to know what really went down, but wiping the slate clean of Montgomerys as mayor should be good enough." Fitz also planned to reach out to the ex-city manager and see if he could give the man a glowing reference to help him out. The Montgomerys had cost him one job. Anything Fitz could do to help him find another was the least of the payback he deserved.

"Yeah. The money was repaid. Too many years have gone by. Dredging it up won't fix anything." Everett pointed finger guns at Fitz. "*Threatening* to, however, should fix all your problems with your parents."

This was shaping into a viable plan. "The cost of my silence will be their promise to stay hands-off from now on. Hallie and her parents will be safe from their games, too. I'll quit the campaign. Then I can live my life."

"I like how you've found a way to stay loyal to your family legacy and still orchestrate what you want. You're not the kind of man who would put your family through that. However, your parents don't know that you don't share their taste for playing dirty. So yeah—you don't end up with any guilt. Way to go."

"Thanks." Fitz glanced at the clock. Problem solved with one minute to spare. His friend was *good*.

"Except for one thing." After a practice flick, Everett whipped another pencil into the acoustic tile overhead. Then he looked Fitz dead in the eyes. "You can't quit the campaign."

"The hell I can't!" Had he even been listening?

Quietly, Everett said, "Hallie wouldn't want to win that way. Not by default."

Shit.

Everett was right. The reason she'd given for initially accepting a slot on the ballot was wanting to get him off of it. This was truly a competition. Librarian versus mayor. He couldn't deny her the possibility of an earned win.

He pushed out of the chair to pace from the windows across to the bank of battered file cabinets. "Okay. This is what brainstorming is about: getting an idea and then patching the holes in it. I stay in the campaign—it's only two more days. If Hallie wins, that's great. If I win, I resign and ask everyone who voted for me to accept her as mayor."

"Will that fly? Legally?"

"Legally, all I have to do is demur. But I want to go the extra distance. Give her the official nod, and make sure that they know I've got full faith in her."

"Might not be an issue. You know *I'll* vote for you, but I heard her suggestion to bring back the position of city manager went over like gangbusters."

"Because it's a damn good one." Fitz had burst with pride for Hallie when she'd laid out the plan at their most recent event. "Ever since Bronson told me the whole story about my uncle, I've been thinking about bringing back the position. It'd mean I wouldn't have to pay the accountant to help me do my job and keep the city's finances safe anymore. It'd be a layer of protection to prevent anyone from abusing the power of the office again. I just didn't know how to bring it up without throwing my uncle under the bus."

There he went again, being torn between family duty and doing the best for the town. *Again.* It had to stop.

A knock on the door was immediately followed by two heads poking in. "Mr. Reynolds, can we talk to you about the candygram delivery schedule for the last day of school?"

"Two minutes, girls." Everett rubbed his hands together as if trying to make a spark appear. "Let's keep working on this plan tonight. It needs to be airtight. Burgers? The pub?"

"Steaks, at the Beaumont. I'm buying. I owe you for helping me come up with a plan to get my life back."

For the first time, Fitz believed it could happen. He'd be able to do whatever he truly wanted.

And what he wanted to do most was check out his librarian…

Chapter Twenty-One

Even though she'd lived in Swan Cove for five years, Hallie had only been inside its iconic opera house once. Tickets to their season were way outside of her price range. So she openly goggled at its ornate Rococo gilt flourishes on every wall and ceiling. It was a stark contrast to the two-story rustic saloon mostly constructed on the stage—sets for *La Fanciulla del West*.

Two months ago, she would've felt out of her element. Today? All she felt was pride that her small town had such a sterling reputation for its summer operas that they pulled in big names from all over the country to star.

Hallie would be walking onto that stage in just a few minutes when the winner of the election was announced. Not as a laughingstock from the wrong side of the tracks. As a genuine contender for mayor who'd garnered votes.

She just didn't know how many…

"How ya holding up?" Ana put an arm around her waist and leaned over to touch heads briefly. "Because you look fantastic. Smart but approachable."

"Isn't that a coincidence? That's *exactly* what you said this outfit would look like when you laid it across the foot of my bed and ordered me to wear it tonight," Hallie said, tongue firmly planted in her cheek.

Still, she was grateful her friends had done the legwork and given her the closet makeover. The white boatneck dress had big watercolor splotches of blues, oranges, and pinks across it—a little dreamy, a little feminine, but paired with a white blazer to keep it businesslike.

Ana beamed, evidently not put off at all by the sarcasm. "See? You're a good listener. Great skill set for, oh, being a mayor."

"Fitz is a *great* listener," she said wistfully. He had such a knack for making a person feel like they had 110 percent of his attention, no matter how mundane the conversation.

"No. Nonononono." Ana shook her head briskly, long dark waves careening over her shoulders. Then she put a finger perpendicular to Hallie's lips to shush her. "You can't mope tonight of all nights. You can't pine after the guy you chose to break up with when you're about to crush him into a fine powder."

Who knew it was possible to spit out so many inaccuracies at once? Hallie batted away her friend's hand. "First off, I'm not moping. I'm *pining*. There's a difference. Moping is just sadness. Pining has a top layer of wishing for what you know you can't have."

"I prefer my thesauruses to be inanimate, thank you very much, and preferably with a speckled calf leather binding and original wrappings."

Hallie would *not* let Ana distract her by dropping rare book terminology that often made her drool with want. "Also? I didn't *choose* to break up with Fitz. I simply acknowledged that it was a foregone conclusion and acted accordingly."

"You can spin it however you want. Bottom line?" Ana

dropped into a chair and put her feet up on the one in front of her. "Fitz didn't dump you. *You're* the one who made the call."

"I ended things so he wouldn't be forced to choose between me and his family. *I* did it to make it easier on *him*, because I care that much." She pushed Ana's dusty boots off the green velvet upholstery. "Besides, aren't you supposed to be on my side, bucking me up?"

A sharp tug at the hem of her blazer pulled Hallie down into the adjacent seat, and then Ana twisted to look at her full-on. "Sometimes being on your side means making you acknowledge the thing you're trying hard to ignore."

"What's that?" Hallie cast a quick glance at the rapidly filling auditorium. She didn't want anyone to overhear this conversation.

She also kind of didn't want to be having it immediately prior to joining her ex on stage, for the simple reason that her breath still hitched in her throat every time she thought about Fitz. Even in a thought as barely there as an air kiss.

There was nothing barely there about Ana when she decided to open the bay doors and drop her classic truth bombs. She was the bluntest in their little group—but also unerringly accurate with her observations.

"There was no foregone conclusion about you and Fitz. The odds weren't impossible, just stacked against you." Ana put a hand on her hip and made the giant silver hoops brushing her collar dance as she shook her head. "Do you want to know my hot take?"

"Probably not."

"You got scared."

Hallie winced. The truth indeed hurt. "I'd like to upgrade my response to *definitely* not."

"You realized it'd be hard to fight the mighty Montgomery machine on two fronts—as mayor and as Fitz's girlfriend. You knew his parents would move heaven and earth to replace you at his side with someone more wealthy, more cultured, and more appropriate. You instantly regressed into that teenage bookworm who never felt like it was possible to fit in. The one who was too smart to have a lowbrow conversation with the jocks or the average students. Who wasn't pretty enough to be catapulted out of nerd-dom, but that was okay because it gave you more time to read."

Wow. *Wow.* "Don't hold back or anything."

Ana smirked. "That ship has sailed, crossed the equator, and dropped anchor." But she squeezed Hallie's shoulder. "I think you're the bee's knees, Hallie. I also think you've got a reverse chip on your shoulder from growing up in Crow Harbor and from being every single cliché about a librarian. You're more than your job. I just wish you could see it."

Oh. My. Goodness.

That was more or less what she'd encouraged Fitz to see about himself.

How could she have not looked in the mirror and realized that, while her hang-up stemmed from a different place, it was essentially the same as his? Somebody stuck in a predetermined box wrapped in other people's opinions, ones that weren't necessarily true at all.

She'd flipped open the flaps of her box to run for mayor, but when it really counted, when she had this fabulous, funny, charming, kind, *hot* man to fight for, she'd hunkered down.

Hallie *had* been scared. Ana was so very right, like always. And she'd put off figuring out how to fight for him until after the election. That'd be fear, yet again. Ohhh, Hallie was so disappointed in herself, and yet so grateful to Ana for helping her figure it all out.

"You're like a really good masseuse. You dig your elbow into that emotional knot until I'm writhing in pain, but as soon as you're done, I feel a thousand times better." Hallie bent and flourished her arm in a half bow. "You're right and wise and I'm so lucky to have you as a friend."

"Damn straight you are."

The revelation had lifted her spirits for about thirty-seven seconds. Just as quickly, though, they plummeted again. Because realizing she'd essentially chickened out meant brainstorming post-election wouldn't make a difference. Breaking it off with Fitz wasn't reversible. "But I'm too late."

"For what?"

"To fix this. I must've hurt Fitz terribly when I didn't bother to fight for him. How could he ever trust me again with his heart?"

Ana rolled her eyes. "Dramatic, much? Just because we're *in* an opera house doesn't mean you have to soliloquize like a dying soprano."

Of course, she couldn't understand. Ana had never teetered on the brink of a great love, like Jane and Rochester, or Claire and Jamie Fraser.

Or Fitz and Hallie…

She wanted the chance to at least *see* if that could be their future. She wanted the chance to be the mayor, be a good girlfriend to Fitz, and not have his family and/or the town hate her. It in no way seemed akin to asking for the sun, the moon, and the stars to be handed to her.

On the other hand…Hallie had zero idea how to make it happen.

Just like she had zero idea if there was a real chance of her winning the election. That was the other thing—okay, maybe the only thing at this point—that Ana got wrong. "Also? I'm not about to crush him. The Montgomerys have been de facto owners, parents, and rulers of this town for generations. They are as uncrushable as marble."

"That's only one way to look at it. You could also point to their long history as making people feel ripe for a change.

Some people vote *for* a candidate. Others just want to vote *against* someone. I think if we get a cluster of people doing both of those things, you've got a solid chance."

Hallie's stomach had knotted when they first began talking about Fitz. It knotted in such a way that even the sailors on the whaling ship *Pequod* would be impressed by their tightness. Thinking about the election, however, gave her a whole new set of knots.

"I'm nervous," she admitted in a near-whisper.

"You can be thirteen percent nervous," Randall said, suddenly joining the conversation from the row behind them. He slung an arm around their shoulders. "Just enough to give you an edge and not be cocky. The rest of you, however, has got to be confident."

The sight of the layers of red, white, and blue bandannas around his neck—that she absolutely recognized as the ones they used on the big dog breeds at his grooming business—should've made Hallie smile. Randall adored all things election/democracy related. He claimed that voting for politicians had all the fun of voting for a couple on *Dancing with the Stars*—just amped up times ten.

"I'm confident that I know the difference between the three Brontë sisters. Even more confident I can name the distinguishing characteristics of each Hogwarts house." Hallie tidied the ends of his red bandanna. "I have no confidence about what will be revealed on this stage in, oh, fifteen scant minutes."

"Uh, were you having an out-of-body experience at your last two campaign events?" Ana tapped the top of Hallie's head as if checking for an echo. "How did you not notice the tide turning in your direction?"

"That's a tad hard to gauge with my opponent sitting next to me." Not to mention all the blood rushing away from her head and ears to keep her heart pumping in triple time.

Felicia had given her the hint. Opened the door, as it were. Hallie had done all the work to verify and then determine how and when she could reactivate the city manager job.

And if the budget allowed for it.

"I'm not suggesting you missed people chucking roses at you, but as soon as you proposed bringing back the city manager position—well, it looked like a flock of prairie dogs...wait, is it a flock?"

Randall gave her the long-suffering look that Hallie gave readers who didn't know if it was John Grisham or Stephen King who wrote legal thrillers. "A group of prairie dogs is called a coterie."

Megan plopped into the seat next to Hallie. "Oh, that's fun! Kind of sounds like they're attending a nineteenth-century salon with tea and macarons."

Ana set her jaw. "Fine. It looked like a *coterie* of prairie dogs popping up their heads and taking notice. There's a buzz all across town that you want to make big moves. At least with everyone younger than Preston Montgomery's cronies. You've got a real shot. People love a fresh idea."

Hallie couldn't wrap her brain around it. "The thing is, I started this to prove a point."

"*I* started it," Megan refuted. "As the best birthday present ever. Well, mostly to get you to shut up about what could be done better."

"*That's* the thing." She patted Megan's thigh in their white capris. "A few weeks ago, I would've said this campaign was all your fault, but now it truly *has* turned into the best gift ever."

"I know." Smugness rolled off her like the smelly waves of smoke from the sage she'd burned when Hallie moved into her apartment.

"I never intended to win, just to shine a light and convince the mayor to make changes himself. But now I actually *want* to win. That's why I'm so nervous. I've met so many people, learned their opinions, and gotten to know Swan Cove so much better in the last two months than in all the years I've lived here."

The campaign had also given her the gift of Fitz. Even though he'd been more of a loan than a gift, Hallie would always remember how he'd made her feel, how much fun it had been to be with him. She didn't regret a moment they'd spent together—fighting and flirting—despite how much it hurt every day to *not* be with him anymore.

"Hallie, will you join me for a moment?" Felicia stood just beyond the doors to the hallway.

She scrambled out across Megan. "Thanks for all your help—"

Felicia wrinkled her nose. "Stop that. No need to get maudlin. I wanted you to know your parents are here."

"But they said they weren't coming. They, ah, didn't want to be a distraction." The story of their bankruptcy, shockingly, hadn't ever been in the *Gazette*. No hecklers had brought it up at any event.

When she'd checked in with them yesterday, they were still loath to "embarrass" her, no matter how many times she'd insisted that simply wasn't possible.

"I heard. It's nonsense." As usual, Felicia wasn't pulling any punches. "I collected them and put them up in the Montgomery box. You need their support tonight."

Hallie wanted to gush out her thanks, but she didn't want to get snapped at. "That's one heck of a favor. I'll owe you."

"I'll call it in right now." She took Hallie's arm and led her backstage. "Give him another chance. You're good for each other. And you'd be an invigorating couple at my dinner parties." A little push at the small of her back sent Hallie toward the dressing rooms.

And the unutterably handsome man standing there.

...

Fitz knew that the record for a human holding its breath was twenty-four minutes. He'd made the mistake of joking about heroically lasting two minutes swimming laps, and his sister had coolly informed him just how unimpressive he was. Trust Blake to bring the science facts (aka, kill the fun) to any and every situation.

Thing was, now it was his turn to contact Guinness because he'd been holding his breath for two hours, ever since he'd gone to enlist his aunt's help. Fitz didn't think Hallie would've agreed to meet him alone at his own request.

He didn't blame her.

She had to be hurting as much as he was. Staying apart was self-preservation. Except he hoped to get her to listen long enough for him to fix everything between them, the way he should've done weeks ago.

Seeing her in the dim lighting didn't relax him. There was every chance she'd bolt away after Felicia, now that she'd seen him, just like she had after dumping his ass. This time, though, he wouldn't let her get away.

"Hallie, please. Five minutes. Just let me talk to you."

"There's nothing left for us to say. We'd simply go in circles and end up in the same miserable spot."

"Not true." He eased forward a few steps as the door clanged shut behind his aunt. "We only go in circles if we stay on the same track. I'm proposing we go off-roading. A whole new path, a whole new direction."

"I'm not trying to be difficult, but car metaphors don't really work with me."

"I'll start over." At least she hadn't budged. Yet. "Hopefully, we both will. Come with me."

Hallie raised an arm to point at the three rows of red-velvet curtains. "Fitz, we have to be on stage soon. You know, so one of us can be declared mayor?"

Precisely why he needed to talk to her *now*. "Rand McCallam likes to give speeches. He rarely gets the chance. He'll be rambling on for ten more minutes than allotted. We've got time." He grabbed her hand and pushed out the heavy fire door.

Nine o'clock on a Monday night meant the streets were deserted. A good portion of the town was inside the opera house, waiting on the election results.

Fitz slowed his walk. Better not to rush the last few steps to the swan pond. It might be the last time Hallie let him hold her hand. No better way to do it than under the winking stars and the bright moon reflecting off the ocean. "You look beautiful tonight."

"Fitz. Don't. You don't have to give me polite platitudes. There's no audience."

"Sorry." Not sorry. He wouldn't, couldn't, hold back tonight. This was a *lay all your cards on the table* moment. "I'm about to offload a whole string of facts on you. That's simply the first one."

Hallie's smile was tenuous and full of regret. Fitz never wanted to see that smile on her face again. "The sentiment is appreciated, then, but we can't go backward."

"Thanks for that segue. I'm all about moving forward tonight." He took a deep breath. Jammed his hands in his pockets. "Starting with the assurance that I've made sure you'll win or lose tonight solely on your merits. There were some, ah, sketchy shenanigans that my parents tried to pull."

"You mean about *my* parents' bankruptcy?"

"Aw, hell, Hallie. I'd hoped you wouldn't find out the dirty depths of it. But yes. I'm really sorry they're having such a hard time. Will they be okay? Do they need a loan to tide them over?"

Hallie's jaw dropped. "You're too good to be true. How

can you be so gracious? Offering to help people you've never met? Offering to loan your own money to people who obviously don't have a great grasp of how to handle it?" Because he wasn't a bank doing a business transaction. He was a man helping out someone who needed a hand to get back up. "I don't need to know them. I know *you*. I know they helped you become the woman you are today. And I know they matter to you. So if they need my help, they've got it."

"Thank you. Sincerely. But they won't even take my help." She leaned a hip against the railing around the pond. "How did you stop your parents from spreading that rumor around? Seems to me it would've been something they shouted from the rooftops to secure you as mayor."

Fitz grinned. "I blackmailed 'em."

"What?" The surprised jerk of her head made her ponytail bob.

"I'll tell you the whole story once the election hoopla winds down tonight. Short answer is that I learned a secret that would reflect *very* poorly on the family name. I threatened to do my own rooftop shouting about it unless they backed off. Off of you and off of me. Off of the whole town."

She pursed her red-slicked lips. "Does this secret perhaps involve your uncle?"

Ha! "Should've known your thirst for researching would've turned that up, no matter how well hidden. Good for you. Yeah. I leveraged that. Turns out my mom is sick—another long story—and they've decided to spend more time at our house in the Bahamas. The weather will be kinder to her. That's the official spin, anyway. End result? They'll both be gone and hands-off of Swan Cove."

A couple of beats went by as she slowly squinted. "You... you wouldn't really play that dirty."

It freaking delighted him Hallie saw through to his core like that, in a way that, apparently, his parents never would.

"Nope, but they don't realize it."

Hallie's suspicious squint morphed into a smirking smile. "I think it'll be interesting—and probably quite good—for this town to figure out how to do things by itself."

"Like I said, a new path. New leadership." Fitz hooked a thumb back toward the theater. "I think you'll win tonight, Hallie. I know you *should* win. You'll be a great mayor for Swan Cove."

"Thanks." Hallie dipped her chin. "You, ah, weren't as horrible a mayor as I made you out to be, you know. Once I dug into how and why things had to happen for governance here."

"I know. It doesn't matter, though, because even if I win, you'd better be prepared to take over—I'll resign right there on the stage." God, it felt good and official to say it out loud. Which was why it'd slipped out loudly enough to startle a swan into a frenzy of wing-flapping.

After a sharp gasp, she asked, "Why?"

"A little personal off-roading. I'm taking your advice."

"I like the sound of that. Doesn't even matter the topic, since I give great advice."

"You'd better be right. I'm going to work at integrating Swan Cove and Crow Harbor. It's a two-pronged plan. I joined the expansion committee."

"Why?"

"To keep them from hurting the fishermen of Crow Harbor. The expansion's a good idea for this town. There's no downside. Only for the fishermen we're cutting off from the access to their route. I'm proposing we build them another one."

"Different access to the harbor?"

"Yeah." He pointed across to the water. "We'll widen that canal and adjust the marina plans by a few blocks. Then build a drawbridge to make it all work, at our expense. Crow

Harbor fishermen won't be impacted at all."

Hallie steepled her fingertips at her mouth. "This is all your idea? Because it's brilliant."

"I had help. Talked to the fishermen. Went down to the docks and solicited ideas. We came to it together, and it's the only way expansion will go forward. It'll have zero to do with who sits in the mayor's office."

"That's one heck of a prong, Fitz. I'm going to stick with calling it brilliant. I'm so proud of you."

That sounded good. He felt like he had momentum with this speech, enough momentum that it might catapult Hallie right back into his arms.

"The second prong is me moving my full-time attention to the community center. There, I'll be working on programming and expansion to benefit as many people as possible. I can still help the people in this town—just on a one-on-one basis."

Another gasp. If this kept up, he might have to get her a paper bag to breathe into. "Really?"

"Everything's in place—except for my title." As if the thought had just struck him, Fitz covered his mouth, then pointed at her. "Maybe *you* could help me come up with one, since you're the queen of words?"

She looked up at him from very coy, half-lowered lashes. "I'd need to hear, in copious detail, what you plan to accomplish, which I'd very much enjoy. I'm just thrilled for you. You've got this desire to connect with people, and a real talent for doing so. It's a perfect fit."

"It's one thing I truly *want* to do. There's one more thing I want, though, a whole hell of a lot more." Fitz took her fisted hands. Gently unfurled each one. "I want you, Hallie."

"Oh, Fitz. I want that, too, but I can't be what drives you apart from your parents."

Selfless and sweet. Was it any wonder he was crazy

about her? "Weren't you listening? I just literally drove them thousands of miles away to a different country. And even if they were still here in town, it doesn't matter what anyone else thinks. Or what they might expect of me. I was serious. I want to go down a whole new road. Not just with my career, though. With *you*."

Her ponytail swished vigorously in the negative. "It's risky."

"Being without you is a bigger risk." And at least she wasn't pulling her hands away...

"The town might not approve."

"The town can suck it," he said succinctly. "They get a vote in who is mayor. They don't get a vote on my personal life. I should've drawn that line in the sand years ago." The ocean breeze dusted them with a shower of pink crabapple petals. Fitz couldn't have engineered a more romantic sight if he'd thrown all the Montgomery influence and money at the moment. Guess Swan Cove itself was pulling for them.

"You need to be who you want to be, do what you want to do." And Fitz could swear her eyes were suspiciously, sparklingly damp at the corners. "I'm so sorry you didn't feel that was possible until now."

"Yeah, well, my parents can shoulder some of the blame. I'll take a healthy portion of it, though. I got stuck in a rut trying to make everyone else happy. That is, until I found the one thing that made me happier than I'd ever been." He dropped a soft kiss on her knuckles. "You. Wanting you made me pull my head out of the sand. Realize that I can be a Montgomery and still be myself."

"It's funny you put it like that. I recently realized that I can still be myself—a woman proudly from Crow Harbor, a self-confessed nerd, a librarian—and that's more than good enough to be anything else I want, including mayor." She inched closer until the tips of their shoes tapped together.

"Including your girlfriend."

So much relief. A tsunami of it. "I like the sound of that."

Hallie tilted her chin to aim those big brown eyes right at his. "I'm so sorry, Fitz. I split us up for what I thought were the right reasons. I thought that proved I cared. Fighting for you would've shown that a lot better. I should've dug my heels in and said that you mattered enough to be with no matter who thought what about us."

"Say that again," he demanded.

"What?"

Swiftly, he bracketed her cheeks with his palms. "That you care about me."

"Nope." Hallie pulled out of his grasp.

He would've been worried if not for the Cheshire Cat grin—yeah, they'd skimmed the book together at the cottage—on her beautiful face. "Why not?"

"It isn't accurate. You know what a stickler I am for accuracy." Backing up, she clasped her hands over the big splotch of pink atop her heart. With a solemn slowness, she stipulated, "The fact is, I'm fairly certain I'm falling in love with you."

Fitz staggered backward a few steps, feigning a direct hit. "Damn it, Hallie. That was the final fact I was about to lay on *you*."

"Is that so? Look at us agreeing on something."

"We weren't particularly good enemies, but I know we'll make a strong team as lovers. I want another chance with you—to be judged solely on my own merits. Not as a Montgomery, and not as a mayor. Just Fitz."

"That's a measure I'm comfortable voting yes on. Because I never should've run scared after your parents applied pressure. I adore you no matter *what* your last name is."

"So we can be just Fitz and Hallie again?"

"Yes."

With a whoop, Fitz picked her up. He started to swing her in a wide circle when the speaker in the pergola crackled and sputtered. "It's official, folks. Swan Cove's next mayor is our librarian, Hallie Scott!" Applause thundered.

As Hallie's mouth dropped open, he took the opportunity to swoop in for a kiss.

The announcer kept going. "It is the first time in two hundred years that someone without the last name of Montgomery has held the role."

Fitz beamed down at her. "You did it."

"Yikes." Her voice wobbled, but her smile just about cracked her beautiful face in half. "Laid out like that, it really sounds like I'm breaking a tradition."

"Well, you never know. Maybe the tradition will stay unbroken."

"How?"

"If things go the way I hope between us, Mayor Scott, you just might consider marrying me and becoming a Montgomery…"

"For the good of the town," she intoned solemnly, and then they both burst into laughter.

Acknowledgments

Thanks to Liz Pelletier for jump-starting this story, and to Heather Howland for buffing and polishing it into shape. To my weekend write-in warriors - M.C. Vaughan, E. Elizabeth Watson & Robyn Neeley - your bi-weekly help is *invaluable*. I'm grateful to everything online for the cities/towns/villages of Bar Harbor, Camden, and Rockport Maine which hopefully reduced my errors in interpretation in small town governance. And to my readers - thanks for cannonballing into another series with me!

About the Author

Christi Barth earned a masters degree in vocal performance and embarked upon a career on the stage. A love of romance then drew her to wedding planning. Ultimately she succumbed to her lifelong love of books and now writes award-winning contemporary romance, including the Naked Men and Aisle Bound series. Christi can always be found whipping up gourmet meals (for fun, honest!) or with her nose in a book. She lives in Maryland with the best husband in the world.

Also by Christi Barth...

THE PRINCESS PROBLEM

RULING THE PRINCESS

TEMPTING THE PRINCE

IMPERFECT ANGEL

Discover more romance from Entangled...

TINKERING WITH LOVE
a novel by Aliyah Burke

As if losing her dream job as motorcycle mechanic after moving all the way from San Francisco to the midwest wasn't bad enough, Dawson finds out that her replacement job as a car saleswoman is now holding teambuilding event in the mountains. And between dodging murderous chipmunks and dreamy dates under the northern lights, she's now falling for the charming ex-pro hockey player Tully Faulkner—the very guy who stole her job.

KISSING GAMES
a Kissing Creek novel by Stefanie London

Pro baseball player Ryan Bower is back in his small hometown, recovering from an injury. All he wants is a little rest and relaxation. But librarian Sloane Rickman has turned his world upside down, with her erotic book club picks and quirky sense of humor. Ryan can't afford to get tangled up with someone rooted in Kissing Creek—his career takes him everywhere but. And these kissing games they're playing could end up being lose-lose...

THE UN-ARRANGED MARRIAGE
a novel by Laura Brown

Mark Goldman has never gotten along with Shaina Fogel. And Shaina would rather have a root canal than do anything with Mark. But a family wedding is about to change everything they thought they knew about their archnemesis. When it's revealed that the wedding events are a weeklong competition—for a dream vacation—Mark and Shaina do the unthinkable: work together. And as the animosity begins to fade, something even more electric takes its place...

IT TAKES A VILLA
a novel by Kilby Blades

Natalie Malone just bought an abandoned villa on the Amalfi Coast of Italy. She's ready to renovate—with only six months to do it. After seeing too many botched jobs and garish design choices, architect Pietro Indelicato is done watching from the sidelines. He agrees to help, giving Natalie a real chance to succeed. But when the fine print on her contract is brought to light, she might have to leave her dream behind.

Asking For Trouble
a Credence, Colorado novel by Amy Andrews

After her first disastrous attempt at online dating, Della Munroe decides she needs a wingman, and there's no better person for it than Tucker Daniels. After all, he is a man who owns a bar, which practically makes him a relationship expert. He's also her older brother's best friend. Tucker Daniels would rather eat broken glass than watch Della go out with a bunch of douchebag dudes only out for one thing. Unfortunately, he's never been able to say no to her. But when Della wants him to tutor her in more intimate arts, he freaks out. Because this little sister is strictly off-limits, and saying yes to Della is asking for a whole lot of trouble.

First Bride to Fall
a Majestic Maine novel by Ginny Baird

Nell Delaney and her sisters would do anything for their family, but an arranged marriage to save the family coffee shop is going too far. The sisters make a deal: whoever hasn't found true love by the end of the month has to suck it up and marry the son of their enemy. Fortunately, homebody Nell is already halfway in love with Grant Williams. Now to convince him she's the outdoorsy girl of his dreams…